CW01430942

"When you're truly free, you're bound to get a little weird."

~Dr. Gatling

Other Sapphic Pixie Tales From Cassandra Duffy:

The
Steam-Powered Sniper
In the City of Broken Bridges

Cassandra Duff
Moil Pressr
2012

Day Moon Press
Sapphic Pixie Tales

All rights reserved. No part of this book may be reproduced or used in any matter whatsoever without written permission, except in the cases of brief quotations in critical articles or reviews.

This is a work of fiction. Names, characters, locations, and events are meant to be fictitious. Any similarity between any persons living, dead, or undead is completely coincidental. The events are fictional. The version of San Francisco, Carson City, and any other location are fictionalized renditions.

ISBN-13: 978-1477509371
ISBN-10: 1477509372

©2012 Cassandra Duffy
1st Print Edition
Cover Design by Katiie Kissglosse
Edited by Nichole Mauer

For Nikki,
The Steam-powered Sniper of My Heart!

Chapter 1:
Out of Time in Tombstone.

The heat of the Arizona summer wasn't abating with the coming fall, pressing hard on the outside of the courthouse turned Lazy Raven headquarters. Claudia slipped from the bed she'd been sharing with Veronica to open a window. The sun was setting. The desert was finally giving up its scorching hold on the day to replace it with a chilly grasp on the night. She stood nude in the open window for a moment, smelling the dry air coming off the fields of marijuana and opium the Ravens were growing. It was a thick, organic scent of earth and plants, with a strange perfume to it as so many of the plants were blooming.

Claudia glanced back to the bed where Veronica was snoozing amid the puffy pillows, downy comforter, and satin sheets. This was a relationship of convenience, Claudia kept telling herself. She didn't really know Veronica all that well, but she knew Veronica was close to Fiona, as close as any two people could be, and that would likely be as close to Fiona as Claudia would ever get. Similarly, Claudia knew Veronica was interested in her simply because she was dimensionally close to the petite Asian pilot that had so captured Fiona's heart. Veronica, who was typically the pure image of feminine glory, was extremely masculine in her sense of attraction—she was attracted to Claudia because Claudia's body looked enough like Gieo's.

This wasn't a source of consternation or oddity with Claudia the way it was with some of the Ravens. Claudia knew a little of Veronica's past, knew she'd never had a feminine influence, and knew exactly what that could do to a girl's sexual development as her own experiences mirrored it. Claudia was raised by a strong man of compelling charisma and had lost her mother young. She'd taken to her father's proclivities as a son would and had so approached the world with a tiny ribbon of feminine grace in an otherwise hardened form.

She and Veronica were alike in two other significant ways as well when it came to romance and love. They both compartmentalized sex from feelings when it served their purposes and they both tended toward myopic obsessions once they found an object of desire. Claudia believed both of these traits made her an excellent sniper, but seemed to complicate her love life in some truly bizarre ways. This was the case with Veronica and Danny before her. Both the sultry White Queen and the bearded young hunter were in love with Fiona, which Claudia admitted had created most of her attraction for them.

Danny had been a sweet boy growing into a remarkable man until that worthless asshole Rawlins shot him down. Claudia had never shut the door on men, although she had long since come to the conclusion that she preferred women. Danny was a special case though. Somehow the difficulties of the new world order hadn't destroyed the human parts within him and he remained sweet and almost gentlemanly as though he were always meant to be a cowboy and waited only for the world to give him the opportunity. Again though, it was a relationship of convenience as they were in love with the same woman who noticed them both only in a maternal or platonic way. Still, part of Claudia grieved that the world had lost Danny even though he wasn't what she wanted for anything more than a passing fling. Given the chance, he might have charmed another woman at some point, one who would need him and appreciate him in ways she hadn't.

Claudia returned to the bed when the sun had fully set and darkness filled the room. Veronica was still asleep, although she'd rolled onto her back, letting the sheet fall away from her chest. A shaft of light from the lanterns outside snaked through the window, across the bed, and illuminated Veronica's left breast with the distinctive knife scar. She really did have glorious breasts, Claudia thought. She liked Veronica well enough as a person. She was interesting, strong, surprisingly caring at times, and as smart of a person as Claudia had ever met, but her real interest in Veronica was carnal—once they had consummated their coalition of castoffs, her body physically ached for Veronica's whenever they were close to one another.

Claudia crept across the bed as not to wake Veronica, keeping to one side to avoid blocking out the shaft of light for as long as she could. Once she'd snuck up on the still, sleeping form of the Raven Queen, Claudia bowed her head and took a long, taunting lick up the curve of Veronica's exposed breast, following the line of the jagged scar. She waited a moment on hands and knees to see if Veronica would wake up. When she didn't, Claudia took a few more licks along the soft curve of Veronica's breast, tasting on her skin the lingering sweat from the heat of the day and their earlier lovemaking excursion. Veronica might not have awoken from the attention, but her body certainly did. Claudia took the hardening of Veronica's nipple as an invitation and flicked her tongue across its tip.

She glanced up to Veronica's face to find her eyes still closed but a smile painted across her lips. "You were awake the whole time, yes?" Claudia asked. Her accent was French Canadian, although she could tone it down or thicken it as needed. Coming from Quebec, she was bilingual and able to speak both languages as a native speaker. She knew what effect the accent had on people, Veronica in particular, and used it to good advantage.

"Yes, but I wanted to see how far you would take your molestation of a sleeping woman," Veronica replied, finally opening her eyes. Her eyes were a lovely hazel with a twinkle of permanent mischief that Claudia suspected mirrored her own. When she smiled as she did in that moment, Claudia believed Veronica was quite possibly one of the most beautiful women she'd ever met.

"I had no concrete plans, although my time spent on your breast was certainly only meant as a beginning," Claudia cooed, returning her mouth to Veronica's breast to suck the pert little nipple into her mouth.

She spotted the red flashing light out of the corner of her eye and her heart leapt into her throat. Claudia knew as well as anyone what the silent warning light meant. She had discussed with Veronica why this time might be different than the repulsion of marauders she'd participated in back in Vegas. Veronica knew Claudia wanted to leave the Ravens to seek out her father, and she'd said her opportunity to do so would be coming soon.

Claudia and Veronica dressed quickly in the slowly flashing red light set above the doorway. Claudia kept chancing glances to Veronica as she equipped herself for battle. She thought there might be something she should say in such a moment, but she couldn't imagine what it might be. She dressed and equipped herself as thoroughly as she was able, knowing it might be her last chance to do so. Finally, she grabbed her rifle from beside the closet, slinging the strap over her shoulder.

"Do you remember where the pilot's motorcycle is?" Veronica asked.

"But of course," Claudia replied with levity she didn't really feel.

"Then I suppose this is goodbye." Veronica turned from her weapon rack, armed to repel the raid she'd suspected was coming for some time. Claudia was waiting to embrace her, but stopped short when Veronica held out her hand.

"I could stay…"

"You can't save Tombstone and you can't save me," Veronica said. "If we lose, you'll die, and if we win, you'll be as stuck as you are now. Take the chance since it might be your last."

Claudia didn't take no for an answer on her second attempt. She grasped Veronica by the back of her neck, pulling her down until their lips met in a fiery embrace. She didn't love Veronica, probably never could, but she cared for her more deeply than she'd admitted to herself. Veronica smiled down to her when their lips parted; her mouth was adorably flushed from the intensity of the kiss as it often was. She left the room through the door while Claudia slipped out the window she'd left open.

Claudia skulked along the ledge outside the window, leapt easily the two feet across to the lamppost nearest the corner, and slid down to the ground. She wasn't just an excellent scout and sniper, she also had almost a decade's worth of gymnastics training that made her amply able to move through urban landscapes as easily as open terrain. If she wasn't also built like a gymnast, she always thought she might have made a good soldier.

She crept through the empty city streets, trying her best to move away from the sounds of engines and gunfire, which were quickly spreading through the darkened desert night. When she reached the oldest section of Tombstone where the replica of the Old West street had been built, she scaled one of the flat roofed buildings via the fire escape ladder along the back wall, and began making her way from rooftop to rooftop.

She stopped short at the final street before she would make a left, slide down from her perch, and escape into the night aboard the pilot's hidden motorcycle. The marauders would be Zeke's men, most likely from Juarez; these were things Veronica knew although she hadn't known when the attack would come or how intense it would be. She'd shared the information among the Ravens, but not with Fiona.

Claudia turned back, tracing a very specific sound through the city. The quad gun was being fired, the one the pilot had salvaged from one of her dirigibles; Claudia had seen it the night they were to defend the high school turned stables against the cultist army. It was Slark technology and Claudia knew the sound all too well. It stopped before she could reach it under the sudden thickening of armed men on decrepit old 4x4s racing through the streets, seeking out easy Raven targets. She raced across the rooftops, her boots finding sure-footing easily among the flat topped buildings.

The giant truck with the gun pod that the bartender and mentally challenged cook once owned was destroyed in the middle of the road with several dead Ravens surrounding it. Claudia lifted her rifle to her shoulder and scanned the bodies with her scope. She recognized Stephanie and what she guessed was the gargantuan cook, but she didn't spot Fiona among the dead. Her focus was snapped from the scope when she heard the telltale roar of Fiona's Colt Anaconda. She chased the sound along the tops of the buildings, quickly becoming winded from the exertion of tracking and backtracking so quickly.

She spotted the redhead gunfighter with her smoking pistol pointed at group of men all but one of which had been felled by her. Claudia shouldered her rifle to see who the lone survivor was under Fiona's gun. She couldn't believe her eyes. The old Texas Ranger Cork stood ready to either finish off or be finished off by Fiona. The question of whether or not Fiona had a cartridge left for Cork was answered when the man began lifting his sub machinegun. Claudia held her breath to steady her aim. The crosshairs landed firmly on his left temple. She gave the trigger a loving squeeze and a firm grip to limit recoil. The rifle jerked in a familiar way and the front of Cork's head came apart in a red cloud.

She wanted to call out to Fiona, to promise cover or tell her where she was going, but there was no time and Fiona wouldn't be interested in any of it anyway. Claudia waved when she thought Fiona traced back the rifle fire to its source. Fiona didn't wave back. She couldn't be sure if Fiona even really saw her.

The swift moving flames, which Claudia had only caught a glimpse of at the end of the street, was in full chase when she slung her rifle back over her shoulder. She ran along the rooftops, outdistancing the fire that was sweeping easily through the dusty desert town.

The lamppost at the end of the row, the one that didn't work anymore but for some reason still had a few pairs of shoes dangling from it, was her goal. The strange steam-powered motorcycle was hidden beneath it behind a half of a propane tank and long dead shrubbery. Still out of range, with one more roof to run across, she heard a decidedly female scream, a spray of gunfire, and then a jarring explosion. The shoes dangling from the lamppost, danced on the ends of their laces when the explosion rippled through the chaotic night. Claudia didn't need to be told what had happened. She'd heard it in Phoenix, Barstow, Las Vegas, and in countless other minor skirmishes when something went sideways for the Ravens.

She slid to a stop at the edge of the last roof, a few feet separating her and the lamppost. At the base of the building, too close to the motorcycle's hiding place for it to be coincidence, was a tangle of obliterated human remains. Claudia leapt out to the lamppost, wrapped around it, and did a half turn to face the building again as she deftly slid to the ground. She hopped free and drew her Walther PPK to cover the bodies and the entrance to the alleyway as she slowly crept toward the scene of a trump card having been played.

She might have known the Raven, but there wasn't enough left to identify her. Claudia suspected even dental records couldn't have sorted out who she was after the grenade had done its work. By the look of the other remains in the area, the girl took at least three men with her.

"Make them pay a precious price, little bird," Claudia whispered the mantra required whenever anyone found a Raven had played their last card. She holstered her sidearm and turned her back on the scene of unspeakable carnage. She couldn't think of what might have been if she'd run faster, if she hadn't stopped to wave to Fiona, if she hadn't stopped to save Fiona…she'd nearly driven herself mad with what-ifs her first few times in combat and she wasn't about to go back down that road simply because it had been almost a year since she'd last seen the after effects of a trump card.

The propane tank half came away easily revealing the bike still in place. Claudia got in behind the handlebars and pushed the monstrosity free of its hiding hole. She'd ridden motorcycles before, but she imagined her experience on the 500cc dirt bikes used by scouts around Las Vegas would count about as much in riding the bastard child of a Slark engine and an Indian cruising bike as knowing how to ride a horse would qualify someone to ride an elephant. Still, her options were to try the motorcycle or get walking, and with those as her choices, the motorcycle seemed significantly less intimidating. She slid her night vision goggles from her pack and settled them into place over her eyes, bathing the world in the strange green glow. Dying in a motorcycle accident was better than a trump card and so she hopped into the saddle of the steam-powered monstrosity.

She roared out into the night at incredible speed, heading north because that was the only direction she knew to go.

Chapter 2:

Into the Dragon's Desert.

Claudia found the pilot's remarkable motorcycle did most of the driving. It needed tending, management on temperature and fluid levels, but it largely knew how to keep to the roads all on its own. Once she figured this out, she pushed it to go fast, as fast as it wanted for optimal fuel and water consumption which was just shy of 90 MPH. She'd skirted the eastern edge of the ruins of Phoenix, knowing Ravens had outposts on the western edge; in the event of a Slark invasion, they could fallback through the ruins of the city and make a fight of it even if they were massively outnumbered. By the time the sky was graying with the coming day, and coincidentally when the bike began to languish too hot under constant use, Claudia believed she'd passed into Utah.

This belief was stymied when she left the highway that would take her west to Vegas in favor of a two lane road that instead brought her near the Grand Canyon. She knew better, knew major landmarks were where she was most likely to run into trouble, but she couldn't help herself. Years ago, before the invasion, she was meant to see the Grand Canyon on a school trip, but hadn't ever gotten the chance. Against the nagging voice of her survival training, she turned off onto the detour to the national park.

The sun was fully clear of the horizon by the time she pulled up to the edge of what remained of the Grand Canyon village. Time and conflict hadn't been kind to the little outpost of tourism. In the early days of the war, she'd heard talk that a band of Apache separatists had held up in the canyon when the Slark were pushing east. Claudia had thought it all sounded too romantic of the Old West to be true, but what she actually found in the canyon closer to confirmed it. The more she explored, the more she found to support the story of guerilla fighters giving the aliens a fight around the canyon. War had indeed hit the national park and it looks like the Slark had paid dearly to achieve their passage. Several of the smaller crawlers littered the canyon floor along with one of the medium sized weapon platforms. She didn't see any army vehicle tracks anywhere in the area, which was peculiar, but didn't necessarily mean the revived Apache nation was responsible. It occurred to her after she'd hiked away from the canyon's edge that she hadn't taken a moment to marvel at the natural splendor of the Grand Canyon; after what she'd seen in the past six years, a giant hole in the ground really didn't seem all that amazing.

She was exhausted, the bike was laboring, and she needed food and water every bit as much as her mount. She pulled up alongside the lone remaining structure, what appeared to be a cinderblock power relay station. The metal door was broken off its hinges allowing her access to the cramped little room. Most of the equipment she expected to find inside had been removed at some point leaving a scraped up cement floor and desert dust blown into the corners. A few lizards skittered into cracks in the walls when she darkened the building's lone doorway.

With enough prodding and more than a little luck, she managed to squeeze the motorcycle through the doorway. She'd pinched her left hand between the handlebar and doorframe at one point and only a quick jerk of the limb back saved her from having her fingers crushed. She tore off her leather glove to inspect the scraped hand, clenching her fingers to be sure they all still worked. A realization came over her—she was on her own. She'd been "on her own" before on scouting missions, but always with the possibility of rescue and a support system to return to once she'd accomplished her tasks. If she made a mistake now even the Raven's thin medical support would be out of reach.

She propped the door back in place and slept through the hottest part of the day, awaking when the cinderblock building became uncomfortably warm. She was thirsty and something in the darkened room was dripping. She pulled her head from the balled up jacket she'd been using as a pillow. She traced the sound of dripping water to its source, finding water tapping its way out of the bike, finally having worn a hole in the sandy coating on the floor to drip against bare cement.

"*Merde!*" Claudia cursed. She crawled quickly across the dusty floor and traced her hands along the cooled metal body of the bike, seeking out the leak. Finally, her hand slipped along the jagged edge of a puncture in one of the brass water tanks. Shrapnel from the grenade must have found its way through the half propane tank to put a dime-sized slice into the all-important water reserve. She still had one, but the re-condensing chamber, helpfully labeled as such, apparently poured the reclaimed water back into the tanks equally. She'd likely run dry in that tank at some point in the night and now lost half her remaining water through the hole as well.

She tore off a scrap of cloth from her shirt and stuffed it into the hole. She scanned the tangle of tubes and metal chambers as if there might be some answer within them to explain how she was supposed to disconnect the wounded tank or prevent the re-condensing chamber to continue feeding that side. The combination of Slark technology, an 80-year-old Indian motorcycle, and the pilot's own eccentricities made a maze of Rube Goldberg-esque complexity. She knew next to nothing about machinery and she imagined even the most gifted mechanic would require days of study to understand what the pilot had created.

Claudia ran her damp hands up into the thick tangle of her black hair and let out a genuine groan of her foolish defeat so early into the trip. It took her a few minutes to rally herself to the problem at hand. She needed something to patch the hole. She needed water to replenish the tanks. And she generally needed supplies of every kind. Maybe she wasn't smart enough to figure out the insanely complex vehicle she was riding, but she was a master forager and scout—she could feed herself and the bike indefinitely if the structure of the motorcycle could be assured. She steeled herself for the work of the day and put her hands to it.

Five hours later, she'd found enough water from a strange little spring tributary and plastic jugs to carry it without having to hike all the way to the canyon's floor. She happened across a fat old rattlesnake out for a hunt in the dusk, and popped its head off with an easy shot from her Walther. Rattlesnakes, as dangerous as their bite could be, were reasonably easy prey as they identified themselves with the telltale rattling and would use their insanely fast reflexes to try to bite at a bullet if they saw one coming, making headshots almost guaranteed. Food and water was easy, but she had no idea if the metal shavings and ancient bathroom caulking gun she'd found would actually plug the hole in the bike's brass tank.

She cleaned the snake and set it to cook over the low embers of a dying fire. The desert sky exploded in crimson and pink as the sun began to set, painting the rust colored rocks of the Arizona desert with a beautiful palette. She stopped in her work to enjoy the little moment of peace and beauty. In the quiet moment, she wondered how things turned out in Tombstone. If anyone had a way out, it would be Veronica. If anyone was too mean to die, it was Fiona. She gave little thought to the resumption of the war and how the pilot's assault on the refineries might go. If the aerial assault failed, the Ravens would find another way. The resourcefulness and determination of her former clan was undeniable.

She shook off the nagging thoughts that Veronica and Fiona might well be dead. She had to see to herself, her mount, and her solitary mission. She set to repair the bike once the snake was roasting happily over the coals. Squeezing the handle on the caulking gun was a monumental task requiring both hands; finally, with an angry sweat rising on her brow, she managed to pour the tiniest rivulet of white caulking material into the crack. She quickly added as many of the metal shavings as would stick. The second attempt went slightly better. Her third and final effort closed the gap and she hoped put an end to the concern as the caulking gun wasn't going to give up anymore of the pungent sealant and she was completely out of metal shavings. She smoothed the plug as best she could with a chunk of wood and prayed it would hold.

She read the dirty and peeling label on the caulk canister. It was silicone based with a set time of 30 minutes and a completely dry time of 24 hours. Not really knowing what any of that meant, she decided to split the difference and wait a few hours before trying to pour water into the repaired tank.

She sat by the low glow of the dying fire, eating her gamey rattlesnake dinner as the sun finally set and the chill of the desert night found its way to her. She'd eaten reptile before and kind of liked it with a bit of salt and pepper, especially fried in oil. Others said rattlesnake tasted like chicken, but she assumed it was just the comment of an unsophisticated palette. Rattlesnake tasted like reptile, which was its own distinct flavor; moreover, carnivorous reptiles like rattlesnakes had a very different flavor than insectivorous lizards. She started to wonder what turtle would taste like with a nice white wine sauce.

She hadn't realized what she was doing until earlier that afternoon, but once it struck her, it was all she could think about. She was heading north. North to Canada. Whatever that might end up meaning. It was a romantic notion and about as good as any direction to head, although she had no idea if it would lead her back to her father. She wanted to believe Canada of all places would weather the Slark storm best, but she couldn't make it stick. The whole concept of a matriarchal society ruled by a Russian mafia queen rising out of the ashes of the invasion to become the new North American super power wouldn't have even been on Claudia's long list of possibilities, but there the Ravens were, rebuilding society like they were always meant to.

She was 14 when the invasion struck, on a school choir trip to Las Vegas to compete in an international competition. Her father had seen her off to the airport, watching her pass through the security checkpoint with his steely eyes, waving only once before she finally passed out of his vision. Her teenage self had been so glad to be free of his rigidity and rules. Her minor rebellions seemed so trivial and petty in light of the past six years. She wished she'd given him the kiss on the cheek he'd asked for when they parted company for what might well turn out to be the last time. Airports were crowded places and her friends were watching, she'd explained. He'd said he understood.

One night out of the Ravens and she was already crumbling to depression. She'd had the morose streak in her and she knew it. Time to think for her was time to count her regrets—she wasn't as strong as she'd thought and she might well be twice as foolish. She wrapped the remains of the snake in the cleaner of the two shirts she'd brought and stuffed it into the nearly empty backpack she'd brought. She wondered if her ill-conceived flight of fancy would kill her before she became too depressed to turn back. In the weakness of the moment, she had to admit the Ravens weren't a bad home for her. They'd completed the training her father began, taught her to be a sniper, taught her about explosives, made a proper soldier of her and gave her a purpose and the protection of community, and all they'd asked for in return was a lifetime of service. No, she decided, that probably wasn't a fair deal after all.

The caulk was dry enough and she even had a little water left over when she'd filled both tanks. As she poured water into the wounded vessel, her heart leapt into her throat as she stared through the gloom to see if the lumpy white seal would hold. As the last of the jug dripped into the tank, she let out a heavenly sigh of relief. The ugly little plug was holding.

She roared out into the night made green by her night vision goggles, turning back to the road labeled 89 to continue north.

†

The second morning was still well on the horizon when the freak storm hit her. The black sky broke out in blacker clouds and then proceeded to drop fat, heavy rain on her. Her speed cut, steam rose off the bike's workings when the moisture hit it, and she quickly became soaked to the bone. She had no idea where she was as most of the road signs on that stretch had long since fallen. More than that, she'd changed directions a few times in the darkness and now she thought she might be on a highway again. Without the North Star to navigate by, she couldn't even be completely certain she was still heading north.

Thunder roared above the sound of the motorcycle's engine and lightning pained the sky in wicked flashes. The first few strobes of lightning illuminated the Painted Desert and the empty highway where only a few derelict vehicles still stood along the sides in random intervals. As she was finally considering stopping to try to take refuge in one of the old cars, a flash of lightning illuminated something truly bizarre up ahead. Colossal rocks, pushed up at an odd angle like a stack of coins fallen to one side, cut directly across the highway with the narrow lane of asphalt carving a tiny path between them. The strange rocks weren't large enough to call a mountain, but were clearly larger than any hill. Claudia pushed on toward the strange rock formation. Each time the lightning flashed as she came closer the more and more the rocks looked like the spine of a great reptile or monster. She passed between the strange reef rock formations and came out on a gentle curve where a rest area indicated she'd reached the southern mouth of Black Dragon Canyon. She pulled off the side of the road and made for the visitor information center. The two bathrooms were connected in the middle by a roof that had long since fallen in.

She tucked her motorcycle under the triangle portion created when the awning fell in nearest the women's restroom, and ran for cover into what remained of the brick building that formerly housed the women's bathroom. Most of the ceiling was gone, allowing the rain to pour inside, pooling in places but mostly running straight down the drain in the middle of the floor. Claudia huddled beneath the last corner of roof near the bank of sinks. It took her several minutes of cursing her weakness and fear of something as trivial as rain before she managed to talk herself into taking advantage of the storm to refill some of the plastic jugs she'd brought. She was cold, wet, and starving before she finally got the jugs set up to fill in the pouring rain. Pure exhaustion settled over her, knocking the fight from her until she fell asleep with her head down on her knees, not sure if she was waiting for the storm to pass or simply kill her.

Almost as quickly as she'd fallen asleep, she was rattled awake by an apocalyptic rumbling. She couldn't be sure how long she'd slept. The rain was easing although the night was still too dark to see even the faintest outline of the crumbling room around her. A lightning flash illuminated the building through the many holes in the roof. Across from her, not ten feet away, standing nearest the stalls, was a large man. Instantly she was on her feet, her pistol jumping to her hand. She pointed the little Walther at the man, unsure if the gun was too wet to even fire.

"I picked up your trail at the Grand Canyon," the man said, shouting to be heard over the storm and the approaching rumble. Of course he had. She should've known better than to leave a trail near a landmark. Marauders picked points of interest to set up their traps for the very reason that unsuspecting people would go out of their way to see the things denied them before the world went to hell.

"What do you want?" Claudia shouted in reply although she knew the answer.

"You're a long way from home with that accent," the man said. "I've heard a man with that same accent before."

"Where?!" Claudia couldn't be certain, but she thought she saw the man reach into his jacket to remove what she imagined was a knife. She prayed for another flash of lightning to tell her what the large man had in his hand.

"In the City of Broken Bridges," the man said, taking a step toward her.

The rumbling had grown so loud, so close, and so constant that she couldn't be completely certain she'd heard him right. Wherever the rumbling was coming from, the echo off the canyon walls was distorting and intensifying it until it became an all encompassing roar from all directions. The night sky lit up with a flash of white and she finally got a look at the large hunting knife the man had in his hand. Every fiber of her being told her to shoot the man, but she couldn't, not until she knew what he meant about the city and the accent.

"What does that mean?!" Claudia shouted her question though the rumbling had long since drowned out her ability to even hear her own voice with any clarity.

She couldn't tell if the man heard her or made an answer, although after a moment's hesitation, he took a step toward her. The brief flash of light over the man's face showed the hunger she'd expected of someone whose prey had grown scarce over the last few years. She didn't know where her trump card was and wasn't interested in playing it anyway. Whatever information the man might still hold would have to be lost with his life. She pulled the trigger. The brief pop didn't tell her if she'd hit. The rumbling finally caught up to them and tore away the half of the building the man was standing in. For a brief, confused moment, Claudia thought the tiny pistol had somehow blown away the entire half of the room. Immediately after, she recognized the work of a mudslide. She pressed her back to the wall behind her as the fast moving river of water and debris continued to erode the floor in front of her. The man was gone, along with any answers he might have had, and if Claudia didn't think of something she would join him miles away and beneath an ocean of debris when the mudslide finally found its ending.

Nothing around her gave her any hope. The wall behind her felt unstable already, far too unstable to climb, the floor was inching back toward her toes, and the stream of black mud was so littered with boulders and enormous debris that she knew death was assured if she fell in. She pressed her back against the wall as hard as she could, her eyes never leaving the deadly river ahead of her. The last of the tiles right in front of her boots crumbled away an instant before she fell back through the weakened wall. She curled into a ball as bricks and other debris fell down around her. She felt a few hit home, likely raising bruises on her arms and shoulders, but luckily not her head. When she was certain the wall was finished raining bricks on her, she pulled her head from beneath the wooden slats that had actually done most of the work of shielding her. The rest area was nearly gone and not just on the side she was on. Another flow of mud was coursing its way along on the men's room side as well having long since worn away the building there. In fact, if one of the reef style rocks from the outcropping hadn't fallen across the highway, and very recently by the look of it, the middle ground where she and her bike stood would have washed away as well.

Claudia worked quickly to free the bike and push it further up near the giant rock shard, larger than most buildings in Tombstone, to take full advantage of its shelter. She sat on the lone chunk of asphalt that was once the tiny parking lot, leaning her back against the bike, watching the river of death flow around her to either side. A strange, thin hope crept into her born out of something she wasn't sure had even happened. The City of Broken Bridges—San Francisco maybe.

Chapter 3:
Into the Wounded West.

The following day brought with it an oppressive heat as though the rainstorm of the night had never existed. Claudia awoke with a start, having slept sitting up in an uncomfortable position. She had a direction, albeit a vague one with little more to go on than what she'd used to decide on north to that point. She briefly considered searching the rubble for the shadowy man who tracked her, but discarded this plan as the mudslide could easily have deposited his corpse, and it would with almost complete certainty be a corpse, miles away and dozens of feet beneath the rubble.

She stood, stretched as best she could and began to survey the state of the world in the harsh light of day. Hunger and thirst were beginning to nag at her. She'd lost the plastic jugs and even if she found them again, the water inside would likely be too foul to drink. The building that was the rest stop was gone as though it had never been there, and with it her satchel, her night vision goggles, and any survival accoutrements that weren't physically strapped to her. Her rifle had been saved only by the luck of her being too tired to un-strap it from the motorcycle the night before. She had her survival knife, her Walther, her rifle, and her survival filtration straw in her battle harness, but little else.

To add to the problem, the mud flow left a river's breadth of debris and mud across the road in either direction. Getting the bike back to the highway would be a struggle and one she wouldn't be able to ride through. There was always the option of abandoning the bike to walk, but she had no idea how far she was from anything and she doubted she could walk for very long without food or water in the oppressive heat of the Utah desert. She removed her jacket, tied it around her waist, and set to the work of walking the bike across the inert mudflow.

†

The sun was setting before Claudia finally pushed the bike through the mudflow. She had to use the engine several times to dislodge the monstrously heavy motorcycle, burning precious fuel. Her entire body, especially her back, ached from the exertion. She'd lost count of how many times the bike threatened to roll over the top of her during the entire process. Back on the road, with the bike struggling to keep a pace of 70 MPH, she felt a little like the banged up, half-starved motorcycle. Her mouth was a desert, her stomach had long since passed from hungry to nausea from want of food, and she was fairly certain she'd done permanent physical damage to herself and the motorcycle throughout the day.

She struggled the bike onto highway 50 heading west. On the map in her head from before the U.S. fell to ruin, she probably couldn't accurately place Los Angeles and New York, let alone anything in between, but she knew a bit more about the lay of the land now that the Ravens had taken over much of the region. Salt Lake City was a smoldering crater next to yet another landmark she knew better than to approach. The Slark hadn't actually destroyed Salt Lake City. They'd hit it, done a number on it, and moved on. The true devastation came when a Mormon Holy Land arose from the ashes to declare Utah once again a sovereign nation gifted to the Latter Day Saints by the prophet Brigham Young. Obviously the Ravens took umbrage at having the patriarchal holy land in the midst of their female dominated territory. The war, if it could even be called such, took place a year ago, lasted only a month, and resulted in heavy artillery shelling of the city until nothing stood above the height of a short woman's knee skirt. The refugees, men and women Claudia helped track down, were brought back to Las Vegas as indentured servants. Claudia didn't know what the U.S. map looked like before the war, but she knew full well what the Raven map looked like as she'd played a small part in forming it. Salt Lake City wasn't worth seeing in its current state and she wasn't interested in what amounted to a detour for past glory's sake.

No matter how she cut the directions, she would have to go through Carson City. If she was lucky, her fuel would last until then. The Carson City area was a hot zone. The war between the Slark and the Ravens was still very much alive on the border between old California and new Nevada. There would be Ravens there, food, water, a comfortable bed, and maybe even fuel enough to finish her trip. Her last hope was that her name and rank within the Ravens was still good enough to get her some pleasant treatment. Word traveled slowly without modern technology. Carson City might not know Tombstone had even been annexed by the Ravens.

With the bike laboring badly and her own situation not much better, Claudia didn't really have a choice. She'd spent so much time in the saddle as a scout that long rides on the motorcycle were heaven by comparison, but she'd gone without water for some time now and she was beginning to feel the effects of extreme dehydration including a splitting headache and slowed reflexes. She would cross the desert on a limping motorcycle with the hopes of collapsing of thirst in Carson City where she might be hung as a deserter. Part of this tragic ending for a lone rider appealed to the macabre sense of beauty she had, and brought a weak smile to her face as she pushed on toward what might well be her ending.

†

The shine of her tragic tale of the Old West was well tarnished by the time she actually rolled into Carson City. The bike's headlight, which she hadn't used to that point, barely illuminated the road before it. This might have been a problem if the motorcycle hadn't lost all ability to run, trundling along with gasps of steam and smoke, barely breaking 30 MPH.

Raven patrols paid her little attention as she clunked her way into the rearguard. She was obviously one of them, and while her ride was peculiar, it wasn't unheard of for someone to still manage a bit of technology and if someone had, it was likely in the state Claudia's motorcycle was. The cantankerous machine, which Claudia had come to love and loathe in equal parts, managed to roll to a stop at the edge of the Raven controlled downtown district. She cranked down the pod to park the bike and nearly fell out of the saddle.

"Well, look at this bit of tumbleweed blown in," a man's voice said from above Claudia. Somehow she'd managed to lay flat on her back across the sidewalk, although she wasn't quite sure how that had happened. "Where are you in from, gerbil?"

She pried her eyes open to see who had just called her a gerbil. Four men, no doubt U.S. soldiers reclaimed by the Ravens at some point, were collected around her. They wore a strange amalgam of metal breast plate armor and modern body armor yet carried the provincial assault rifles of their own era. When Claudia's response only came out as a strangled croak through a parched throat, the hardened men all looked to the largest of the bunch, the one she assumed spoke to her.

"Medic!" the largest man bellowed down the street.

Heavy boots came clattering toward her. Above the sound of the medic's approach, she heard the familiar sound of heavy cannon fire and assault rifles in the west. She knew the line was lively at Carson City, but she hadn't really known how lively. The lack of information exchanged between outposts apparently worked both ways. She still had her Raven credentials on the dog tags around her neck. The medic would no doubt find them, know her name and rank, and then she would find out if she was to be labeled a deserter or simply a rider off course. Being hung for desertion sounded unappealing, although she didn't think she'd survive her dehydration without help at that point. Two days crossing a desert in summer without water was a feat unto itself.

"Hang in there, gerbil," the big man said. He smiled down to her in a way that made her feel like she could hold out a little longer. She struggled against the rising tide of unconsciousness, but lost that battle a few moments after the medic arrived.

Chapter 4:
Meeting the Owl.

Claudia strolled the railroad tracks in her native Quebec. She knew she was dreaming, knew the world of her childhood was not reality. She was still her adult self and she hadn't been back to Canada since age 14. The granite gravel between the railroad ties crunched beneath her boots all the same. The richly green triangles of pines still framed the railroad tracks that cut a straight swath ahead and behind her. She could hear her father calling to her, his voice just on the edge of hearing and well beyond understanding.

She knew a train was coming. Every now and then, she would adjust her path from walking between the tracks to balancing on one like a tight rope walker. When she did this, she could feel the vibrations of a freight train coming down the iron rails. Playing chicken with the train that passed by her home was a game she'd enjoyed her whole life. She would wait until she knew it was coming and stand in the center of the tracks, eyes closed, arms outstretched. The train's horn would blare at her, the rocks would bounce a little around her feet, and the tracks would tremble at the approach of the thousands of tons of train bearing down on her. She would keep her eyes clenched tightly shut though, wait as long as she could stand it, until she finally threw open her eyes and leapt away from the tracks. She was always sorely disappointed in herself when she would open her eyes and find the train still hundreds of meters away. Each time she resolved to be braver and each time the result was the same—the train would be too far away to be any danger and then roll by her at what she guessed to be a paltry speed designed to bring it to a stop at the depot on the edge of town.

Her father had only caught her once playing the potentially suicidal game. She thought he would rail at her, tan her hide, and drag her home to restart the whole process. He'd surprised her ten-year-old self by racing to her, scooping her off the tracks, and then cradling her in his arms at the edge of the tree line. He'd stroked her hair, clutching her head to his chest, whispering again and again: you're safe now. She'd believed his words and felt safe in his embrace. Still, she couldn't quit playing the game, only hiding it better to spare him.

In the strange world of dreams, she could see her younger self and her father's younger self from her memory off to her right. He was cradling her, whispering the promise of safety, waiting for the train to pass through without taking his daughter. She ignored the touching scene. She wasn't that person anymore. She closed her eyes and walked forward, arms outstretched to prove the train didn't frighten her.

She could hear her father's voice more clearly now as he no doubt raced through the woods to reach her in time. His calls varied, but the one that stuck out to her was a question: why have you waited so long? She didn't understand the question. It wouldn't matter. The train would get to her before he did this time and then she wouldn't be able to hear him above the sound of its passing.

She walked on, the train's horn blared from what seemed like just up ahead. She knew better though, knew it was simply a product of the alley created by the trees to funnel the sound to her to make it sound closer than it really was. She hadn't known this when she was a child, but she knew it now and walked on. The ground beneath her began to shake and she could hear the clicking and clacking of the train as it approached. The horn blared again, this time closer. She clenched her eyes tightly closed. Not this time, train, she told herself and walked on.

Her father was close now, close enough to be heard above the roar of the train. She could hear him screaming from behind her. "You have the ruinous streak of your mother," he shouted to her. This was true, and not the first time he'd told her so. She wanted to correct him, to tell him she'd survived all the same, ruinous streak or no; it would have been a hollow statement in light of what she was doing though and so she ignored his words and walked on.

The train roared through the Canadian wilderness like an angry god. She could feel her heart thundering in her chest now, beating quickly to match the clacking of the train down the tracks toward her. She clenched her eyes even tighter, refusing to show the train her fear. The horn blared again and this time she knew it was no trick of sound. The train was upon her. She opened her eyes to the glare of the lone headlamp in the center of the engine as it was a mere inches from her face.

She tried to awake into action, but her body rebelled in its limp, semi-conscious state. She was in a hospital bed. A man in a white lab coat had awoken her by checking her pupils with fingers to pry her eyelids open and flashing a small flashlight into her eye. She shook her head to get away from the light.

"I was asleep, not in a coma," Claudia hissed.

"You were in deep REM," the doctor replied. "I should have been able to check your pupils."

"Yes, well, they are fine," Claudia replied, batting away the flashlight the man was still holding entirely too close to her face. Her headache, the one she'd almost grown accustomed to over the past two days of dehydration and heat exhaustion was gone. She could feel the IV in her arm and knew the source of the restorative fluids although she could remember little of how she came to be where she was.

"Don't get your feelings hurt over it, Doc," a gruff woman's voice sounded from the other side of the bed in the darkened room. "You should know better by now than to manhandle a sleeping Raven."

The doctor, who was little more than a shadowy figure in the darkened hospital room, scoffed and took his leave. For a brief moment when the door opened, bathing the room in faint light, she could see she wasn't the only patient in the room. A match struck to light an oil lamp and her little section of the hospital room was bathed in a soft, warm glow. The woman who had spoken and lit the lamp sat back in the chair, which she'd occupied, to that point, in the dark. She was a stout woman with a round face, a flattop haircut in her graying hair, and half a dozen scars lining her stern face. Everything about the sturdy woman spoke of authority derived from her attitude as much as her rugged appearance.

"We're supposed to get reinforcements," the woman said. "I'm hoping you were sent as an advanced scout and not as a messenger to tell me they aren't coming."

"Neither," Claudia croaked around a dry mouth.

The woman poured water from a canteen on her belt into a little plastic cup and handed it to her. Claudia drank greedily, swishing the obviously boiled water in her mouth to clear away the dryness before swallowing. Despite the lukewarm state of the water, she could tell it had been boiled—water purified by fire had a taste to it like tea without the tea; thinner somehow is the only way Claudia could think to describe it.

"Then what are you doing this far north if you're supposed to be attached to the White Queen's expeditionary force?" The woman spun the cap back into place on the metal canteen and resettled herself into the little arm chair.

"I'm on a scouting and mapping mission to Oregon and Idaho," Claudia explained quickly. "The White Queen wants to know if there is a newly opened route around the northern edge of the Slark line." She'd always lied well under pressure. She assumed the woman she was speaking to was probably used to ferreting out lies though and so she only gave herself a coin's toss of a chance at being believed.

"I'm sure you've got orders to prove this too?" the woman said shrewdly.

"I lost all my supplies, my orders, and most of my gear in a mudslide in Utah," Claudia said. This was the truth, at least in part. She hadn't lost her orders since they'd never existed, but the rest was true. "I wasn't even supposed to be this far west yet."

Claudia couldn't tell if the woman believed her or if there simply wasn't enough proof to the contrary to confront her with a proper accusation. Regardless, the woman didn't seem all that interested in pushing the issue. "Well, Corporal Marceau, I'm afraid I must impose on you a few more questions before I let you get back to sleep." The woman leaned forward in her chair, settling her massive arms along her knees. She was dressed like a soldier in dirty camouflage with the sleeves rolled up to above her elbows. "I am the Red Rook Bancroft—have you heard of me?"

Claudia shook her head.

"Never mind that then. Count yourself lucky you'll be able to formulate your own opinion of me before the well is poisoned." The woman didn't smile at this although Claudia guessed it was meant as a joke. The woman nodded to Claudia's empty cup. Claudia handed it to her. Bancroft refilled the cup and handed it back. "I find myself in need of a sniper. The rifle strapped to your bike wasn't just a prop, was it?"

"No, ma'am." Claudia shook her head.

"Good." Bancroft stood slowly as though her joints had already settled into the seated position too much to return to life easily. "One more question: where the hell did you get that motorcycle? My mechanics have been looking it over for a couple days now and can't make heads or tails of most of what they're seeing."

She'd been out that long, a couple days, Claudia mused to herself. "It is a prototype created by the White Rook Gieo," Claudia said. "Beyond its basic operation, I know only that it is beyond my understanding."

"Get some more rack time," Bancroft said, not really interested in Claudia's answer after it had been given. "I'll be back in the morning to take you over to meet the Owl." Bancroft walked from the room with something of a limp in her sturdy right leg.

Claudia thought her mind would refuse to return to sleep. There was too much to think about, too much to plan. Her body thought otherwise though. She finished her second cup of water and immediately fell back into a deep slumber.

†

Claudia awoke several hours later with sunlight streaming in through windows above the headboard of her bed. A doctor, she guessed the same one from the night before, was hovering in her general vicinity and came rushing over when she sat up. Bancroft was close behind as though she too were waiting only for Claudia's recovery. The doctor quickly checked her vitals, removed her IV, declared her fit for duty, and sat back smiling as though some great miracle had been performed.

Claudia gave him a false smile and thanked him. The tall, slender, doctor, well past his prime with a lot of miles on bald tires, looked like a bedraggled Irish Setter gone completely white. He took no notice of the thanks. He beleaguered the moment before reluctantly turning to other duties in the chaotic room of patients. Claudia wondered how she'd slept through the chaos as she was normally such a shallow sleeper.

Bancroft helped Claudia from the bed and pointed her to under the bed to find the gear she wasn't already wearing. Claudia was interested in a hot meal, some sort of bath, and maybe another nap, but Bancroft had other ideas. She waited only as long as it took Claudia to collect her things and lace up her combat boots before ushering her quickly out of the main infirmary.

"Are all the medical staff so attentive?" Claudia asked as they wound their way deeper into the hospital. The more of the building Claudia saw, the more she suspected it was actually a school converted to a hospital at some point. This wasn't surprising as the Slark targeted hospitals first as standard operating procedure.

"You met the one and only doctor we have," Bancroft said. "The medics and nurses we can still scrounge are burned out on the worthless side and I had thought Dr. Granger was too until you came in." Bancroft moved Claudia with gentle nudges on her shoulder in the direction she wanted her to turn, ushering her away from the loudest parts of the converted hospital to more genteel settings. "You were a special success for the good doctor. You came to his care in rough shape and are leaving in pristine condition. That doesn't happen around here."

Every glance into the various rooms they passed confirmed this statement. Claudia spotted at least a few makeshift morgues and every wounded soldier she saw appeared to be maimed for life by their injuries. As if to embody the point, the final room Bancroft ushered her into contained one man, burned horrendously yet on the mend. Half his face, scalp, indeed, the entire right half of his body appeared to have suffered severe burns giving him the look of being half-comprised of thoroughly chewed gum. Through the extent of the burns, it was difficult to tell how old the man was. In the lone remaining brown eye, Claudia caught a sense of something wily.

"Meet, the Owl, Corporal Marceau," Bancroft said, "the last survivor of our scout sniper corps and my husband."

It was clear that the Owl would never again practice the art of the distant strike. His right hand, and likely his trigger hand, was burned into a useless stump, fingers either fused or missing, and without a second eye for depth perception and range finding, he likely wouldn't be able to determine shots with any reliability or speed. Bancroft ushered Claudia to a wooden chair next to the hospital bed the Owl occupied, placing her on the left side, and not coincidentally the good side while Bancroft sat on the burned side of her husband.

"A pleasure to meet you," the Owl said, struggling to form the words with only half a functional mouth. "Don't mind my face. If it hurts you to look at, imagine how much it must hurt me to have it."

Claudia smiled and looked brazenly at the wounded part of his face. "It does not bother me in the slightest," she said, meaning every word of it.

"The scaly fucks have been breaking open the unusable cluster bombs they used to drop from their giant walkers and are hurling the bomblings like grenades," Bancroft explained. "The Owl was trying to kill the Gator when his sniper nest got hit by a salvo of the things."

"I fired one too many times," the Owl said, "and didn't hit anything of value."

"The Gator?" Claudia asked.

"The Slark commander on the other side. He came in from who-the-hell-knows-where about six months ago and has pushed our line back from Lake Tahoe to the western edge of Carson City and now he's threatening even that," Bancroft said. "If you kill him before you leave, you'll be doing us a world of good."

"Leave us to talk, my dear," the Owl said to his wife. "I'll make sure she learns from my mistakes."

Bancroft stood reluctantly, placed a sweet kiss on the burned side of the Owl's face, and took her leave. The Owl waited a good while, more than long enough for his wife to be well away before returning his attention to Claudia. A few birds, actual song birds, chirped in the trees outside the window of what Claudia guessed used to be an office of some kind. It was a strange turn of events to hear them in such a mournful place.

"Everything I have of value came from before the war," the Owl explained. "My wife, my name, my skill with a gun...it's all from before. I was a vermin hunter in a trailer park outside Vegas before the war; my wife was a pit boss at a fading casino in the old dregs of Las Vegas. It was a lean, but good life. In case you're wondering, that's where I got the name: the Owl, by killing rats, opossums, and raccoons at night to keep the trailer park clean. Tell me, Corporal, what were you before the war?"

It was taboo to even speak about the before times within the Ravens. What you were, what you did in life before you became a Raven was irrelevant—the society that had made people what they were had been burned out, replaced by what the Ravens built. The skills acquired afterward or use made of any skills carried over determined worth; the hierarchy created by a worthless, opulent society mattered not at all in a world with no need of accountants, lawyers, CEOs, or politicians. As much as Claudia appreciated the new world order, she didn't see any harm in talking of the past.

"I was a high school freshman," she said. "I sang in the school choir and was on the gymnastics team."

The Owl actually laughed at this. "That'd be the truth of it," he said. "Neither of us could return to what we were before even if the world went back to the way it was."

Claudia realized too late why the Ravens demanded a purging of one's past life. The Owl looked at her differently knowing she was an innocent when the invasion began regardless of what she'd become after. There was no such thing as an innocent anymore, but she could see in his remaining eye that he didn't see her as a viable option to kill the target he'd failed in assassinating. With his livelihood stolen from him, he could only see himself as a defunct exterminator and he could only see her as a choir girl.

"I have seventy-nine confirmed Slark kills, and forty-three confirmed human kills," Claudia said. "Have no faith in what I was—have faith in the numbers I claim. I swear, I will kill your Gator."

"Good enough for me," the Owl said. "Listen and learn from my mistakes…" He rested his head back on the pillow as though he were unloading a great weight, closed his remaining good eye, and began retelling the story of how he'd failed in killing the crafty old lizard.

Chapter 5:
Slaying the Gator.

Claudia checked and rechecked the plan. She scouted the nest and the kill zone on her own and then with her team of three others—coincidentally the three men who had found her near her bike. She didn't actually remember them, although she was assured they were the same three, not that she cared. Their task was simply to ensure her safety to and from the sniper's nest, although Claudia suspected the *from* part wouldn't be as important as the *to* part.

Bancroft's scouts mapped several kill zones along a proscribed path for the plan of luring the Gator into sniper fire when the Owl was to be the assassin. The one Claudia chose of the remaining three had a shot already known to be around 400 meters from fifty or so feet of elevation. She would take the shot from the fourth floor of what appeared to be a shelled out hotel. Of the remaining three firing positions, it was the last before the Slark fully pushed their way into Carson City. Fire pots were set along the route for light, the sniper's nest was prepped with metal plates along the front of the building to prevent return fire should the Slark spot her before or after her shot, and three escape avenues were mapped; Claudia spotted a fourth route for escape, a long, winding path through the ruins of the western suburbs, but she didn't mention it during the pre-battle briefing. Claudia and her team bunkered down in the fourth floor of the Ormsby House Casino in the early afternoon, and waited.

The three men kept their own company, silently playing cards well away from the windows on the attack side of the floor. The carpet was already stripped and the interior walls knocked down, leaving only a cement tomb broken up by an occasional pillar or pile of useless rubble. Claudia made a show of dozing against the wall even though she was too excited to actually sleep. She got the usual butterflies of performance, the same ones she'd always gotten before a choir concert or a gymnastics competition, but in more recent years before battles in which she was to take a vital shot. The last time she'd gotten the butterflies was south of Tombstone when she'd made good on her promise to Fiona by killing Yahweh Hawkins with a beautiful headshot at 350 meters. The shot to come that night was farther out and the target bigger, still the butterflies were the same.

Time to close her eyes and reflect turned into questioning her own sanity. The man at the rest area, if there had even been a man, said he recognized her accent from a man in San Francisco. This was, quite frankly, the flimsiest evidence for anything...possibly ever. Maybe she'd imagined the man. Maybe in her delirious state of dehydration, exhaustion, and fear, she'd imagined a shadowy figure. Tracking her bike at night during a torrential rainstorm seemed nearly impossible. To add to this, her accent was thin and vaguely French sounding—most Americans couldn't even place the origin language causing it let alone know it was that of a Quebecois and not European French. Even further doubt crept into her when she thought of exactly how deranged and delusional most desert folk became, especially marauders, after long stretches alone without prey. The man might have been crazy, so crazy as to never have been to San Francisco save in his own diseased mind and even if he had, he might not be able to split the differences between her accent and that of Wayne Gretzky, if the man even existed. She was such an idiot sometimes.

Claudia bonked her head back against the cement wall.

Veronica would cover for her. She could stay in Carson City, or go back to Tombstone, or Vegas, or...returning to the machine was not an option. Nor was heading blindly north any sort of plan now that she stopped to think about it. Autumn and winter would be upon her soon and Canada, especially the open lands of Saskatchewan, Manitoba, and Ontario, could be unforgiving and brutal as early as October.

Something else strange occurred to her. If her father did live, the last place he would have known to search for her was San Francisco. Her itinerary was a tour, on a bus, that had started from San Francisco, traveled east to Sacramento, down to Las Vegas, with the final stop being Los Angeles, a stop that never came as the Slark invaded less than twelve hours before they were supposed to leave. Her father knew the general idea of the trip, but in her misguided teenage independence, she hadn't remotely kept him in the loop of where she actually was on any given day. If he was to search for her, San Francisco was likely to be where he would start.

The joy of her concocted thin hope faded when she mused about what might remain of San Francisco. She didn't know what became of Los Angeles, but none of the stories carried by refugees were good. California certainly seemed to belong to the lizards. She shook this off; whatever was there, she would see it, and then decide what could be done about it all. She was uniquely qualified to survive for quite awhile without society should the need arise to eventually make her way north.

A gentle hand on her shoulder tore her from her musings. The sun was fading in the west, and one of the soldiers with the strange metal breastplates was holding up a hand-cranked radio with the incoming signal light flashing. They weren't to receive or send any actual radio transmission as some soldiers speculated the Slark were tracking patrols by radio signal. This sounded out of character for the Slark, but so too did a leader of the skill and organization the Gator supposedly possessed. No sooner had she seen the flashing signal light on the drab green handheld than she heard the sounds of battle echoing through what remained of the southwest commercial district.

She slipped into position, settling her rifle amidst some plastic sheeting and rags she'd draped around the window and several other windows throughout the building. She could hear the fighters luring the Slark, their automatic weapons clattering as they retreated in an orderly fashion, drawing the body of the Slark column into new territory. As the battle neared, she could hear the diesel engine of the Slark crawlers giving chase as the mechanical centipede-like walkers clanked along the rubble strewn roads. Through the scope and the haze of the early evening, she could follow the fires lit by the soldiers as they baited the Slark toward the trap. The ground was too open for a traditional ambush in numbers and the Gator's support force was well known to be larger than anything the humans could muster on short notice. Bancroft's plan counted on the Gator having the military knowledge to understand his advantage, using his confidence to lure him into a lone sniper. The fires served three purposes in keeping the Slark to a specific line, throwing off their normally acute night vision for anything outside the realm of the fire pots, and showing Claudia the exact path they were taking.

This was the point of exaltation the Owl had warned about. He'd fallen prey to it, thinking everything going to plan meant everything was going well. Just because they were following the path, just because the Slark made a show of letting themselves be lured, didn't mean anything else would work or that they would be helpless when they arrived. They'd easily sniffed out his sniper's nest and assaulted it expertly. Claudia took a deep breath, calming herself for the coming onslaught, steeling herself for a difficult shot as she'd made up her mind she would only be taking one.

The fighting men of the Ravens came into sight first. They were indeed working well together in luring the Slark, keeping their distance but never too far, and always pressing an attack should the Slark appear to waiver in their resolve. The ebb and flow of battle was nothing new to Claudia. She'd been in more than a few and always felt the flow as if standing in a storm with shifting winds. This one was a flood gate though, waiting to burst through, and it finally did shy of her position. The Slark made a terrible charge, frustrated by their numerical advantage being stymied again and again by the fleeing Raven soldiers. The rush didn't entirely catch the Raven men off guard, although enough damage was done to put a hopping step in the three men of her escort. She held out her hand to them, palm down, and gestured for them to hang back. They were acting, as she'd instructed, as decoys at other windows, and now she was regretting the instruction. If she'd held them back near the stairs, they wouldn't have been able to see the battle turning against the men below and they wouldn't be antsy to flee or join the fight. It was too late now to remedy that mistake in judgment.

The Slark crawlers pushed into view finally, three in all. The laboring engines running on barely processed diesel fuel struggled to move the heavy machinery at much more than a crawl, forcing most of the Slark soldiers to walk alongside, reserving the fortified positions on the crawlers for the most important of the lizard army. For what it was worth, and Claudia didn't think it was worth all that much, the Slark soldiers appeared to have suffered some pretty extreme maiming of their own in the standoff. Many were scarred or missing limbs as well although the aliens had more limbs to lose before becoming useless in combat. There was speculation among the Raven scientists charged with learning and understanding the Slark that they behaved much like earth lizards in being able to regenerate even severe body damage when they shed their skin. From the look of the Slark army, soldiers couldn't be spared to allow this level of healing without depleting the force needed to keep pressure on the Carson City humans.

Claudia scanned the first crawler and the escorts on foot around it. The Owl said he'd fixated on the first one when he'd made his attempt, and he believed this might have led to his missing the Gator. She searched again and again, checking and re-checking the lizard men, finally concluding, the Gator was not among them. The three men, her escorts started to move toward her, she could feel their eyes on her, but she held out her hand again and for the moment they returned to their positions. They were eager, unused to the patience required of the scout sniper, and she was now regretting their very existence in the building; Bancroft's reasoning behind the escort was sound as the Owl might not have suffered such grievous injuries had someone been there to put out the fires on him. Still, Claudia wasn't planning on getting set on fire, so they were more of an irritation for her than a source of security.

The second crawler through was the one she believed the Gator would be on, in the middle of the formation, able to rely on defense from the first and third in case of an ambush. She didn't like the third for it, didn't believe the Gator would lead from the rear, although she tried her best not to fixate as the Owl had. On the second crawler there were two possible targets, one on the crawler and one walking beside it. She moved on from these two, noting their positions, but not taking her initial impression as solid—this too was a mistake the Owl had made. He'd stuck the Gator label to a target too easily and only learned after that the one he'd killed was a decoy. By the time he learned this lesson, his advantage was gone and he had to scramble to find a specific target within a kicked hornet's nest. Surprise was an advantage Claudia had no intention of relinquishing.

The third crawler, which the Owl said he hadn't even really known was coming, didn't appear to be anything but support crew working to rearm the first two crawlers and their fire teams. Claudia inspected it in disbelief, not that she thought the Gator would be on it, but simply out of shock at the organization level the Slark were showing. They'd lost their command structure—they weren't supposed to know how to organize military raids anymore than human farmers, mechanics, and fishermen were. There was something indeed special about this Gator. He was either a soldier who had survived the cataclysm or he was smart enough to learn how to become a soldier under pressure. The Slark on the re-supply crawler were all too small to be the Gator. They were what the Ravens referred to as whelps—smaller Slark trusted only with menial tasks and cowardly in the extreme typically. Claudia was a little surprised they would be trusted anywhere near combat.

She returned her focus to the second crawler to check down the list of known traits of the Gator that the Owl had walked her through half a dozen times. There were a few Slark large enough to be the Gator, but only two of them were missing the lower left arm as the Owl had stated was true of the Gator. Claudia inspected these two closely. The Slark column was coming ever closer to the kill zone and the men on the ground charged with luring were on the verge of breaking. Try as she might to see the Gator in either option, neither target worked. The first one, the one on the crawler, was big enough, healthy enough looking, and appeared to be giving orders, but he was too obvious. If the Gator was this foolish, Claudia was certain the Owl would have killed him.

He also didn't have the slash scar on the left side of his face the Owl said would be there.

She checked the other possible target, walking slowly with the crawler to defend its flanks. This one too was missing the scar and actually seemed a little rattled by the conflict. She flitted back and forth between the two that were missing their lower left arm, the limb the Owl said the Gator had lost in a rocket attack two weeks earlier. Neither fit perfectly and neither felt right. She'd learned to trust her instincts, her sixth sense that sparked up when something didn't feel right. It was a natural sniper trait and one she'd learned to rely upon. The kill zone was nearly upon her though and she didn't have a target.

She wondered if limb regeneration or scar removal was possible with enough skin shedding. She didn't know how often a Slark could shed their skin or how much it would even help with a lost limb if at all. She rechecked the possible targets on the crawlers and finally spotted something strange. The co-pilot, the one beside the drive, was maneuvering the levers and buttons normally on the right side, but not on the left. From what Claudia had seen, crawlers required four arms to drive. The co-pilot was only using three, moving his upper left arm between the levers meant to be operated by two arms. Claudia focused on the immobile arm—it was a fake limb hidden by a leather, armor sleeve. The co-pilot had the scar, had the size, but she'd passed over him at a glance because he'd seemingly had all his limbs.

Wind was neither present at the height of the hotel or on the street level; her shot would be undisturbed from her rifle to its target. It was a perfect night for an assassination. She centered her crosshairs over the Slark's head, adjusted a tick to the left to compensate for the crawler's slow yet reliably steady progress. She waited for the upswing that would violently drop the crawler and its co-pilot into the path of the bullet and then gave the trigger a squeeze so gentle she may as well have been making love to it. The shot cracked out above the sounds of the fire fight. Her target, her kill, her Gator, was grasping at his throat as an ocean's worth of green blood flooded from the wound he could not gain purchase on. He slumped free of the crawler. His lifeless body was kicked a few times by the churning crawler legs until the pilot managed to get the vehicle stopped.

Claudia slipped from her nest. She made it several feet toward the proscribed exit before one of the men grabbed her arm.

"You missed," the man said too loudly for their silent work.

"No, I didn't," Claudia hissed.

"How do you know that was him?" another of the men asked.

They were all closing in on her now, and she wondered how strained these fighting men really were. She tore her arm away from the grasping hand and shot the man a reproachful glare. "Because I know," she said through clenched teeth.

"Shoot the big one, the one giving orders," the man who grabbed her demanded. "Make sure you get him."

"I'm not shooting again," Claudia said. One shot, that's what the Owl said she would have. One shot or they would figure it out. The Owl only took two, and that's all the Slark needed to find him.

"Fine," the first man said, making a grab for her rifle. "Give me your gun and I'll do it since you're too afraid to do the job right."

Claudia pulled the gun back from his initial grab, although she knew if he wanted it and his friends wanted to help him get it, there wasn't much she could do. She jumped back far enough to buy herself a couple of seconds, and ripped the bolt action free of the gun in a smooth, practiced pull. Her rifle was special, modified by her to be rendered useless with a technique she'd practiced until it was second nature and kept secret so she was the only one who knew how to perform it. She tossed the metal bolt of her rifle down a hole in the cement floor, hearing it clatter into the darkness and debris.

"Nobody fires my rifle but me," Claudia said.

The man's eyes followed the bolt as it vanished into the hole in the floor. When his vision returned to Claudia, rage had washed over his eyes. "Stupid bitch!" he bellowed. Claudia didn't see the strike coming—she honestly didn't think any Raven man would be so stupid, and she paid for this hubris when his closed fist made solid contact on her left temple and the outside of her eye.

She dropped with a fast moving fog covering her senses. She fought back against the darkness to prevent the punch from rendering her unconscious. Her skin already felt puffy with the numb, hot needles of being hit engulfing the place he'd struck; it had been so long since she'd been struck in the face she'd almost forgotten how much it could hurt. He made a grab for her, but she was ready, rolling to the side, kicking her leg out to make solid contact with the side of his knee with a thrust kick. He fell awkwardly and his two friends made the fatal mistake of grabbing to help him rather than grabbing to catch her. She rolled back and up to her feet, immediately retrieving her Walther from its holster on her battle harness. She had the three of them covered before they could be sure of what had happened. Their guns were with them, but uselessly slung along their backs. At such a short range, she could kill all three before even one of them could get a shot off. She knew it—moreover, they knew it—she'd gotten the drop on all three of them.

"I'm leaving," Claudia said. "Do not follow me." She backed out toward the stairs, never wavering in keeping her gun trained on the three stunned men. They would follow, but it wouldn't matter. She'd kept the longest of the escape avenues to herself; besides, they couldn't catch what was behind them.

Down the stairs, she doubled back to the other stairwell on the floor below and ducked into the alcove of what she guessed used to house a water heater for one of the rooms. The second floor was unimaginably dark as most of the windows were still boarded up. Darkness alone might have concealed her, but the alcove offered auditory protection as well should one of them be smart enough to listen for her breathing. She heard the thumping of the men's boots on the cement stairs and then heard them split up. They covered the three escape routes they knew of and were gone without as much as a word passing between them. Claudia waited for a good while before sneaking from the darkness of her hiding spot. She slipped out one of the side windows, walked around to the back of the building on the tiny ledge provided, hopped down a single floor, rolling to dissipate the impact of the jump down to the loading dock, and she was free of the building to head back through the suburban side, blocks away from any other escape route and several minutes behind them.

She would have to return in the morning to try to find the bolt from her rifle. By then, Bancroft's men would be pushing the Slark back toward Lake Tahoe.

Chapter 6:
Hanged.

During the long walk back, Claudia vowed to herself to become more cautious. Her talk with the Owl had done her a world of good in improving her target selection skills and her throbbing eye was an ever-present reminder of what misplaced trust might do. She'd simply succeeded so easily in the past. She'd taken to the fine art of the distant strike with ease and flair. Scouting and survival built on the lessons her father had taught her in such a familiar and natural way that she wondered if it all wasn't a fated part of her. The Raven instructors who trained her in sniping and scouting gave glowing reports that she was meant for the work and possessed natural affinities that simply could not be taught. And this, combined with easy success over the last couple of years of actual combat, had made her lazy and reckless.

The mission held darker connotations as well: the Slark were recovering from the blow they'd taken. The cataclysm was a stout blow, a destructive blow, but not a killing blow. The Gator would be the first of many to pick up the cause that brought them to earth and do so with renewed fervor. More would learn and adapt. Veronica believed they would. She'd told Claudia as much on several occasions. The quirky little pilot also seemed to think so. With ample evidence before her, Claudia had to admit she'd erred in doubting them. Still, the pilot believed humanity could outrace the Slark to new and better technology while Veronica thought brute force and eradication would suffice. As with most things, Claudia imagined the answer rested somewhere in the middle.

The background noise of battle gave way to the foreground noise of celebration as she neared the security lines of the occupied Carson City. She was identified by the soldiers on post and enthusiastically, if a little roughly, escorted toward the heart of the celebration. The loop at the front of what used to be the Carson City Community Center was abuzz with a full blown carnival atmosphere. The closer Claudia came to the center of the throng the more the zeal increased around her specifically.

A Slark body was hanging from scaffolding in front of the community center. Claudia knew the giant beam and platform well as a gallows for multiple simultaneous hangings. Men were hoisting the Slark body in the center now. Claudia was pushed forward into the focus of the excitement. Bancroft personally bent low on the edge of the great wooden platform to help Claudia up. A second guest of honor, the Owl, made his slow, shuffling way through the crowd to join them. Even battered and dusty as it was, Claudia recognized the Slark as her kill and likely the famed Gator. The Owl took a long, lingering inspection of the dangling lizard corpse. Finally, he declared in his out-the-side-of-his-mouth way of speaking that it was indeed the Gator. The gathered Ravens erupted in applause and cheers. It was a roar on par in intensity and envelopment with the rumble of the mudslide in the canyon.

Bancroft wrapped her massive arm around Claudia's shoulder, holding her close enough to speak to her, raising her voice to be heard above the adulations. "We sent some RPG equipped shock troops in after your shot. If the Gator was still in the mix, the Slark line would have hardened under his orders and we would have been pushed back by good use of reinforcements."

Claudia didn't need to hear the rest. The very presence of the Gator's body told her all she needed to know. Bancroft, sensing Claudia's shift in attention, continued by directing the rest of the information to the army around her. She held out her hands, finally releasing Claudia and silencing the masses.

"For the first time in months, the Slark showed us their backs," Bancroft shouted, waiting for the army's whooping and hollering to subside before she continued. "The famed Gator is dead and brought back as a trophy of war." Again, more cheering followed. The crowd was working themselves into a proper bloodlust and Claudia suspected they would have marched to the ocean that night if Bancroft so much as glanced to the west. "Before the autumn frost, we will push them back to the lake and reclaim our wall in time for the first snow!"

The next part, Claudia recognized in usual patterns of victory speeches as she'd attended a few over the years, would be to thank those responsible, and this she needed to stop. Claudia stepped close enough to Bancroft's side to be heard, speaking quickly in her ear before the last of the applause died out. "Broken Heiklen Law," was all Claudia whispered. Bancroft's facial expression went stone solid with fury when Claudia pointed to her swollen eye.

Heiklen was a doctor, more specifically the Black Queen's personal physician before the Slark invasion. She'd been beaten to death by her husband shortly after the war began and Las Vegas fell into an intense civil war. The punishment of Dr. Heiklen's husband helped carve the Raven Legal Code.

Bancroft abandoned the speech, leaving the rest to her husband who seemed overjoyed to simply be out of his hospital bed let alone presiding at the victory wake over his mortal enemy. The Owl took his wife's place at Claudia's side, wrapping his burned arm around her shoulder while he finished thanking her. She was barely aware of the words he spoke or the response the crowd gave. Claudia focused on Bancroft, following her with her eyes as she barked orders to a few female MPs at the edge of the stage. During a break in the noise, Claudia thought she heard Bancroft practically shout, "…they'll hang by dawn."

The speech continued on as she'd expected, even with Claudia's attention only half in the moment. It came her turn to talk when the Owl asked her how she'd managed the feat. Part of Claudia wanted to leave out the last part, the treachery, but she knew she couldn't. Rage at the code being broken was a powerful propaganda tool and the Ravens demanded she keep this rage stoked with the telling of fresh atrocities against it. And so she told the captive audience of the events of the night in her beautiful French accent, flourishes blossoming in the story as needed, until she came to the part of the story where she'd dropped the bolt action of her rifle down the hole and the betrayal that followed.

The quality of the collected army's energy mutated before her very eyes, never losing in intensity, yet no longer the same creature it was before she'd finished her story. They were angry, men and women alike. The code of the Ravens meant continued survival for so many who had believed the end of humanity was inevitable. Ruthless, yes that was the word Claudia knew for it—ruthless and necessary. Her word was evidence enough. The three men's absence, the rising black eye, and the missing bolt action from her rifle were irrelevant, archaic holdovers from a society that valued a man's claim of innocence while demanding overwhelming evidence to support a woman's accusation. In the world of the Raven, Claudia's word was enough.

Bancroft ushered Claudia toward the back of the gallows. "Let's drink away the unpleasant stain on the otherwise glorious night," Bancroft said.

Claudia couldn't agree more.

†

The private officer's lounge, the one Claudia would not have normally been admitted to as an enlisted scout, was little better than the tavern in Tombstone and in many ways not nearly as charming. The lounge was likely the community center cafeteria at some point, although it had undergone some strange transformations since then. Men and women, grimy and exhausted from war, populated the mismatched collection of tables, drinking grain alcohol from metal cups, their hands never far from their weapons. The only lights in the room came from oil lamps at each table and along the walls giving the effect of a much lower ceiling than actually existed.

Bancroft and Claudia had been drinking the epically foul liquor that was the only alcoholic drink option in the entirety of Carson City. The Red Rook Commander, despite her fearsome appearance, wasn't much of a drinker and Claudia's prowess with a bottle had long since put her at a distinct advantage over Bancroft.

"You're a liar," Bancroft slurred, nearly knocking the bottle of undoubtedly flammable alcohol into the oil lamp in the center of the table. "I'd be inclined to try to keep you here.

We could use you. I won't though. You'd just run away from here too." At this Bancroft erupted in awkward, drunken laughter. "And who could blame you? Here is a shit hole."

Enough of a fuzzy edge found its way onto Claudia's mind to loosen her tongue, but not so much to make her trample on her new vow to stop being so reckless. "You are right in that my mission is not official Raven business. I do, however, have the permission of my commanding officer the White Queen."

"What are you really doing out here?"

Claudia weighed her options. She could drink Bancroft into a stupor fairly easily if things went sideways on her. A drunken blackout might cover the memory of Claudia saying something potentially treasonous. Or, she could simply trust Bancroft.

"I am going to San Francisco to look for my father," Claudia said.

Bancroft's head nodded and continued nodding until Claudia wondered if it was a nod of understanding or a drunken sway picking an odd direction to manifest. "I understand. Maybe not the father thing as my dad was an absentee career loser, but the seeking out a loved one thought lost—that I understand," Bancroft said. "If you don't find what you're looking for out there, know that you could do us a lot of good here."

"Even though here is a shit hole," Claudia said with an inebriated wink.

This brought another laughing fit to Bancroft. "We'll fuel you up, give you what you need, and you can be on your way tomorrow," the commander said. "I don't think thanking you would cover quite what you've done for us here. We were on the point of breaking to retreat." Bancroft poured herself another drink although she appeared to be more interested in holding it than drinking it. "On a personal level, you did the Owl a world of good too in finishing the work he'd started but didn't think would ever get done. Take a wife's thanks for helping out a husband who has known enough hurt already."

Claudia reached across the table to stay Bancroft's hand before she could down the drink wrapped in her fist; she wanted to be sure Bancroft could remember her words and she suspected the drink she held might jeopardize that. "He has a gift for instructing. Perhaps he might still find his worth in guiding a new generation of scout snipers to their potential," Claudia said. "I would not have succeeded tonight without his words."

"I may do just that," Bancroft said. "Can you imagine him becoming a proper teacher after starting out a vermin...?"

"In the world of the Raven, he is what he is, not what he was," Claudia said quickly to cut off the drunken confession Bancroft was about to make. The words the Owl imparted taught her both intended and unintended lessons. As much as Claudia wished to be free of the Ravens, she knew the construction of society it was based upon was precisely what humanity needed in the world thrown down into chaos. In breaking those rules, the Owl showed her how valuable they were.

"As it should be," Bancroft said, steel returning to her spine.

The Red Rook's wallowing, albeit brief, gave Claudia hope for herself and Bancroft. Melancholy was understandable, eradicating it impossible, but with practice it might become fleeting. Claudia lifted her glass, clinked it to Bancroft's and they both drank.

"Should I ever love in the way you love the Owl, I am certain it will be my death," Claudia said, unsure of where the leak of honesty came from.

Bancroft shook her head, this time violent enough to let there be no doubt it was in rejection of the statement. "No, no, a good love, a solid love grants life. We're both still here because the other needs us to be. Find that, and love will keep you from death."

Maybe she was drunk. Maybe she was pining for Fiona and Veronica and even a little for Danny. Maybe she simply wanted to believe Bancroft. Regardless of the reason, Claudia thought it was the most brilliant thing she'd ever heard and willed herself to remember it regardless of the inebriated state she found herself in.

✝

The following morning, with her motorcycle repaired, refueled, and refilled with water, Claudia believed her mount better prepared for the journey than her. She had a hangover of biblical proportions that refused to abate even after she delayed her departure for more sleep. Staying another day to recover could too easily turn into another day and another and so on until she found more than enough reasons to abandon her search permanently; she couldn't let her hangover be a snowball to start an avalanche no matter how hard Bancroft tried to encourage it. Bancroft and the Owl came out to see her off. She was loaded down with more than enough supplies to make it to San Francisco and back again should she feel the need.

They stood by, awkward in the farewell, as though they were reluctant parents seeing their only daughter off to college. Claudia liked the comparison. It felt normal. It was also something she didn't get to experience and she doubted Bancroft and the Owl had either.

"If the White Rook built this monstrosity, I'm glad she's on our side," Bancroft said, making idle conversation about the most prominent thing in the area.

"You should see the flying machines she built," Claudia said with a little wink that left ample room to wonder if she was joking.

"One more gift before you go," the Owl said.

"I am sure I have no more room," Claudia replied, making a bit of a show of searching the laden bike for further space.

"It's not so big a gift as that." The Owl produced a metal rod from his jacket pocket, holding it out in his burned hand by a curved ball handle.

Claudia immediately recognized the bolt action from her rifle. She took it with reverent fingers, confident it would take days to locate, days she didn't have to find it among the rubble after she got a daylight look at the floor it fell to. She slipped the rifle from the holster along the side of the bike and slid the bolt back into place.

"How did you find it?" Claudia asked.

The Owl pointed to his remaining good eye with the burned stump of his right hand. "This one still works," he said with a single-sided grin.

"Thank you," Claudia said, "truly, thank you."

She left them with those words hanging in the air. It was a goodbye, of sorts, and one of the most honest she'd ever managed. The way she'd left things with Veronica churned in her. She didn't know how she was meant to say goodbye to the White Queen, but she knew how she'd done it wasn't going to offer closure of any kind for either of them. She couldn't even consider how useless and futile her goodbye with Fiona had been, if it could even be called that. Thank you, truly, thank you, felt like a worthy way of leaving things with people who helped her more than she helped them.

The bike wound its way through the remains of Carson City heading northwest to find the highway. She spotted the gallows and the fat, black crows atop it. She wondered after the birds eating Slark carrion. She knew they would if they were hungry enough, but she couldn't imagine that would be a problem in Carson. As she neared the plank, she saw they had indeed passed on the Gator's battered body. Three humans, the three men who were to be her protection, were strung up beside the Gator. The metal bands wrapped around them at mid-arm/chest level, wrist/hip, and knees told of the pain they'd suffered before being hanged. The metal bands, like rungs around a wooden barrel, were tightened until they constricted breathing, broke bones, and contorted joints. This was ended by the slow strangulation of hanging as Raven gallows held no trap doors to break necks. Criminals convicted of capital offenses were lifted off the ground by the ropes and left to dangle. Death sentences were rare as the crimes to earn them were few and the belief in the code was nearly absolute. It had been years since Claudia last saw an ironclad hanging.

She stopped in front of the gallows a moment to watch the bodies gently swaying as the crows picked at them. The daughter her father knew would be horrified. The woman she'd become saw only justice of a valiant system. Her aching left eye acted as a reminder, not of what was done to her, but what the laws really represented. If their word was held as truth, all four of them would have died in the building even after the Gator was long dead. In the Ravens, her word was law, not theirs. If they'd listened to her, they would have lived.

"Fools," Claudia muttered under her breath as she roared away from the macabre scene.

The Ravens were already pushing out the Slark, widening their holdings to the original battle lines. Claudia wouldn't have to swing nearly as wide to the north to find the end of the Slark line. Maybe, if she wasn't fast enough, she might even get swept up in the fleeing Slark if Bancroft decided to keep pushing them west. It was a silly thought. Even still, it brought a smile to Claudia's face.

Chapter 7:
Mutants of a Forgotten City.

Shooting the gap was what Claudia considered it. She skirted the southern edge of Reno, as far from the heart of the city that would contain another Raven outpost that might draw her in with more work and might not be nearly as willing to let her leave as Bancroft. Still, she needed to make the crossing far enough north to avoid the end of the Slark line. With a map and a compass in her possession, this gap shooting took place easily, keeping to unused roads that weren't nearly as choked with derelict cars as the major freeways of California still were. She broke west onto a two lane road named after a real person. The tall trees and sylvan wilderness shielded her, reminded her of Canada, and sent her morale soaring. Roaring down the open road, through a true forest, toward a possible reuniting with her father, felt right for the first time since she'd parted company with Veronica.

She marveled at the beauty of northern California as she passed through forests, around mountain lakes, passing through the most beautiful parts of the Sierras at one of the best times to do so. As the Tahoe National Forest finally broke around her, she followed Marysville Road down toward Yuba City. Here her swift progress hit its first snag of the day, coming late in the afternoon. Claudia stopped the bike well away from the edge of where Marysville Road emptied into Highway 20. She lowered the pod legs, slipped from the saddle to stretch her back and legs, and took a brief walk to look down into the lowlands below and the devastation they'd suffered. She slipped her map from the pocket of her jacket and re-checked her route. Directly south of her was supposed to be Beale Air Force Base—in its place was an entirely devastated wasteland. To the southwest, Yuba City didn't look to be much better. Her hunch, not really needing to take a closer look, was that she would lose the road entirely if she tried to pass through the field of utter destruction. Curving south to cut around would require her to rejoin Interstate 80 at some point and would take her directly into what she believed would be Slark occupied territory. To head north around would add hours to her drive and would make no promise of things getting any better. She would begin losing the light in another two hours and would have to make her attempt soon if she was to make it at all.

Claudia returned to the bike, retracted the pod, and gunned the engine down toward the ruins of Yuba City.

She didn't know what Yuba City was supposed to look like, but she didn't think it was supposed to be the strangely dusty and dry wasteland it had become. Almost immediately, passing through the shattered city, her sixth sense screamed to her that something was very wrong. She'd passed through several abandoned towns to that point without ever getting such an unwelcome sense. Her rational mind wanted to explain the ominous feeling away as a product of the level of destruction Yuba City had suffered, but Claudia knew better than to listen to her rational mind over her danger-sensing gut.

On the map, highway 20 cut a straight line exactly west through Yuba City before resuming its meandering into the coastal mountain range. If she kept this exact heading, even if she lost the road, she would end up more or less where she should. She'd attached the little ball compass the Owl had given her to the center of the handlebars on her motorcycle. Normally Gieo seemed so detail oriented and fond of multi-functional gadgets that Claudia wondered why the pilot hadn't done this when she was building the bike. Perhaps the pilot planned on celestial navigation night and day, perhaps she had a better innate sense of direction, or perhaps, and this was what Claudia thought most likely, the pilot simply wasn't done fine tuning the bike when it was stolen. Regardless of why a compass hadn't been included in the vehicle's standard package, Claudia quickly became grateful she'd added the aftermarket feature when the road fell away entirely into a post-apocalyptic wasteland of war-torn rubble.

She veered as best she could among the largest chunks of upended asphalt. The bike rattled beneath her all the same, crunching through a layer of debris and rocks of almost unperceivable thickness. With how focused she was on trying to traverse the shattered ground directly before her, she couldn't even scan the area for a better option to try to make her way toward. The vibrations even rattled the compass so severely she couldn't accurately read it to know whether or not she was still heading west. With frustration mounting, her speed plummeting, and no way of knowing if she was even still going in the right direction, Claudia finally slowed to a stop, praying she would be able to get the motorcycle moving again.

She lowered the bracing pod, which struggled to find purchase among the rocks. When it clearly wasn't going to help hold the bike stable, Claudia retracted it and tried her best to balance the bike between her legs with aid from the internal gyroscopes that held the bike upright during riding. From the look of destruction of Yuba City, the war had taken place a hundred years ago or more. What remained might interest an archaeologist but wouldn't even be given a second glance by most scavengers. A few trappings of what society once existed still remained among the destruction and dirt that had blown in from somewhere. She could see what she guessed was a McDonald's sign listing heavily to one side a few hundred meters to the south. The posts for a gas station alcove or some other lofted structure were still standing a little ahead. The top of a bus, or part of the top anyway, poked out a dingy yellow between two huge mounds of gravel to the north. She checked the compass again; she was already quite a few degrees off course, heading in a slightly southern direction now. She slid her rifle from its holster along the side of the bike and scanned the horizon with the scope to see if any roads survived.

Her sixth sense of something being off went into full blown paranoia when she spotted a dusty figure shuffling between the jagged rocks and ruins of old cement buildings. The sun was at her face now, heading quick to the southwest and an eventual setting. Getting a clear picture of what was ahead would be difficult only to get even more difficult. She tore her gaze from the scope to briefly scan ahead. She still couldn't spot anything approaching a road, though she could see other dusty figures moving among the ruins, no doubt brought to attention by the roar of her bike engine and its colossal tires crushing rocks as it roared into the devastated town.

She focused on one of the figures ahead of her, angling as best she could until the sun's glare wasn't obscuring her scope too severely. There was something very wrong with the figure. It was humanoid, yet didn't move quite right to be a person. She lowered the rifle and glanced around again for a closer target to get a better look at the strange figures wandering around her at an extreme range. She knew two things for certain: they weren't Ravens and they weren't Slark. Beyond that she had no way of knowing if they were dangerous or how dangerous. To the north, near a flat area that could possibly be an intact road, she spotted one of the hunched figures.

She lifted her rifle and inspected the figure closely. It was most likely male from the heavy set to its shoulders. It seemed to be short an arm. She turned the aperture on her scope a click to increase the magnification. Entirely swaddled in rags, the man was indeed missing his right arm, but also his left leg below the knee. He was scrambling among the rocks and rubble in a strange crawl using his left arm and right leg as his primary limbs. His head was entirely stripped of hair and his face looked as though it was melted over in plastic; not the familiar chewed up look of burn scars, but literally melted like dripping candle wax.

Claudia didn't need to see any more—she needed to get the fuck out of there. She strapped the rifle back into its case on the side of her bike. The first rock thrown at her landed woefully short, clattering among the other stones of similar size. The second rock hit close enough to send a spray of shards into her hair. She cranked the engine up and gunned it. The bike wallowed in the loose gravel. She cranked one gear higher and gave the throttle a slow squeeze, repeating a mantra of 'do not panic—if you panic you are dead' to herself as she walked herself through the steps of extracting the motorcycle from the mire she'd just put it in by cranking the engine too hard. More rocks and other items began raining down on her, a few even clinking off the bike's flanks. She finally broke free of the debris, but try as she might, she couldn't gain any true sense of control over the motorcycle's path. It bounded and leapt beneath her like a raging bull, bouncing off whatever came into its path, and all she could do was hold on and hope it remained upright.

The dust she'd kicked up seemed to serve a dual purpose. She could no longer see anything through the haze, and she had to squint to see anything at all as she'd only been using sunglasses to that point to protect her eyes and those were immediately flung from her head by a violent jolt during her bull ride. Additionally, the mutants didn't seem to be able to see her anymore either as their hurled projectiles became increasingly inaccurate into the ballooning bank of dust.

Flat ground and a light breeze at her back righted her path. The needle on the compass, nearly obscured by the dust on the plastic cover, snapped to the north and Claudia knew her course albeit in the wrong direction. She didn't dare gun the engine again, for fear the obscured road and dust stinging her eyes would suddenly end in a pit, a wall, or some other catastrophe before she could react. As the dust began to clear, slowly expanding her field of vision, she pressed harder on the engine, picking up speed, although she didn't know how much as all the gauges were covered over in a thin layer of dust. Her exhilaration of possible escape came to a crashing halt when humanoid figures began shooting past her on the road. In the dust cloud, which was clearly following her, it took her a moment to realize they weren't whizzing past her, she was driving past stationary figures going far faster than she could tell without a real reference point.

The reaction to this realization came a second too late as she crashed through a group of the mutants at a speed she could only guess at. For this moment alone, she was glad to be partially blinded by the dust in her eyes as the carnage was undeniable. Something hard knocked her right hand from the handlebar in a painful jolt. Something bigger and wrapped in rags made full impact on the front of the bike, shattering the headlamp and knocking the compass off with such force that Claudia had to duck to avoid being smacked in the face by the plastic ball. Falling back on the only information she had regarding road kill, something her father once said to her when they'd nearly hit a deer in the wilds of Manitoba: "If you are about to hit a deer, and you cannot swerve to avoid it, it is better to speed up—make the animal go high over the top." Of course, he'd swerved to miss the deer. It was just on the edge of what he and their old Toyota Land Cruiser could handle to stay on the road. The near roll over at highway speeds had rattled them both, but not so much that he couldn't impart the advice and she couldn't take it to heart. She cranked the engine, prayed to whoever was listening, and roared farther into the collection of mutants. The bike didn't catapult the mutants over the top, as her father said would happen with a deer, but began rolling over them like some demonic steed on a grisly rampage. They howled inhuman shrieks of pain and curses at her. They ricocheted off the motorcycle when they weren't sucked under. And the smell, the horrible scent of rotting flesh still clinging to bone, fetid breath, body odor, stale urine saturated cloth, and the putrescence of spilled bowel all combined into a horrific bouquet that threatened to knock Claudia from the bike.

A moment before she believed she would retch, the dust cloud broke, the open road yawned wide before her, and the mutants found room enough to scatter out of her way. She drove hard, dodging between derelict, rusted out cars, striving to put distance, regardless of the direction, between her and the mutants of Yuba City. She could still hear them behind her, screaming in their unintelligible tongue. Even after she was certain she was too far away to still hear them, she still heard them.

The sun was setting over her left shoulder—she was heading north, into what used to be farmland. She'd no doubt lost most of her supplies again and the bike was once again laboring. She needed to make camp, to give the bike time to cool down—more than these things though she needed to put space between herself and Yuba City. She pushed the bike hard, nearly to the breaking point before she swiped her hand across the gauges to clear the dust and know precisely how close the bike was to catastrophic failure. Everything was in the red. Steam was pouring out of every gasket, threatening to cook her like a lobster in the saddle if she didn't back off immediately. She pulled off on a small road to the west in the midst of pasture gone to fallow, and finally let the bike lumber into the soft, green grass between the barbwire fence and the road's gravel shoulder. She had to hand crank the quad-struts to hold the bike up, which was made difficult by the metal handle having heated to almost an almost unbearable temperature with the rest of the metal on the bike.

She rolled feebly from the motorcycle, gasping and coughing in the grass as her new and different movements kicked up more of the Yuba City dust off her clothing. She finally did throw up, which only made her feel sicker. The hangover that she'd thought might be on the verge of leaving her became a secondary concern. She didn't know what she'd breathed in during the course of her mad dash through hell, but she had to assume whatever made the mutants what they were hadn't gone anywhere simply because the Slark moved on.

Claudia crawled weakly back to the motorcycle and searched for three necessities. She hadn't lost all her water, she hadn't lost the map that was folded in her jacket, and her rifle was still strapped snugly in place.

She coughed violently several more times and threw up again. She couldn't tell if the sun was setting or if her vision was going dark. Regardless, she tumbled into unconsciousness unwillingly with the daylight fading.

Chapter 8:
A Spirit Guide to a Bridge of Fool's Gold.

Dreams, feverish nightmares haunted Claudia's sleep, scarring her mind with visions of Veronica and Fiona being torn apart and worse by the mutants of Yuba City. She startled awake, screaming so loud she wasn't even sure of the source of the noise until she'd stopped. She glanced around the gathering dusk to make sure the mutants hadn't actually chased her. The fields were quiet with only the sound of a few cowbirds chirruping their way across the man-made grasslands and the far away sound of wind blowing through open country. Her head was throbbing, her fingers were numb, and she thought she might be coming down with a migraine of epic proportions.

She came a hair's breadth from draining the last of her canteens down her throat. She checked her bike's recollection tanks first to see if the bike needed water. Miracle of miracles, the motorcycle's re-condensing chamber had functioned perfectly, recapturing two thirds of the bike's water supply and pouring it back into the two tanks. Claudia drank greedily from one of her remaining two canteens, stopping short of overdoing it as the water almost immediately threatened to come back up.

She checked the map, checked the mile posts, and even checked the scant few signs around her, all of which offered her no real information. She'd turned left while going north, which mean she was pointed west and that was all she needed to know. She slid into the saddle on the bike and started the engine. It rebelled at first but fell into the increasingly familiar dull thunder on the second attempt.

Her eyes itched and the open air blowing across them as she rode didn't help. The sun was long below the horizon and soon she was driving blind with only a couple lights on the bike offering any illumination with the main headlamp destroyed by the mutant who had nearly come up over the top of the handlebars. All of these problems seemed fine to Claudia though. She could follow a road knowing little else about it than it was beneath her.

It didn't take a doctor to know she was having fever delirium, but the thing about having fever delirium, even if one knew they were having it, was that one couldn't be made to care. Claudia laughed to herself at this realization and drove on deciding a swift death in a motorcycle crash was preferable to a slow, delirious death and certainly better than becoming one of the monstrous mutants.

She found signs, found the markers that would guide her back to her route. But then she picked up a hitchhiker, although she was sure she hadn't stopped. Veronica was with her, sometimes on the bike behind her, sometimes running alongside, and sometimes simply talking in her ear. Claudia tried to ask her how she'd found her way to western California. Her mouth refused and the words wouldn't form.

"Like a champion of perdition, you ride into oblivion," Veronica said to her. "When you reach the Pacific, will you point the gnarled front of your motorcycle toward the Far East and drive resolutely off a cliff like Thelma and Louise?"

Claudia wanted to answer, wanted to tell Veronica that she never got the references she kept making to that movie as Claudia had never seen it. Veronica was always doing that, referencing movies that Claudia had been too young to see when they existed and would now never get a chance. Movies were gone forever. That seemed sad to Claudia. She liked movies. Movies were extinct. Like dinosaurs. Movies were dinosaurs. In her fever delirium, these thoughts seemed profound although she suspected they were actually rather simplistic.

Claudia mechanically made turns along her trip. Signs told her she was passing through Santa Rosa heading south on the final leg of her quest. If she was lucky, she would have just enough left in her to cross the Golden Gate Bridge and collapse among the ruins of San Francisco so the mutants there could feast upon her. Santa Rosa was alive and well, people walking the streets, tending their yards, and out on random errands. Of course, everyone in Santa Rosa was Veronica. They all knew her though and they were all glad to see her. Claudia wanted to stop, wanted to live in this dark city that was entirely peopled by glowing specters of the White Queen, but they were all cheering her on, encouraging her to finish her trip. And so she drove on into the darkness, following the winding roads leading south.

By the time she'd reached the overlook leading down toward the bridge and the city of San Francisco, she was aware her hallucinations had completely replaced reality in such a seamless way that she couldn't be sure if she was even really awake. The city, which she'd only seen briefly when first arriving in the states, had undergone a truly bizarre change. The only building left stretching into the skyline was the Transamerica Pyramid. It stood tall and lonely above a field of black, illuminated white against the night sky as the sole remaining beacon of how to find San Francisco.

From her vantage point above, she could also see the Golden Gate Bridge was missing a significant section out of the middle. The suspension lines still flowed from one end to the other, but they were the only part of the bridge complete enough to make the entire trip from shore to shore.

Claudia wound her way down to the bridge and began her trek across it. Several chunks of the railing were missing where people had no doubt driven off the bridge in the distant past. The lanes were clear though and she was free to press the bike to its limits. She struggled to keep the motorcycle in a straight line when winds began kicking up toward the middle, setting the crumbling bridge to sway beneath her. Maybe that's where the gaps in the railing had truly come from, people trying to drive across and getting hurled off by an unexpected shifting of the bridge. Claudia found the swaying of the bridge nearly matched the swaying in her head brought on by the fever, making the entire experience rather soothing when it should have been terrifying.

Her headache was gone, replaced by vertigo and a strange sense of euphoria. Despite being freezing cold and overly hot all at once, she couldn't figure out how the two extremes weren't canceling each other out. She wondered if maybe falling off the bridge wouldn't feel kind of nice—she might have even tried if she could be sure of the water's temperature.

She pulled up nearly to the edge of the crumbling pavement, far closer than her right-minded self would have. She knew she wasn't in her right mind and didn't care. She un-strapped her rifle from the bike and slung it lazily over her shoulder.

"If you want to reach the other side, you have to climb," Veronica told her.

"I know," Claudia said, finally finding her voice. She couldn't find Veronica anymore, but she knew she was somewhere nearby.

Claudia scrambled almost drunkenly over the railing, grasping onto one of the last two suspension tethers on the right side of the bridge. Climbing it was difficult, especially with the constant swaying of the bridge and the vertigo spinning her head. She made it to the top, even managed to free climb around the outside of the massive suspension line that arced across the entire expanse of the bay, and she began walking south. Her headache was returning, the footing was slippery, and the little lines along the side meant as possibly handrails for maintenance people had huge gaps. Rather than kneel and crawl, as would have been prudent, Claudia brazenly high-wire walked these handrail-less sections.

She struggled getting down. The ribbed points in the massive cable was how she'd gotten up from the suspension wires, but getting up was apparently far easier than getting down. She slipped in the very early going, shrugged hard to keep her rifle strapped to her shoulder, and lost her handhold in the process. Were it not for a solid grip for her left hand and a fortunate weakness in the structure to create a hole for her foot, she would have followed her rifle into the bay hundreds of feet below. She watched the rifle go with a strange detachment. She needed the gun, had an emotional attachment to it, but couldn't think of anything she could do to change it or her fortune at that point. Somehow she found herself walking down the centerline between lanes on the opposite side of the bridge, beckoned on by the white pyramid jutting into the sky. How she'd completed the descent from the bridge, she couldn't be sure, and the more pressing concern was how itchy her eyes were. Veronica was gone now. Her rifle was gone. The cantankerous bike that had brought her so far, complaining the entire way, was gone. The only thing not gone from her was the will to walk toward the pyramid.

She stumbled once, but managed to keep her feet. She stumbled again and this time went over although she managed to rise again. The sun was coming up, pinking the sky in the east, and bringing with it a clearer vision of the pyramid that was her surviving focus. Ocean birds squawked, soaring nearby on their morning fishing expeditions. The water beneath her roared as the ocean struck the bay. Her focus remained on the pyramid. She stumbled again, fell, and this time stayed down. She was so close, on the other side of the San Francisco side towers of the bridge. Even still, she was done, spent, not to rise again.

She heard men, real men with real voices speaking accented English although she couldn't understand what they said. They flashed lights in her eyes. She tried to apologize to the doctor since she didn't imagine she would leave his care in pristine condition this time; it took her a moment to realize the lights probably didn't belong to the doctor from Carson City.

"Only one sparkler," one of the men said after he'd finished flashing the lights in her eyes.

"Claudia?" a familiar voice called to her. Not Veronica this time, a voice so long unheard that she almost couldn't even be sure it was the voice she remembered. "Claudia, is that you?"

"Papa?" Claudia choked out. The rising sun was over his shoulder, obscuring her view of him. Moreover, one of her eyes was refusing to work, as though she was viewing the entire world through frosted glass over her right eye.

"This one is too far gone. Over the edge with her, Marceau," a stern man's voice spoke from farther back on the bridge. "We don't have time for your flights of fancy."

"This is not a flight of fancy," her father growled. Claudia recognized the voice as a rarity. He spoke softly most often, a hard man, but with a subtle exterior. Should his angry voice arise, she didn't envy who it was leveled at. "This is my daughter, finally found her way to me."

"You've said this before, made this same mistake more than once, and this infected will not be allowed back in my city," the man's voice said. He had an accent, a British accent, high end like aged scotch and London Fog hound's-tooth clothing.

"It is me, Papa," Claudia said. "Veronica helped me, but I lost my rifle…"

Claudia was dropped from her father's arms, landing harshly on the pavement though she'd only fallen a foot or so back to where she'd originally landed. She heard a scuffle, but she couldn't regain herself enough to see what was happening. Rough hands grabbed her by the arms and began pulling her toward the edge. She heard her father's voice shouting in French after her. She could see him again, although just barely. He was being restrained by two men while a third stood by, hands behind his back, supervising. She was being lifted toward some purpose as another man grasped her ankles.

Over the side, the British man said again. He was too focused on watching Claudia's removal to notice that her father had broken free—indeed, had broken one captor's nose and the other's arm in the process. The British man didn't see her father coming, didn't seem to really understand what was happening even when her father's knife cut into the side of the British man's neck and slashed out through the front of his throat. Claudia watched the blur of her father scoop the British man's pistol from its holster on his hip even as he was falling forward, gurgling blood. Claudia's father pointed the strange looking gun in her general direction and fired off two odd sounding shots. Normal gunfire had a distinct pop, but these shots sounded more like quick hisses followed by a snap. The two men holding her fell, letting her go. She bounced softly on their tangled legs and slid down the pavement ledge of the narrow walkway on the side of the bridge. Her father turned his attention to the two men who had tried to hold him. They were still licking their wounds, shocked at his ferocity, and made little or no fight when her father shot them as well with two more of the peculiar sounding shots.

Reality began to flicker around her. Her father, strong as an ox even now, hurled bodies over the side of the bridge over and over until Claudia lost count and wondered if maybe he hadn't always been locked in this Sisyphean task and she had always watched him. Reality faded to black and she was being carried by her father toward the pyramid although he was calling it the white tower. The white tower, he told her, would be their salvation. Reality faded again only to return to what she thought was a laboratory of arcane origin. A man with a salt and pepper beard and a strange magnifying apparatus over one eye was inspecting her even as she was carried by her father.

"Possible, but not probable," the strange little man said in another British accent, this one lower, more common, but not quite Thames dredge low.

"This is my daughter," her father repeated.

The man's skepticism appeared to match his dead countryman's on the bridge, although he was hardly as dismissive. He wore his doubt plainly on his face but made no comment.

"I found you, Papa," Claudia said, reaching for her father's stony face to offer evidence for her father's words.

This seemed to change the little bearded man's position on the matter, galvanizing him to remarkable action that only a moment ago seemed unlikely. "Blast me from the rock's fort," the man said, "it really is your daughter!"

Claudia was given over to medical hands, laid on a table with wheels, and gentle hands began the work of removing her clothes. She wanted to ask after where they were going, but the question was voiced by a female assistant behind a breathing mask of some sort before she could. The incinerator was where the man instructed his assistant to take the clothes. The woman in the strange rubber breathing mask hurried off with Claudia's belongings to burn them. An odd metallic clicking followed the woman when she walked away.

"Where's the rest of your patrol?" someone well out of Claudia's view asked. She was moving away from her father and the asker of the question. She desperately wanted to hear his answer, although she couldn't be sure of why.

"Mutant attack," her father said. "They followed my daughter across the bridge."

Claudia knew the lie, knew her father's eyes would narrow when he told it, and she suspected he wouldn't be believed although she couldn't hear the rest of the conversation before she was wheeled into another room, whiter than the inside of a fluorescent light bulb.

Chapter 9:

The Girl in the Jar.

Olivia walked the halls of the White Tower with her mechanical leg straining to keep one foot in front of the other. She was growing tired of the mechanical monstrosity attached to her from just above her knee on down to the ground. It worked well enough, in short spurts, but malfunctioned occasionally and required far too much maintenance. Her reasons for visiting Dr. Gatling were twofold that day as were most of her trips lately.

Gatling's office was a wonderworks of science unleashed upon a world that craved its discoveries more than gold. A mind like Gatling's came along rarely, found its way poorly in the old world, and often pursued flights of fancy deigned useless by most, but all encompassing by the doctor. Ideas that formerly received a 'there isn't a viable market for this' response now were given a 'Godspeed, good doctor' by a society who ceased to care about profits when simple survival came at a premium. Many of these flights of fancy remained on shelves around this laboratory, stacked to the ceiling, triaged as failures, projects to return to, and projects that hadn't quite failed yet would never be completed. Dr. Gatling was at his workbench, among his inventions, tinkering with something or other when Olivia limped through his door.

The room smelled of burning plastic, metal shavings, formaldehyde, soot, and a great many other unidentifiable chemicals and scientific nonsense. Olivia had long since lost the ability to marvel at the machinery he'd managed as she wore one as part of herself and it wasn't all that wonderful.

Upon her entrance, the hunched little man extracted himself from his work and wheeled over toward her. He had also lost limbs although his were double and from the hip down. He had long since given up on creating prosthetics for himself. His time went into enhancing his wheelchair, a marvel in itself, raising him to the height he'd held before the accident that claimed his legs. The three sets of wheels in a strange triangle pattern on the side of the chair's waist-high tower, along with their corresponding gears and levers, actually allowed the chair to climb and descend stairs, an obvious necessity in the new world of very few ramps or elevators. The chair drove under battery power, guided by movements of his hips, or through manual power via fold-down flywheels for his hands.

The doctor motored out to greet Olivia, running his hands feverishly through his salt and pepper beard as though the project he'd just left had launched a face-full of itching powder at him during his work, and for all Olivia knew, it might well have. His ruddy skin, cleanly picked bald head, and beady little eyes spoke of a man who had never much thought of women and likely had never been thought of much by them. Still, Olivia would consider him charming in an odd sort of way, although she was a bit odd herself and perhaps she was mistaking fondness for a sufferer of a mutual malady for actual charisma.

"Leg acting up again, is it?" Dr. Gatling asked, knowing full well it was.

"If I wasn't having bad luck with it, I wouldn't be having any luck with it at all," Olivia said. She put her right leg forward and pulled up the cuff of her tan woolen trousers. The brass plated leg, a marvel really matching her real leg in almost every dimension excepting composition and color, required opening smooth plates to find the inner workings that might have gone awry.

The doctor popped a plate off her thigh with practiced grace and clicked his tongue in a disapproving tsk tsk tsk. "You've been hyper-winding the down thrust gears again, haven't you?"

"Not more than it can handle…"

"I swear by the…" Dr. Gatling quickly removed the bent gear rods, the gears with the worn down teeth, and replaced the main spring on the down thrust mechanism. "…I'm going to weld this plate shut and you'll just see what a time you'll have with this leg when I'm dead and gone. I didn't show you how to tinker with it so you could go over-clocking the thing. Because a clock is precisely what it is; you're wearing a glorified Swiss pocket watch in your bloody leg. Stop treating it like a battering ram."

"Fine, you have my word," Olivia said, rolling her eyes.

"I'll have your bloody leg and stick you in a chair not so nice as mine if you don't knock it off. Or a peg for a leg, like a proper pirate, wooden and stiff. People will start calling you Peg, they will, and so help me, I'll be the one to get the ball rolling." He chuckled to himself, in spite of himself, at a joke meant really only for himself as he constantly muttered such nonsense under his breath whether or not anyone was listening.

The doctor worked so quickly to replace and repair the offending parts that Olivia wondered if maybe he didn't enjoy when she broke her leg to give him a handy excuse to show off his alacrity. Still, she decided it wasn't wise to push him too far, even if he did seem to enjoy the work. She couldn't very well fight from a wheel chair and she doubted a peg leg would be much better.

"On an unrelated matter…"

"No, that patient still hasn't woken up yet," Dr. Gatling said, knowing full well what the other matter was. "Feel free to go stare at the bubbles if you like though. I'm done with your leg and don't want to be seeing it in here again anytime soon." He slipped the tools he'd used into the leather vest he wore with all the other countless tools in it and turned back to the workbench, signaling for good and all the end of the conversation.

Olivia passed through the double doors between the laboratory cluster and the clinic side of the doctor's floor. Things went from being a combination of auto repair shop and a high school science lab to an only slightly less preposterous combination of a mad scientist's laboratory and a modern hospital.

The patient in question, the one with the answer to the question asked by everyone in the City of Broken Bridges, was in a giant glass jar, filled with vaguely green suspension liquid, and supported by countless tubes and wires. Olivia stood outside the glass, as she always did, staring into the medical marvel keeping the woman alive, waiting to see if any sign of life came to the petite girl who was definitively the commander's daughter.

The girl was hauntingly beautiful, with a very slender face, a squared off chin, much like her father's in a more delicate size, and had the slightest upturn on her nose and the outer corners of her lips as to give her something of a natural bemused facial expression. Her long, curly black hair floated ephemerally around her in the suspension liquid, catching occasionally on the compression bandages held firmly over her eyes. Olivia wondered for the millionth time what color those eyes really were.

Commander Marceau, executive officer and hero of the city, said his daughter's eyes were dark blue. Olivia wanted to know what blue specifically. Gatling had said after the radiation doses she'd taken more likely than not, those eyes would be milky white like dead fish eyes at best or decayed enough to require removal at worst. Only time would tell, he said. The radiation weapons used by the Slark in the early stages of the war created different radiation than anything on earth and did very different things to people than even atomic bombs. Dr. Gatling was figuring it out, albeit slowly, and his guesses as to its effects in what doses was still fairly unreliable.

This wasn't the first time Commander Marceau had believed he'd found his daughter—this was simply the first time he was right. The commander had mistakenly identified runaways and random urchins with black hair and blue eyes as his daughter so many times that people were beginning to ignore it as a simple eccentricity of post-apocalyptic stress. Aside from the odd proclivity of seeing his most likely dead daughter everywhere, the commander's mental ship seemed to be stout and sound, which led most to be forgiving of his occasional misidentification. It was almost inconceivable to everyone when the daughter he wouldn't believe was dead actually showed up, infected with the strange radiation sickness, coming across a bridge nobody had crossed in years, and identified her father even with completely fouled eyes. Dr. Gatling had checked the DNA without the commander's knowledge, and sure enough, the girl in the jar was in fact

Claudia Marceau. Dr. Gatling had made a joke about a broken clock being right twice a day, which was far more often than the commander was in his search for his daughter, but apparently he only needed to be right once for it to all be worthwhile.

She'd been in the stasis jar for a month with November coming on quick. Her father had spent the entire time in a prison cell awaiting his daughter's words to free him. Dr. Gatling said it would be a miracle if Claudia's lungs ever worked right again. Olivia knew they only had to work right enough and long enough for her to confirm the commander's story about what really happened on the bridge, and then she could cough her lungs up onto a plate and eat them with hot sauce for all Olivia cared.

Commander Marceau's story went as follows: his daughter came across the bridge, oddly enough showing the mutants chasing her how to make it across as well. The commander moved to save his daughter, fouling the line of sight to shoot the mutants, and sadly it all went horribly wrong after. General Hastings went over the side fighting two of the mutants and his men didn't fair much better. There was blood and radiation enough on the bridge for the story to hold some water, but the possibility of five seasoned fighters all falling off the bridge held a vague scent of seafood. When none of the bodies were recoverable by boat as they all seemed to have fallen directly in the current heading out to sea, the commander was jailed on suspicion without accusation to await the only corroborating witness's version of the story.

For the hundredth time, Olivia spoke to the glass in hushed tones, telling Claudia exactly what her father said happened. Should she ever awake, the investigators would question her before she could speak with her father, and if there were any discrepancies in the stories, Commander Marceau would have a lot to answer for. The city was in enough trouble after losing General Hastings. Olivia didn't know what might happen if they lost the commander too.

Genera Hastings, the commander of the British flotilla that had shipwrecked in San Francisco right before the whole world went belly up on them, was the supreme ruler of the City of Broken Bridges. In his absence and with Commander

Marceau, the obvious heir to the despot's throne incarcerated, Olivia's own father had taken up leadership of the city. Her father was a smart and capable man, the former head of the philosophy department at U.C. Berkeley, but they were still at war, and he was a devout pacifist. They needed the commander to take Hasting's place, and they needed him soon.

Olivia stared at the petite woman in the jar for the millionth time and wondered what sort of daughter Marceau had spawned. His love for her was obvious, even to a fault in many people's estimation. Olivia wondered what this frail little creature had done to earn such adoration from such a great man beyond simply being his only child.

Olivia turned from the tank and made her way from the building. After a short elevator ride to the ground, she collected her heavy woolen pea coat at the security checkpoint. The cold, foggy day greeted her back on the street.

Her own father, the Grand Keeper of Knowledge as the city's commoners called him, earned respect easily from everyone but his daughter. Olivia loved her father to the point she thought a daughter was required, but no further. It was only happenstance that she and her father were both in San Francisco, which made her wonder how remarkable it was that both Claudia and the commander both found their way to the city independently in search of one another five years apart. The bond between them was something Olivia couldn't grasp in terms of her relationship with her own father and she came just short of comparing how far she would go to remain near Commander Marceau should they be separated. She had to remind herself that she wasn't his daughter; his daughter was in a decontamination tank in the tower.

She strolled the barren city streets with brazen, long-legged strides. Her mechanical limb whirred and clicked with every step, a sound she could still focus to hear, but one that had long faded into the background of normalcy. The war shattered most of the city's buildings save the Transamerica Pyramid. Bombardment by Slark artillery continued to tear down structures even after the great wall was built. Her father's recycling programs dismantled the rubble and cleared it leaving a great grid of what the city once was in the shape of empty foundations. The bombardments might have even continued had Commander Marceau not pushed the Slark back out of no man's land into the ruins of San Jose.

The true City of Broken Bridges lay beneath the earth, buried by earthquakes, built over through the decades, and mostly forgotten until the new inhabitants unearthed the relics out of necessity. Before the war, Olivia's father said a few blocks of the underground city of San Francisco functioned as a tourist novelty. But they'd dug deeper since then, rebuilt more, and rediscovered much of what was lost until the population of nearly 100,000 pure humans were able to exist in an entire city beneath the ground, five levels deep, sprawling over most of the oldest parts of San Francisco, and incorporating long lost sections of the city dating back to the early 1800s. There were a few thousand surfacers still, partially mutated people who hadn't quite recovered even after Dr. Gatling's attempts to cure them, still living among the older buildings of Noe Valley and the Castro. But these were not thought of as real citizens of the city—indeed, many didn't even think of them as human anymore.

Olivia strolled past one of the guarded gates into the under city, immediately being greeted by the chaos of the Chinican District where the Chinese and Mexicans melded nearest the entrances as the bastions of commerce and labor. Before the war, the two cultures had little to do with one another, but once national pride was stripped of humanity, the Chinese and Mexicans blended seamlessly into the Chinican people as though it was what they were always meant to do. Patrons crowded vendor stalls, seeking out the best prices on chickens, strange vegetables, beans, rice, and seafood. If it was grown, caught, raised, or slaughtered in the City of Broken Bridges, it was likely done by a Chinican. The first level didn't look significantly different from a modern city marketplace, albeit one completely underground. The streets were still asphalt and the buildings still of recognizable architecture.

Olivia's stop was still one level lower. The deeper into the city one went, conversely the higher they went into social standing with the Keepers occupying the lowest and oldest tier in the darkest section dating back nearly to colonial times. The second level, the one she felt most at home in, was occupied by the Cons, short for Conscripts. The drafted British soldiers and sailors who had unwillingly been forced onto ships during the earliest stages of the war, who eventually found themselves shipwrecked in San Francisco. They were the dregs of their own society and took in other dregs and immigrants along the way. Olivia, a former yeoman on a British destroyer, had joined the military willingly, which held her apart from the Cons who had been forced. She was a Bowler Con rather than a Rag Con.

Yellow, flickering lights lined the labyrinthine tunnels of the under city. Buildings dating back to the Old West held a few modernized trappings on the second level although most remained in roughly the same shape they were in when that part of the city sunk beneath progress. The streets here were dirt and rock, the sidewalks made of plank, and the architecture was that of a bygone era kept fairly congruous even in the required repairs that had to be made. Men and women in simple woolen and linen garb strolled the street, many staggered drunkenly, too inebriated to stroll effectively. She could hear the Ukrainian Cause long before she saw it. The bar, her bar, was a raucous affair owned mostly by an old Polish couple with a minor interest owned by Olivia. She'd bought her share a year ago to prevent from being thrown out so damned often.

She pushed open the heavy steel door with the spray painted U.C. scrawled across it. The interior was louder and more chaotic than the outside. The original use for the building had been a tavern of some kind, with plank floors, and the serving bar restored. Windows, two to either side of the door, were boarded up permanently as glass to fill the oddly sized panes couldn't be found anymore. Even if glass was plentiful, Olivia didn't think it worth procuring anymore since people kept getting thrown through the wooden slats they'd tried to use until they'd boarded them up permanently.

Olivia counted the top hats among the patrons and found the numbers to be about even across the boards. A smoky haze obscured the low ceiling, making all but top hats difficult to discern in the crowded bar. Top hats were worn by the eastern Europeans while the cockneys favored bowlers or bare heads.

If she belonged to a group, it was the bowlers—not necessarily cockney and still fancy enough to use a fork instead of their fingers when eating.

She pushed aside two top hats at the bar to find her place. One was a man she'd pummeled earlier that week; he gave his ground as easily as a beaten dog. The other was a top hat she hadn't yet bested, and he seemed rather perturbed about being shoved aside.

She beckoned the bartender over with a flash of her ring-bedecked hand. The bartender Orlovsky, a limping, hunched man in his seventies, dressed in a stained apron, tattered undershirt, and battered leather trousers, made a slow trip down the bar toward her, throwing a ragged bar towel over his shoulder where the stout, gray wires of his shoulder hair held it in place.

"Gimp bowler bitch, I was next," one of the top hats protested.

"And now you're next to be next," Olivia replied, not bothering to turn back. She didn't need to look to know her retort had set his bushy moustache twitching. She could pick a fight with a look or a word if she wanted. She liked to draw it out a bit more as of late, savoring the adrenaline high of combat at every opportunity.

"Step aside or you'll feel the back of my hand," the top hat said, putting his hand on her shoulder.

Olivia allowed herself to be turned, giving the top hat a coy smirk. He was bigger than her, but not by much. His protruding lips were already wetted and red beneath his impressive handlebar moustache. He had the Ukrainian accent and red swath of alcohol blush across his cheeks and nose common to the breed. He raised his hand as if to backhand her, more in threat than in action.

"It's to be fisticuffs then, is it?" Olivia asked with a little wink.

The man didn't recognize her or the challenge, new to the bar most likely. The crowd around her on both sides knew what her words meant and gathered close to catch their own glimpse of what was to come. Realizing a moment too late what was coming, the Ukrainian took a single step back as his only act of preparation. Olivia lunged forward, driving off her mechanical leg to increase the power of her left jab. The punch caught the man square on the chin, sparking blood among the stubble when Olivia's brass rings did their work. She followed it immediately with a right cross before her left even fully pulled back to cocked. The second strike sent the Ukrainian's jaw swinging like a rusty gate.

She backed out to savor the moment. The crowd gave her space, their dusty work boots dancing across the bloodstained plank floor in a familiar jig. The Ukrainian wasn't done despite the first two hits raising significant lumps. He came at her enraged, throwing a left cross followed by a wild right haymaker. Olivia easily dodged the man's left with a step to her left and ducked the follow up right. She countered with two quick strikes into his exposed stomach, doubling him over.

She set her audience to the beat of the fight music they were to dance to by straightening up, clapping her hands in the cadence, and stomping her flesh foot as the backbeat. The crowd quickly picked up the drum line of Freddie Mercury's *Mr. Bad Guy*.

The Ukrainian righted himself and threw a couple wild crosses at Olivia, who danced back out of range easily, letting him nearly stagger into their audience from the overreach. She was about to finish him, about to put him into the purple sleep of a boxer's dream when she heard the bartender, old Mr. Orlovsky, shout above the backbeat she'd put the bar into. Somehow his voice could carry about the fight like no other, cutting with clarity and strength to reach every ear.

"Get your head out of your work, Olivia, the jar girl's awake," he bellowed, holding his hand away from the receiver of the strange phone used among certain buildings in the city.

Olivia's attention flickered to the news just long enough for the Ukrainian to land a violent strike to the side of her head. It hurt, sent little stars of pain across her skull, but didn't rattle her. Before she could respond, the bar erupted around her in a dozen other brawls when the bowlers took offense to the top hat's perceived bad form against one of their own. The Ukrainian in question swamped under in a pile of three cockneys that smelled easy prey in him after seeing Olivia quick dismantling of him.

Olivia did her best to extricate herself from the bar, taking a few more lumps and having to give quite a few more before she was able to push her way back out to the street.

Chapter 10:
Friends Nearby.

Olivia could no longer run. The gears and mechanisms of her leg simply wouldn't function at anything above a brisk walk and any attempt at ramping them up only resulted in structural failure. It was a life changing factor. She'd run track at university. She'd jogged to clear her head. In boot camp, she'd finished first on most runs. But no longer. Unable to run, she lost her position as a soldier. She fought now to clear her head, only in bar fights anymore, and even then, being unable to run shaped how she fought, leaving her with no way out other than to win. She hobbled back to the tower in hopes of being there when the girl was extracted from the jar.

The sun was going down when she stepped back onto the surface. She could hear the Irradiated top dwellers scavenging among the ruins of the old city on their nightly errands. In the distance, to the south, the thunder of artillery sounded like concert drums. Even though it would fall woefully short of the wall, the Slark never quit firing the shells into no man's land, possibly defending against expansion against them, possibly as an impotent display of their faded might. Regardless of which, it kept the field clear of the true mutants that had long since followed the example of the City of Broken Bridges, burying themselves in dug outs and caves when the shelling began.

Olivia could see by the trench coat clad men heading into the tower that she was too late. The inspectors would be by the bedside when the girl awoke, spoiling any chance Olivia had to talk with her first. As futile as the errand was now, Olivia still had the morbid curiosity of seeing what sort of state the girl would be in. Dr. Gatling said it was one of the severest cases of radiation poisoning he'd ever tried to treat, but hope arose as she'd taken well to the stasis chamber. Olivia wondered after the ultimate result.

If her slow walk was frustrating, the elevator ride up to the clinic was maddening. At least when she was walking she could feel like she was in control of the pace, at least as much control as she could exert, but in the elevator, all she could do was watch the numbers tick by. She emerged on the floor of the clinic to the expected chaos of jar extraction.

The girl was out already and the tank's priming had begun anew. Dr. Gatling and the rest of his staff, which included Olivia as a volunteer from time to time, were already checking over the patient on a gurney. The three inspectors in their trench coats stood in the corner, watching with detachment. They were hard men, older men, with furrowed brows, longer graying hair, and cleanly shaven faces. There wasn't anything remarkable about the inspectors aside from the possible need for three.

Olivia positioned herself close enough to the gurney to overhear the medical assessment without drawing too much attention. Dr. Gatling was reasonably satisfied by her recovery. A few more weeks in the jar would have done her good, but that was up to Claudia, not him. Each person had their own specific tolerance to the process that allowed them a unique amount of time before rejecting the stasis—apparently Claudia's was about a month and no more. Dr. Gatling ran a specialized Geiger counter above Claudia. It crackled a little, more than normal, but not what Olivia believed would mark the girl as an Irradiate. This would matter for what Gatling would do, although not necessarily how the city would react to her. Olivia hadn't noticed any physical deformities when the girl was in the jar, but that didn't necessarily mean there weren't any or some wouldn't show up later.

"Keep her sedated, replace the compression bandages in a dark room, and run a blood panel to be safe," Dr. Gatling instructed.

The gurney wheeled away with Claudia on board, attended by four nurses, one male, three female. Before Dr. Gatling was even fully turned, and long before Olivia could reach him, the three inspectors blocked his departure by standing in a half crescent across around the front of his wheelchair.

"When can we speak with her?" the largest inspector asked. He was American as evident by the accent. Olivia didn't know if that was a good thing or a bad thing though—it was tough to tell where the Yanks fell when it came to loyalty to Hastings or Marceau.

"When I'm sure that coming out of sedation won't be agony for the girl," Dr. Gatling said, clearly more irritated than cowed by the three men blocking his way. "I must warn you though, she may not be able to speak, and she may well have been blinded long before the incident on the bridge."

"We'll determine that," one of the other inspectors said. This man was British, a Coventry man by the sound of his accent, and this worried Olivia.

Dr. Gatling seemed a little taken aback by the comment. Of the three statements he'd made, two of them were completely up to Claudia's luck, good or ill, and the third was what Dr. Gatling considered to be his call to make. "You'll not be getting the Narcan from me, nor will you compel me to administer it."

"Maybe not," the Coventry born inspector said, "but we can certainly prevent you from administering any more sedation."

The three men parted around a stunned Dr. Gatling to walk down the same hall the gurney had vanished down. Olivia took her cue to step to Dr. Gatling's side.

"Worthless bastards of..." Dr. Gatling stammered to Olivia, not really seeing her in the midst of his rage. "Those growling dogs better hope they don't ever need a doctor because I'm likely to sew their heads up each other's asses if this ends up costing my patient even a moment of pain."

"I think there was a movie about that sort of surgery," Olivia said.

Now Dr. Gatling saw her, his head of steam undiminished by the tirade to that point. "Who the hell would watch a movie like that?"

Olivia shrugged. "I guess we leave it in her hands now."

"Like hell..." Dr. Gatling wheeled away with a determined slant to his shoulders.

†

Claudia couldn't describe the truly bizarre sensations that greeted her. It was as though she'd awoken to find herself scuba diving in complete blackness. This was followed by the most wondrous drug high of floating, cushioned euphoria. This absolutely wonderful feeling evaporated like a puddle in the sun, so quickly and completely that Claudia, try as she might to hold it, found herself instead dropped into a new world of agony. More than simply being rid of the agony, she wished for a return of the euphoria. She became aware, reluctantly, that she was in a bed, in a room, with her eyes held shut, and machines beeping out her heartbeat. She must have moved or shifted to let someone know she was awake, because immediately following, she heard a growling voice to the left of her bed.

"This is pointless. What the hell information could we even get from a burned up Irradiate anyway?" the growling man said.

"The doctor says he ran the DNA," another man, this one with a British accent to go with his growling voice, said from the other side of her bed.

"So it's Marceau's daughter? So what?" the first man said, sounding increasingly frustrated. "Sounds to me like that'd make her more likely to lie." She could feel the man's breath as his face came closer to hers, blowing hotly against her cheek. "Wake the fuck up!"

"I'm awake, I've been awake," Claudia said. "Watch how you speak to me. The code of law forbids…"

"Get a load of…code of fucking law?" the British man laughed. "We are the fucking law, girl."

A horrible realization came over Claudia. Wherever she was, it wasn't Raven territory. She was blind, felt weaker than if she'd spent six weeks battling a flu bug, and she believed, as all Ravens believed, that any society ruled by men would have very few, if any, laws to protect women.

"No need for all that," a refined, softer voice said from behind the first speaker. He had a British accent, but none of the harshness to his tone or timber. "We are inspectors of the City of Broken Bridges. I am Cavanaugh, and these are my associates: Billings and Anders. Around the stationhouse, we're called the ABC Detectives. If you can believe it, we were matched numerically, not alphabetically."

"Stranger things have happened, I suppose," Claudia said. She desperately wanted to remember how to placate men. The truth was, she hadn't been in such a weak position in so long that she couldn't even remember the last time it'd happened, let alone what she'd done. She knew to make her voice soft, to lull with her accent, but didn't know what to say once she had.

"Stranger things indeed," Cavanaugh said. "Like a young woman making it across the Golden Gate Bridge in the middle of an extreme case of radiation poisoning."

Claudia could hear chairs moving, clothing rustling on both sides of her, and then smelled a strangely warm cologne or aftershave reminiscent of spice and leather. "Was that what happened to me?"

"Why don't *you* tell *me* what happened to you?" Cavanaugh said.

Claudia knew to lie, and typically lied well under pressure. Training as a scout sniper included a few courses in counter intelligence to resist interrogation should the often lone operating sniper be captured; she excelled at this too, building on her natural urge to lie anyway. Still, she typically could see facial cues to tell her whether or not a lie landed and where to take it next from reactions of the listener, which was obviously out of the question. Omit the unimportant, seek verbal clarification where possible, and reveal weakness only with reason—these were the counter-terrorism techniques she could remember off the top of her addled head. She ached, felt nauseous, her sinuses were dried and uncomfortable, and her head felt tingly; what she really wanted was more of the euphoria drug and to be left alone to enjoy it.

"I crossed the bridge on the suspension wire, looking for my father," Claudia said, waiting for a few moments after for verbal confirmation, hoping to force Cavanaugh to come to her for more information, possibly providing some of his own in the process.

"Go on," Cavanaugh said, giving her nothing.

"And I found him. Where is he now?"

"Your father is busy at the moment," Cavanaugh said. "Was he alone when you found him?"

Claudia wanted to smile. She'd gotten an answer that told far more than Cavanaugh probably wanted her to know. "No, there were five men with him, soldiers I would guess by the look of them." Claudia waited until she was certain Cavanaugh was about to speak before she continued. "Can I have a glass of water?" Someone walked from the room after a few seconds and Claudia guessed one of the men had been unwillingly dismissed to fetch the water by Cavanaugh.

Cavanaugh waited until the footsteps returned. He touched her hand with one of his and gently guided the plastic cup into it. His hands were soft and his touch even softer, which surprised her as most men she knew in the new world order had long since lost any trappings of self-tending. Claudia took the cup and sipped a few times from it. There was a strange, malingering taste in her mouth that she hadn't really wanted to swallow, but didn't really think trying to spit it out would be a good plan while blindfolded. That was a distinction she was becoming increasingly aware of—she was blindfolded, not blinded.

"Now, what happened to these men with your father?" Cavanaugh asked, waiting long enough for Claudia to drink quite a bit of the water before he continued. He didn't seem remotely concerned with giving her time to collect her thoughts—a worrisome trait.

She certainly couldn't tell the truth now and she doubted a half answer would suffice. "I don't know," Claudia said. "I passed out in my father's arms when I saw him. Is my father okay?"

"Your father is fine, for the moment," Cavanaugh said.

This statement, Claudia accurately identified as a threat. She had misjudged Cavanaugh as simply playing the good cop, waiting for the time to hand off the interrogation to one of the other two to play the bad cop. He was both good and bad cops rolled up into one with the bad part likely being the truth of it.

"Are the men who were with my father okay?" Claudia asked, perhaps a little too slyly.

"Would that upset you if they weren't?"

He was smart, probably smarter than her, and he had her at a ridiculous disadvantage. If their cat and mouse game continued, she knew he would find a way to slip her up eventually, and she guessed he had the patience of stone to get there no matter how long it took. With the fuzziness still floating around her head, she wasn't going to be able to think fast enough to plan several moves ahead and she wasn't sharp enough, especially not without visual cues and facial expressions, to wing it.

"Mind your toes boys," a gruff voice echoed across the room, "my patient needs her bandages changed and her eyes checked."

"Turn the lights back on. We're in the middle of..." Cavanaugh began.

"You're in the middle of blinding an innocent girl if you don't let me do my work," the gruff man said. Whirring and clicking of spoken wheels powered by a motor brought the gruff voice closer to Claudia. "I don't know what nonsense information you're after from her, but you can get it when her bandages are changed and her eyes are checked." Something bumped the side of her bed with a metal on metal clink. "Mind the tray table, will you? I'm not exactly in a good position to bend over and pick things up if you spill them, Inspector." Claudia felt something rattle her bed from beneath, but couldn't be certain if she was simply being jostled from a different angle.

Cavanaugh apparently relinquished his position beside Claudia's bed as the scent of aftershave lingered a moment before being replaced by the smell of adhesives and possibly gun oil. Careful hands made quick work of the bandages Claudia had mistaken for a blindfold. The room was dark and whoever was tending her did so by a faint light over his back shoulder, creating a shadowy silhouette with frizzy beard and some sort of headgear. She didn't know who he was or what he was about and she didn't care—her loudest thought was simply glad she hadn't actually gone blind. The careful hands, which seemed so eager a moment ago, were slowing their inspection of her eyes and bandaging work intentionally. Claudia didn't want to have her eyes covered again, but it was clear that was the task ahead. As the world vanished under the cotton and gauze of bandages, she heard a soft, insistent voice whispering in her ear opposite the side of the frizzy silhouette tending her eyes. The woman's voice was husky with a pleasing British accent.

"You were chased across the bridge by mutants," the voice whispered into Claudia's ear. "Your father was the lone survivor of his patrol. The rest went over the side of the bridge. Take strength in these words and know you have friends nearby." A strong, yet soft hand gripped Claudia's in a reassuring squeeze. "I will be under your bed should this interrogation turn violent."

And just as quickly as the voice came, it was gone. Claudia was once again bathed in the darkness of bandages over her eyes and her hand was once again left alone. She felt someone shift the frame of the bed, presumably the owner of the voice keeping her word in hiding beneath the bed.

"We'll have to keep the lights low in here," the gruff voice said, probably to Cavanaugh. "I've given her drops to dilate her pupils and even with the bandages on she shouldn't be exposed to light."

Claudia knew this was a lie. She'd had such eye drops before during eye exams as a child and she'd only been given plastic goggles that didn't block out even a fraction of the light the bandages did. More than that, she didn't remember the gruff man giving her any eye drops. The gruff man knew about the whispering voice, knew she was hiding under the bed, had likely brought her in beneath the tray table he clanked against her bed, and wanted to make sure Cavanaugh didn't discover her. Perhaps Claudia had two friends in this.

The scent of spicy cologne returned with an audible sigh as Cavanaugh sat back into the chair, pushed slightly out of position now. "Where were we?" he said.

"You were asking about the men with my father," Claudia reminded him.

"Yes, of course, what happened to these men—you said there were four of them, correct?" Cavanaugh asked.

"No, I said five," Claudia corrected him, knowing full well his game.

"Ah, yes, of course. Go back a moment if you would, what happened before you saw your father?"

"I was chased across the bridge."

"There were people chasing you?"

"Yes, but they weren't normal people."

"Mutants, perhaps?"

"If that's what you call them. The soldiers with my father must have fought them as they were sure to catch me soon. I was very tired and very sick."

Claudia could hear Cavanaugh exhale heavily out his nose. He shifted in his seat and she heard the scratching of him writing something on paper with a pencil. "And what happened after that?"

"I don't know," Claudia said.

"You didn't see anything else?"

Claudia laughed and tapped the side of her fresh bandages beside her left eye. "I feel lucky to be seeing even the backsides of my own eyelids."

"Indeed, thank you for telling us what you know." Cavanaugh flipped the cover of something shut, Claudia guessed the notebook he'd been writing in, and then stood from the chair.

"That's bullshit, Cavanaugh," the American man said from across the room. "She knows something."

"Perhaps she'll remember more later," Cavanaugh corrected the angry American. "We'll let her rest and see if something else comes to the surface."

Three sets of shoes walked across the room and out the door. Claudia waited for some time after the men left, wondering if the voice had indeed hidden beneath her bed. Her answer came after a few minutes when she felt the bed shift again. The soft hand was once again holding hers lightly with the gentle voice whispering in her ear.

"You did well," the voice said. "They'll have to free your father now."

"Who are you? Where am I?" Claudia whispered.

"I am Olivia and you are in the City of Broken Bridges," the voice replied.

"Is my father okay?"

"He is jailed the last month, waiting for your words to free him, which you just did."

A month, Claudia mused, she'd lost an entire month to a coma. It was better than being dead, blind, or mutated, she supposed. "Would you stay with me awhile?" Claudia asked.

"I've visited you so often, a little longer couldn't hurt." Olivia held her hand still, although shifted until she was clearly sitting a little higher than the floor. Again, Claudia heard a strange ticking and metallic clicking like a clock when Olivia moved. "I've wondered for weeks now where you came from and how you found your way here."

Claudia sighed and began telling the bare bones of her story, of the Ravens in Carson City, the mutants in Yuba City, the accursed motorcycle, and even the man swept away by the mudslide who had given Claudia her only lead. Without seeing Olivia's face to judge her reaction, Claudia was left to wonder what impact her words might have had on the silent holder of her hand. Finally, Olivia responded, her voice closer and lowered by emotion.

"You and your father are cut from the same cloth, Claudia Marceau," Olivia whispered to her.

Chapter 11:
Sights Unseen Not to be Believed.

A week passed under the cover of bandaged darkness. Claudia only caught brief glimpses of the room she was in, always in darkness, and outlines only of Dr. Gatling and Olivia. Thankfully, the inspectors did not return, although Olivia informed her they were doing their best to delay the release of Commander Marceau.

Claudia split her waking hours between telling Olivia of the outside world and listening to Olivia read to her in the lovely accent Claudia was increasingly enamored with. She still couldn't precisely say what Olivia looked like, but she found her charming and dedicated, which increasingly drove her attraction.

When the time finally came to remove the bandages and offer Claudia her first darkened look at the world, she requested that Olivia be the first face she saw if her father was still not free at that point. Dr. Gatling waited until nightfall to remove the bandages, keeping the room dark as a precaution. A faint candle, heavily shaded, offered the only light, kept far from the patient in the corner of the room. Claudia's bleary eyes scanned the room as it slowly came into focus, finally settling on the woman sitting half on the foot of her bed, head cocked to one side in a quizzical pose.

Her sandy blond hair was cut short and styled messy. Freckles dappled her cheeks and forehead. Her eyes were large, rounded, and the pleasant color of chestnuts. She had the look of a World War II bombshell dressed in an appropriate fleece-lined leather bomber jacket. Claudia smiled to her and the woman smiled in return with her pert, chapped lips.

"Olivia?" Claudia asked.

"In the flesh, more or less," Olivia said.

Olivia moved closer and took a harder look at Claudia, which offered Claudia the same opportunity for close inspection. Olivia had a slight bow to the right in her flat little nose indicating a badly healed break. Her lips had a few scars indicating they'd been split repeatedly with several cuts that likely required stitches to close. A large, jagged scar cut its way from Olivia's hairline above her left eye down, skipping over her right eyebrow, and then completing its run on her right cheek. Among Ravens, scars were badges of honor—Claudia envied Olivia's.

"Is that normal?" Olivia asked, looking very closely at Claudia's eyes.

"Talk about things not to say to someone who just got eye bandages off after a week," Claudia said.

"Five weeks," Olivia corrected her. "You keep forgetting about the stasis chamber."

"She's irritating like that, isn't she?" Dr. Gatling said, roughly turning Claudia's head to face him. A faint headlamp illuminated Claudia's face, although the good doctor was careful to keep it from directly shining in her eyes. "Well, that'd be a new one on me."

"What?!" Claudia said.

"Maybe something, maybe nothing," Dr. Gatling said. "Were your eyes always two different colors?"

"No, of course not," Claudia said.

"Not different colors," Olivia interjected. "The same color—different shades."

"Hold your hand over one eye and then the other," Dr. Gatling said. "Is there a difference in your vision?"

Claudia did as instructed, holding her hand over her right eye and then her left. Something indeed did seem strange when she looked only through her right eye. The green lights on the display of the heart monitor machine looked strange, as if they were more multi-chromatic, not quite rainbow level, but definitely with more variation in color than the plain green her left eye saw.

"The light on the machine looks different," Claudia explained. "More colors mixed in."

"More colors…" Dr. Gatling mused. He continued musing under his breath as he wheeled out of the room, returning shortly with a strange device that looked a little like an electric lantern but with a strangely small bulb. "…more spectrum maybe…pigmentation problems could have a lot of explanations…worth a look regardless." He guided his wheelchair to the opposite end of the rather large room so he was well concealed in the darkness away from the flickering light of the candle. "Tell me, both of you, how many fingers am I holding up." He snapped a button and a faint buzzing filled the air.

Olivia strained to see through the darkness. "I don't know—four?"

"Two," Claudia said, "your thumb and your index finger."

"How did you see that?" Olivia asked.

"The light he turned on," Claudia said, still holding her hand over her left eye.

"She's seeing outside the normal visible spectrum," Dr. Gatling explained. "The lamp I turned on is a chromatograph for a radiant color of an ultraviolet wavelength humans can't see."

"Why would you even have a thing like that?" Olivia asked.

"To check if I could see it," Dr. Gatling said. "I've been experimenting with Slark radiation treatments on lenses to create bifocals that see outside the normal human spectrum of light. What we see is highly limited in the grander scheme of all radiant light. I believe the Slark see in a spectrum we don't."

"You call them Slark too?" Claudia asked, momentarily distracted from the bizarre news about her eyes.

"Yes, of course," Dr. Gatling said. "It came from the military—Six Legged Artillery Rover…it's what the military called the giant platforms before we knew what was on them. They added the 'K' to mean 'kill' when they finally started downing them. But that's neither here nor there." He set aside the lantern and wheeled back over to the bed. "The real developments began when we started taking their technology apart. They have radiation unlike anything on earth. I thought I could use it to create a lens that could see a broader range of UV light. We have bulky, delicate machines that do this, but I thought I could create a simple lens with no moving parts perfectly attuned to the Slark spectrum because it would be created by the Slark spectrum. Your eye proves my theory correct. Certainly, the lens is the natural lens inside your head, but the principle is sound!"

"Wait, you were irradiating spectacles?" Olivia asked. "Weren't you concerned about giving yourself eye cancer or something?"

"Oh my goodness no," Dr. Gatling said with a dismissive flap of his hands. "I didn't wear them myself. I used the Irradiated patients to test them—they're reasonably immune to Slark radiation, as, I might add, is Miss Marceau now." Dr. Gatling clearly lost himself in thought again, tapping a little copper lever on his headgear against the prickly beard on his cheek. "But she's worthless for testing the lenses...she can already see the UV spectrum beyond normal parameters. The practical applications still remain, jumping my research over the prototype testing to actual field work..."

"What practical applications are you on about, doc?" Olivia demanded.

"The Slark use lights for communication that we can't see," Dr. Gatling said. "I was going to build detectors to try to find them if the lenses thing never came together, but now we have a working human eye, lighter and more portable than anything I could build."

"I can see the Slark's communication?" Claudia asked.

Dr. Gatling nodded. "In theory, anyway. We still need field tests. It's a shame we only have one..." and then he was gone from hearing range, out the door, and back to the lab.

"Is he coming back?" Claudia asked.

"Probably not for a few days," Olivia explained.

"Do you have a mirror?"

"Worried you'll look strange with an eye two shades lighter than the other?" Olivia asked. "Whatever doesn't kill you makes you a little stranger."

"True, although I'm not sure that is how that saying goes," Claudia said.

"It is now." Olivia sat on the edge of the bed, closer to Claudia. She pulled up the cuff of her trousers to display her mechanical leg with the lustrous copper plating. Claudia looked deeply into her own reflection on the prosthetic's surface. It was difficult to tell color in the golden mirror of Olivia's leg, but she could definitely make out the drastic difference in color concentration between her eyes.

"How did it happen?" Claudia reached out a tentative hand and touched the metal leg. It was vibrating at a highly regular interval and almost sounded like it might be ticking.

"One of the Lasher Trees got me," Olivia said.

"Lasher Trees?"

Olivia pulled the cuff of her trousers down and gave Claudia a questioning look. "I forget, you've never seen Slark occupied territory," she concluded. "They brought their flora and fauna with them and it's pretty horrible stuff. Didn't you wonder what they were doing here?"

"All that is above my pay-grade," Claudia said, borrowing a line her father was fond of saying.

"The Keepers think they're probably colonizer refugees from a dead or dying world," Olivia explained. "They brought their menagerie and equipment to make good use of them. We destroyed their fishing fleets a dozen times before they ran out of Slark who knew the trade. I'm not sure what they use the lasher trees for."

"Fishing fleets? They brought fish with them?"

Olivia smiled and shook her head. "What have you been fighting them with in the desert? Pointed sticks and heavy rocks?"

"Guns, mostly," Claudia said, feeling a little foolish for the answer. "Horses too."

"The fish are where they get their fuel," Olivia said. "It's from a gland or some such squishy bit that turns the blood into…I don't really understand the process, to be honest. Dr. Gatling figured it out almost immediately. We've been plucking them from the sea and making our own version of the fuel for years now."

Claudia's eyes went wide, which kind of hurt a little. "How…?"

Olivia stiffened a little at the implication. "We're English," she said. "We're the island nation who took to the sea and forged a global empire with limes, pluck, and wooden ships. The oceans are ours and always will be. Hell, sometimes we run our ships down to Los Angeles just to fire a few volleys into their home."

The last bit was a boast, and one Claudia easily spotted among the braggadocio of it all, but she didn't doubt the rest of it. If the Slark had been able to fish the waters, they would have had Slark fuel to fight the Ravens with, and they didn't. It was a vital piece of the puzzle, and one the Black Queen or even the pilot would have been able to make astounding use of if someone could actually carry the information to them.

"I could scream or kiss you or both," Claudia said. "If only there were a way…"

"I wouldn't say no to a kiss," Olivia interrupted.

Claudia glanced down to find Olivia's fingers with the scarred up knuckles were fidgeting among the sheets of the bed. The accursed romantic in her, the one who came along with the ruinous streak inherited from her mother, set aside all concerns. Claudia watched the fingers, considered the offer, and planned her next move. She lowered her head just enough for some of the black curls of her hair to fall across her face. She looked up through the curtain she'd created and smiled impishly. The effect on Olivia was obvious and precisely what Claudia hoped for.

"You're looking for appreciation, yes?" Claudia asked. She waited for Olivia to answer, wetting her lips when her flirting partner began to speak.

"I wouldn't say…" Olivia trailed off, her full attention drawn to the glisten on Claudia's lips catching the faint candlelight from the corner of the room.

"Thank you," whispered Claudia. She slid closer to Olivia, placing her hand on Olivia's to soothe her fidgeting fingers. She waited again, showing patience in the dance, until Olivia looked ready to speak. Before she could, with the words left unformed in her mouth, Claudia kissed her.

Olivia's offhand comment was the only spark needed to ignite Claudia's tinder. From what little she'd learned of Olivia over the past week, Claudia knew the respect and admiration she received from Olivia was at least partially based in being the daughter of someone the Brit greatly admired. Fantasy, regardless of the bizarre source, was something Claudia thrilled at fostering. She thought herself a talented gardener of romantic desires with a red hot thumb for the work.

Olivia cupped Claudia's face, taking the cue as aggressor when Claudia began pulling her toward the bed. Claudia let Olivia lower her head to the pillow in an ineffably sweet gesture that maintained the escalating contact of the kiss. Olivia's lips were so full, so lovely, with just a little rough edge from lack of tending in a harsh land—Claudia loved them as she imagined they were what Fiona's lips would be like. She lifted her hand to grasp the back of Olivia's neck, drawing her down to deepen the kiss.

A man cleared his throat from the doorway bringing the kiss to an end with such suddenness that Claudia wouldn't have been surprised if it made a snapping sound when it broke. Olivia and Claudia whipped their heads to look to the door in unison. Standing proud and tall, backlit from the hallway, was Commander Marceau. He had a slender face similar to Claudia's although his features jutted with prominent structures on the jaw, chin, and cheekbones in ways hers didn't. His eyes matched her left eye in piercing, deep blue, but unlike her, his hair was tan on the border of blond, clipped short with graying edges around his temples. From the last clear image in Claudia's head, he looked older, more rugged, with a few extra scars and a little less muscular bulk, but the eagle's sharpness in his eyes remained stronger than ever, perhaps even more so.

"I am glad to see my daughter fit enough to flirt well," Commander Marceau said, "although I am surprised you would fall so easily for her charms, Ms. Kingston."

Olivia pried herself from Claudia's grip and stood as quickly as the whirring gears within her leg would allow. She saluted crisply, staring off into a space that was neither at the commander ahead of her or the commander's daughter directly before her. "My apologies, commander."

"Never mind that, Kingston, but if you don't mind, I would like to speak with my daughter."

Olivia saluted again, took one glance down to Claudia who rolled her eyes as though she should have stood up for herself regarding the kiss, and then Olivia walked briskly from the room. She stopped briefly at the doorway. "It is good to have you back, commander."

"It's good to be back, Kingston," he said over his shoulder. He waited a moment until the clicking of her leg fled down the hall beyond hearing. His attention returned to Claudia and a proud father's smile painted his lips. "My daughter, still kissing the boys *and* girls, only to break their hearts, no doubt."

"I am my Papa's daughter," she said.

"You are more than I would have expected from even myself." He crossed the room to her, scooping her into his arms, kissing her hair as he did when she was a child. "My little Claudia, my world, I never stopped hoping…"

Claudia cried tears of joy into the shoulder of his gray, tattered jacket. She knew his words were spoken with the purest truth, not simply because she remembered what was said on the bridge or what the inspectors had alluded to, but because she hadn't ever stopped hoping either, and she believed their hearts had always beat as one. "Neither did I, Papa, neither did I."

Chapter 12:
Wonders Never Cease.

Days passed and Claudia still didn't feel completely well. Her lungs burned with even minor exertion, requiring constant treatment with a nebulizer. She walked the halls of the White Tower, which was the new and proper name for the building, with her father or Olivia depending on who was able to get away from their duties the longest. More and more frequently, it was Olivia as her tasks as a part owner of a tavern were significantly lighter.

"There is talk of a permanent split in the power structure," Olivia explained on one of their strolls around the building.

The interior of the building, which once served as office headquarters had long since transformed into a multilayer government building, hospital, scientific research station, and from what Claudia could tell, a military command center. She preferred inspecting the interior of the building to the exterior as what was going on outside was fairly disquieting.

"You mean nobody offered to step into the role of supreme ruler since Hastings' death," Claudia said.

"The only man who could is your father and he doesn't want the job," Olivia said.

Claudia knew this wasn't entirely true. Her father mentioned that there was still a significant contingent among the civilians and likely within the military that thought her father had killed Hastings to do exactly what Olivia said he didn't want to; only she and her father knew they were partially right in their thinking. This concerned Claudia. She knew why her father had done what he'd done, but she couldn't be sure if he wasn't taking Hastings' spot because he didn't want the job or because he didn't want to be perceived to want the job. She had a lousy head for politics, indeed interpersonal back biting nonsense in general as she saw it.

That was Veronica's thing, never Claudia's.

"I would assume it is to be a split between your father and mine," Claudia said.

"My father claims it would be between the military council and the entire Oligarchy of the Keepers, but yes, in essence it would be them." Olivia seemed antsy, her leg clicking and ticking as they walked appeared a little tightly wound, like she would rather be running.

Claudia reached over and took her hand to calm her. "Do you not think this is a good idea?"

Olivia calmed some, but there was still an edge to her posture and words. "Why would I?" she said sourly. "My father is no leader. It should be your father entirely as it was with Hastings."

They stopped at the corner windows of the floor they were on to look out over what had become of San Francisco. To the west, rolling hills, newly green with crops marked out what had once been a bustling city that was there no longer. The setting sun struggled to press through the cloud cover above the sea, giving enough golden light at the end of the day to illuminate the meandering appearance of giant metal monstrosities walking out of a great cavern in the ground amid the fields. Claudia let go of Olivia's hand and walked to the window for a better look.

The robots, for lack of a better word, stood thirty or forty meters tall a piece. Half a dozen of them walked from their earthen realm in surprisingly fluid motions. They looked slightly different, although all were more or less humanoid in shape. Some had multiple limbs, longer limbs, differently jointed legs and arms, various metals for plating, but all were exceedingly beautiful as though Leonardo Da Vinci decided to build robots out of old Aston Martins. The impression Claudia got from the robots, not only because the Irradiated field workers didn't seem to mind their sudden entrance, was that they were calm and definitely not dangerous despite their size.

"What are they?" Claudia asked in reverently hushed tones.

"They're the Transcended," Olivia explained. "The Keepers say it is what they become when they choose to move on, whatever that means."

Claudia glanced over her shoulder to Olivia and cocked her head to one side as if to say the explanation was lacking in sense and content. "What are they, though?"

Olivia walked over to the window as well. "Exactly what they look like: giant freaking robots. I've been around them for so many years, I guess they don't seem that interesting to me anymore. They build and invent, recycling whatever they find into something more useful. They took apart the entire city over the course of a couple years, built a wall spanning the entire width of the peninsula, and now they simply build things they think will be useful to us out of the scrap they pull from the ruins of what was San Francisco."

"Are they dangerous?" Claudia asked, although she seriously doubted it.

"They don't seem to have any notice of anything living at all," Olivia said. "They won't fight the Slark, they won't help with growing of crops, and they don't even seem to see the Irradiated surface workers although they would never step on any of them. They simply exist in a world beyond what we can know or understand, building whatever they feel like for as long as it takes to be built, and then returning to the underground for rest, I suppose."

Claudia watched them for a time, sorting through piles of already sorted scrap, plucking pieces out as they saw fit, and then beginning some construction project using the tools that were part of their bodies.

"I guess your saying applies to humanity as a whole: whatever doesn't kill us simply makes us stranger."

"Close enough, although from what you've told me of your Lazy Ravens, I think it also gave us an opportunity to set things right."

Claudia shrugged to this. She didn't really know another way. She had a childish, vague understanding of the world that came before the power structures that ruled it. She was a fairly sheltered 14 year old girl from an idyllic town in one of the most peaceful countries in existence when the Slark invaded. What she knew of the world was simplistic at best before the Ravens and what she knew of them…she was beginning to understand better.

"I believe I made a mistake of the 'grass is greener' variety when it comes to the Ravens," Claudia said. "It's easy to become complacent and spoiled in a society built for you."

"Yes, but I envy that you have that concept," Olivia said. "Most women go their whole lives without knowing what it feels like."

Claudia smiled to her and leaned lightly against her shoulder. "You would be highly prized among the Ravens for your courageous heart, willingness to fight, and military training."

Claudia found out earlier that week that Olivia was thirty and well on her way to thirty-one years old. She'd taken her university training and military service all before the Slark were even known to exist. She'd lived her entire life within the construct of men. Claudia was barely twenty years old, but she wondered if maybe she and Olivia weren't coming to the same point of world weariness—more macabre thinking born out of the ruinous streak from her mother, Claudia surmised, but she couldn't shake the feeling.

"You're a morose little thing," Olivia said, giving Claudia's side a playful tickle.

"*Oui*," Claudia replied, "and to think, I have not yet known the heartbreak of a lost love. How insufferable I will be when this finally happens."

"I'm going to talk to Dr. Gatling about letting you get some time out of the tower," Olivia said. "I fear you're in danger of becoming a Bronte sister without the writing talent."

"*Merci.*" Claudia smiled as if she knew what that meant.

Claudia was exceedingly worn out by the walking and talking of the afternoon. Olivia walked with her back to the room, gave her a cordial kiss on the cheek, and took her leave. As Claudia passed into sleep, she wondered after how truculent Olivia had become since their kiss; she wondered if Olivia was afraid of offending Claudia's father in some way. Such a strangely honorable woman to find in truly bizarre world.

†

Later that week, after a day of thundering boredom, Claudia demanded clothing and permission to leave the tower. Dr. Gatling, who had come in to run a few tests on her eye, didn't seem to care what she did once his tests were done. He had clothes fetched for her and told her to come back before the end of the week so he could compile some more data.

She dressed in the offered charcoal gray cotton peasant dress, strapped knee high boots, and a heavy, wool belted jacket. The air outside was cold and damp when she walked from the tower. She couldn't even truly get her bearings in the fog of the stripped ruins of the city. Chilly air heavy with the scent of salt water blew in from the ocean, unhindered by the farming hills in the way it had been by the buildings when last she set foot in San Francisco more than six years ago.

She briefly considered wandering the fields although she wasn't sure she trusted the Transcended yet. To the south, the fog blew slowly across a more jagged landscape. On brief occasion, Claudia caught a glimpse of something colossal near the horizon only ever in snippets when the fog cleared a little. She wanted to go see what on earth could be so big as to be seen from such a distance, but she also didn't think she would have the energy to get close enough to make a determination and certainly wouldn't have enough to get back.

Instead, she followed a handful of people who were making their way from the surface down into the lower levels where the true city was supposedly held. Immediately down the staircase that might have been borrowed from a BART station, the quiet solemnity of the surface was completely shattered. An enormous market place stretched out before her with shoppers packed shoulder to shoulder at stalls while barkers called people to their shops in a language that sounded equal parts Spanish and Chinese.

The mélange of scents, roasting meat, spices, smoke from cooking fires, and sweat all mixed together to create an overpowering aroma that Claudia could only describe as ancient—she assumed it was the same scent that hung over bazaars going all the way back to the beginning of civilization. She walked through the gaps between the people as best she could until a specific scent caught her attention. It was an impossible smell and one she was quite certain she would never smell again. It lingered just under the surface, threatening to be overpowered at any moment by chilies and fish. Still, she tried her best to follow the thin, attractive ribbon of the familiar smell to its source until she found herself outside a happy little shop tucked away in a corner near an elevator to the lower levels. The bedrock came out on both sides of the white and yellow slat building that looked like a cottage transplanted into a subterranean world. The hand painted sign above the door, with flourishing pink letters and flowers on a white washed board confirmed what Claudia had thought impossible: donuts.

Claudia pushed open the shop's windowed door to find the smell of cooking donuts wasn't the only familiar scent rediscovered that she thought long gone. Coffee was being brewed as well. The sudden rush of sense memory was almost enough to knock Claudia from her feet; if someone in the shop happened to light up a hand-rolled cigarette, Claudia knew she would burst into tears. When she was little more than a girl, her maternal grandfather took her to a donut shop in Montreal. He would buy her whatever donut she wanted, get her a glass of ice-cold whole milk, and tell her stories in French while he smoked hand-rolled cigarettes and drank black coffee turned nearly to syrup by the amount of sugar he put in it. Grand-père Dupuis knew English, but refused to speak it, especially to his only granddaughter.

"Can I help you with something?" a sweet voice asked from behind the counter.

Claudia realized she must have been standing idly, adrift in the world of her memory. She glanced around the shop to catch her bearings. Strings of lights crisscrossed the ceiling, providing a soft white light, almost like daylight in their effect. A handful of petite chairs and tables, painted white and yellow like everything else about the shop, stood empty on the restaurant floor. Claudia walked further in, drawn by the glass display cases and counter where actual donuts awaited her.

"Are you okay?" the voice asked again, and for the first time, Claudia realized the person speaking must be speaking to her.

"Yes," Claudia said, "I'm just a little lost in thought." She looked up from her inspection of the donuts to find the woman speaking to her was actually a little hard to find. She was short, possibly even a little shorter than Claudia, wandering amid the crowded service area behind the display counter. The woman was petite with thick, black hair held back in a long braid. Her large doe eyes were dark brown on the border of black, yet lively and warm.

"Can I get you something?" the woman asked.

"Maybe," Claudia said. "I'm just a little overwhelmed in learning that donuts are not actually extinct."

"Yes, my grandmother and I resurrected them the first chance we got," the woman said with a little grin. "Esmeralda's Donuts has served the City of Broken Bridges for three years now. Before that, it served San Francisco for thirty years."

"Esmeralda is your grandmother? Is she here?" Claudia really hoped the woman's grandmother was around. A little old Hispanic woman amid the entirely feminine donut shop would perfectly complete the picture.

"In a sense," the woman said. She lifted a pendant from the front of her white apron and dangled it out until the light caught on the gold. "She is always with me now although she has been dead a few years. I am the Esmeralda of the shop now, but people just call me Esme."

"I am Claudia."

"It's nice to meet you, Claudia," Esme said. "Are you hungry?"

"I wasn't until I smelled your shop, but I certainly am now." Claudia's eyes traveled down from Esme's face, back to the row upon row of donuts within the display case.

"If you have your labor punch card we can fix that right up."

"My…what?"

The smile vanished from Esme's face as she took a closer look at Claudia. "You're awfully clean for an Irradiated laborer. What exactly do you do?"

"I'm a scout sniper," Claudia said, falling back on the only job she'd ever had. She'd tried her hand as a showgirl in some of the Raven's shows, singing ballads under a red lantern, but it was little more than a gimmick, and she doubted there were cabarets in the City of Broken Bridges to revive her dead act.

"Try again. Irradiates aren't allowed to use weapons." Esme folded her arms over her chest giving Claudia a stern stare that no doubt emulated a look favored by the original Esmeralda.

"Why do you think I'm an Irradiate?" Claudia asked. She vaguely knew the term from her talks with Olivia. Irradiates were surface dwellers. Individuals cured of a mild case of radiation poisoning by Dr. Gatling's stasis chambers, but still slightly radioactive. Olivia hadn't said as much, but Claudia gleaned from the way she talked that Irradiates were second class citizens, little better than true mutants.

"Because of your eye," Esme explained. "There's always something at least slightly off about Irradiates."

Claudia had almost forgotten her right eye didn't match her left. She was neck deep in an entirely new society with rules she hadn't remotely started to learn. If she was going to pass as anything but a tainted field hand, she would need to start wearing colored goggles to cover her eyes.

"Look, I'd love to be able to give you something without punching your labor card, but if word got out among the Irradiates that I was giving away food, I'd have an endless stream of open hands running me out of business and scaring away clean customers," Esme said.

"I understand," Claudia said. "I'm new here and still getting used to things."

"Where did you come from?" Esme asked with a skeptical eyebrow raised, her arms still crossed over her chest.

"Quebec originally, but more recently Las Vegas."

Esme's eyes went wide, which was remarkable considering how large and round they already were. "You're the commander's daughter."

The bell on the door rang and heavy boots stepped onto the plank floor. "She is indeed," Commander Marceau's voice boomed through the tiny shop. "My little Claudia, how did I know you would find this place among all the shops in the Chinican market?"

"I am so sorry, commander," Esme stammered. "I didn't know."

Claudia rolled her eyes and leaned back against the shop counter to face her father. Of course Esme was just another attractive woman who was completely cowed by Claudia's father. Claudia wondered how far outside the City of Broken Bridges she might have to go before she found a woman who would have that reaction to her rather than her father.

"Papa, do you know Esme?" Claudia asked.

"Everyone knows Esme," her father said. "She might be the only living donut artist left on the planet. I got to know her well in the years I searched for you. I came here often as I believed it would be a place that would speak to you, and as you see, I was right."

Claudia had to admit that was true. The shop called to her on more than just the scent level. She enjoyed the décor, the exterior, and it did hearken back to the shop of her childhood. In truth, Claudia didn't like the masculine intrusion of her father upon the feminine space of the shop. He was a strong, brutish, male figure, armed and armored in a shop meant for pleasantness. Her father strode deeper into the shop, wrapped his arm around Claudia's shoulder, and rested a kiss atop her head. Her minor, inner objection to him being in the shop melted under the warm embrace. Sure, he had pistols on his hips, a shotgun slung over his back, and a metal chest plate on, but beneath all the warrior accoutrements, he was still her father.

"What jewel among these riches would you like to end your long fast of donuts?" her father asked as he bent low to look within the glass-front display case. "As I recall, you liked sugar-dusted crullers."

"Yes," Claudia said, getting a little choked up at his perfect memories of her, "those were my favorite."

Esme plucked one of the twisted knots of dough, glittering with sugar crystals, from the case with metal tongs. "Would you like one as well, commander?"

"My stomach is too occupied with thoughts to eat anything," Commander Marceau said. "If possible, could you wrap this treat to go? My daughter has an appointment to meet the Keepers that we should make our way to."

"Absolutely, commander," Esme said. She quickly wrapped the donut in a clean sheet of cloth in such a way that

Claudia could still bite one end. When Claudia reached to take the offered cruller, Esme caught her hands in the exchange. She leaned in close to whisper across the space to Claudia. "Please, forgive me for assuming you were an Irradiate. Feel free to come by any time."

Claudia had a biting comment rise in her throat, but she tamped it down. As much as it irritated her that Esme would only fawn over her after learning whose daughter she was, the pragmatic part of Claudia's mind refused to condemn her for adhering to societal norms of a city that Claudia didn't truly know yet. She resolved to get to know Esme better before she could know if she was worth knowing—especially if the process involved eating donuts in the cheerful little shop.

"You'll be seeing a lot of me," Claudia said, opting for the friendlier, almost flirty comment instead.

This seemed to please Esme immensely. As Claudia and her father walked from the shop, she glanced back over her shoulder to see if she could catch Esme in a more honest moment of watching them. To her surprise, the little donut shop owner actually seemed to have been looking at the backs of Claudia's legs.

Chapter 13:
What Lies Beneath,

The elevator down to the Keeper's sanctuary wasn't the elevator next to the donut shop as Claudia suspected. It would have satisfied an Occam's razor sort of suspicion that her father actually just lucked across her on the way to somewhere nearby. The truth was far more flattering and in line with what Claudia actually wanted to believe; her father knew her and still wasn't done searching for her.

She ate her cruller as they walked, finding it was everything she'd hoped it would be. Esme was as talented as her father said she was, although Claudia began to wonder where she might have come by flour and milk to make such a treat, or the far more exotic items like sugar and coffee.

The elevator they were seeking was across the Chinican market from the donut shop, down a few streets, and guarded by little more than the unassuming façade of an orange mining basket dangling from a heavy winch. They rode down the old mining elevator into the rock of the earth. The lone light in the cage above them lit the damp stone walls of their chamber as it slowly crept by. Claudia and her father stood on opposite sides of the elevator, facing and mirroring each other in their casually leaned postures.

"Fathers make obvious mistakes," her father finally spoke. The deep rumble of his voice carried above the squeak and squeal of the elevator's descent. "Most fathers mistakenly chase after their daughter's love, ignoring the need for respect. Likewise, fathers will expect their sons to be perfect extensions of them, continuing work and dreams left incomplete by the father. The lucky few of us will grow up with our children to realize these are both foolish dreams. Children will become the people they are meant to be regardless of a father's wishes."

Claudia knew this to be true from watching Olivia. Her father wanted nothing more than her love and had lost her respect in the process. From what Danny had told her during their brief, yet eventful relationship, his father expected to raise an accountant only to end up with a surfer. Danny had laughed at the thought; his father was petrified of the ocean and Danny was terrible with numbers. Claudia wasn't sure what her father had done so right that so many other fathers failed at. She loved her father, respected him above anyone, and wanted nothing more than to follow in his footsteps.

"You managed to avoid those obvious mistakes," Claudia said.

"This is true, but in doing so I made others." He tapped his thick index finger against the side of his nose in the classic pose of thinking he always adopted when he didn't wish to give words to his thoughts right away. Claudia wondered if she'd unconsciously picked up that from her father as well. "I left you to your independence, did not protect you as well as I might have, and thus made you someone very similar to myself."

"I'm proud of who I am—prouder still that you think I am like you."

"Yes, I know you are, and a foolish father might be proud of this too," her father said. "You are not supposed to continue my work though. I am meant to complete my work, leave the world a better place for you so you might have your own work. I failed in this, but I have been given another chance."

"What do you mean?" Claudia didn't like the look in her father's eyes, the distant quality of a man who had stared too long at the ocean and lost his place on the shore.

"I have to create for you a world where survival isn't a daily concern, and I know how…" the rest of his words were cut off by the elevator's slow stop. Her father pulled himself from his leaned position against the railing and opened the gate for her.

They exited the basket into a hallway that was blacker than anything Claudia had ever known. Outside the halo of the elevator's light, the cavern stretched into complete darkness. They were deep in the earth after a long elevator ride that started well below the surface already—for the first time, she felt that depth.

"Touch your hand to the wall and follow it," her father said. "I am behind you."

She touched her right hand to the stone of the wall as she was instructed and walked carefully with her other hand outstretched in front of her. At first, she took mincing, cautious steps, but as nothing about the passage seemed to change, she gained the confidence to walk more boldly. After a few twists and turns, a faint, golden light began to illuminate the passage and the sound of great machinery reverberated through the stone. Claudia's hand left the wall as they continued on toward the light.

The passage was chilly, not necessarily cold, but definitely of a brisker temperature than the marketplace. As they neared the source of the light and sound, the passage became almost uncomfortably warm.

The passage opened up into an underground cavern that Claudia imagined would have taken millennia to construct. She'd seen the Grand Canyon earlier in her travels and now she was seeing the subterranean Grand Canyon. The passage they'd used opened somewhere in the middle with equal space above and below. The roof of the cavern above appeared to be lined with strange metal panels while the bottom of the canyon, where the river would run was actually an open thermal vent of lava. Amid the many walkways crisscrossing the canyon, men and women walked amidst numerous Transcended robots.

"Startling the first time you see it, eh?" her father leaned over to ask her. As they walked deeper into the lair of the Keepers, her father directed her to points of interest. "In their digging, they discovered a fault line and opened it to get at the geothermal power source. They bring in sea water from the pipes you see along the walls and boil it with the heat from the lava. As far as I know, it powers everything in the city. We used to use the nuclear reactors from the ships for power, but they phased those out entirely and now they remain functional only for emergencies."

"How could they build all of this in a little less than seven years?" Claudia asked.

"The Transcended can build incredible things in no time at all," her father said. "Imagine a world where society was wiped clean and anyone who wanted to remake the world in new and interesting ways need only convince others to follow them. Apparently, very few people liked society as it was. The Ravens you told me of are just one incarnation of that longing for the world to be different than it was—the Keepers are another."

The people they passed paid them about as much attention as the Transcended, which was to say, absolutely none at all. Claudia guessed them to be the Keepers although they didn't look like she expected. Many were older, but nearly every age range was represented in some number. The clothing worn by the various Keepers was as eclectic and strange as everything else in the cavern. Suits, lab coats, robes, and more comfortable clothes mixed in an endless array of uniforms that spoke of a society that put no importance on appearances and at the same time astounding importance on appearance judging from the suits and elaborate robes.

"There were no guards anywhere," Claudia said. "Are people simply allowed to come down here as they wish?"

"They can," her father said. "Nobody is denied access to knowledge of the Keepers. Most do not come down here though. I think the entire thing frightens most people."

Claudia could understand that. Open rivers of lava and giant robots walking on stone pathways was pretty damn scary. Add to that the fact that they appeared to be nearly a mile below the surface of the earth and she could see why visitors were rare. If she weren't in the company of her father, she likely would have turned around and gone right back up after a single glance.

"Professor Kingston!" her father shouted to a man walking amidst a flock of students.

The entire scene was bizarre. There was a man dressed as a college professor walking amid a group of younger men and women who were dressed like students, talking with them as though he were passing between school buildings rather than walking amid giant robots on a ledge above a fault line filled with lava. The professor took his leave of his students. The gathering of a dozen or so dispersed without their center.

"Commander Marceau," Professor Kingston said, "how good of you to come see me."

The two men met in the middle with a warm handshake and smiles on both sides. Olivia may not have respected her father, but it was clear Claudia's father did. More than that, if Claudia was still any judge of her father's behaviors, her father liked Professor Kingston.

"Professor, this is my daughter Claudia," her father said, guiding the conversation toward where Claudia stood.

The professor was smaller than her father in most ways, being of slighter build and shorter stature. He wore his receding, gray hair short and swept back. His face, which mirrored Olivia's in many ways, was clean shaven and pleasant. The man dressed in a sweater vest, an oxford button up shirt, and a bowtie, which was precisely what Claudia always imagined to be a professor's standard uniform, although her only point of reference was television shows and movies from before the invasion.

"It is a pleasure to meet you at last," Professor Kingston said, offering his hand to Claudia. "My daughter and your father have told me so much about you, I feel like I know you already."

Claudia shook his hand, which was soft, warm, and immaculately tended. "All complimentary things, I hope."

"Indeed, and Dr. Gatling has even been down a few times to speak with me about your condition. He is the only surface Keeper you're likely to meet. If you'd like to get a rise out of the old doctor, I encourage you to call him the Wizard of the Tower." Professor Kingston and Commander Marceau laughed in unison at this. They walked together toward some goal known only to the two men. Claudia fell in a step behind them as they walked and talked ahead of her. Apparently, her part in the meeting was over and now she was meant to observe the action from her position down stage.

"There are grumblings out of Hastings' old command structure," her father said.

"No doubt upset at the sudden dispersal of power," Kingston replied.

"They'll get over it, or they won't," her father said. "We have more than their aspirations to think about."

"Olivia said she wishes you would worry more about their grumblings."

"Olivia worries enough for all of us."

"True enough," Kingston said. "On that topic, I would ask that you find a way to help her back into some work. She's chaffing under the discharge Hastings gave her. Nothing so grand as direct combat, but perhaps security on the Balclutha."

"Consider it done."

"While I'm asking favors, I might impose a couple more upon you."

Claudia recognized something strange passing between the two men. She wished Veronica was there to see and explain what was going on. All she could tell was that Kingston was building toward asking for something long denied to him by Hastings.

"What might those impositions be?" her father asked.

"I would like to sit down with your daughter and record what information of the outside world she would be willing to share with me," Kingston said.

"I'd like to do that myself. Why don't we make a week of it up in the tower?"

"Certainly," Kingston said. "Finally, I know you are planning on anti-incursion assaults on the Slark squads planting the lasher trees. While I can't condone the resumption of conflict, I would ask if a Slark prisoner of war could be supplied for our research that you might find your way to deliver one."

That was the one Hastings had denied; Claudia could see the tension jump to attention in her father's shoulders to verify this. She also knew from her time with the Ravens that taking of Slark prisoners was a giant waste of time. Capturing them alive was difficult as many committed suicide before it was possible, but even if one could be caught, they were nearly impossible to communicate with. The Raven scientists spent years trying to crack the language barrier with limited success. Although, Claudia guessed the Keepers might have an easier time of things if her surroundings were any indication of what they could accomplish.

"I will not risk the lives of any of my soldiers in such a pursuit, but if an opportunity should fall in our laps, I will instruct my men to take one of the lizards prisoner rather than execute it."

"That is all I can ask."

They parted ways amicably. Immediately after Professor Kingston walked away from them, the flock of students returned to gather around him. Their stroll ended near another passage leading to an elevator, which Claudia guessed was entirely planned by Kingston.

"Hastings didn't want to take the Slark captive," Claudia said once she and her father were riding up an elevator toward the surface again.

"He did not."

"Because he didn't want any chance of a peace being brokered with the aliens," Claudia surmised.

"Precisely."

"There were people among the Ravens who thought that would be possible too," Claudia said.

"What conclusion did they reach?" her father asked.

"As far as I know, we gave up on trying to talk to the lizards," Claudia said. "Back then, we didn't think there was anyone on their side worth talking to anymore. I think that's changed though."

"Because of what you saw in Carson City?"

Claudia nodded. She'd told her father the whole story about how she'd come to be in the City of Broken Bridges, including the assassination work she'd done in Carson City. He hadn't said much at the time beyond expressing praise for a job well done. Either his stance on the topic was changing or at the very least evolving.

"I believe I want to find one of these gators," her father said. "We can see then what the Keepers might make them say."

Claudia didn't know Hastings or what kind of leader he might have been. She knew what her father was like though and suspected the Slark had never faced an enemy like him. When she was little, she used to watch him play chess in the park. He never attacked the same way twice, never defended in a structured way, and confounded opponents with maneuvers that looked like chaos only to discover they were all part of a bizarrely grand plan. She had no doubt the fall of society and the years of searching for her had made him stranger, maybe even a little unstable, which she guessed would alter his already eccentric plans in some truly unpredictable ways. Claudia came to the conclusion that the war with the Slark was about to get very interesting.

Chapter 14:
A Question of Perception.

Olivia received her posting on the Balclutha as promised. The Balclutha was a proper three-mast, square-rigged, 256 foot windjammer built in Scotland in 1886. The ship sailed north along the coast to set up lumber camps or drop off foragers to collect livestock and survivors should they find any. As the northern California and Oregon coasts were cleared of survivors and livestock, the primary focus of the ship was to collect the cut timber and exchange laborers from the camps. Refitting the museum vessel hadn't taken much effort and as one of its original purposes was hauling lumber, putting it to an old task seemed only natural for the black, red, and white square rigged vessel. The long term security details assigned to the various lumber camps required more physical capabilities than Olivia could boast and so she was relegated to the ship's touring squad, returning to port after every tour.

The first sojourn on their most recent voyage was Crescent City and the redwood lumber camp there. The bay was dredged deep enough for the Balclutha and the observation dock on the other side of the lighthouse peninsula had been repurposed to accommodate the mighty ship. Late morning rain fell heavy on the deck and insistent winds snapped the sails before they could be trimmed. Olivia stood tall near the prow of the ship, getting the first view of the city and the storm rolling toward it out of the north as they rounded the mountains guarding the city to the south. Even in the dwindling days of autumn, the northern California coast was lush and green.

Olivia's security detail was comprised of four former San Francisco police officers and four former enlisted men from the Royal Navy's shipwrecked battle group. It was actually rather fortuitous that Olivia returned to active duty when she did as the officer she was replacing had taken ill with appendicitis at the apex of a tour near the mouth of the Columbia River and died before the Balclutha could return him to the City of Broken Bridges for surgery.

Olivia rallied her men with a sharp whistle that followed the ringing bell to assemble the unloading crew. Her eight man squad fell in to a perfect line at full attention along the railing. "Quick and quiet work of it, gentlemen," Olivia told them as she walked in front of the line on her whirring and ticking leg. "Set up shop in the old roundabout parking lot with two by two watches."

"Aye, aye, ma'am," the men said in unison.

She'd received the affectionate nickname 'Pirate Kingston' which was later shortened to 'Pirate King' by the end of her first tour. The source no doubt was her leg and the way it caused her to limp like an old pirate with a peg leg. She didn't mind the moniker because her mechanical leg, which was a disability on land, found perfect use on the open seas as a magnificent anchor point to balance upon a rolling deck. She'd had good sea legs on the missile frigate she'd served on during her navy days, and now she had unshakable balance due in no small part to the gyros in her prosthetic leg.

They were greeted at the dock by the security detachment assigned to the lumber camp as was routine, although the numbers seemed strained with only the base commander and one bodyguard attendant. Olivia's team disembarked first under a strange sense of foreboding.

"Major Bradley," Olivia greeted the once retired marine corps officer, "why are you traveling in such lonely company?"

Major Bradley stood haggard and exhausted, a man in his late sixties with a lot of miles having passed beneath his combat boots. His face was chiseled from stone with lines gouged deep, but his brown eyes were still sharp. "Warder Kingston, I'm afraid the news isn't good," Major Bradley said, offering a crisp salute in reply to the one provided by Olivia. They began walking back down to the docks to the convoy of old diesel trucks in the roundabout set to unload goods for the Balclutha's hold. "We were suddenly flush with the first livestock survivors in ages, but as soon as we started sorting the sick and radiated from the healthy, the mutant attacks began."

"Mutant attacks this far west?" Olivia asked.

"It caught us by surprise too."

Olivia mounted the carriage among the trucks as directed by Major Bradley while her men began the work of overseeing the offloading of supplies. The Major's bodyguard saw to the horse team to drive them back around the edge of the bay toward the town. Olivia always wondered where the Major had even found the reasonably nice covered-carriage or the horses to drive it for that matter.

"It's going to take us a few days to sort the animals now that we're having to patrol pretty heavily," Major Bradley said, raising his voice above the clomping of hooves and the creaking of the old carriage. "Most of the livestock is mutated cows with a few half-feral pigs in the mix. We've had to put down and burn almost 80%, but the remaining 20% is beautiful and healthy."

"We can certainly prolong our stay," Olivia said, "and if my team can aid in anyway to the town's security while we're here…"

"You read my mind," Major Bradley interrupted her. "I'd like to give you a truck to take up the highway a ways to see if you can figure out what is riling the mutants up."

"We're more than equal to the task, Major," Olivia said, "although I might have a theory already."

"Don't keep me in the dark, Kingston, what do you know?"

"Since the mutants are sterile, there would be no reason to expand their territory since their population is finite. Commander Marceau's daughter mentioned a new civilization pressing the Slark across the eastern border of California. If the map is as Claudia Marceau says it is, then the Slark being pushed west would push the mutants west and the mutants being pushed west would push any remaining pockets of livestock…"

"Right into our lap," Major Bradley grumbled. "If that's true, things are likely to get worse all up and down the coastline before they get better, and we'll be seeing Slark by spring."

"Indeed," Olivia said. "As I said, it is just a theory and I intend on seeing for myself."

†

Olivia's new duties left Claudia with an astounding amount of time on her hands that she hadn't realized had previously been consumed by Olivia. She decided the time could be well spent walking down into the Chinican market to drink coffee, eat donuts, and talk with Esme. Her first few attempts hit at busy times in the day, preventing her from doing anything but collecting a cruller to go, until she found the perfect lull in the late afternoon.

Esme was behind the counter, cleaning the mostly empty trays from the day. She was so engrossed in the work of collecting the day-old donuts into a sack that she hardly noticed Claudia's arrival until she was standing at the counter.

"Oh, hello there, Ms. Marceau," Esme said. "Would you like a cruller before I bag them for the evening?"

"If I keep eating every time I come here, you're going to be rolling me back out eventually," Claudia said, although it wasn't likely to be true anytime soon. She'd lost a significant amount of weight during her stasis from an already petite frame and it was coming back painfully slow.

"I would doubt that, and besides, if not a cruller, why would you come down here?" Esme asked as she plated one of the last twisted donuts all the same.

"To talk to you," Claudia said. She'd taken to wearing sunglasses and a few trappings of a military uniform although her father hadn't explicitly said she would return to work as a scout sniper under his command. The sunglasses she removed as their primary function was to prevent people from spotting her irradiated eye, which Esme already knew about.

"Certainly." Esme collected the plated donut, set aside her sack, and walked around to the front of the counter to join Claudia at one of the tables. They sat across from each other in silence for a time before Esme spoke. "What did you want to talk to me about?"

"I hadn't thought much about that," Claudia said. It didn't make any sense. She was normally so articulate and smooth around people. She could flirt and banter with the best of them in nearly any setting. Yet a donut shop girl was tripping up her game. "You were checking out my legs," was all Claudia could finally blurt out.

"There were a lot of things I could have been looking at yesterday," Esme said, a touch of red finding its way to her cheeks.

"No, I meant the first day I was…were you checking out my legs yesterday too?"

"I'm allowed to look at things." Esme's blush had gone from a light touch to a full swatch of red that began to leak down to her upper chest.

The warmth of familiar territory washed over Claudia. She had a degree of certainty that was formerly lacking— Esme was indeed interested in her. "Had I known, I would have worn daring skirts to give you more to look at," Claudia said.

"Now you're teasing me."

"No, I am saying I wish I had done more to tease you." Claudia gave her a wink and a faint smile that tugged only on the right corner of her mouth. "There are things I want to know about the city, things I could ask most anyone about, but I'd rather hear the answers from you."

"Why?"

"Mundane information is always easier to understand if it's explained by a pretty girl," Claudia said.

"Go easy on the charm, Ms. Marceau," Esme said. "I have a tolerance for the stuff."

"Please, call me Claudia."

"Okay, Claudia, but if I'm going to answer your questions, you have to answer a few of mine."

Claudia shrugged. "Sure, what would you like to know?"

"No, no, you go first since you asked first."

Her deference was kind of endearing; Claudia decided it might be easier to take Esme seriously than she initially thought. "Where did you come by coffee and sugar?"

"The arboretum in the park had coffee trees and sugarcane plants before the Slark invasion," Esme said. "We've been growing greenhouses full of the stuff for years now." Esme leaned forward and pinched the end off the cruller in front of Claudia. She tucked the little bite of donut in her mouth and smiled. "Does it worry you to send your girlfriend into possible combat?"

Claudia furrowed her brow. It sounded like a pointed question, although she couldn't imagine how Esme would know about past girlfriends in the Ravens or Veronica or… "Do you mean Olivia?" Claudia asked.

Esme nodded.

"She's not my girlfriend and I'm certain she can take care of herself on fluff runs up the coast."

Esme quirked a curious eyebrow and shrugged. "The talk around the tower says she is your girlfriend."

"My relationship status has been mostly single for more than a year now," Claudia explained. "Beyond sexual entanglements and flirtatious fun, I remain unfettered."

"Fair enough," Esme said. "What do you plan on doing for work, or are you just going to become the princess of the tower?"

"I think it was my turn to ask a question, but I'll answer another," Claudia said. "I plan on going back to what I'm best at, what I was trained for: scout sniper."

"Women aren't really soldiers in the City of Broken Bridges," Esme said. "Hastings thought it was foolish to throw away fertile women in combat so he all but outlawed it. Olivia was the last woman to really wear a uniform and when she lost her leg, Hastings put an end to it all."

"Yes, well, Hastings is dead and I'm not planning on getting pregnant anyway," Claudia said.

"That's a shame—you'd look cute pregnant."

"Is that a fact?" Claudia asked.

"What can I say? I like the look of pregnant women. I want kids; family is important to me."

"Then wouldn't it make more sense for you to be the pregnant one?"

"Oh, I plan to be, but I want my wife to carry a child as well."

And just like that, Claudia was right back where she started. Esme had her tongue tied and confused. She rallied as best she could, a little thrilled by being unbalanced by an unassuming shop girl with big brown eyes. "I would like to see more of the city and I would like you to show me," Claudia said.

"Are you asking me on a date?"

"Do you want it to be a date?"

"I wouldn't have asked if I didn't," Esme said with a knowing smirk.

"Be still my heart," Claudia teased, "a clever girl who can make a good cruller."

Chapter 15:
Unlikely Harbinger.

The truck promised to Olivia and her crew was actually an old Suburban retrofitted to run on the mixture of bio diesel and ethanol that was the predominant fuel before Dr. Gatling unlocked the secret to Slark fuel. The roads were rutted and ruined into the rain-drenched forests heading east and the poorly maintained Suburban struggled to crawl over the multiple washouts.

Her men hadn't asked their purpose in heading east in such an obviously untrustworthy vehicle. They were stout sailors and good soldiers. They also possessed the funk men can get on a sailing vessel, which prompted Olivia to roll down all the windows even though it was raining.

The road they'd chosen wound its way through thick sylvan forest, following a river back to its source in the mountains. The forest seemed almost primeval at times. Tree branches grew thick enough to create something of a tunnel above the road. Without regular truck traffic, the branches encroached more and more on the space until they were often scraping along the roof of the suburban. A break in the trees opened up on a large, rocky lobe surrounded by a river bend. On this outcropping of an acre or so of river stones, a cluster of mutants had pinned something at the river's edge.

"Stop the truck," Olivia said from her position in the passenger seat.

The driver brought the truck to a stop in the middle of the road and they all exited the vehicle armed with their modified carbines. The weapons were also of Dr. Gatling's design, using a different byproduct of the Slark home planet fish that provided the fuel. The solid propellant created by drying something or other from some gland or other replaced gunpowder and provided a lot more bang for the amount needed. The existing guns required added reinforcement to fire and rotating pieces to prevent fusing of moving parts due to overheating. All things considered, Olivia liked the old gunpowder weapons to the new guns.

"Skirmisher line," Olivia ordered her men, "and watch your footing."

"Warder Kingston, ma'am, perhaps you should…" her second in command began.

"Perhaps you should carry out the order you've been given," Olivia interrupted, settling the matter of her leg before it could even begin.

They climbed down the larger boulders nearest the road toward the rocky flats. Olivia's leg did indeed give her difficulties in the climbing, although she refused help when her men offered until they simply gave up offering. They scattered into the skirmisher formation as soon as they hit the flat of gathered river stones.

Above the sound of the mutants howling and the rushing river, Olivia heard something she hadn't expected to hear again—dog barking. Dogs were the only version of livestock in the early days of the City of Broken Bridges and were eaten almost exclusively during the early years of the war until they were extinct for all Olivia knew.

"Hold your fire until we're sure to hit," Olivia instructed as they advanced on the gathering of a dozen or so mutants.

The dog barking intensified as they crept up on the mutants. The howling, gibbering forms barely resembled humans anymore. Their limbs were mismatched, their skin strangely colored and distributed irregularly. To add to the disquieting physical appearances, on full display as most didn't wear much beyond a few tattered rags, was the smell. Olivia had almost forgotten that mutants smelled horrible. Beyond simply being unwashed human, which was a scent they had in droves, Olivia identified the real stench as open bowel. It was a distinct scent somewhere between feces and vomit with a peculiar blood tinge running through it. She wasn't sure why mutants smelled like disemboweling, but they did.

The mutants were thoroughly distracted by the pack of wild dogs they'd apparently pinned against the river. The sound of the rushing water and the barking dogs covered the sound of her squad's approach even as they disturbed stones with every step. As the squad neared, Olivia could see the mutants had already felled a handful of the dogs with their rock throwing. The remaining four or so skeletal German Shepherds were guarding their fallen comrades with snarling teeth and vicious barking.

"Put the mutants down," Olivia gave the order.

Fire rippled down the squad's line. Olivia selected her target in the middle of the main cluster of the mutants. They advanced slowly on the mutants popping off shots when the footing allowed. The mutants turned to the new threat. A few managed to get a badly thrown rock off in defense. All their projectiles fell woefully short and the thrower always drew the attention of a bullet shortly after. When the tide was clearly turning against the mutants, the remaining few tried to flee into the river. The swift moving current made short work of the ill-equipped creatures, dashing them across rocks before sucking them below.

The wild dog pack, or what remained of it, took the opening created by the obliteration of the mutant tribe and ran north along the bank. In their wake, the dog pack left several dead and one wounded.

"Been a long time since we've shot mutants, eh, ma'am?" her unofficial second in command asked with an adrenaline induced grin painted on his unshaven face.

"Like riding a bike, I'm sure, Lane," Olivia said, although her heart wasn't in it. She'd shot mutants, countless droves of them in the securing of the lower peninsula before the wall was built. It never felt like combat to shoot half-naked whelps armed with rocks. As much as the idea disagreed with her view of a soldier's work, she always thought of shooting mutants as putting terminally ill people out of their misery. Olivia could tell from the combat rush her men were enjoying that they didn't see things the same way.

"Uh oh, Johnnie has an upset stomach," Lane said, motioning to the youngest of their group as he doubled over to take another look at his lunch.

"It's just the smell," Johnnie managed to croak after throwing up.

"Set up a defensive perimeter." Olivia cranked open the heat port on her carbine and blew across it to speed the gun's recovery. She slung the cooled weapon over her shoulder and made a slow approach on the wounded dog. "Here's a good boy," Olivia whispered soothingly to the dog.

The primal part of the dog brought to the surface over nearly seven years struggled against the domesticated part that recalled a youth in contact with humans. The gangly German Shepherd growled at her initially followed immediately by a submissive whimper.

Olivia pressed on fearlessly. She held out the back of her hand to the dog, which eyed it warily but made no further aggressive move. She inched closer to let the dog get a smell of her hand. By and by, after another bout of growling, the dog finally extended his muzzle to gently sniff at her hand.

"That's a good boy," Olivia cooed to the dog. "We'll have you seen to in no time at all."

†

It took an hour or so and a hammock made of their coats to get the wounded dog back to the truck. The Brits among the bunch took to calling the dog Roger along the way. When the Americans asked why, Olivia told them Roger Davis was a cricket player who lived through being hit by a cricket ball a couple decades earlier. They pointed out that plenty of baseball players were struck by baseballs every season, how could they all seem to remember one player's name? Olivia asked how many baseball players died from being struck by a baseball. None of course was the answer. And that was the difference, Olivia informed them.

Roger apparently enjoyed the good natured banter about baseball and cricket as he calmed significantly with the jovial discussion going on around the edges of his makeshift gurney. Olivia was glad her men all appeared to be equally concerned with the dog's life. By the look of things, the more difficult conversation would come when they would decide who got to keep Roger, should he survive.

Olivia rode in the rear cargo boot of the Suburban with Roger on the way back. She guessed from the way he was sitting and the pained yelps he would let out when a bump in the road rattled him against the rear gate that he likely had taken a wound to his right rear leg.

It was nearly dark by the time they pulled back into Crescent City. Roger was sluggish when they tried to unload him at the strip motel repurposed into a veterinary clinic and livestock corral. They may as well have brought in a unicorn for the reaction Roger got from the veterinary staff.

A Geiger counter confirmed Roger was not irradiated beyond normal levels. A few other pokes and prods by the remarkably efficient staff confirmed a broken hind leg along with a likely concussion. "We'll have your dog fit to travel within the week, Warder Kingston," was the official word from the staff, and thus Roger became Olivia's dog, much to the chagrin of the other men in her squad.

Olivia was barely back out to the highway at the edge of the fishing fleet's dry docks when Major Bradley caught up to her.

"You came back with a witness," the old Major said with a smile. "Did the pup have anything to say?"

"Concussed, I'm afraid, sir," Olivia said, matching the major's smile. "We'll interrogate Roger once he's recovered."

"Why don't you debrief me at dinner? The old restaurant across the way was turned into the mess hall. We've got a feast of the sea's bounty waiting for us." Major Bradley motioned for Olivia to walk with him. As they neared the old two story restaurant and club, the lumberjacks, fishermen, soldiers, and sailors from the Balclutha thickened, all heading in for the raucous environment within.

Olivia was slower than Major Bradley, but he slowed to match her pace. "Sadly, there's not much debriefing to do," Olivia said. "We came across a dozen or so mutants attacking a pack of wild dogs. We killed the mutants with a staggered skirmisher line, the dogs that were well enough ran off, and we brought back the injured one."

"A dozen is a good sized group," Major Bradley mused. "Glad you cleared them out though. From what we've seen, the mutants talk to each other. If even one survived to tell his tribe, they'd be riled up by the killings."

"I didn't know the mutants were that organized," Olivia said, a cold tremor of foreboding running up her spine.

"Neither did we until recently," Major Bradley replied.

"We could stay on awhile and see to bolstering your security."

"That'd be a bucket to bail out a barge," Bradley said. "If you want to do us a favor, find out if the other outposts are having the same troubles and take what you know back to the City of Broken Bridges. You've seen it first hand, which is the real reason I sent you out. If Commander Marceau, your father, or whoever else is in charge these days asks, you can say you saw the mutant encroachment with your own eyes."

"Can you hold out until help arrives?"

"That'll depend on a lot of things, but we've started practicing evacuation drills using the fishing fleet and some rafts. If worse comes to worse, I believe we can limp to Gold Beach."

"I'm friendly with the commander's daughter," Olivia said. "After what she went through, I imagine she'll be helpful in preventing others from falling prey to the mutants."

"Here's hoping for all of us then." Major Bradley held open the door to the restaurant turned mess hall. The warm glow of lamp light and the cheerful reverie of working men poured out. Olivia and Bradley entered the festivities under storm clouds nobody else saw or felt.

Chapter 16:
With Just the Right Eyes.

In the early dawn, with a chill and bank of fog lying over the city, Claudia's father came to her in the White Tower with a gift. He gently shook her from sleep in the hospital bed she was still convalescing in. He held a gun case in one hand and her robe in the other. Without a word, he handed both to her and escorted her from the room.

The halls of the tower were quiet in the small hours surrounding dawn and Claudia felt she should be quiet as well. The floor chilled her bare feet as she followed her father up the stairs a few flights to the opposite side of the tower from where her room looked out. When the case became heavy for her and her breath became short from the exertion of climbing stairs with her still recovering lungs, he slowed to wait for her, but didn't offer any help. She took this as a sign of confidence and a challenge at once, resolving to make him proud.

They reached the floor he had in mind toward the top of the tower. He guided her to an empty office at the end of a hall on the abandoned floor. When he opened the door, frigid, wet air flooded into the hallway. The windows along the wall were missing along with most of the wall itself. She followed him through the scant rubble clinging tenaciously in the exposed room to look out over what the city had become from the lonely vantage point. The sun rising in the east across the bay picked up on only the highest points able to reach above the layer of fog, which were the mountains on the northeast edge of the bay opposite them and a lone broken stump of a building on a rise between them and the water.

"The Slark destroyed most of the city in their initial invasion," her father said, staring over the ruins of the kingdom he'd inherited. "Down to the ground destroyed, I mean. What remained, and there was very little, Hastings and his flotilla destroyed in taking it back after the cascade momentarily struck technology from the world." Her father pulled her closer to the edge he was standing at so she might better see the view and feel the thrill of the precipice. "The tower you see standing above the fog was once Coit Tower. It sits upon Telegraph Hill as a final gift to the city from a remarkable woman, although I believe it was built after her death. The Slark that once held the city used it for their last stand."

Claudia shifted her attention fully to the tower, seeing in it something suddenly interesting. She'd glanced over it meaninglessly a few times in her few brief walks among the ruins of the city, but never gave it much thought. She couldn't be sure if the Transcended left it as it stood because they didn't want to climb the cratered hill or because it held some greater meaning. Black smudges from fires and explosions scarred the exterior of the tower even when viewed from the great distance and she suspected it was probably riddled with bullet holes. The top of the tower was clipped off with a jagged edge leaving a question of how tall the tower had ever actually been. In a landscape completely swept clean of signs of war by the Transcended, the tower stood as a lone reminder of the war that wiped out the San Francisco that was. Before her father could even say what happened, Claudia pieced together why the Transcended hadn't cleared the tower—its destruction was owed to humanity, not the Slark.

"Rather than fight them for it, Hastings destroyed most of the tower from a distance with artillery and starved out the rest," her father said. "Your Ravens may not know this, in truth, I didn't either until I inherited Hastings' papers and began reading them, but the cascade was a worldwide effort. The ship we felled in New York that irradiated the entire northeast was one of many. London is likewise destroyed...Moscow, Tokyo, Berlin, Rio, Mexico City, Beijing, and a few dozen other cities stand like the toxic graveyard New York is or are inhabited by the fallen ships and Slark survivors as in Los Angeles. Hastings knew this when he gave the order to destroy Coit Tower." Her father placed his hand upon her shoulder in a gesture that seemed partially for his own support and partially to comfort her. He looked older and sounded tired from the weight of what he'd seen and now knew. "It was meant to be a killing blow," he finally said, his voice husky with an edge of frustration, "but it simply crippled us both. We're a cancer patient on the other side of chemo therapy but we still have cancer."

Claudia knew the analogy hurt her father and she knew he'd used it to drive the point into her heart. Her mother was such a patient, weakened and sick from chemo therapy that was supposed to eradicate her cancer along with her own health; she'd come through on the other side too weak for another round yet still riddled with pockets of cancer. Ultimately, the cancer won.

"I cannot wage war with just the army we can raise here," he said. "There are too few soldiers left and too many Slark. Nor can I abide further destruction of our home in the pathetic hope of eradicating the invaders. Hastings' destruction of Coit Tower must be our last failed attempt at chemo therapy." He turned her away from the tower to look him in the face. His eyes, bloodshot from lack of sleep and edged in tears, no doubt matched hers. "Can your Ravens do it? Can they finish this Extinction War?"

Before Tombstone, before she'd seen what Juarez was willing to risk to take a single Raven stronghold from female hands, she would have said yes without a moment's hesitation. Combining the hard lessons she'd learned in Carson City with her frantic escape from Tombstone, she didn't believe anymore. If Veronica survived Tombstone, she would continue colonizing to spread Raven influence, but it would be far too slow if what her father was saying was true. The Red Queen Carolyn and The Black Queen Ekaterina could spread Raven influence at the point of a knife, which would move faster, but leave more dead than could be spared. No, too much of the old sexist guard remained for the Raven model to wrest control over the tattered remains of humanity from the hands of men, not with their brutal tactics and not with the Slark encountering no such gendered opposition to their recovery. Humans didn't seem capable of cooperation anymore, or maybe they never really were.

"No," Claudia finally said. "If it was just Los Angeles, they might be able to, but if what Hastings' papers say is true, it will be a momentary victory with a final loss to come." He'd used the phrase she'd only heard in the early days of the war. It was based on supposition since knowledge of the enemy was almost non-existent. With the tenacity of the enemy known, scientists had hypothesized the Slark were on a last ditch effort to save their own species by populating a new planet. If they succeeded, humanity would go extinct; if they failed, they would go extinct. This created the phrase Extinction War—she'd heard it a few times in radio transmissions before the cascade, but not since. Apparently, everyone but her father had forgotten the direness of the stakes for both sides. "We need more," Claudia said, not wishing to extinguish hope entirely. As much as she hated to admit it, the Ravens needed at least one male leader to rally other societies to their cause. "If we seek out the Ravens, we cannot do so fragmented and we need to come to them as equals, which won't be easy. They have armies and have won wars against the Slark and other human factions. They don't share because they haven't had to, or maybe they've spent their lives sharing too much and have decided they won't anymore."

Her father nodded, but seemed to have spoken his last on the topic. "Open your present now," he said.

Claudia settled the gun case along the cement floor and knelt before it to unclasp the latches with reverent hands. Her fingers were quaking from excitement and cold as she opened the case to reveal a sniper rifle of entirely unknown design. It looked to be made of piping in ways other rifles weren't and had chambers in addition to magazines. To add to the strangeness, in place of a bipod at the front of the rifle for stability, there was a cluster of six tentacles, like a small robotic octopus had buried its head along the underside of the tapered barrel.

"The design is Dr. Gatling's," her father said. "The weapon is one of a kind. It'll take you some time to train on, and I don't want you fighting until you do, but once you understand one another, I suspect everything else you know will fall into place."

Claudia touched the strange tentacle pod at the front. The little, prehensile limbs retracted from her touch. "What are these?"

"They're from a captured tackle box off a Slark fishing trawler," her father explained. "They grasp inorganic things and let go at the touch of something organic. I think they're used to gather the strange net things the Slark use to catch fish. Gatling surmised they would make a good bipod to offer stability. What we learned of robotics from the Slark has jumped our own technology ahead centuries, but apparently we're still clumsy students needing to repurpose what we can't build."

"I'll begin training immediately, Papa," Claudia said.

"Good, I have plans that will need you, including the training of a new scout sniper corps." He helped her to her feet and slid the strange rifle strap over her shoulder. "We will find our way forward, *tourterelle*."

He kissed her on the forehead and she wanted to believe the Ravens would see in him the great man, the warrior, and the father that she saw. He would be a marvelous ally and a banner to draw the men of the world to their cause as the organization's first White King, if only he could bring the whole of his own city beneath his rule. Others might suggest Professor Kingston and still others, like the remnants of Hastings' guard, would likely reject anyone but their dead commander. She didn't know what he was planning to surmount what she thought was insurmountable, but she had to trust he had a plan. She would do what he asked for the moment and the future, starting with learning her new rifle.

†

Bundled in heavy wool coats, hand knit scarves, and berets, Esme and Claudia stood on one of the remaining streetcar platforms along what used to be the Market Street F-Line. Most of the street was gone. Stretches of asphalt remained of the road, but generally the tracks cut across flat gravel land as though the street cars were normal trains. Claudia had no idea what the Transcended were doing, stringing lines and repairing rails, until Esme finally pieced it together that they meant to rebuild the streetcar and trolley tradition of the city.

Esme was a bundle of excited energy at Claudia's side, smiling from ear to ear. A Transcended stood beside the raised cement platform, staring in the same general direction as Esme and Claudia. Standing still as it was, the Transcended could easily have been a sculpture rather than an autonomous robot. Claudia kept glancing up to the colossus waiting for the street car with them. It couldn't be waiting to see them get onto the streetcar it so carefully restored as the Transcended didn't seem to even see people. Claudia kept glancing out across the rolling hills of crops, trees, and grasslands that the San Francisco peninsula had become, wondering what the Transcended was looking at. This particular Transcended was made of mostly copper plating and steel tubing. The copper was tarnishing in places, going from the cheery bronze glow to a green similar to the Statue of Liberty. A few faint orange lights flashed along its body at specific points, which Claudia guessed made it easier to avoid at night as they were placed on the robot's extremities; it might not see people, but it clearly wanted people to see it. Up close, standing perfectly still, Claudia was able to give one of the Transcended a proper inspection. The only true similarity she saw between any of the others was the murky blue globe. This particular Transcended's globe was in the center of its chest, roughly the size and shape of a basketball, guarded by copper grating. She'd seen the globes on the others as well, all in different places. Some wore the globe like a cyclopic eyeball, on the shoulder like an epaulette, and one even had it as the pommel of a cane permanently attached to its hand.

"What do you suppose is inside those glass spheres they all have?" Claudia asked.

Esme glanced over as if seeing the ninety foot tall robot beside them for the first time. "I don't know," she said. "Robotic stuff I guess. To be honest, I don't even notice them anymore."

"How is that possible?"

"After enough years of them not noticing us, it gets easy to not notice them back," Esme said with a shrug.

Claudia wondered how many years it would take for that to happen to her. Esme drew her attention away from the Transcended to the approaching streetcar as it clacked its way down the tracks toward them. The car, which looked like a prop from some 40's movie, had been repainted by the Transcended with a mural depicting a city. When it got closer, Claudia surmised it must have been Los Angeles from the inclusion of the famous Hollywood sign.

"The streetcars were all taken from other cities at one point," Esme said. "I guess the Transcended liked the idea."

The doors opened, and they stepped on board. The interior was that of a normal streetcar, bench seats, bars to hold onto, straps dangling from the ceiling, with the one obvious difference of all the people inside being bronze statues. Claudia and Esme both stopped just inside the doorway when they were greeted by a bronze statue in the driver seat, followed by several other statue passengers in various positions. There was a man in a suit with a fedora, standing with his hand looped through a ceiling strap, reading a paper with his other hand. A woman with a bag of groceries was looking out the window, peeling a bronze orange. As Claudia and Esme ventured farther into the street car, they marveled at the remarkable detail of the passenger statues. Their faces told stories, some sad, some bored, some excited, but all remarkably human.

"It occurs to me that we are the only living passengers," Claudia said in a hushed tone.

"Most people are afraid," Esme said.

"I can imagine," Claudia replied. "Wait, why are you unafraid?"

"I feel safe with you." Esme blushed and nodded her head a little. "You make me bold."

Claudia smiled to her and linked their arms. "Then let us find a seat not occupied by a metal ghost of the past."

They sat by the rear entrance with Claudia nearest the window upon Esme's insistence. She watched the countryside as it rolled by. It was incredible to think it once was all a city. The peninsula looked more like the moors of England rather than the ruins of San Francisco. Fog rolled across the fields only partially broken up by lines where streets and buildings once stood. An occasional piece of architecture survived to be restored by the Transcended and inhabited by the Irradiated, be it a house, a store, a warehouse, or an apartment complex.

"What happened to the capitol building and the churches?" Claudia asked, finally realizing what was strangely absent among the few surviving structures.

"The Slark destroyed those first," Esme said. "It's sad really. The city once had some beautiful cathedrals and government buildings. Didn't that happen in Las Vegas?"

"Probably," Claudia said, "but who would notice their absence?"

This seemed to strike a chord in Esme, "what do you mean?"

"I mean there weren't many government buildings or churches to speak of and they certainly weren't noteworthy in such an eclectic landscape," Claudia said.

"Las Vegas wasn't destroyed the way San Francisco was?"

"Hardly touched," Claudia said. "Most of what was damaged was damaged by us fighting over it. The Slark wiped out the military and the airport and moved on. The city has no tactical significance, few natural resources, all the food, water, and electricity is shipped in from elsewhere—they probably thought us insane for even creating such a place."

"They probably thought you would starve and kill each other off," Esme said sourly.

"We would have, were it not for Ekaterina," Claudia said.

"Tell me about her, the great Raven leader."

"I only ever met her once. She seemed the perfect Russian mix of anger and sadness."

"Is she beautiful?"

"Not anymore, although she might have been at one point, long ago. She is fifty something now, having lived a hard life for many years. She is strong though, and ruthless in ways that still make me shudder."

"Do you admire her?"

Claudia considered the question for a moment before answering as she'd never actually stopped to question how she felt about Ekaterina other than grateful for survival. With distance from the situation and her survival now guaranteed by other means, she could be honest with herself. "In truth, I do not know. I am French—we must have music in our lives and she has gone deaf to all kinds of music to become what she is."

"French Canadian," Esme corrected her, giving her a quick kiss on the cheek.

"That is a joke with a rapidly approaching expiration date," Claudia said.

"It's true though. Quebec is in Canada, not France."

"We do not see it that way," Claudia said.

They rode in silence for awhile, cuddled close to one another. The sun began to break through the cloud cover and fog, casting shafts of light along the reclaimed moors and farmland they passed down toward the wharf. As they neared the docks and the defensive parapets created by the Transcended, they began to see people running and walking in the same direction the streetcar was heading. As the car rounded the corner to head along the old waterfront, the crowds thickened, taking on an excited tone. Claudia pulled the cable to notify they wished to get off at the next stop. She didn't even think until after she'd done it that the cable running above the windows might not do anything anymore, what with the driver being a bronze statue and all. Either it did still serve a function or the next stop was intended anyway as they were let off at the remains of the old Pier 39, right in the thick of the gathered throng.

"What's happening?" Esme asked of the first person to cross their path.

The person shook her off and continued along their way, forcing Claudia and Esme to push along with the multitude down toward the water. A familiar voice with a soothing British accent spoke behind them when the gathered people thickened too much to continue forward. "They're excited about the return of the sea lions," the man said.

Claudia and Esme both wheeled around at once to find Inspector Cavanaugh behind them, dressed smartly in a three piece hound's-tooth suit with a matching wool tam and a gray trench coat. Claudia recognized the voice but not the face. Esme seemed to truly know the man.

"I heard rumors you were involved with the commander's daughter," Inspector Cavanaugh said. "I hoped they weren't true, Mouse."

"Why do you call her 'Mouse'?" Claudia demanded. The fear she'd had of him when she was blind, weak, and disoriented evaporated. She was strong now, guarded well by her father, and had long since lost the fear of men from her years with the Ravens. She could see now, could still shoot a gun, and couldn't see Cavanaugh as a threat so long as she was armed, which she'd been whenever she left the tower once her father had returned the Walther he'd found on her the night she arrived.

"You'll have to ask her that yourself," Cavanaugh said. "As for our earlier discussions, Miss Marceau, there are some important discrepancies between your rendition and the facts that have come to light since."

"Are these the sorts of facts that will resurrect your beloved General Hastings?" Claudia asked with a sly smirk. "Because, if not, I fail to see why you would care or why I should be concerned about them."

This barb didn't seem to land on the unflappable Cavanaugh, which deeply disappointed Claudia. Perhaps she mistook Cavanaugh's interest in the Hasting case or his true motives in the matter or perhaps he simply had a remarkable poker face. Regardless, he'd tipped his hand in saying anything to her about the investigation continuing.

"We'll have eyes on you and your father," Cavanaugh said.

"Obviously," Claudia replied. Counter-intelligence and spying was a game, and a game Claudia was good at. It might take awhile to determine who was to be the cat and who was to be the mouse, but Claudia had every intention of winning regardless. She smiled to him to let him know she was eager for the game to start in earnest; Cavanaugh did not smile back as he took his leave, tipping his hat curtly to Esme who actually flinched at the gesture.

When Cavanaugh was thoroughly out of earshot, pushing his way in the opposite direction of the crowd, Claudia took Esme's hand in hers. "Why does he call you Mouse and why are you afraid of him?"

"In the early days when Hastings fought the Slark to liberate the city, before the Transcended, before your father came, children were used within the tunnels of the city below.

We were spies, carriers of information, and when the liberation war turned against us, suicide bombers. The information network, the one Cavanaugh was in charge of, didn't let us keep our names. I was Mouse so nobody would mourn me if I was captured, killed, or sent on a suicide bombing."

Claudia did some quick math in her head, determining that Esme must have been twelve or thirteen at the time, probably even slighter of build, and petite to begin with. Yes, the Ravens had done similar things with willing volunteers though. Children stopped being children at around age ten in the new world, but suicide bombings and stripping them of their names…barbaric wasn't a strong enough word for it.

"You said it was before my father?"

"When your father came, looking for you as the stories go, he turned the tide. We had a true champion of the field where Hastings had simply been a tactician moving pieces around on a board. He outlawed suicide bombings, which was easy to do since we didn't need them anymore once he started winning fight after fight."

"How did you never get sent on a suicide run?"

"I was good at spying. I grew up here, knew the city better than the Slark, and survived by being too valuable to throw away on a single strike. Many of my friends weren't so lucky."

Claudia gave Esme's hand a reassuring squeeze. That explained Cavanaugh. He was a man who had willingly thrown children into the war machine to die. Whatever blink or flinch might exist in Inspector Cavanaugh was long gone. Claudia had met such men before—the world was sick with them now as they tended to survive when most fell to their hesitations and humanity. As with the promise she'd made to Fiona in regards to killing Yahweh, Claudia made a silent promise to herself that she would be the one to kill Cavanaugh for Esme. Addition by subtraction, as Veronica was so fond of saying; the world would be a better place without him.

"Come, let us see if the rumors of sea lions are true," Claudia said.

They made their way through the crowd, guided by Esme as someone who knew a thing or two about sneaking through tight places. They found their way to the front of the docks where rocks were piled by the Transcended as sea lion refuge. The rocks, which Esme explained had sat vacant for six years, were now alive with the barking sea lions. The brown aquatic hunters lounged, played, and cuddled upon the rocks, somehow used to an audience.

Claudia glanced from face to face in the gathered masses. Men and women, hard men and women from the under city, Irradiated field workers, and Chinican merchants all had happy tears in their eyes and hopeful smiles on their lips. Claudia looked to Esme and found the same expression of fragile hope. Claudia recognized the feeling as a strange and frail pride. The people weren't Americans, Californians, or humans so much as they were San Franciscans. The identity of French that Claudia clung to for her sense of self seemed paltry in comparison to the identity of San Franciscan that Esme and the gathered people had. Claudia was struck by a powerful urge and acted on it, scooping Esme into her arms to kiss her fiercely. She could taste Esme's tears in the kiss and reveled in the salty edge they added to the passionate moment. The slender woman in her arms was Mouse of the City of Broken Bridges and this seemed like a marvelous thing to be; Claudia felt honored to know her and be adored by her.

On the ride back up the hill, the street car was full of living bodies to go with the bronze riders as the native San Franciscans found their courage and faith in the return of a symbol of recovery to a city that had somehow survived.

Chapter 17:
Mapping the Radioactive Tides.

Olivia didn't like leaving the Crescent City lumber camp. It felt like a tenuous hold on their southern most outpost. The Balclutha's captain and Major Bradley both insisted though, and soon they were on their way to Gold Beach.

Roger was declared fit to travel and found a comfortable spot with Olivia in the Balclutha's chartroom. The little cabin atop the poop deck living chambers was once the sewing room of a captain's wife more than a century prior. Under Olivia's ownership, the chartroom was transformed into the ship's armory and her living quarters. She left the door open onto the port side of the deck to let people come and go during the day to see Roger. It also allowed the sea air to blow out the stench of unwashed dog, which was a little overpowering if the windows or door were closed for too long. To his credit, the skeletal German shepherd seemed reasonably comfortable at sea. The pitch and roll of the ship didn't seem to bother him in the slightest so long as Olivia was within view of his hastily constructed bed of a rag stuffed old sleeping bag.

The Balclutha had a schedule to keep and they were already a few days behind. They dropped off supplies, fresh laborers, and machinery on their way up the coast, and then picked up raw materials collected by the outposts, mostly lumber, on the way back down. They would return to Crescent City in a week or so as their last stop on the way south to collect the rough cut lumber and the livestock deemed suitable to return to the City of Broken Bridges. Olivia took the time between to chart the movements of the mutants. She drew and redrew the map as though she were charting the tides of the sea. If the Ravens were responsible for pushing the Slark back, which in turn were pushing the mutants west, using Carson City as the genesis point heading directly west wouldn't make sense; Crescent City was too far north to feel any effect. Using radiating patterns, not too dissimilar from those used to calculate underwater explosion impact patterns, she determined the Ravens must be trying to flank the Slark line to roll it south. The mutants might not be pushed by Slark, but rather the Ravens trying to create space enough to move large troop quantities.

She didn't quite know what to make of the new theory. If the Ravens were motivated in forcing out the mutants, Crescent City was likely to see a huge influx of attacks. If the Slark were heading north to try to escape a direct westerly assault, the mutants would be slower, but likely followed closely by Slark. She desperately wished she knew which was happening so she might warn Major Bradley.

The Balclutha's northern most stop was the fisherman's village at Winchester Bay in what used to be Oregon. The fishery that harvested and processed salmon was a tiny camp with next to no defensive positions as it didn't sit on a former population center. If the mutants made it far enough north to attack the two dozen fishermen camped out on the dunes beside the bay, they would be slaughtered. Olivia resolved to leave a contingent of her men there just in case. The food provided by the fishing outpost was too valuable to risk losing for want of a few defenders she could easily spare.

With the charts drawn, Gold Beach on the horizon, and her orders planned for the rest of the trip, Olivia lay out on her bunk to remove her prosthetic leg to let her stump breathe. She felt more comfortable with the leg in place, but Dr. Gatling had made it all too clear that she shouldn't wear it indefinitely, especially not in the salty, dirty air aboard a ship. She unbuckled her belt, undid her trousers, and slipped them off. Her brass leg was losing some of its gleam from so much work without tending and so she resolved to polish it a bit at the same time. She unhooked the banding and clasps that held the metal limb to the stump of her leg that ended at mid thigh. Dressed in just her t-shirt and underwear, she hopped across the room, leg in hand, to her workbench where she maintained the ship's small arms. Roger erupted in a furious barking fit at the sight of her leg or perhaps it was the stump.

"What are you going on about?" Olivia asked of the frantic dog. She took a seat on the stool at her workbench and slipped her leg back on. Roger's barking ceased. She removed the leg again and he resumed barking. "You're becoming an irritation, boy." She didn't have the maternal instincts required to be anything but annoyed by the pungent dog scent and the raucous barking at her fake leg. She resolved to feed him up, help him recover from his injuries, and then give him to someone who felt a kinship with dogs. Idly thinking, with her chin rested in her hand propped on the workbench, something fairly ingenious occurred to her—she could give Roger to Claudia. She'd mentioned having a dog when she was younger and it would be a gift unlikely surpassed by the donut shop girl who had become a romantic rival at some point.

Her attraction to Claudia had only deepened over the past few months. She was charming, beautiful, and the daughter of the commander she respected so much. These were the obvious qualities that drew her in, but the real draw quickly became her war record. Olivia had never met another female soldier of such quality. Claudia could spin a masterful story, no doubt about that, but it was the content of her war stories that really impressed Olivia. Hearing about her assassination work in ridding the world of the mad cult leader Yahweh and then turning the tide in Crescent City by eliminating the Gator was music to Olivia's ears. She wanted Claudia to be every inch the warrior her father was, but in a less idealized, more feminine package. Olivia could never get past her hero worship of Commander Marceau or the fact that he was male, but she would do every depraved or loving thing Claudia could want if she would simply ask.

She looked over to the resting Roger with a newfound interest. If the ship's cook could be persuaded to feed up the dog and one of her men could bathe him in Gold Beach, Roger would almost be presentable. "I'll bet dogs to donuts she'll like you more than a cruller," Olivia said to Roger who quirked his head to the side as though he were trying to understand her.

†

Olivia left Lane and his pick of two others at the fishing outpost in Winchester Bay. The fishermen seemed largely unconcerned about the threat of mutant attacks. That particular section of Oregon was lush and nearly untouched. They'd constructed a few log cabins along their new beachfront property and were making good use of the blackberry bushes that grew like wildfire along any stretch of open ground. In addition to the processed salmon haul, the Balclutha also picked up an impressive amount of blackberry preserves, promising to bring glassware on their next trip. Standing amidst the barely re-tamed wilderness in what was formerly a lovely national park, Olivia understood the cavalier dismissal of mutant attacks by the fishermen. They lived in a world so set apart from the war it might as well be on another planet.

They were a week and a half out of their original stop at Crescent City when they finally departed Gold Beach for the second time. Olivia was glad to see the Gold Beach lumber camp boss, although not a military man, had done well in fortifying the position after the initial warning. An autumn squall slowed them further, forcing them closer to the rocky shore than most were comfortable with. The Balclutha's captain masterfully skirted the margin of the storm and the killing zone of the coastal rocks with only a torn sail to show for it. Olivia couldn't imagine where the old man had learned to sail nineteenth century windjammers with such skill. She'd gone to him when they were clear of the storm, standing beside the wheel he was guiding one handed. She'd told him how impressed she was, thinking the endorsement of a career navy woman might mean something to the captain. He'd shrugged and went right on staring ahead into the gray skies ahead. His soaked gray beard jutting from beneath the yellow hood of his rain slicker dripped water like a spigot to which he also paid no mind.

When she turned back toward her cabin, he finally spoke. "She survived too long to give it up now," he said.

Olivia stayed with the captain atop the poop deck the rest of the day until the clouds finally broke in the west. They rode easily the rough sea and the pitching of the deck, both practiced sailors with impeccable balance. They didn't speak again as simply sharing the space felt like company enough.

Crescent City was just on the edge of visible with the naked eye when the watch at the bow rang the alarm bell. Smoke pillars, he screamed.

"Get your team ready and take the fast boat out," the captain told her. "We'll anchor past the breakers until you give an all clear flare."

Olivia moved to carry out the order, kicking herself with the leg she didn't have anymore for leaving almost half her squad in Winchester Bay. In the cabin beneath the wheel and charthouse, her squad was already armed and ready to put to water. She grabbed her own carbine and accompanying pistol. A shock of cold fear ran through her—she'd have to climb down the side of the Balclutha in a rolling sea to sit inside a rubber boat with an outboard motor while it drove through rough waters toward a turbulent beach landing. There was no doubt in her mind, if she went into the water, she'd drown. Her leg wasn't made for swimming and there wouldn't be any way to get it off in time, nor did she know how well she could even swim with one leg as she'd hadn't tried since losing the limb. If she hadn't left Lane in Winchester Bay, she could have trusted him to lead the shore party; without him, she'd have to go.

The storm had drenched the entirety of the ship, and the indentation ladder on the port side was no different. She slipped twice, nearly falling the second time before she finally mastered climbing down the pitched side of the ship using her prosthetic leg only sparingly. She was exhausted and shaky when she finally settled into the "fast boat" so named as the Balclutha's wooden long boat was still powered with manual rowing. Her men gave her wan smiles, clearly just as nervous as she was about her falling and missing the boat. Or they were perhaps as concerned about possibly capsizing the boat in the surf where she would drown and they would lose their weapons.

"It's not going to get any easier by waiting," Olivia said through clenched teeth, reading their reticence.

The outboard motor sprung to life, and Johnnie nosed them toward the shore. The spray off the bow and the wind in their face made it difficult to see much of anything on their approach. They made for the lighthouse and the pebbly beach strewn with driftwood along its southern edge. Olivia briefly thought of directing them around the jetty into the bay proper, but decided against it. There wouldn't be anywhere to land the rubber boat that wouldn't also leave them entirely exposed. The lighthouse's beach was clear, she could see that much from the Balclutha, and it had cover almost immediately in the giant rocks and driftwood piles. It was as good a place as any to establish a foothold since she didn't know if the town fell to Slark or mutants or maybe even human marauders.

She gripped the side rope for all she was worth when the boat crested over the first breaker near the beach. The bow shot up and fell even faster on the other side. Johnnie gunned the engine to get clear of the wash, almost losing the boat when it turned diagonal on them. Somehow he corrected and got them pointed at the shore again just in time to jump over the next, smaller wave. This one, coming so close on the heels of the first, nearly unseated Olivia, but one of her men, an American sitting on the other side of the same bench from her, managed to grab her battle harness with his left hand to pull her back down. She almost screamed in joy when she felt the plastic bottom run up on the pebbles of the shore. The two men at the front leapt from the boat into the waist deep surf and hauled for all they were worth, bringing the fast boat well up onto the shore. The remaining men followed suit, including Olivia, covering the first two as they secured the boat.

Out of the turbulent chaos of the surf, Olivia was shocked at how calm the beach was once she was on shore with the tiny waves lapping at the heels of her boots. She slowly, quietly advanced up the beach to take point, her carbine trained in front of her, expecting an onslaught at any moment. With the boat pulled up far enough out of the surf and tied off to a heavy piece of driftwood, her squad fell in entirely behind her as she guided them in a waxing maneuver to face the lighthouse. Their stealthy assault was halted by the unlikeliest of warnings. Little red dots sprung up on all of them, two to a man and three on Olivia. Her first instinct was Slark, but she'd never known them to use laser sights.

"Put the weapons down," a woman's voice called from somewhere unseen.

Olivia slipped the strap of the carbine off her elbow she'd wrapped it around to steady her aim and set the gun in the pebbles at her feet. Her men followed her lead. Olivia didn't need to guess at how badly they were outnumbered. Whoever got the drop on her team was at least ten strong and aiming from cover. If they'd wanted to kill them, they could have done it without a moment's thought, making surrender an appealing option to still have.

"We're the security detail from the Balclutha out of the City of Broken Bridges," Olivia said to the unseen force. "We're looking for Major Bradley and the Crescent City logging camp contingent."

"That's all a lot of gibberish to me," the unseen woman replied.

A squad of fifteen emerged from cover in the rocks and driftwood. They were commandos of remarkable skill to hide so completely that she hadn't seen a one of them when they'd landed. More surprising than their ambush was the squad's composition—they were all women.

"Ravens…" Olivia murmured, stopping the women in their tracks.

"That's right," the lead woman said. She was tall, taller than Olivia even, and dressed in the traditional Special Forces attire of a battle harness, camouflage clothes, tightly cinched boots, and grime across her face to obscure her features. Her light brown hair was pulled back in a tight braid, leaving her brilliant green eyes as the only distinguishing feature. "I'm Captain Dylan Watson of the Voron Dagger."

Olivia only barely recognized the words Voron Dagger as something Claudia had mentioned. It was the designation for the commando vanguard she'd once been a part of—the Raven's advanced scouts and Special Forces units trained in the tactics of the Russian Spetsnaz.

"I am Warder Olivia Kingston of the Balclutha's security detail," Olivia replied.

"What are you? Marauders? Pirates?" Dylan asked.

"Fishermen by the look of how they hold their weapons," one of the other Raven women said. A small chuckle ran through the group.

"We're a cargo vessel," Olivia replied flatly.

"You're not going to find any cargo here, Warder," Dylan said. "We came upon the mess after the fact and had to wipe out an entire tribe of creepers."

"Creepers?" Johnnie asked.

"She probably means mutants," Olivia said.

"I actually like creepers better," Johnnie said. "They do sort of creep, don't they?"

"Whatever they're called," Dylan said, "they came here in force and swamped the city's defenses. A few men, former Marines by the look of their uniforms, made a last stand in the lighthouse. They were overrun a few days ago judging from the state of the bodies. Your Major Bradley might be in that bunch."

Olivia ran through all the worst case scenarios she'd charted and none of them were accurate. The Ravens were already sending teams to the coast which could only mean they'd already turned the corner and flanked the Slark line. Every outpost and the City of Broken Bridges itself would be washed over in mutants in no time at all.

Dylan, reading the obvious frustration on Olivia's face, took a few steps closer. "I'm sorry to be the bearer of bad news," she said. "Were you close to the Major?"

"No, well, kind of, I guess," Olivia said, and she didn't know why or maybe what quality about Dylan made her continue, but she was driven to admit more. "I've made several mistakes in my command lately and it seems they've started to cost me."

"Something I know all too well," Dylan replied. "Tell me though, how do you know about Ravens?"

Olivia couldn't think of a reason not to tell Dylan about Claudia. From all the war stories she'd told, Claudia seemed like a Raven hero. There was the other name, the important name Claudia had mentioned with some fondness and deep-seated reverence, Veronica. Olivia wasn't sure if they were out of the woods yet with the commando women, but she thought it was as good a time as any to play the familiarity card.

"One of your scouts from the Voron Dagger group Draco made her way to the City of Broken Bridges, what you would probably call San Francisco."

This brought only a glimmer of surprise to Dylan's face, which was immediately banished. "What is this Draco scout's name?"

"Claudia Marceau."

"That's bullshit," the soldier who had made the joke about Olivia's men being fishermen interjected. "Marceau's unit was wiped out in Tombstone."

"Easy, Garcia," Dylan said. "There were a lot of MIA after Tombstone, most of which turned up later in New Mexico, but I'm curious, how did Marceau get so far northwest?"

"She said the White Queen Veronica sent her here," Olivia said, parroting almost verbatim the vague explanation Claudia had given her to a similar question.

"Veronica died in Tombstone," Dylan said. "I'm curious why Claudia wouldn't know that."

It was hard for Olivia to fathom the word in connection to the remarkable soldier Claudia claimed to be, but the word refused to leave the forefront of her mind: deserter. Whatever shift in demeanor surfaced on Olivia, it seemed to satisfy many of Dylan's questions.

"Have a look around, if you want," Dylan said, "and when you see Claudia again, tell her the Voron will be on the coast soon." The commandos left the beach in an orderly skirmish line, melting back into the brush and cover as though they'd never been there.

Olivia's men retrieved their weapons immediately, although their commander continued to stand stunned on the beach.

Chapter 18:
Commissions of Fire and Disappointment.

Shortly after seeing the sea lions, Claudia began sleeping at Esme's home behind the donut shop on a dark, narrow little lane in the Chinican District. Shortly after this, Claudia's feet began to itch in a familiar way.

Lying in the darkness of Esme's bedroom, wrapped in the light sheets and blankets common to the underground dwellings of the City of Broken Bridges, Claudia struggled with a desire to flee even while she attempted to sleep. She nudged the curtain over the vent window open with her toe—such was the size of the tiny room on the back of the house. The head, foot, and one side of the bed Esme slept on were all against walls. The vent window, which many houses along the rock walls had, opened up on tubes that ran down to the giant chamber below where the Transcended and Keepers made the city's electricity in the volcanic canyon. Faint, hellish red light filtered up along with an abundance of heat. With the added light in the room, Claudia looked over Esme's sleeping form. Her hair had fallen most of the way over her eyes and her thumb was in her mouth.

There were two sides to the donut shop owner—the public side of business as usual and this quiet, private side of a deeply traumatized, fearful girl. Claudia didn't plumb the depths of Esme's history in the war, although Esme had seemed eager to talk about it, simply because Claudia didn't want to know what horrors had befallen Esme. War stories were supposed to be grand, triumphant, and remarkable; she suspected Esme didn't have any stories like those. There are people suited to war and there are people who are not, was how Veronica had put it, always adding as an afterthought: and the world doesn't give a shit which you are anymore. Claudia thought she was born to fight, just like her father, and regretted a world that would ask someone like Esme to see combat of any kind.

The depth and severity of the damage done to Esme's mental and emotional health aside, which was daunting and frightening all on its own, Claudia also began to suspect they weren't all that sexually compatible. To that point, after a week of sleeping in the same bed, they'd only had sex twice, and both times were brief, uninteresting affairs. In the past, when Claudia grew bored of a lover, she simply changed dance partners or skipped town. As Esme increasingly began to rely upon her for emotional support, Claudia wondered if she might not do some serious damage to the girl if she followed her usual pattern.

This was almost certain to happen with the good news she'd left unspoken at dinner earlier that night. Training with her new sniper rifle was going so well, her father offered her a field commission to go out with the torch brigades to clear the lasher trees growing in and around Half Moon Bay before they could encroach on the no man's land that was the ruins of South San Francisco—outside the wall. There would be mutants to shoot, sniper support to provide the burners as they were called while they saw to their work. Most burners were what Olivia referred to as rag bowlers from the second level. They were poor and without the business sense or abilities of the Chinicans, so they worked the violent jobs the city still valued like harvesting rats or, in the case of particularly brave bowlers, working as burners in the torch brigades. Burners were adorned in metal helmets with welder masks, full-body leather aprons, and carried elaborate flamethrowers designed to kill the lasher trees. The cover fire for the torch brigades stood atop a scissor lift affixed to a platform driven along on modified tractor treads. They would always go out in squads of three burners, one driver, one shooter, typically sixty or so squads at a time so nobody would ever be too far from help. The driver would park the scissor lift in a central area, not too close to the lasher trees, and then send the shooter skyward to watch for mutants. The burners, barely able to see in their flame-resistant getups, would then triangulate a lasher tree and work it from the top down until it crumbled over. Most mutants had moved south and the Slark seldom ventured past

La Honda anymore. It was a cake walk mission, but her father called it an important first step in teaching his daughter to be a leader of men.

She hadn't told Esme about her new post, about her return to the uniform, about the chance to finally take on a leadership role. Esme was not going to like it. This presented Claudia with a conundrum. She could tell Esme and let whatever anger she had over it put an end to their romantic entanglements, and that would be a way out of the relationship for Claudia, or she could try her best to ameliorate the news by lying and calling it something else. She didn't feel like lying and she doubted it would do her much good beyond a momentary reprieve as it would no doubt get back to Esme what she was really doing.

She'd made it clear to Esme that they were not an exclusive couple, although she wasn't sure if Esme believed her. It was shortly after Esme had said, "You talk like a lesbian, but fuck like a man." The words had stung and Claudia responded with a sting of her own, reminding Esme that their relationship was without strings, that she wasn't the type to settle. Settle was her exact word and she regretted using it after although not enough to apologize.

She considered waiting until the morning to tell her. She didn't sleep well in Esme's bed though. It was small, felt enclosed, and the concept of being several stories underground bothered her immensely. The impenetrable darkness reminded her of the restroom in the canyon in Utah where she'd nearly died in the mudslide—most nights, she still woke up with a start, thinking she heard rumbling. If Esme was mad enough about the news, she might send Claudia back to the tower where she could sleep comfortably.

Claudia awoke Esme with a gentle nudge. She came to the world afraid, disoriented, and a little surprised to find her thumb in her mouth. This happened nearly every time she awoke, Claudia had learned. Although she carefully arranged her hair over her eyes before sleeping, Esme didn't start out with her thumb in her mouth; it always made its way in there after she lost consciousness.

"What? Is something wrong?" Esme asked.

"I have to leave tomorrow," Claudia replied. "My father found a posting for me in the defense force."

"You're going to walk around on the wall, patrol the bridge stumps, or train recruits?" Esme asked, settling back onto her pillow. "You can still sleep here during that if you want."

"I will be providing sniper support for the torch brigade."

This brought Esme fully from sleep. She sat up and stared down at Claudia with an expression equal parts fear and rage. Her face, half-lit by the red glow from the vent window, looked strangely plain to Claudia as though it could be anyone's face or everyone's face. She was any woman who wished conflicts would pass them by. Claudia didn't think it was the face of the brave Mouse that had convinced her to join Esme in her bed a week ago.

"You know how I feel about combat," Esme said sternly.

"I do, but you know I do not feel the same way," Claudia replied.

"Would you stay if I asked you?"

"No, but I would be flattered if you did."

"Would you stay if *she* asked you?"

"She would never ask me to."

"No," Esme said, "she will probably be thrilled for you."

"I am sure she would be as I was thrilled for her when she was given the post on that red and gray ship. I did not understand her desire to go to sea again, but that did not stop me from feeling happy for her. Why would this be different? I am a creature of wilderness and war. You should be glad to see me return to my home away from…" she stopped short of saying 'this hell' although those were the words she wanted to use to describe the underground world of the City of Broken Bridges. "…you should be glad for me is all I am saying."

"I told you what I went through during the war, I told you how many friends I lost, I told you…"

"Yes, I know, and I was honored you trusted me so much…"

"I didn't even carry a weapon. I never told you that part. They wanted to give me a gun, bombs, a knife even. I always refused. Dying with a weapon is…is a sin."

This threw Claudia from the bed. They'd been down that road just once and Claudia had made it clear her immortal soul, if it existed, was too far removed from any higher power to be cleansed now. She grabbed up her pants and began dressing.

"You know I do not believe in such things," Claudia replied tersely. "Does your god look over the Slark as well? Are they his creations, huh? Did he destroy their planet and send them here to take ours?" Claudia pulled on her boots and stood, stepping far enough away from the light of the vent window that only the tips of her toes would show, leaving the rest of her in silhouette. "You did not carry a weapon in war. I respect your bravery in this, but do not think we are the same. I am a warrior, like my father and his father before him. Did you know my grandfather was one of the youngest soldiers to assault the Juno beach at Normandy? At fifteen, he did not turn his back when the Germans occupied France and so what would he say to me if I set down my rifle to become a shopkeeper when the Slark are still on the other side of the wall you seem to have forgotten exists?"

"Lovely speech," Esme said, resting her forehead on her knees as she folded over herself. "I'd ask what your grandmother might have thought, but you've made it clear to me we are not truly together, so I don't know why you're asking me what I think."

Claudia pulled her hair back into a ponytail and tied it off. She didn't have anything else to do to get ready to leave, but wasn't ready to leave the conversation just yet. For a moment, a brief, angry moment, she considered telling Esme about the warrior women who captured her heart or made her hot, wet, and wanting. Whenever she'd tried to talk about Fiona or Veronica in the past, Esme always stopped her with the trite saying, "less history—more mystery." By the third time, when Claudia simply wanted to tell Esme about the kindness Veronica had shown her in letting her leave, and how she suspected it was likely the last time she would ever see the remarkable woman, Esme had repeated the mantra, and Claudia wanted to slap her for the disrespect.

Claudia rushed to the edge of the bed and grabbed Esme by the shoulders, pulling her face from her knees until they were looking each other square in the eyes. "What do you see when you look upon me?" Claudia demanded. "What am I if not this?"

"You are...sweet, with music in you," Esme replied.

Claudia shook her head and let Esme go. It was a simplistic and easy answer—neither description particularly true anymore. She couldn't sing anymore, not since the radiation damage to her throat and lungs, not that she felt like it anyway. Nor did she feel all that sweet. In truth, she felt like killing something, many things, starting with Inspector Cavanaugh and then any Slark or mutant stupid enough to cross her path. For a brief, angry instant, she flashed upon the moment in the old casino in Carson City when the men meant to assist her had tried to kill her. The satisfaction of seeing them dangling at the ends of ropes followed. No, she was definitely not sweet.

"All this time I thought I was the one with the messed up eyes," Claudia replied as she made for the door.

"What do you see when you look at me?" Esme asked before Claudia could leave.

Claudia stopped with her hand on the doorknob. She wanted to close the literal door, but not the figurative one, not yet anyway, although she couldn't understand why just yet, and so she didn't say the first thing that came to her mind, the thought about Esme being anyone or everyone who never wanted to face down a conflict.

"A clever woman who can make a good cruller," Claudia replied.

Chapter 19:
Beyond the Wall in Good Company.

Claudia waited in the gray, pre-dawn hours amid what looked like a combination of an army and a tree trimming crew. A chilly fog hung over the day, dampening the mood of the men when combined with the early hour.

Her father specifically hadn't come down to see her off. His presence, as he'd explained, would undermine her authority if she was perceived as a child being dropped off for her first day of school by her father. He was the commander of all military forces now, and she was at the bottom of the officer hierarchy—the appearance of nepotism needed to be avoided at all costs. Still, as Claudia looked around to the gathered families and friends seeing off the men of the torch brigade she wished someone had come to see her off. It had been so long since she had anyone staying behind to wish her luck as most of her lovers to that point went off to war with her. Now she had a father and two pseudo-girlfriends to wish her well, and none of them were there.

"You must be the Marceau girl," a gravely man's voice snapped her attention away from the several dozen touching scenes around her.

Claudia looked ahead to address the person speaking to her. She found a gray uniform with three bars up and three bars down—a master sergeant to be addressed with respect but not a salute as she was technically commissioned as a second lieutenant.

"Yes, master sergeant," Claudia replied, "ready to receive my posting."

"Walk with me, lieutenant," the master sergeant replied.

They set off at a slow walk as the sergeant had a pronounced limp in his left leg. Claudia glanced down to find he had one of Dr. Gatling's mechanical legs in place of his right limb below the knee. This brought Claudia's attention to the rest of the support staff fueling up the scissor lift vehicles, arming the burners, and issuing duty commands—all of them were missing one or more limbs to have them replaced with the bronze mechanical arms and legs designed by Dr. Gatling.

"Normally, I would have questioned putting a woman on a shooting tower, but after seeing you on the range, I think this posting may be a bit beneath your abilities," the master sergeant said. "Here's your detail, Tractor 23." The sergeant checked a few pages down on his clipboard. "You'll be clearing grid delta-niner. Don't worry, Alfie here knows right where that is. Good luck out there, Marceau." The sergeant limped away, leaving Claudia in the company of her new men.

Claudia's men snapped to attention upon her arrival, offering her a sloppy set of salutes to which she responded with one of her own. The driver that the sergeant had referred to as Alfie was a gangly young man, no more than sixteen or seventeen, with a shock of dirty blond hair and a missing front tooth. The burners consisted of two burly men in their thirties, brothers or cousins by the similarity of their jagged facial features and curly black hair, and a stocky bulldog of a man with an ornate handlebar moustache.

"I am Lieutenant Marceau," Claudia said to her men. "My history is with scout sniper units so my military decorum is a bit lacking. Can we dispense with all the saluting from here on out?"

"That's dandy-candy with us, LT," Alfie said. "We're an informal lot down here in the pits. As the sarge said, I'm Alfie, the two towers at the front of our rig are the Hungarian brothers—they've got names none of us can pronounce, so we just call them Ben and Jerry." The two brothers nodded to Claudia before returning to their chores of helping one another into their leather protective gear. "The man with the mighty moustache goes by the Greek."

"We lose angry, drunk Russian and get tiny woman with face so pretty it remind the Greek of his own daughters," the moustache man said in a thick Mediterranean accent. "I like this plan. I like this rumor I hear that small woman shoot dots off dice to win bet."

"Is that true, LT?" Alfie asked. "We heard you shot a set of dice off a target at three hundred yards."

"It was four hundred," Claudia corrected him. "I'm guessing you're the man that hands out the names, Alfie."

"Sure-sure, if you don't like LT, I can conjure up a new one, but it's best not to change them up too much as the Greek gets confused easily since his English isn't so good, and the Hungarians don't speak much English at all." Alfie hopped off the edge of the tractor tracks he was lounging on and took a step closer to Claudia to whisper as not to be overheard easily by the other three. "I'm the only one what knows you're the commander's daughter. I'll keep it under my hat if you like or tell them if you like that better."

"LT is fine and I'd prefer if you kept that bit of information to yourself," Claudia said.

"As the officer bids, so do we go," Alfie said with a grin, showing off the gap left by his missing incisor. "Grab your seat, LT, and we'll be underway in a jiffy."

Claudia climbed up the ladder at the back of the strange vehicle until she stood in the armored basket atop the scissor lift. The two Hungarian brothers took their positions along running boards with handles to hold onto on the sides of the vehicle while the Greek secured himself to the front, slightly off to one side, so Alfie could still see where he was driving from the sunken cockpit between the two tractor tracks.

The massive wall, towering in front of them, taller than any free-standing wall Claudia had ever seen, stretched off in both directions beyond sight. Up close, Claudia marveled at the wall's construction, looking as though the city itself had somehow influenced the flavor of the patchwork structure in remarkably aesthetic ways. The wall began to open at the base as a section lifted much like a hundred yard wide garage door.

The sixty or so similar tractors around them started up, sending blue puffs of diesel smoke into the air as the squads made ready to depart. With a few lurches, they were off, heading out under the direction of the lead tractor a few ranks ahead of them. Alfie pulled on a leather helmet reminiscent of a World War I pilot's, pulled goggles over his eyes, and spoke loudly into a metal cone in front of him to check in as ready. The whole column of gangly vehicles departed at a turtle's crawl. The metal and stone wall of remarkable sturdiness and architectural beauty loomed large above them as they dipped into a trough beneath. The sound of so many engines in such an enclosed space was deafening, the smell of the exhaust choking to the eyes and throat, and entirely dark for the fifty or so feet they were under the wall. They popped up into the remains of a true war zone that Claudia expected of San Francisco.

The rolling hills and valleys of what used to be the suburban sprawl of South San Francisco was rubble on par with the bombed out husks from old war movies. The column of tractors broke up into the ruins, visible at a distance only by the spires of their blue exhaust smoke rising into the fog and overcast sky. Claudia kept her eyes scanning back and forth as they made their clanking way through the debris of shattered city streets and fallen buildings. As they got farther and farther away from the wall, the column spread so thin she couldn't even see any of the other tractors around them. She suspected mutants to leap from the ruins at any minute to set upon them, but she was alone in this as the three burners looked almost bored in their perches on the edges of the tractor. The posting was said to be routine. They needed to keep the lasher trees from getting close enough to the city so they couldn't spread their spores on the populated side of the wall. With how often the torch brigade burned out the no-man's land, the Slark and mutants seemed to get the message about staying out of the way.

At a top speed of about seven or eight miles an hour, it was almost noon before they broke free of the war torn no-man's land of South San Francisco. Trappings of true wilderness began to pop up around them, but it seemed to have an alien tint to it. Grasses and shrubs looked normal for coastal California, but among them were peculiar looking flora as well. Occasionally a grayish trunk, almost razor straight with a tiny taper at the top, jutted from the landscape.

"What are those?" Claudia shouted to be heard above the clanking of the tracks.

"Lasher trees, LT," Alfie shouted up to her. "Those are just saplings though, and not in our grid. The squads behind us will take care of them."

Claudia spotted movement off to the right, far enough away to be indiscernible with the naked eye. She lifted her rifle to her shoulder and sighted through the scope to see what it was. A few mutated deer were moving through the grass near one of the lasher saplings. Most of the deer lacked full coats of fur, most had odd numbers of limbs, either five or three, and none of them had a regular head shape. Claudia cringed at the sight of them, but watched on with the same morbid curiosity attributed to watching a car wreck. One of the deer came close to the lasher tree, not close enough by Claudia's or the deer's estimation to be in range, but sure enough, the gray spire snapped open from a seam on the side, and a thin, pink, ropey tentacle shot out, snatching the deer from the ground. The entire gray spire bent under the weight, trembling as the deer tried to escape. Two more tentacles, blue and smaller than the first, followed the pink one, and sliced off the deer's hind legs with the surgical precision of a laser.

Claudia tore her vision away from the rifle's scope, not wanting to see any more. Olivia mentioned losing her leg to a lasher tree, but Claudia didn't know what that truly entailed and Olivia hadn't wanted to go into detail. Seeing how lasher trees actually removed limbs, Claudia could understand why. The shocking number of amputees in the support staff for the torch brigade suddenly made a lot more sense.

"The trees don't attack the Slark?" Claudia asked.

"They don't seem to," Alfie shouted back. "They don't smell like prey or something. Dr. Gatling said lashers are a lot more like our jelly fish than our trees, but I think they've got to have some shark in there too since they can smell prey a mile away."

"What about mutants? Do they eat mutants?" Claudia asked.

"It would solve problems if they could," the Greek bellowed, "but mutants have learned the trees and do not get eaten so much now. Trees eat up all dumb, slow mutants. Leave only smart, fast ones."

"It's a proper messed up Wild Kingdom episode out here," Alfie added. "The mutants learned to come after us when we're burning the trees down. Those mutants may look all messed up and wrong, but they're still as smart as most people."

"There are million, maybe two of the millions," the Greek rumbled, "we in torch brigade kill hundred or so two time a month. It only take thousand years to get rid of them all."

"With LT on our tractor, you can cut that time in half," Alfie replied.

They rode on for an hour more in conversational silence, although the tractor itself made every manner of noise as the bio-diesel engine rumbled, the tracks squeaked and squealed, and the metal pieces rattled against one another. The forest, a true forest of redwoods, firs, and pines loomed ahead and Claudia found she was a little excited to return to the wilderness. They stopped short of the actual tree line by almost a quarter mile. Alfie stopped the tractor and shut down the engine. The remarkable silence that followed was nearly deafening until the sound of wind across the open grass and down out of the hills filled the void left by the tractor's racket.

"Are we in Half Moon Bay?" Claudia asked.

"We passed to the east of those ruins awhile back," Alfie said. "We went right down the middle here toward the lowest grid. The old freeway through San Mateo is to our left, the ocean is to our right, and our task is directly ahead."

The two Hungarians and the Greek hopped off their perches on the tractor. They assembled in something of a ring, facing each other's backs, and did the final preparations on the tanks strapped to the next man in line's back. They pulled on their huge, bronze helmets that looked like older diver equipment but with welder shield slots along the front. Alfie made a few strange bip and boop noises into the cone on the tractor and all three held up their thumbs.

"About to send you skyward, LT," Alfie said. He threw a lever forward and the scissor lift extended, hoisting Claudia and her little armored platform up into the air thirty feet or so. "They'll work left to right across the grid," Alfie explained. "The mutants will come up behind them if they're going to come at all, usually popping right out of the ground. The real fight out here for you is going to be boredom."

"Boredom I can handle," Claudia muttered.

She watched the three men in heavy leather drapings with their brass flamethrowers and divers helmets first with her naked eye, and then the scope of her rifle when they were a hundred yards out or so. They triangulated one of the pointed gray spires of a lasher tree, keeping a good distance from it always. The Greek crept up closer and sent a couple sprays of fire, stepping several paces back when the seam along the side opened. The tentacles lashed out, although not nearly far enough to grab the stocky little burner, and the Hungarians pounced, at least as much of a pounce as massively encumbered men could make, spraying at the opening along the side with jets of strange, blue fire. The entire process was kind of remarkable. The lasher tree didn't burn like a plant, which was what Claudia expected, rather it exploded like a water balloon sending semi-clear liquid spraying in all directions.

"That's weird," she said. "It popped."

"Like I was saying—they're basically jelly fish," Alfie said, never looking up from the torn remnants of the paperback he was reading. "The water boils in them, expands until their skin can't take it, and then sploosh! They're gone."

"Why did the Slark plant them?" Claudia asked.

"No earthy clue, LT," Alfie replied. "We made sense of the fish they brought right quick, but these things...who the hell knows? They started planting them before the cataclysm, says Professor Kingston anyway, so it can't be to keep us in line since they had their crawlers doing that just fine. Got any theories?"

"A food source is all I can think of," Claudia replied.

"I like that," Alfie said, "simple, easy to remember, and makes us seem like proper ruffians running around burning the other bloke's crops and all."

Claudia returned her full attention to her vigil over the three burners. They were making good time sweeping the sapling lasher trees away, still staying well away from the actual tree line of more traditional trees and shrubbery. The grasslands that looked to have grown to about knee high on the Hungarians and mid thigh on the Greek were clear of any mutant attackers. Boredom indeed, Claudia thought.

"Are we going into the actual forest?" Claudia asked although she knew the answer. Using flamethrowers, even carefully, would start a forest fire, which she knew California was already prone to.

"Nope," Alfie replied. "The lashers in there have grown tall, strong, and hide well among the real trees. In there is a proper killing zone."

"Hang on, I think we have our first customer," Claudia said, catching a flicker of movement near the edge of the forest out in front of where the three burners were making their sweep. She zeroed in on the shape, expecting one of the lumpy, amorphous humanoid mutants she'd seen in Yuba City. What she actually saw made her blood run cold. It was gray, scaly, and definitely not alone. "Slark!" she shouted.

Alfie snapped to attention and shouted into the cone, "skate, skate, skate!"

Claudia didn't know what the warning meant initially, but apparently the burners knew as they dropped their work of triangulating one of the lashers and began trundling back toward the tractor. They swung wide through the area they'd cleared rather than try to dodge the line of lashers between them and the tractor that they hadn't cleared yet. Claudia thought they were moving painfully slowly, although she didn't know how fast she could run through tall grass with limited visibility and all that gear on.

She settled the tentacle pod of her rifle on the lip of her armored basket. The little arms gripped hard, steadying her rifle better than and bipod. She zeroed in on the first Slark she'd seen through her scope. The scaly invader had figured out his position was compromised and launched his attack early. Claudia fired. Her rifle let loose with a whirring hiss, and the round lanced through the Slark's chest as though he were little more than tissue paper. Dozens more followed the downed leader's attack, flooding from the woods like the proper army Claudia secretly dreaded was hiding among the trees.

She didn't lack for targets, and couldn't spare the time to see if the burners were making good time. The Slark were moving faster and they didn't need to mind the lasher trees. If she didn't slow them, they would easily catch up to her men.

She found a target, fired, downed it, found another target, fired, and felled that too. This continued until the gun in her hands began to radiate with such heat it threatened to cook her. She reluctantly pulled herself from her scope to see to her weapon. She followed through the cooling process of turning the heated sections out to replace them with the cooled portions that formerly faced out. The entire process of turning parts of her gun inside out felt like it took an eternity, but probably only soaked up less than thirty seconds.

When she returned her attention to the field ahead of her, she saw one of the Hungarians had taken a round from a Slark weapon. Four arms and the Slark still used projectile weapons mounted on their wrists, as though they couldn't be bothered to hold the things. The uninjured brother returned for his limping kin while the Greek continued plowing forward through the grass, leaving a wide trail of stomped down vegetation behind him.

Claudia covered the brothers as best she could. The pressure of the situation along with the increased heat of her rifle made her shots slightly more erratic. She hit four out of every five, but she could tell the misses were leaving cracks she couldn't afford. The uninjured Hungarian did his best to help defend himself and his brother by spraying at the grass behind them with his flamethrower, wielding it one handed. The wet grass reluctantly caught fire at first, but quickly took to the flames, creating huge infernos across the field, slowing the Slark, but also threatening everything, including the tractor.

"Bring me down," Claudia demanded. Alfie did as he was ordered, lowering Claudia's pod at an agonizingly slow pace. The tapped the little tentacle pod on her rifle with a bare finger and it released the edge of the basket. "Abandon the tractor," Claudia ordered him as she slid down the ladder to land on the ground. "I need you to head back, warn the others, get to the city."

"What about you, LT?" Alfie asked.

"I'm going to try to get to the other advanced position squads before the fire or the Slark surprise them too." Claudia began walking out into the grass toward her fleeing men and the fire chasing them. She found targets dancing among the flames, smoke, and grass. She felled what few she could, wounding others, and missing a couple entirely.

The Greek ran past her first. Alfie did his best to help the stocky little burner get his helmet and gear off to run faster. The Hungarian brothers limped in close on the Greek's heels, although Claudia could tell from all the blood slicking down the brown leather apron on the wounded brother that he wasn't long for the world.

"Why not take tractor?" the Greek asked as Alfie pulled him back down the path they'd blazed getting there.

"If it burns up and the Slark find it, they might think we burned up near it, giving you a head start," Claudia replied. "Now get going."

Her four men did as ordered, although Alfie kept looking back to her as he fled. She turned toward the battle, pulled her scarf up over her mouth to block out the smoke, and charged into the field. She needed to get onto the other side of the fires, onto the other side of the Slark line, to pick her way along the trees. The smoke and brushfire might work as cover, but her window was closing. If she planned her shots right, she might have cut a proper tunnel through the inferno. As she ran into the burning field, she hoped she was right about the Slark formation being a skirmisher line or she'd be running right into a second wave.

The smoke made her eyes water, burned her throat, and sapped her already waning energy, but the only bodies she saw among the grass were the bloody corpses of the enemies she'd felled, finally releasing her on the other side of the line, a few dozen yards away from the forest.

She smiled in spite of herself. She figured she might owe Esme an apology. As exciting as it all was, Esme was right, Claudia was a danger to herself in combat situations.

Chapter 20:
Found Beyond the Vale.

Claudia stood on the other side of the line for a moment, mostly to catch her breath, but also to collect her thoughts. The sun dropped swiftly in the west, casting the last of the light of the day across the hills, creating long shadows of the smoke. If it was just a raid, she could find another tractor to return on. If it was more than a raid, as she supposed it to be, the Slark line likely stretched quite a ways in either direction. Alfie had said the coast was to the west and the freeway to the east. The freeway and the ruins of San Mateo likely had traffic of Slark and probably mutants, but the coast could be rocky and impassible if she didn't know the way, and she didn't. Plus, if the setting sun was at her back, she'd be harder to spot by any Slark she came up on. East was the best of two iffy options.

She took off at a light jog, rifle slung across her back. Her stamina in running, which used to be marvelous, was long gone from easy months and whatever damage she'd done to her lungs from the radioactive dust in Yuba City. She was walking soon, slowing even further when she started spotting the spires of unburned lasher trees. She considered briefly heading into the woods, but with twilight coming on fast, she suspected it would be a fantastic way to have all her limbs torn from her body by an unseen lasher tree that could be as tall as redwoods by now for all anyone knew.

Toward the top of the highest hill in the area, which took nearly everything she had to climb, she turned back to look down on the grasslands behind her that were nearly fully engulfed in flames and smoke. The already burned areas were scorched, black smudges across the landscape. A light wind had turned the fire to the west, further supporting her already made decision to head east. She was glad for the bit of luck for her fleeing men that they at least wouldn't be pursued by the fire and even happier that the western edge of the Slark line would likely burn or have to retreat for a time.

Gunfire and shouting drew her away from her inspection of the inadvertently brilliant fire the Hungarian brothers started. She was well away from the tree line now without much cover. She crouched low in the grass and snuck up over the crest of the hill. With any luck, anyone in the vale below wouldn't be able to see her with the setting sun fully at her back. She knelt at the apex and slid her rifle from her back to look through the scope. She spotted the Slark first, running in their strange gait after something that clearly had them confused and disorganized. Two of them ran past a lasher sapling and for some reason the tree opened up and snatched them both from the ground, taking special care to remove their legs before starting in on their arms. Claudia scanned farther up the valley toward the tree line to the southeast of her position, trying to find the source of the gunfire. A lone man with a rifle that looked like one of Dr. Gatling's insane creations was firing back at the Slark, daring them to come get him, and landing well-placed shots on his pursuers.

She made the decision to help the man, who appeared to be on the numerically unfavorable end of a twenty to one situation. She scanned back to the Slark in time to spot two more passing by another lasher sapling. As they neared it, something shot into the frame of her scope. A rag wad or something dark and soft anyway, because when it struck the Slark, the alien registered momentary confusion, but no real injury. An instant after the ball struck the Slark the lasher tree opened wide and snatched the confused lizard from the ground. Claudia noted with some amusement that the Slark weren't putting up even the token struggle the mutated deer had. They must really never have thought they'd be on the receiving end of dismemberment at the hands of their own crops, she surmised.

She found a target, exhaled slowly to steady her breathing and heart rate, and fired. She toppled a Slark from the middle of the pack where she suspected they might not notice. The man felled two of the closest ranks to him after taking cover behind a few glacier washed boulders in the widening of a creek bed. Claudia sighted in on another Slark, popping one of the lizard's eyes with her shot. The man behind the rock clearly figured out he had help on the ridge as he pressed the attack back up the valley when the Slark turned to escape the unseen sniper fire.

Claudia didn't bother shooting after the fleeing dozen or so Slark. She couldn't get them all anyway, and they weren't posing any immediate threat worth wasting ammunition on. She honestly didn't know exactly how long she could fire her new rifle before it would need more of the strange Slark fish juice or specialized metal shards. She had a few pouches of each on her belt, but ammo conservation was always smart behind enemy lines.

The man scanned the exact ridge Claudia was on, holding his hand above his eyes to shield them from the sun. He seemed to vaguely figure out where she was and waved in her general direction. Claudia sighed and began walking down toward him. She was going that direction anyway and the man had somehow figured out how to make the lashers eat Slark, which was worth asking about. The man, finally seeing her on the shaded face of the hill, began walking toward her as well.

"I don't know who you are, but I'm mightily happy to see you," the man said in a velvet smooth Scottish brogue. On closer inspection, he was tall, wiry, and in full possession of the boyish good looks most college advertisers would go nuts for. His eyes were sharp, pale, and green. His messy auburn hair threatened to fall in his face with every turn of his head.

"I'm Lieutenant Marceau," Claudia said, a little surprised that he didn't make a comment on her gender or size.

"Corporal Liam Gregory of Tractor 17, at your service, lieutenant," Liam said with a sloppy salute as his attention kept returning up the valley to where the Slark had vanished over the next hill. "Think we ought to get moving? They've got a whole army somewhere back there."

"I'm heading east, hoping to pick up stragglers to return to the City of Broken Bridges by the freeway ruins," Claudia explained.

"Sounds better than the last plan I was following—I'm with you."

They headed off immediately up the next rise to the east, having to double back a little to get fully around the creek bed, which was dwindling to a trickle in the late autumn. Claudia marveled at Liam's height as they walked. He was nearly a full foot taller than her but moved with the agility and effortlessness of a mountain goat up the side of the bluff.

"What was your plan, exactly?" Claudia asked between increasingly heavy breaths as she was struggling to keep up.

"The plan you saw the end of wasn't mine," Liam explained, waiting a little for her to catch up. "Some sergeant or other from one of the other tractors came through, gathered up everyone's shooters, a dozen in all, and said we were going to draw the Slark off to let the rest of the brigade get clear."

"What happened to the others?"

"We got the Slark chasing us, far more than we expected even. Once we figured out we were on the other side, it was too late to head back through. The Slark got some, the lashers got others, until there was just me, and apparently you."

"How did you get the lashers to kill the Slark?" Claudia was sick of seeing Liam having to stop to wait for her, although he clearly didn't seem to mind. His eyes were constantly to the horizon, his attention all around him in equal parts, as though he couldn't see enough of the world.

"Bloody rags and body parts," Liam said cryptically. "I scooped up remains of the other shooters or scraps of their clothes that tore free readily enough, and threw them at the Slark chasing me. Lashers love the smell of our blood and don't much care who it's on."

"That's actually…brilliant," Claudia said.

"Thanks, that plan was mine," Liam said with a wink.

Claudia glanced to his gun. It was obviously made by Gatling as it had the eccentrically functional look to it commonplace to all his inventions. It was a six barrel rifle, set in a wheel pattern like a Gatling gun. The front brace and rear grip were both handles with a folding stock and open sights along the top. Liam must have amazing eyesight to shoot such a weapon at distance without aid of a scope. Liam caught on her inspection of the gun and flipped it into one hand to show it to her.

"I call her Six-shooter Sally," Liam said with a silly grin, his hair falling across his left eye.

"It looks like one of Gatling's weaponstrosities," Claudia replied.

"Yep, he was particularly proud of this one and even equipped some of the other shooters with them," Liam said as they walked on once Claudia had caught her breath. "I was joking about the name. I didn't really name my rifle. That always seemed like such a juvenile thing to do with a weapon. Unless you named yours, in which case I was joking about joking."

"No," Claudia said with a grin, "I've never named my rifles."

"I thought not," Liam replied. "You have the look of a sensible woman."

They walked on, heading east into the growing darkness. At the bottom of the next valley over, with a hill that might rightly be called a small mountain ahead of them, they found another creek, this one healthier than the last with a proper flow going down into the forest. Claudia made for the water to fill her entirely dry canteen and splash some of the water along the back of her neck. Liam caught her by the shoulder before she could do either.

"Whoa there, lieutenant," Liam said, "that's likely as radioactive as everything around here. It might not hurt you to splash around in it, but you certainly shouldn't drink any."

"I'm…"

Liam nodded and let go of her shoulder as if seeing her peculiar eye for the first time. "Irradiated."

"Yes," Claudia replied. She dunked her canteen into the water and dropped a couple iodine tablets in after. "I'm probably more radioactive than the water."

They stood in silence for a bit at the edge of the stream. Darkness was nearly fully upon them when Liam finally spoke. "We can't keep going in this. We'll likely get snatched up by a lasher or stumble right into a Slark camp."

"The former, but not the latter," Claudia replied. She closed her normal eye and pointed along the sky. "I can see their communication beams. There's a whole army out there talking through those flickering lights." The strange beams of light that she knew no human besides her could see drew in from the entire peninsula north of them, heading toward a single point in the south somewhere in the forest. It was just as she'd feared. There was an invasion force headed toward the wall and she was on the wrong side of both.

Liam proved to be a remarkable wilderness survivor in his own right. He found a few bushes along the edge of the stream, hacked away a handful of branches, and constructed an impromptu shelter between two rocks. A fire wasn't out of the question as there were plenty of other fires around the valley that might dilute the threat, but Claudia and Liam agreed even the tiny risk it would pose wasn't worth the fraction of warmth they might get from it. They crawled into the little shelter on the back of the creek and huddled closer to one another for warmth.

"What did you mean when you said you could see their communication beams?" Liam asked in a whisper.

"My irradiated eye changed enough to see in other light spectrums outside the visible range," Claudia explained the concept she wasn't entirely clear on herself. "Dr. Gatling said he thought the Slark communicated through light beams we could not see—now I can see them."

"I'm just a foot soldier, shooting in the direction they tell me to shoot, but that sounds like a skill we'd want to make use of. Why would command risk putting you on a tractor?"

Claudia considered the question for awhile. She didn't think Liam knew she was the new supreme commander's daughter, nor was he likely to know her father was a firm believer in making a person earn their place. It was a valid question though and one she didn't have an answer for. "Beyond my pay grade," Claudia replied.

They drifted off to sleep, only to be awoken by the reason wildfires struggled to find purchase in the late autumn. Rain, like cold daggers, began falling, accompanied by an oppressive fog. Claudia and Liam both awoke when their branch roof began leaking in on them. It was pitch black and freezing. Fixing up the shelter wasn't an option and building a fire was an impossibility. Instinctively, Claudia and Liam pressed against one another to maintain what little warmth remained.

The embrace, born out of the need for survival, felt far more intimate than Claudia thought it would. Liam wrapped around the outside of her in something of a protective shell with her face pressed close to his chest, just below where his collar bones ended. When she'd slept with Danny, the quiet, intimate moments of intertwined bodies after sex almost always resulted in Danny taking on a protected posture with his head near her chest. Danny was so strong in his public persona that it was strange to find him vulnerable when they were alone. In juxtaposition, Claudia rather enjoyed the protected feeling that having Liam wrapped around her provided. The fresh rain and wet vegetation aside, which had a pleasing scent all on its own, Liam had the difficult to describe smell of a man. Claudia had nearly forgotten how enjoyable the scents of leather, gun oil, and male sweat could be up close.

"Not that you'll hear me complaining, but you're quite the little heat reactor," Liam said loud enough to be heard above the rain.

Claudia didn't know how he knew she was awake or if he was just talking to talk. "Someone told me it was an Irradiate trait to exude heat, although I think I was always somewhat hot blooded."

"If that's true, you'll be popular in the winter," Liam said.

"Who is to say I'm not already popular?"

"Touché, lieutenant."

Silence hung between them for awhile. Liam's shivering stopped, which Claudia had barely noticed until after it was gone. His breathing was evening out and she suspected he was going to fall back to sleep soon. There were questions she wanted to ask him in the darkness, questions she might not be as interested in asking tomorrow. "What brought you to San Francisco before the war?"

"I was supposed to play professional football...er...soccer for the L.A. Galaxy team, but I never saw the field. A month after landing in Los Angeles, it was overrun with those giant metal machines of death. Bad luck or good, I'm still not sure which, and a few different evacuations landed me in San Francisco right before it fell," Liam said. "Do you mind answering the same question?"

"Maybe later," Claudia replied.

"I don't mind a little mystery, but my natural curiosity and active listening skills will win out eventually," Liam said.

"I'll watch for that."

They fell asleep again, this time to a more restful slumber. When Claudia came to the next morning, the fog had abated, but the sky was still overcast and the smoke of war and wildfires still hung low in places. Her beret was a little off kilter and when she looked up to Liam, she figured out why. At some point in the night, he'd rolled his head almost entirely to one side to sleep with the top pressed against the ground. In turning into the position that looked remarkably like something only a housecat would find comfortable, the auburn stubble on his solid chin had caught on the felt of her hat. She nudged him in the stomach with her thumb and he came to the world with fluttering eyes and a little yawn, calm as if he'd awoken in his own bed.

"Mind putting the kettle on while I get the paper?" Liam said with a little grin.

"Sleeping cold, wet, and on the dirty ground, yet he wakes up with a joke," Claudia murmured. She extricated herself from his embrace and the nearly toppled shelter roof to stretch beside the stream. She spun off the cap of her canteen and took a drink of the hastily purified water. It had the unpleasant chemical taste of iodine, but it was refreshing in her dried mouth. Liam would need water soon. If she'd realized that earlier, she might have rigged up something to catch rain water when the deluge started the night before.

Liam slipped from the shelter as well, dug around in the roof a bit, and pulled out his half-full canteen from the branches. He took a sip and winked to her. "My mom used to say, 'if you can't wake with a song in your heart, what's the point of waking at all?'" Liam rustled his hand through his messy hair to dislodged the bits of dried mud collected from sleeping on the ground. "Of course, she was a proper bipolar nutter who spent quite a bit of time not getting out of bed because of her depression."

Claudia smiled and shook her head. It'd been a long while since she'd had company out in the wild, and even longer since she'd had company she actually enjoyed on her scouting missions. "We should get moving," Claudia said.

"Right you are, lieutenant." Liam removed a wide brimmed British Special Forces hat from his jacket pocket and settled it over his head. When Claudia gave the hat a weird look, he shrugged. "I'm Scottish," he said with a laugh. "I'll burn to a crisp when the sun comes out, even in the fall."

"Where did you get the hat?"

"Raided a military surplus store at one point or other. Why? Where did you get yours?"

Claudia straightened her beret. The insignia patch on the front identified her as a Canadian Special Operations Commando. Technically, it was her father's hat that he'd given to her before she left on her choir trip to America, back when there was an America and a CSO. Strangely, Liam was the first person to actually ask her about it although others had made vague comments about it through the years. She still wasn't ready to tell him who her father was, or give him a hint that would help him figure it out. She liked how casual he was around her; she liked his jokes and easy manner. If he knew she was the great commander's daughter, he might back away to a formal distance the way Olivia did.

"I won it in an arm wrestling competition," Claudia replied.

The answer seemed to please Liam as he smiled and nodded with an appreciative grin on his face. "I'll consider myself warned not to bet anything I'm not willing to lose in an arm wrestling contest against you," he said.

Chapter 21:
Options Being What They Are...

It didn't take long to figure out the mountain wasn't going to be passable with the limited supplies of a couple rifles, knives, a grenade or two, and the clothes on their backs. The hill wasn't a hill, but probably a mountain that was part of a range, and may have even had a name before the Slark came along and destroyed California, irradiated the soil, and planted horrible lasher trees everywhere. They'd had to see the now nameless mountain first hand as he was Scottish and she was Canadian, and neither of them knew California as it once was. They turned back, and while the failure hit Claudia in her already morose-leaning core, it did little to diminish Liam's good mood.

"I mean to say, four hands and they can't be bothered to hold something in any of them," Liam continued his diatribe about how ridiculous the Slark were in how they held their weapons. "What did Slark criminals do back on their home world if the Slark police caught them? 'Twiddle your weapon thumbs idly while we gather enough handcuffs to fit all your gangly arms.'" He'd already pointed out that their weapon triggers were actually rings on the ends of wires attached to what he believed was the thumb on their three fingered hands. Claudia was glad to find someone else thought it was equally preposterous that their weapons were wrist mounted, although she hadn't put nearly the consideration into it that Liam clearly had. Still, something he'd said resonated with her.

"What do you think their home world is like?" Claudia asked. They'd been heading back in the general direction they'd come. Early in the day, the sounds of war echoed in the north, but as noon came and went, the sounds faded beyond hearing, indicating to Claudia the battle was heading toward the wall.

"A dead, useless rock by now, I would imagine," Liam replied. "I read a book once, I can't remember who it was by, that spoke about an alien race whose planet was all used up and they started killing each other off until a race of pink jellyfish people came and saved them in space ships."

"That was from a video game," Claudia said with a smirk.

Liam winced and shook his head. "I knew I gave too much detail. You bloody well caught me; I'm not much of a reader, but I used to enjoy a good video game."

"I'll forgive it for the moment, but only because I need you to consider an unappealing proposal," Claudia said. They stopped for a minute for her to point out what she'd been pondering since they were forced to turn back from the mountain. "We're stuck between a hostile army on the north, a forest of certain death on the south, and a mountain on the east, which means we have to keep heading west in a no-other-options sort of way. You're going to run out of water if it doesn't rain again soon and we're going to need food. While I can eat the game around here..." Claudia shuddered inwardly and wondered exactly what it would take to convince herself to eat one of the abomination deer if they couldn't find something less mutated. Liam looked to her as though he'd nearly worked out where she was going with the seemingly unsolvable problem. "...there's only one source of meat around here that isn't irradiated," she said softly.

"You can't mean..."

"I heard the feudal lord of Tombstone ate Slark all the time and he seemed healthier than anyone."

"Then why are you talking about him in the past tense?"

"We sent him packing into the desert where I would imagine he ate several more Slark before dying of thirst." Veronica hadn't thought he'd really died and neither had Fiona, but that was all semantics as far as Claudia was concerned—she'd watched Zeke walk out into the desert as good as dead.

"I'll try to muster up the courage by the time we get back to the bodies we shot yesterday," Liam said.

"If it helps your resolve, the other option is to die," Claudia said.

"And don't think I won't be considering it seriously," Liam said, trying his best to keep a straight face, although a flicker of a smile worked its way in.

They walked on, finding the bodies of the Slark they'd shot the day before by mid afternoon. The sun had burned through the fog and cloud cover at some point in the late morning, and the Slark bodies were bloated and already beset by flies, several of which looked mutated. Claudia was starving, and she'd already seen a few rabbits on their trek that didn't look too deformed, but she didn't want to eat while Liam went hungry. For a brief, impetuous moment she even thought she might try eating Slark meat with him so he'd feel better about the whole thing. She'd only known him for a day and she was already concerned with his happiness and comfort—she cringed inwardly at what that could mean.

They soon came across where the wildfire started on its westward tear through the rolling grasslands. A few spires of weak smoke said the fire had mostly burned itself out, leaving the overwhelming scent of burned grass in the air. Trudging through the tall grass to that point was tiresome, but walking over the charcoal remains of the increasingly alien landscape was downright unpleasant, although the scorched, ashen remains of the field were far easier to walk over. They'd encountered very few lasher trees to that point, and judging from the blackened field stretching out as far as the eye could see Claudia suspected they weren't going to see anymore anytime soon.

"I don't mean to point out your future misery here, but this will about eliminate wild game from your diet," Liam said, kicking up a bit of ash.

"I guess we both get to find out what Slark tastes like." Claudia couldn't decide what was more repellant to her: eating the green Slark meat or eating one of the five legged deer with the Picasso heads.

"Is there a reason you're acting as though we might be out here awhile?" Liam asked.

"You can never tell with these things," Claudia said, although she could tell. The more she saw of the communications beams above her head, the more she doubted there would be a gap for them to slip through anytime soon.

She'd counted two dozen the first night, and though they weren't as easy to see during the day, she suspected that number had doubled. The western flank was lighter when it came to the beams, likely because of the fire that swept through, but this seemed to be only a momentary setback as new beams were cropping up in front of them every few hours.

"Then we best get to work shooting some fresh Slark," Liam said, "because I'm hungry and only planning on getting hungrier."

"Speaking of which…" Claudia whispered under her breath. She pointed, although she knew it wouldn't do Liam any good. "There's a beam coming online right over there." The beams always started by flickering in intervals with a light pink color and then turned to solid blue streaks when they were in use and likely hardened against interference. The beam in question was just over the next rise and it was still in the flickering pink state.

She grasped Liam by the arm and pulled him back from hiking up the hill right away. "We'll stick out, you especially, in this landscape," Claudia said. Most of her clothing was black or gray, and her hair was black, meaning she'd only need to conceal her face to cover her appearance in the burned up landscape, but Liam didn't have a scrap of black on him aside from the soot clinging to his boots. "Start rolling around on the ground."

Liam reluctantly did as he was told, humming a tune to himself as he did, only singing softly the chorus which mentioned something about a roll in the hay with a sweet maid. Claudia tried not to laugh out loud for fear of alerting the Slark to their position. She scooped up a handful of the ash from the ground and poured water from her canteen over it. The ash turned into black slurry in her palm and she quickly coated her face in the mixture. When Liam's clothes were dusted by the soot on the ground, he rolled onto his back and looked up at the sky.

"That was easily as weird as I suspected it would be," Liam said.

"It's about to get weirder." Claudia knelt beside him and began painting his face with the black mixture. He made a few faces of discomfort at the cold, scratchy stuff being rubbed across his skin, but didn't move away. His face and clothes were reasonably camouflaged and for the part of the plan he was playing, he simply needed to be slightly less easy to see while she was the one who truly needed to hide. She helped him to his feet and handed him his rifle that he'd set aside to start his rolling.

"If we are where I think we are, my tractor should be just around the base of this rise," Claudia said. "If you circle around to the south, you can use it as cover to draw their attention away from the beam." She plucked the two pineapple grenades from her belt and handed them to him. "Use these only if there's more than ten. Less than that, we can take out with gunfire without alerting too much support. We're far enough behind the main line that they likely don't have much security for this location."

"Where will you be?" Liam asked, clipping the grenades to his belt.

"I'll go right over the top of the rise, find a comfy place to lie down, and flank their position when they turn back toward you," Claudia said, pointing to the hill above them.

"How lucky am I that the officer who found me knows more than a few things about waging war in the wilds," Liam said with an appreciative nod. "Luckier still that she's a looker even covered in black smudges."

Claudia was glad the charcoal mixture on her face covered the blushing she was likely doing. "Focus," she snapped, trying to banish the warming effects of the flattery, especially since she'd just told him she planned on using him as bait, which he hadn't mentioned. "You don't need to kill them, so don't take any risks with your cover. Just draw their attention and their fire."

"I will endeavor to be enticing and unattainable at the same time," Liam said, adding a sloppy salute.

The impetuous, romantic side of Claudia snuck up on her, and flirty words exited her mouth before she could wrangle them, "reserve the unattainable part only for the Slark." Before he could reply, she pushed him toward the south. "Now go."

He jogged off with a spring in his step, although she attributed it to his natural affability and not necessarily that she'd said something mildly suggestive to him. She started her slow, deliberate walk up the hill, dropping to crawl on her stomach as she neared the top of the ridge. She moved leisurely, adding more and more soot to her own cover as she went. The top of the hill had a few natural undulations which she settled among. Below her, possibly four hundred yards away, she spotted the Slark position.

Half-a-dozen of the aliens were collected around a tripod device that stood three times as tall as on of them with a spike on the top, fitted with a strange, green lens that was the source of the flickering beam heading south. Claudia waited as long as she could before pulling her rifle up to use the scope. Any glinting of light off the metal weapon with the glass lens scope might give away her position prematurely. Out of the corner of her eye, she spotted Liam skulking up low and fast in a crouched stance. He was to the burned out remains of Tractor 23, across an impressive expanse of open terrain without being seen. For such a tall man, he was remarkably stealthy.

Claudia flipped open the cap on her scope and settled in to observe her enemy. The Slark were clearly a communications team as only two of the six were actively armed and none were paying much attention to their surroundings. This was true of most Slark she'd fought—adept at their tasks, but with poor discipline. Until the Gator, she'd actually started to think the Slark didn't even have soldiers and only succeeded in the earliest stages of the war because of their ridiculous technological advantage. Without the command structure of military minds, the Slark seemed no better than humans at keeping their soldiers in line, especially conscripts. She suspected she was likely looking at the Slark equivalent of six cell phone salesmen instructed to set up and guard a communications relay in a support position.

Liam seemed to be taking a long while lining up his first shot. Claudia began to wonder if he was waiting for a signal from her when he finally fired. She heard the shot and saw the round hit home. He was maybe a hundred and fifty yards from the targets, yet he made a solid first shot with an open-sight rifle. The Slark he'd hit in center mass, dropped onto its strange backward knees, and then pitched over sideways, obviously dead. The analogous organ to a heart on the Slark was actually lower and set slightly to the right—Liam's shot, intentionally aimed or not, had hit it dead on.

Claudia zeroed in on the remaining armed Slark, found its head as soon as its attention went from its fallen compatriot to search for the source of the rifle fire. He glanced up almost directly at her position before she put a round through his head. She looked for another target, but found the Slark dropping like flies. Liam had switched the setting on his rifle and was putting a spray of bullets onto their clustered position that was tearing through the unsuspecting Slark. One managed to take refuge behind the support leg of the mobile relay tower, and this one Claudia shot down, landing her bullet high on his chest. The entire conflict was over and done with in a matter of twenty seconds or so. The tower continued flickering with its pink, broken light.

Claudia slipped from her position, sidling down the hill to keep an eye toward the north, the direction she thought help would come from if help were to come for the dead Slark. Liam was at the tower when she finally crossed the open field at the bottom of the hill she'd perched upon. He was scavenging useful items from the dead, bits of plastic sheeting, a coil of wire, a bag or two of items neither of them could identify, but the bags themselves would likely prove useful.

Claudia set aside her rifle and rolled the largest of the Slark over to begin the work of butchering the carcass. The sound of her knife slipping from its sheath drew Liam's attention to what she was doing.

"I feel like the chivalrous thing to do would be to offer to do the cutting," Liam said.

"Do you know how to quarter a kill?" Claudia asked, deciding just the limbs would likely work for their purposes.

"I haven't the foggiest," Liam said.

"Then it's best to leave it to me," she said, adding a wink so he would know she wasn't meaning to be rude. "Do you know how to rig a grenade trap though?"

"More than one as it turns out." Liam apparently caught exactly what Claudia was thinking. He unclipped one of the grenades she'd given him and went straight to the access panel on the communication relay left open by the Slark. She didn't even need to watch him to believe he would do a competent job of it.

Quartering the Slark kill wasn't too significantly different from butchering a deer. Of course, quartering implied four limbs—she couldn't immediately think of the corresponding phrase for six limbs. She was most of the way through sextupling him when Liam finished rigging the booby trap on the communications relay. He offered one of his salvaged bags to her and several sheets of the plastic the Slark were using as clothes. They wrapped the Slark meat in the plastic and tucked it safely away in the odd backpack thing the Slark had used to carry some of their spare parts.

"Anything else we need to do here?" Liam asked.

"Nope," Claudia replied. "Now we continue west toward the ocean and find a way to set up a dew trap to collect water using some of the plastic you collected. Tonight, we dine on green meat!"

Chapter 22:
Help Comes in all Forms.

Olivia knew something was wrong long before they sailed beneath the ruins of the Golden Gate Bridge. The sounds of war were in the air and the Hercules, a classic tugboat formerly of the same docked nautical museum as the Balclutha, was out in the bay, armed to the teeth, and chasing Slark swift boats out of the space between the peninsula and Alcatraz.

The Hercules, which was a remarkable vessel in its own lifetime, found new service as something of a destroyer. The hull was retrofit with armor, gun mounts were fitted wherever they could, and the engines, once meant for heavy torque, were exchanged for salvaged Slark models meant for speed. The Slark seemed to be having trouble taking on the Hercules even with their twenty to one advantage.

The side-wheeler Eppleton Hall, another historic ship from the nautical museum, spared as the Slark hadn't thought they were worth destroying, steamed out to meet the Balclutha. The Eppleton was the primary tug of the bay now, fitted with some weapons, but not nearly as swift as the Hercules as the main means of propulsion were the two paddle wheels along the sides while the Hercules had a more efficient propeller setup. Olivia briefly considered ordering the signal flagger at the bow of the ship to tell the Eppleton to give them a push back out to the open sea, but the captain seemed fine with bringing her into the bay. If the Slark caught them on the ocean with their swift boats, the Balclutha wouldn't be able to out run or out fight them. The captain clearly thought the Hercules had the bay well in hand, or at least well enough in hand to bring in his cargo and let the sea wall's defense cover things from there.

The realization set Olivia's stomach to churn—the sea wall defenses, built by the Transcended on both sides of the peninsula and on Alcatraz, weren't firing. In fact, there looked to be a few battles raging on the shore as well. She ordered to arms and on deck for the remaining men of her squad.

They were armed and at attention when the Balclutha was tied off at the pier that once served as the nautical museum. Her men followed her down the gangway first, but made it no farther than the end of the dock.

"Hold this position," Olivia ordered. "The Balclutha must not be boarded by anyone but the port authority until I return."

She hadn't made it far before a small, yet surprisingly strong hand grasped her arm, stopping her dead in her tracks. She turned to find Esmeralda holding her back.

"She went outside the wall and didn't come back with the others," Esme said. "Nobody will tell me anything and nobody has gone to find her. You have to help."

They were in the same situation of not knowing where Claudia was, but only Olivia was in a position to do anything about it. Part of her felt sorry for Esme and the horrible sense of helplessness she must have felt. They might be rivals for Claudia's affections, but that didn't mean they had to be enemies.

"Come with me," Olivia said. "I'll see what I can find out."

The surface was in full battle mode as they strode toward the town. The street cars weren't running and the Transcended were nowhere to be found. Olivia led them toward the White Tower where she suspected she would find Dr. Gatling or Commander Marceau. Esme kept up with her easily, actually seemed at times eager for Olivia to move faster than her prosthetic leg would allow.

They crested the edge of Telegraph Hill to find the valley between them and the tower filled with the militia. They were still in a clump that indicated mustered, but not put into rank and file yet. She pushed her way around the edge of the gathered men readying themselves for orders to defend the city. Before she could reach the base of the tower where she suspected she would find the Commander and Dr. Gatling, she was cut off by Inspector Cavanaugh who was dressed in the uniform of a military officer under General Hastings' command. The uniform, which Commander Marceau hadn't supported the use of any longer, was a holdover from the days right after the cataclysm and the war they'd waged in the broken streets to deliver the city from the Slark occupiers. Olivia had once worn the same uniform before it was stripped from her after her leg was cut off by a lasher tree; she would have lost the uniform a month after anyway when Hastings officially banned women from combat.

"Get back to your ship, Warder Kingston," Inspector Cavanaugh barked.

"I don't take orders from constables dressed in outdated finery," Olivia said. "Unlike you, I hold a commission in the defense force, so why don't you tell me what is going on here before I have you thrown into the mix with the rank and file militia."

Cavanaugh didn't flinch in the slightest. In fact, a strange, angry grin pressed across his tight lips. "Fine, Warder," he said through clenched teeth. "The Slark are assaulting on two fronts and the mutants are attacking us on several more."

"Get out of my way," Olivia said, "I need to talk to the commander." Olivia pushed past Inspector Cavanaugh, leading Emse farther up the hill. Cavanaugh caught Esme's shoulder before she could follow.

"The Mouse stays here," Cavanaugh said. "We could use her to run messages and report back on troop numbers."

Without even thinking, Olivia slipped the steel ASP sentry baton from her belt, extended the telescoping club, and swatted Inspector Cavanaugh on the upper arm with a three-quarters force strike. He immediately recoiled and grabbed his arm.

"Count yourself lucky I don't have time for your shit," Olivia snarled. "A break in military protocol like that would normally dictate I give you a public beating." Olivia grabbed Esme by the hand and continued dragging her toward the White Tower. Before Claudia, before she'd heard of the Ravens, Olivia would never have brushed aside Cavanaugh so easily; having met real Ravens recently, everything Claudia told her was verified and she couldn't go back to being cowed by men, especially not ones she outranked.

Commander Marceau was in the midst of a hornet's nest of activity. Olivia had to wait her turn in something of a makeshift queue, refusing to let go of Esme's hand while they waited quietly for their turn to speak with the commander. She let go of Esme's hand and saluted Commander Marceau when her turn came. He responded in kind.

"The Balclutha is safely docked and under guard," Olivia reported. She faltered before continuing, knowing the rest of the news would not be so innocuous. "The Crescent City lumber camp is gone, wiped out in a mutant attack. No salvage operation was attempted as I left half my security detail in Winchester Bay fishing village and didn't think I could ensure the ship's security without them. Gold Beach was as hardened against attack as could be managed though."

"When it rains, it pours," Commander Marceau replied. "Good work regardless, Warder Kingston. We'll see about sending proper guards to the remaining camps when our current situation is stabilized."

"Permission to ask what the state of affairs is, sir?"

"We've got mutants in the BART tunnel and coming across the broken bridges," the Commander said wearily. "Only a fraction of them are making it across the bridges, but even they number in the thousands. I'm regretting not destroying the bridges entirely after Claudia managed to get across. We're trying to choke them off in the tunnel without sacrificing it, but we lost a mile in the first hour of the attack and have been steadily heading backward since." The commander signed off on a few orders offered by his support staff who immediately handed them off to runners. Olivia followed him as he made his way out of the cluster of questions to head down the hill toward the assembled militia. "This would be bad enough on its own if the Slark weren't attacking at the same time. They've got two or three divisions right outside the wall and they're doing their best to land another division around the Bay Bridge base while we're busy with the mutants."

"The mutants and Slark are coordinating?" Esme asked.

"I don't think it's as dire as that," the Commander said. "I think the Slark saw what the mutants were going to do and decided it was an opportunity to throw two armies at us at once."

Olivia knew exactly why the mutants were hitting the city and she knew exactly how much warning the Slark had in it to plan their coordinated attack. Rather than let the Ravens roll up their line, the Slark must have withdrawn and let them push against the mutant population. Once the mutants were on a stampede toward the sea, the Slark simply organized their reserve troops and followed them across the bay. There was no way the Ravens could know what they'd done, but they had seriously fucked the City of Broken Bridges.

"Why aren't the sea wall defenses active?" Olivia asked.

"The engineers, who can't normally make heads or tales of the Transcended's work, think it's the mutants. Apparently they act like little nuclear weapon EMP bursts when they get shot, destroying electronics and frying computers, which is probably why the Transcended headed underground," the Commander said. "If there's any good news in this, it's on the west. No mutants are coming up the ocean side, so the defenses there still work. Once the Hercules has cleared the bay, we can send our support fleets off the western shore to sit in a defensive flotilla under guard of the western sea wall."

"Esme said Claudia was still outside the wall," Olivia said.

"Two of the four men from her tractor returned this morning as part of a makeshift column," the commander said. "The driver said she was still alive when he last saw her. He said she went back into the fray to find more survivors."

"I request official permission to lead a rescue effort beyond the wall, sir," Olivia said, stiffening formally with the request.

"Would that I could, Kingston," Commander Marceau said, his voice cracking a little at the end. "With the mutants wreaking havoc on our sea wall defense weapons, I don't have the men or weapons to spare. We're spread thin and barely holding. Anyone I take off the line now leaves a crack in a very delicate defense."

"If I get you the soldiers, get the guns from somewhere else, can I lead the mission?"

"If you can find at least fifty able bodies not already in the militia and arm them with civilian weapons, I'll even get you the remaining tractors to take out," the Commander said. "Right now, I really have to get to work putting the militia to work plugging holes."

Olivia saluted as the commander walked away. When he was out of hearing range, she turned to Esme. "Can you get your hands on weapons stashed away in the Chinican District?"

For a moment, it looked as though Esme would play dumb, but the moment passed and she nodded. "I'll see what I can scrounge if it means getting Claudia back."

"Go, and meet me back here before sundown."

Olivia and Esme parted ways. Esme headed down into the first open tunnel leading into the city below while Olivia headed in the direction of the torch brigade staging area. Her plan was ludicrous on the surface, but brilliant in its pragmatism. They had a store of military trained, battle-hardened soldiers who were not on the field and wouldn't likely be sent to it anytime soon. If Olivia could convince them to join her and Esme could convince the Chinican trade guilds to arm them, they could be outside the wall within a day.

Working with Esme toward saving the same woman they were both chasing seemed strange. Olivia resolved to keep her head down and work the plan she'd concocted rather than think too much about it. She wouldn't want Claudia making up her mind based on a feeling of onus toward either of them anyway.

Near the base of the wall stood the staging depot, which apparently was once part of a warehouse district near the old mint. There Olivia found what she was looking for. The support staff for the torch brigade, all of them amputees like her, were waiting in a fretful holding pattern over. They spotted her and several of the uniformed men moved to speak with her.

"Her men, Alfie and the Greek made it back," the old master sergeant said as the de-facto spokesman for the group. "They were both on the edge of hysterics after seeing her run headlong into the fire, to draw the Slark away as they saw it.

Alfie spilled about her being the commander's daughter and suddenly everyone was mourning her as a martyr for a lowly cause."

"You're not a lowly cause and I don't think she's dead yet," Olivia said. "I know what she came through and the shape she showed up here in. If anyone can survive out there, it's Claudia Marceau." This seemed to breathe a little life into the gathered men of the torch brigade. "We have a chance to rescue her if you join with me to take on the Slark once again. We are stronger for what we've suffered." Olivia knocked on her metal leg for emphasis, which clanged a little under her fist. "They say we cannot serve in forward combat areas because we are not whole anymore. They say we can't run, swim, or fight, but they're wrong. If I can still take to the seas on a sailing ship, who among you can still fire a gun? Drive a tractor? Show the Slark we don't need a full compliment of limbs to make them die?"

The men of the torch brigade's support staff, some of them missing an arm and a leg, all knew the horror of the lasher trees just as Olivia did, and so many of them were looking for a new emotion to replace the deeply seated terror still within them after their dismemberments. She'd caught on something, a pride in honor, a rage at being overlooked by the enemy and their own command structure, and they let themselves be heard. Slowly, the sound of fists pounding on brass limbs echoed against the wall like a hale storm on a metal roof.

"Come with me now and help me show the commander he has two hundred men more in his army, soldiers of metal limbs, iron wills, and full hearts. Claudia Marceau is one of our own, and we will not leave her outside the wall," Olivia said, shouting to be heard above the din.

They took to the street en masse, still rattling fists against metal limbs as they marched in an orderly rank and file behind Olivia. They were incomplete soldiers reborn. Olivia knew the resurging pride they felt since she'd felt it on her last tour on the Balclutha. She'd spent so much time feeling worthless because of her lost leg. She'd fought with her fists within the bars for so long in hope of meting out some of the anger she felt at herself mostly and in turn receive punishment for the shame she felt at losing a limb. It was an odd, horrible emotional state to try to exist in and the person who had pulled her from it was beyond the wall. Claudia had shown such strength and resolve in reaching her father; it was inspiring enough to pull Olivia from her highly complex depression to watch Claudia's recovery from radiation sickness. She'd felt pride and a restored worth when she fought the mutants outside Crescent City, saved Roger, and then braved an aquatic insertion onto a beachhead. She wanted to share that renewed sense of purpose with the men behind her, her men now, because they'd earned it, paid for it by surviving what killed so many others.

By the time she got back up to the White Tower with her new battalion, Olivia saw that Esme had finished her part of the plan as well, although in a seemingly odd way. She'd expected workers to carry the weapons from the Chinican hidden caches, but what she saw were top hats intermingled as well. The top hat leader, if there was such a thing within the loosely organized dichotomy of top hats and bowlers, was a man named Bruce Coffey. He, like Esme, was a San Francisco native and a generally reasonable man as far as Olivia knew. Only arbitrary tribal lines drawn by heritage, wealth, and delineated by headwear separated them.

"So the sweetshop sweetheart wasn't lying," Bruce said, coming away from the two dozen or so other top hats who had followed Esme and her Chinican workers out of the wards below. He tipped his top hat to Olivia and smiled. "You've found some men, or most of them anyway, and you're going to take this hair-brained plan to the commander? Amputees and scavenged old slug throwers, is it, Olivia?"

"I'm happy to show you again what an amputee can do so long as she has two healthy fists," Olivia said. She'd bested Bruce four of their last five tussles, and she was eager to make it a solid five of six.

"Not where I was going with that line of questioning," Bruce said, holding up his hands in mock surrender. "I've got an eye toward the militia and you've got a mission you need to survive. I think we can help each other out."

"I'm listening," Olivia said, relaxing a little.

"I don't like Cavanaugh or his crew," Bruce said flatly. "They treat us like shit in our own city and they trample on our contributions to her liberation. Sure, Hastings provided the soldiers we didn't have, but those days are over and we've got plenty of men *and* women who became trained warriors during the fighting. The captain of the militia should know and respect this. The captain of the militia should be a handsome devil like me." He smiled and twirled the end of his impressive black, old school handlebar moustache that bisected his pale, narrow face.

"If we succeed, you think I'll have new pull with the command structure?" Olivia asked.

Bruce laughed and shook his head. "You mean to ask me, if you march a few hundred amputees into a war zone and return with the supreme commander's beloved daughter without risking the security of the city in the process, will you have some new pull with the command structure? Yeah, I think that's a safe bet."

"Okay, let's call that a given," Olivia said, feeling a little foolish, "but what can you give me in exchange for my support in ousting Cavanaugh?"

"You won't make it, not on foot, and not just with the weapons the Chinicans have to offer," Bruce said. "Let me help arm you, let my men fix up the tractors, let me give you a fighting chance."

"A truce of convenience then?"

Bruce took on a strange stillness that denoted remarkable seriousness. "I've always respected you, we all have. You've been a trustworthy, honorable, and ferocious enemy in the street fights that forged the two houses of top hats and bowlers, but it's time to hang up the brass knuckles and unite. The city needs us and we need each other."

"You've got yourself a proper alliance," Olivia said, taking Bruce's hand when it was offered.

Chapter 23:
Guerilla Warfare.

Claudia and Liam continued west for several more hours before she heard the distant pop of an explosion behind them. She glanced back over her shoulder to find the flickering pink beam she'd been keeping tabs on since they left the communication tower was gone entirely. She wondered how many they got with the grenade trap.

"I've been thinking," Liam said, snapping Claudia's attention forward again. "Even if we get back to the wall, I'm not sure how we would get onto the right side of it. We could hope to be spotted by a patrol on it I suppose, but most of the patrolling is automated or done remotely."

"We can try to hold on out here for awhile and see if a search party is sent out to look for survivors, but that might not happen until after the Slark are pushed back," Claudia said. Adding quietly after, "*if* the Slark are pushed back."

"They will be," Liam said. "This isn't the first time they've tried to breach the wall. I'd give it a few days before they figure out that thing is still impenetrable and nearly self-healing with the Transcended constantly patching it up."

"A few days of camping in a radioactive wilderness filled with lasher trees and Slark military units doesn't sound so bad."

"Nope, it's practically a vacation when you think about it."

Claudia and Liam smiled to each other.

They found the remains of a winding road out of the hills and began following it. Before long, the smell of salt water filled the air as they neared the ocean. They passed down a valley between two forests. Houses and farms apparently cleared the trees far back from the road a few hundred yards on either side. Bisecting the road, going from one forest to the other, they found crawler tracks having worn a trail going north and south. The trail looked hard packed, but some of the tracks were fairly fresh as the dirt was still wet where it was churned up by the clanking legs of the little centipede-like walkers the Slark used to move troops and supplies.

"I have a partially formed plan in my head," Claudia said. "I am wondering if you could help me finish it now that we've found what I hoped we might."

"Don't keep me in suspense, lieutenant," Liam said.

"You used human blood and remains to trick the lasher trees into eating the Slark," Claudia said. "What if we combined that idea with a trap of some kind to put the scent of prey on anything trying to use this supply line?"

"I like it," Liam said, "perhaps deer or some other game's blood though since I don't fancy donating my own to the cause."

"That's what I was thinking, but I still need help divining a delivery method."

Liam seemed to stare off into space for awhile as he thought. Claudia wondered if it was the sort of brainstorming she should offer her help with, but if she could have figured it out on her own, she probably would have an hour or two ago when the thought first occurred to her. A look of pure joy flashed across Liam's face; whatever idea he had was a good one.

"I've seen the butchers in the Chinican district when they're slaughtering something. They hang it by its hind legs and cut its throat," Liam said, leading Claudia down the Slark trail toward the forest on the southern side of the road. "There's blood, a lot obviously, but it goes in something of a stream. We have the wire we took from the Slark communication camp. Stay with me now. If we can find a tree on the edge of the forest that isn't too close to a lasher, something one of us could climb, we could dangle the deer above the trail, fix a trip wire across the path, and wrap the other end around the deer's jugular. When the wire pulls tight, it'll cut the vein, and start a deer blood car wash for their column to drive through."

"How on earth did you even think of such a thing?" Claudia asked.

"When we were fighting to rid the city of Slark after the cataclysm, those of us without military training were loosely organized into militia bands. We had to be pretty clever in our guerilla style fighting since we didn't get the good guns or gear," Liam said. "We did our best with what we had. It's how I learned to shoot an open-sight rifle and set traps."

"I heard about how rough it was on the civilians during the…wait."

Liam shrugged. "Yeah, I know who you are, and know you weren't here during those dark days. And if I wasn't sure before, I know now. It's pretty easy to spot the commander's daughter based on the stories alone even if you've never seen her."

"I was so concerned you would behave differently if you knew."

"You worried over nothing then," Liam said with his increasingly charming grin. "I only know how to behave the one way—badly."

Claudia suspected his smile was like candle wax: the more it was poured on, the more the charm built up. She hadn't really thought much about what kind of men she was interested in. In truth, she hadn't thought about what kind of women she liked until Esme showed her how much she didn't like timidity. Tall, brave on the edge of foolhardy, and dangerously clever were all traits Liam had and Claudia decided she liked them all. Personality wise, he was a strange mix of Danny and Veronica, which was a brilliant combination of caring and crazy in her estimation.

"Let's find a deer and a tree," Claudia said, slipping her rifle from her shoulder as she walked toward the tree line.

"Not so much as a 'thank you' for putting the finishing touches on your plan?" Liam asked.

Claudia glanced back over her shoulder to him and let her sly half-smile slip across her lips. It was as if he knew exactly how to set up her flirty comments and never missed on the timing within their little dance. "Your plan has not worked yet," she said, dropping her voice a tiny bit to add a hint of flintiness to it. "We will talk rewards if it succeeds."

Finding a deer to use as bait was the easiest part of the plan. The Slark didn't seem at all interested in hunting deer and even though the peninsula was bathed in the strange radioactivity and blighted with lasher trees, the deer population seemed to be doing far better than when humanity was the obstacle. Claudia shot a deer, one of the most mutated she could spot in the bizarre herd at the edge of the field north of the road, but getting the deer into the tree took quite a bit of doing.

They used the scope on Claudia's rifle to inspect the forest from a safe distance first. It didn't take long at all to spot the colossal gray spires within the trees on the southern edge. Most of the lashers were as tall as the old growth forest around them and unlike the saplings of the fields, these lasher trees left to grow unchecked were thick, looked incredibly hard, and were covered with foot long spines. Neither Claudia nor Liam had any interest in finding out exactly how far lasher trees of that size could reach, and so they turned their attention to the trailhead out of the woods to the north. Claudia really wished she'd thought to check that side first when they were already nearer to it while shooting the deer. The wasted exertion and time normally wouldn't have mattered, but she and Liam were both flagging under the lack of food, and Liam was beginning to show signs of dehydration.

The northern edge, which they vetted extensively, even throwing one of the chunks of Slark meat they were still carrying, covered in deer blood, into the forest to see if a lasher tree would snatch it up. When the limb sat unmolested in the middle of the trail, they entered the forest to find a tree that would serve as their trap's dangling point. This also proved difficult.

They ended up quite a ways into the forest, still carefully creeping and using the blood-coated Slark arm as their litmus test for unseen lasher trees, before they finally found a fir tree Claudia suspected she could climb that had a limb above the trail sturdy enough to hold the deer carcass. Liam offered to do the climbing, but Claudia managed to convince him to stay on the ground by pointing out the limb might not hold both him and the deer. She imagined it probably would, although he was looking so tired and thirsty she wanted to spare him the effort.

She climbed the trunk like something of a rock climber for the first dozen or so yards until the branches began. Once she was able to use actual limbs to climb, the process became a whole lot easier. Liam tossed the wire up to her, weighting the end with a rock. She wrapped her legs around the branch and inched her way out, dropping the wire on the other side of the branch. Liam replaced the rock with the deer's back leg, and hoisted the deer up into the tree. He'd removed his jacket at some point. As he pulled at the wire to haul the deer, his arms strained, sweat rose on his skin, and every muscle in his taut form became visible through his tight, tan shirt. Claudia was a little sad when the show ended and it became her job to secure the deer and transfer the wire to the jugular vein. She'd thought Liam was on the skinny side, but it was clear after seeing him with his shirt off that he was simply tall, packing his lanky frame with long, lean muscles.

He'd given her a strap from one of the satchels to use. He pointed out that they didn't really need the center band of cloth meant to go over a second tier shoulder on the Slark. She secured the deer's hind leg to the tree branch using the double bolen knot that Olivia had shown her. With the carcass in place, she unwound the wire used to hoist the deer, and wrapped it around her wrist.

"Don't freak out," Claudia shouted down to a confused Liam.

Before he could reply, she sat sideways on the branch and rolled backward off, dangling by her legs with the branch behind her knees. She hadn't told him this was her plan all along. She was far too tired and hungry to explain her gymnastics background or spend the time necessary to convince him it was the fastest, easiest option since they didn't have enough wire to tie off the snare with a separate length from the one used to hoist the deer. To his credit, he didn't freak out, although he did look concerned and conspicuously moved below her position as though he would somehow catch her if she fell. She wanted to bark at him to get back, that he would only serve to get them both injured, but she decided against it. He could be as chivalrous as he wanted because there was no way she was going to fall.

Digging around in a deer's neck while dangling upside down, twenty or thirty yards above the ground, seemed a lot easier in her head. It took her quite awhile to get the wire secured and her hands, which were sore from climbing the tree trunk earlier, were now also slick with blood before she'd finished. Her lower legs had gone numb and shot through with hot pins and needles when she pulled herself back up onto the branch, making getting down from the tree unpleasant, and slow work. By the time she'd climbed down, Liam had already finished setting up the trip-line snare and was mostly done with concealing it. She heard the clanking of crawler tracks and the rumble of engines the instant her feet hit the ground.

She grabbed up her rifle, handed Liam his, and they ran for the tree line. There wasn't any way they'd make it out of the woods in time to conceal themselves in the grass. They spotted the Slark supply convoy heading north across the road when they neared the edge of the woods. Claudia pulled Liam off to the side and found a clump of ferns and other underbrush thick enough and large enough to hide them both. The camouflage job was a quick one, but she suspected more than adequate.

Lying on her stomach, pressed closely to Liam's side beneath what she suspected was an Oregon-grape shrub and several large fern plants, her breathing quickened from the excitement, taking in the earthy scent of the forest floor and the man beside her.

The crawlers clanked along past them, belching diesel smoke. Three in all, the convoy appeared to be a sustenance supply drop. Claudia recognized a few of the strange casks the Slark packed their food in on the sides of the crawlers. She couldn't hear the wire's trip line above the sound of the clanking crawler legs, and she suspected the Slark couldn't either. Once the convoy was well enough past them, Claudia wriggled out of their hiding spot toward the edge of the trail, dragging Liam behind her.

They stood at the edge of the trail, watching the Slark convoy as it slowly lumbered up the hill. The deer was still dangling amid the branches, dripping blood in a fairly impressive stream. Nothing happened for so long that Claudia began to wonder if the trap failed. As if on cue to quell her doubts, the forest came alive around the three crawlers. Gray trunks bent toward the trail, dozens of hellish tentacles, all thicker than her arm, shot out of the woods, snatching Slark off the crawlers and then tearing off parts of the vehicles themselves. The carnage was unimaginable in its ferocity. Without even knowing she'd done it, Claudia took Liam's hand in hers to draw comfort from him at what they'd done. Yes, the Slark were the enemy, and no, they hadn't done anything outside the bounds of normal warfare when it came to brutality. Still, Claudia couldn't help but feel a little twinge of horror at how well their plan worked.

They began walking back down the trail, out of the forest, still hand in hand. Claudia flashed back on the first time she'd felt such agony over killing. She'd experienced the revulsion of dealing death after her first solo kill of a human being, and then again for her first Slark, but in both of those instances, she'd flashed back to the chipmunk. She'd made her first kill of a mammal when she was eleven. She'd fished with her father before that, squashed bugs as any kid did, and even hunted frogs for her grandfather when he wanted to show her how to cook frog legs, but the chipmunk was the first mammal, which seemed an important distinction to her.

She'd borrowed a book from the library, some boy's guide to wilderness survival and fun published in the fifties or maybe even earlier. She'd hated the idea that only boys got to have fun in the woods and so she proudly checked out the book to prove she could do anything a boy could. Most of what the book tried to teach her was beneath what her father had already shown her excepting when it came to snares and traps. She'd turned to this section first and found the wiliest game the book promised to catch—chipmunks and squirrels. She'd followed the directions exactly, located a likely tree by the droppings around the base, set bushy branches around the trunk, and looped tiny nooses within the tunnels created by the little limbs of the underbrush she'd created. It was less than an hour of waiting, an eternity for an excited eleven year old, before a chipmunk ran for the tree. It hadn't hesitated at the new branches resting against the tree he must have climbed a hundred times. He raced right through them, right into a noose, and kept on going until the snare, anchored to a heavy stone at the base of the tree caught and stopped him. The line went taut with the chipmunk six or so feet up the tree, wringing its neck with its own momentum. The little chipmunk had fallen back into the bushy limbs. Claudia's triumph at her snare working so brilliantly was short-lived. When she saw the lifeless little body among the branches, she remembered thinking its stomach was so white—too white for something that lived in the dirty forest. It was senseless death for the sake of death and she couldn't undo it. She cried rivers as she buried the little chipmunk by the creek, in a nice spot, because she felt bad for killing him. Her father had asked what was wrong when she came home, and she told him. She thought he would be angry with her, but he only nodded in a sad sort of way. "It's natural to feel curious about our power over life," he'd said. She'd never forgotten his exact words. "Feel bad now, but understand, for people to live, something must die." In retrospect, it was a surprising thing for a father to tell his eleven year old daughter, but this was all after Claudia's mother had died. Her father had hardened and so had Claudia in following the example set by her last living parent.

"I'm strangely bothered by this," Liam said, snapping Claudia back to the present.

"Me too."

"I'm not sure if it'd help or make things worse to eat Slark meat now."

She understood completely. If they could view the Slark as a food source, like chicken or fish, what they'd done would simply be wasteful, but if Slark were thinking enemies, and she couldn't see them as anything else after the Gator, eating them now would be something of a war crime on the heels of an atrocity. Still, her father's words called to her, and she used them to tamp down her regret.

"For people to live, something has to die," she said.

"Sure, but I doubt vegetarians feel remorse for their rampant cabbage genocide," Liam said, trying to inject some levity into the conversation.

Claudia found she didn't need to force her little laugh at his joke. She turned to look at him when they reached the road. They were flanked by the setting sun, which broke through the clouds at the last moment to light their path in a golden glow.

"You are a good reminder to me to not be so serious," she said, meaning it as a compliment for him and a reprimand for herself.

He took her in his arms and kissed her. It wasn't a surprise, nor was it unwelcome, but it felt sad that it came when it did. She grasped the back of his neck with one hand and his muscular shoulder with the other. He tilted his head down to hers, and she lifted hers to meet him. The passion of the moment, kissing on the lonely road lit by the setting sun, didn't fizzle with the direness of their situation as Claudia suspected. Rather, the kiss, which stretched on long past what either of them likely intended, built something of a fire in Claudia, bright enough to outshine the primary concerns of survival. When their lips finally parted, she was a little frightened about how easily desire for him distracted her from the task of keeping them both alive.

Chapter 24:
A Night Interrupted.

They walked on until the evening threatened with darkness. Their path was all downhill toward the ocean, ending in what looked to be old little league fields. The silence of the uninhabited peninsula base and the calmness of the night let them hear the distant crash of waves. They sought out shelter in one of the old dugouts as the sky darkened under gathering storm clouds as well as the coming night.

Claudia thought they were probably far enough away from any position of tactical importance and well away from any travel routes the Slark might use. A fire would be safe, and probably preferable, since the only thing less appetizing than Slark meat was raw Slark meat. They created a low fire, shielded slightly at the open mouth of the dugout, below the cement lip. The cave-like structure intended to hold a baseball team caught the warmth of the cheery little fire, and soon they were comfortable in a way they hadn't been since leaving the City of Broken Bridges days prior.

Unfortunately, the dugout roof, in addition to the heat, caught the vile smell of cooking Slark meat. Cooking the alien meat over the fire was simple as the limbs seemed tailor-made for spit roasting, but the smell, the unbearable stench of the meat, was something neither of them anticipated. Liam gave description to the stink in saying it smelled like someone dropped a burning hunk of plastic into a bag of wet dog hair. Claudia had no idea how he would know what that smelled like, although she agreed the odors were probably similar.

They ended up throwing the meat out into the dirt field, completely unconcerned that it would attract any predators. Liam postulated it might even keep animals away. The only benefit of the failed experiment in Slark meat was a momentary relief from their hunger. As the memory of the smell faded and the stench itself floated away on the ocean breeze, their hunger returned in full force.

They cuddled into the back corner of the dugout resting with Liam's back against the wall, and Claudia curled up along his side with her head against his chest. She could hear his heartbeat, slow and regular, as though he didn't have a care in the world. She could also hear his stomach complaining bitterly about the promise of food not being fulfilled.

The rain began to fall, knocking out their fire and dropping them into blackness. They fumbled to set up rain catchers for their canteens and returned to their huddled position in the dry corner.

The darkness and the pounding rain brought Claudia back to Utah and the mudslide that nearly killed her. She imagined if Liam could hear her heart, it would be pounding frightfully. They drifted off into sleep troubled by hunger with Claudia drawing comfort from Liam's protective arms around her and Liam pulling warmth from Claudia's irradiated heat.

†

Claudia's dream came in as vivid as reality, which was unusual for her. Most of her dreams had a fuzzy edge with bleeding colors and muffled sounds. This one rivaled reality for its clarity. She knew she was in Tombstone from the people, but the building was Bill's Gamblin' Hall from Las Vegas. She was dressed to perform in her black fishnets, shiny blue hot pants, matching go-go boots, and a frilly black bustier. Her hair was up in tight spiral curls in an ever shifting hairdo possible only in a dream.

She was singing her usual set of Katy Perry songs with a few Taylor Swift numbers interspersed. Her audience of Tombstone men and Raven attendants paid close attention to her every word, her every move, and her writhing, changing hair. In the audience, walking among the darkened faces gathered around the tables was Veronica, dressed entirely in white. Claudia felt unreasonably happy to see her. She held out her hand, offering to bring Veronica on stage with her.

Veronica took her time making her way to the front of the crowd. She accepted the offered hand, and Claudia helped her onto the small, round stage, lit in pale blue. Veronica was in her typical saloon girl attire of knee boots, cleavage creating corseted dress, and feather boa, but it was all white, where Claudia remembered the outfit having a lot of pink and green before.

"You abandoned me on the bridge," Claudia said, ending her set prematurely.

"You abandoned me in Tombstone," Veronica replied.

"I am here now."

"So am I."

Veronica walked behind Claudia, gently nudging her shoulders whenever Claudia tried to turn to follow her. Veronica seemed determined to keep Claudia facing her audience in the darkened hall, and Claudia relented. She waited while Veronica walked back and forth behind her. Finally, Veronica's fingertips grazed across Claudia's exposed shoulders, sending tingles shooting across her skin. Soon Veronica's lips and hot breath followed. Claudia could smell the strawberry lip gloss Veronica favored. She had no idea where or how Veronica kept finding it in a world that had long since lost any interest in manufacturing such frivolities. Her musings on Veronica's remarkable scavenging skills were interrupted by Veronica's hands making their way up the backs of Claudia's legs. Veronica's fingertips plucked across Claudia's fishnets until they finally came to rest on the swell of Claudia's ass.

"Sing for me," Veronica purred into Claudia's ear, accompanying the command with a firm squeeze of her behind.

Claudia opened her mouth to sing, but her throat suddenly felt too dry to manage the notes. She licked her lips and swallowed to no avail. Veronica, for her part, didn't seem deterred by Claudia's sudden performance anxiety. She pressed on, sliding her hands around Claudia's hips from back to front. Claudia could feel her stepping in closer, pressing her breasts against the backs of Claudia's shoulders. The firmly held cleavage, encased in lacy frills was thrilling and welcome after such a long absence.

Claudia tried to sing again, this time finding enough space in her parched throat to eek out a soft melody belonging to no particular song Claudia could think of. Veronica seemed pleased by the tiny success. She nibbled at Claudia's earlobe, sending shivers down Claudia's spine. Veronica's hands parted ways from their tandem work; one came up to cup Claudia's left breast while the other pressed down along Claudia's stomach until it slipped into the top of her hot pants.

Claudia sang, full throated, in French, the old Edith Piaf song *Non, Je Ne Regrette Rien.* It seemed like such a horribly inappropriate song to sing to Veronica of all people. Regretting nothing, the good or bad she'd done in the past, was all necessary, even abandoning her Raven sisters and her lover in Tombstone. It seemed like a lifetime ago, as though it happened to someone else.

Veronica's hands were heavenly, one massaging her breast with gentle, urgent caresses and the other teasing her lips through her fishnet leggings. Veronica's voice came to her ear, whispering the lyrics to the song Claudia was singing. Claudia was glad of the help as she imagined she would lose her place otherwise. She wanted more of Veronica, wanted desperately to turn and kiss her former lover, but Veronica held her fast to the performance.

"*Avec Mes Souvenirs J'ai Allume Le Feu, Mes chagrins, Mes Plaisirs, Je N'ai Plus Besoin D'eux,*" Claudia sang— Veronica's left hand slipped in the side of Claudia's bustier to caress her bare flesh. She was hot, only getting hotter, and dying for more when Veronica finally slipped a single digit between the netting guarding her pussy and inside her.

Claudia could feel how easily Veronica's finger slid between her lips, how much she'd really wanted to be touched in such a way for too long without relief. Esme, Olivia, and Liam were forgotten in the moment, only to appear before Claudia's very eyes. The trio was walking among the audience, just as Veronica had, curious eyes locked on her, all dressed in white. Claudia sang on, her voice picking up tiny gasps between the lyrics as Veronica's soaked finger made its way up to Claudia's clit, accompanied with a near electrical surge of pleasure. Claudia's body wanted to buckle around Veronica's hand, but she held her up, never relinquishing the hold she had on Claudia's breast.

The audience picked up on the beat of the music and the building pleasure of the public sex act. The faceless patrons of the saloon stomped in unison, missing several beats at a time before bringing in another thunderous stomp that threatened to shake the room. The lights above the stage flashed in odd intervals, illuminating Esme, Olivia, and Liam's faces when they did. The trio looked on passively at Claudia's building pleasure, watched without expression as Claudia writhed lewdly in Veronica's embrace.

Claudia knew it was a dream, knew it was a product of sexual frustration brought on by Liam and guilt left over from Veronica, she knew it wasn't real. She didn't care. It was an earth-shattering sexual experience to climax on stage at the hands of such an insistent and wanted lover in full view of the three sexual partners she would gladly invite into bed at a moment's notice.

She climaxed screaming, losing the song entirely in the act. Her voice vanished in the thunderous stomping of the audience. A crash and a white flicker of light over an inhuman face in the audience shot Claudia from sleep.

She couldn't remember where she was in awaking to the storm. Part of her thought she was still on stage and part of her thought she was back in the hellish canyon in Utah. She didn't recognize the field or the dugout in the darkness, didn't really recognize the world until a flash of lightning brought a strobe's worth of daylight to the stormy, black night. It was enough, just enough to catch another glimpse of the face from her dream. Across the field from them, at the edge of the derelict fence they'd hurled the cooked Slark limbs at, was a wicked, reptilian face, with eyes that reflected a red glow from the lightning.

Claudia leapt to her feet and out of Liam's arms, startling him awake as well. The storm raged down on them, pouring rain, roaring with thunder, and flashing with cracks of lightning. The next strobe of light confirmed what Claudia's mind might have confused in coming out of sleep. Worse still, the Slark on the other side of the field wasn't the most immediate concern. What she could only describe as mutant Rottweilers were racing toward the dugout.

"Skate, skate, skate!" Claudia shouted, repeating the alarm she'd heard Alfie use.

It seemed to work to galvanize Liam. He was on his feet, rifle in hand a moment after. She tore at the holster for her Walther beneath her coat, getting it out an instant before a heavy body slammed into her, knocking her to the cement floor.

The dog creature reeked of spoiled fish and death. The lightning flash illuminated its mangled maw coming toward her face and Claudia knew she was going to die. An instant before the creature's jaws could clamp over her face, Liam's rifle tore off several rounds into the beast. His next few shots sprayed upward as a second monstrosity struck him. Claudia struggled to extricate herself from beneath the dead mutant hound. She'd dropped her pistol and couldn't imagine she would be able to find it in the rainy darkness.

She drew her hunting knife and leapt to Liam's aid. He was fairing better against the creature than she had, keeping his feet beneath him even after it leapt on him, although the next flash of lightning showed he'd sacrificed his arm to its mouth to keep it from finding his throat. Claudia found the dangling beast with her left hand to be sure she wouldn't hit Liam in the darkness. She grabbed hold of it around the middle and stabbed hard several times, hoping to find a kidney or knick the liver. The dog yelped, released Liam's arm, and began thrashing against her. One of its front paws swung around, knocked her head to one side, and raked down her shoulder. Talons shredded her jacket and buried themselves in her flesh. She shrieked, stepped back, and tripped over the corpse of the first mutant dog. The wounded animal in her arms managed to squirm from her, limping away with her knife still buried in its flank.

She struggled to her knees, unsure if she would make it to her feet or if it was even a good idea to try. The lip of the dugout was protecting her from incoming fire like an army trench so long as she stayed low. Her plan, which was fear-based and shaky to begin with, backfired immediately when a powerful hand grasped her tangled, wet ponytail and yanked her off her feet by it. She screamed, grabbed at the hand to prevent it from tearing her hair out at the scalp, and kicked her legs to try to get them under her. She was pulled painfully out of the dugout and hurled into the field. She slid across the mud on her side, coming to rest several yards out.

A flash lit up the sky. A Gator, perhaps even larger than the one she'd killed in Carson City, was the unseen attacker who had thrown her aside so casually. Liam was climbing out of the dugout to give it a fight even with his tattered right arm at his side. He'd found her Walther somehow, but rather than use it in his own fight, he looked her straight in the eye on the next lightning flash and threw it to her.

It was a miracle of astounding proportions that the pistol even made it to her and even more amazing that she caught it despite the lights being turned out again before it reached her. The gun struck her in the chest, and she managed to get her arms beneath it to clutch it against her stomach. She heard heavy paws splashing through the muddy field toward her at a full charge on her right. She barely managed to roll away from the sound, taking a glancing blow from the attacking hound that knocked her backward, but didn't contain the same force or fangs as the first hit she'd taken. She waited for the lightning flash, hoped it would come before the unwieldy and heavy animal could get itself stopped and turned around to make another charge. She yanked the slide to chamber a round. The sky flashed in white, just enough to see by. Claudia found the snarling, drooling monstrosity. It had lumpy flesh with patchy fur and pulsing, vascular muscles below its sore-riddled skin. She fired off three quick shots, satisfied with the hits as the dog yelped and fell before the lights went out again.

She couldn't shoot into the fight between the Gator and Liam. In the darkness and rain, she would hit them both or nothing at all. As futile as it was to try, she lunged at the barely visible wrestling match that Liam appeared to be losing. One of the Slark's upper hands managed to swat her across the face with a remarkably hard backhand that sent stars flashing across her vision. Before she could recover from the staggering blow, he had her by the throat.

A flash of lightning illuminated the world just long enough to see Liam's knife come down on the Gator's hand around Claudia's throat, cleaving it off at the wrist. Claudia fell backward with the lopped-off hand still at her throat while Liam and the rest of the Slark tumbled into the dugout. An instant later, the night lit up with an explosion not from the sky as Liam's remaining grenade exploded inside the sunken, cement baseball team bunker.

Only the sounds of the storm remained after the lingering effects of the concussive explosion wore off. Claudia sobbed weakly as the rain fell on her. It took everything in her not to simply lay there until morning. She rolled onto her stomach and crawled tentatively toward the edge of the dugout where impenetrable darkness once again overtook the cement enclosure. She waited at the edge, listening hard for any signs of life. There was no groaning, no faint breathing, and nothing stirring.

"Liam," she called weakly into the darkness, waiting for a response, any kind of response, which never came. "Liam!" she cried again, this time loud enough to be heard not only by a wounded man in front of her, but anything else in the area that might be listening. Still, no response.

She pulled herself to her feet, wrapped her arms around her chest to hold in what little heat she could, and began walking. The destination wasn't important. She was fairly certain she was heading north, although she doubted direction mattered either. She was freezing, wounded, bleeding, unarmed, and now completely alone. More than that, with death so obviously chasing her down, she started to welcome its arrival.

Chapter 25:
Trudging Toward Glory or Something Like It

Bruce Coffey and his top hat mechanics worked straight through the 24 hours given to them to upgrade the torch brigade tractors into something useful for war. Olivia asked for thirty useable platforms—the top hats delivered sixty. Bruce pointed out not all were armed or armored for frontline combat, that some were fitting only for support, but he assured her at least forty were ready for full-scale war. Olivia looked over her new column of armored vehicles and could see what he meant. Many looked like World War I holdovers, back before tanks became gargantuan feats of technological triumph, and some were clearly just mobile, armored machinegun nests. They would still be slow, loud, and likely couldn't hold more than four people each including the driver. She thought the tanks fit her soldiers well—they weren't fleet-footed, but they likely had more fight in them than met the eye.

The families and friends of the support staff, the top hats who had worked on the tanks, the Chinicans who helped armed them, and a few gawkers came out to watch Olivia's column depart. Among them was Esme, holding tight to her own arms like they might fly away. Before Olivia mounted the lead vehicle, the largest by far with the main cannon on an armored pod on the front and two lobes on the sides for machinegun nests, she went to Esme. She hugged the diminutive donut shop girl who seemed to be shrinking by the moment. Olivia didn't need to ask to know that Esme loved Claudia. Whatever had gone on between them while Olivia was at sea clearly deeply affected Esme.

"I'll bring her home," Olivia said, making no further promise. She had no intention of relinquishing her tenuous claim on Claudia simply because she saw the depth of Esme's emotional bond to her. Olivia might not be as certain in her feelings for Claudia, but she wasn't about to give up now on someone so clearly remarkable.

She climbed the ladder up the side of the armor on her command vehicle and stepped inside among the men who were to be her crew. She'd held over Alfie as her driver and the Greek as her loader for the main gun. Among the two hundred soldiers under her command, only those two still had all their limbs.

They rolled out at a crawl beneath the gateway under the western edge of the wall, following the same path Claudia's torch brigade had taken, guided by Alfie in the lead tank down a path he knew all too well. Their progress was slow, about ten miles per hour at their cruising speed, which slowed further when they hit the ruins of South San Francisco. Torch brigade columns were usually around the same number, but they were lighter in armor and armaments, and spread readily from one another to cover a lot of ground. Olivia refused to let her column get too far from each other and the support they might provide with their numbers. The trails forged by the torch brigade through the ruins were soon choked with the tractors turned tanks as not all the drivers were as familiar with the terrain as Alfie.

They were still mostly in the ruins when noon hit. Olivia could only tell the hour by her watch as the sky was overcast and the air was thick with a mixture of fog and smoke of the battles raging to the east. They were making slow progress. Steady progress, but very slow.

A flare shot up to the southeast, sparkling green as it descended through the haze. The forward elements of her column had struck their first resistance—light resistance from the color of the flare. Olivia watched closely to see if a red or orange flare might follow. When none did, she directed the primary elements within the center of the column, her tank included, to wheel left to support while the rear guard and southwest forward vehicles hardened the right flank.

Olivia was eager to see what her men and new vehicles might do against the Slark.

The engagement they advanced upon was on the southern face of one of the many rolling hills that formerly held South

San Francisco's closely clustered suburban sprawl. Her forward elements, ten vehicles in all, were advancing in good order. Machinegun fire and the occasional hollow pop of mobile artillery explosions brought the ferocity of the battle to her ears before she could even spot the tanks among the ruined husks of houses and apartment buildings.

"Tank Commander Biggs says they're pushing back a light scouting patrol," Alfie shouted above the sound of the engine, relaying the information coming into the shortwave radio earpiece in his leather pilot's helmet. "He says the Slark thought to take a torch brigade by surprise and ended up getting taken by surprise themselves when they hit a dozen gun platforms."

Olivia could hear the joy in Alfie's voice, and by proxy, the joy that was likely in Tank Commander Biggs' voice. Giving back a little pain felt good after being torn out of the combat rotation and giving the pain back specifically to the invaders, rather than mutants, was downright euphoric.

"Move us onto their southern flank to support their push," Olivia directed Alfie. The flagger on the back of her tank, visible to the spotters on the other vehicles directed out the maneuver. It was remarkable how easily the nautical communication flags worked for directing tanks. Sure, they were close enough to one another to shout the orders over, but with the deafening sounds of the vehicles, visual cues were easier. They were a land flotilla of tiny battleships sailing across rough seas as Olivia saw it, and while she had no experience in tank battles, she knew quite a lot about the sailing of it all.

As they rounded the southern flank of Biggs' position, Olivia got her first view of the conflict. The Slark recon platoon was getting solidly routed by the numerically inferior tank squadron. The handful of centipede crawlers the Slark brought to the fight were smoking wreckage or limping slowly away by the time Olivia's tank got into position to support. The four hundred or so Slark foot soldiers were in full retreat, losing dozens more as the machinegun gunners found easy targets on their backs.

"Tank Commander Biggs wants to press the attack, chase them down as it were," Alfie shouted. "Your orders?"

"Denied," Olivia said. "Our mission of search and rescue takes priority." It was true and something Biggs would respect, but not the only reason she denied him. They were slow, too slow to chase anything down, and a dozen tanks repelling a lightly armored surprise attack by a scout recon team was one thing—giving chase to a retreating platoon only to end up making a charge on an entrenched division was something else entirely.

They turned back to the south, fanned out to their skirmisher line in hopes of widening the search, and continued on. She could see for herself what the likely toll was on the Slark and imagined the estimates given by Biggs and his men would only be inflated. They'd taken down three crawlers and maybe a couple dozen Slark in the process without losing a man. Those were numbers Olivia could live with. Losing someone, anyone of the two hundred under her command seemed unthinkable. They were throwaway troops to anyone else in the City of Broken Bridges, but to her, they were as precious as surviving pre-war technology.

She knew she couldn't hold the leash so tightly forever. Soldiers died in war. It was a truth every officer who led troops had to accept. She hadn't truly been in charge of the men under her until the Balclutha's security detail, and to her knowledge, she'd never truly ordered someone into a fight that would mean their death. During the liberation battles for the city, she'd always been part of a command structure, relaying orders from above, leaving the onus on those with more uniform decoration than her. Now, as on the Balclutha, she was on her own, and she was determined not to make the same mistakes she'd made then.

Once they found Claudia and any other survivors they could pick up, then she would let her men fight an offensive war in earnest. She needed an unquestionable success first—a completed mission that resulted in more than just nobody dying or the rescue of a single wounded dog. She needed this for her own morale.

†

Claudia was surprised when she saw another sunrise. She'd expected more of the mutant dogs to chase her down, more Slark to come after her, or exposure to the elements and her compiling wounds to finally finish her off. The rain had stopped before the sky grew gray with the light of the coming day. It was still cloudy, hazy, and cold, but the rain was done for the moment. It hardly mattered though as she was still wet from the soaked, tattered clothes she wore that she was in no position to repair or replace.

All she knew was walking. One weakly placed foot in front of the other. Her eyes never left the ten feet or so of pavement in front of her. She only knew the sun was behind her, which would keep her heading vaguely north. The fever and delirium that caught up to her in the morning wasn't surprising, although the hallucinations accompanying it seemed far more vivid and horrible than simple disorientation from hypothermia, loss of blood, infection, and whatever else was wrong with her at the moment.

Her vision narrowed to a tiny tunnel with only what was directly ahead remaining clear. Gray haze encroached around the edges, preventing her from seeing anything out of her peripheral vision. She knew Veronica was on her right though and Liam was on her left. They were walking with her, but didn't seem to want to talk to one another. In Claudia's befuddled mind, this made sense—they didn't know each other well enough to have much to say.

"I might not be much to look at anymore, but you still could have waited until morning to see if I was truly dead," Liam said to her. "You might have even learned something about the Slark that killed me or the dogs he had with him if you'd just waited to see."

"I couldn't, not again," Claudia said.

"He doesn't know about trump cards," Veronica told her. "How could he?"

"They had something similar," Claudia said. "Mouse's friends did suicide bombings." Claudia couldn't remember what Mouse's real name was. She could sort of picture her face, knew it had something to do with donuts, but the name refused to come to her.

"That is nothing like what we did," Veronica snapped. "The trump card is a final valiant rejection of oppression. Ordering children to kill themselves in hopes of taking a few Slark with them is cowardice at its worst."

"The end result is the same," Claudia said.

"What couldn't you see again?" Liam asked, filling in the portion of the statement she'd left out. She felt a little triumphant in using his question as proof to show herself he was just a hallucination. Despite knowing the real Liam was dead, it seemed important to further prove the Liam beside her wasn't real by pointing out he couldn't know what she was thinking unless he was a figment of her imagination.

"In Tombstone, the night I left, I saw a girl, a little bird who had taken that last, valiant stand," Claudia said. "She was blood and pulp, impossible to separate from the men she'd killed. We could not have truly buried her alone. I did not know her, but I did not need to. She was me."

"I'm not you and the Gator wasn't a man meaning to take us captive," Liam said.

Claudia wanted to point out that the Liam hallucination was indeed a part of her, but she couldn't even completely form the thought let alone articulate it. The concept was well beyond the current state of her conscious mind.

"I couldn't see you like that either," Claudia said instead of giving the other explanation an awkward try. "I need to keep you in my mind as you were, not a mangled mess of flesh mingled with a dead Slark."

"Plus, she always walks away," Veronica said. "Sometimes it is reluctantly, but make no mistake, she always walks away."

"We aren't the father she doesn't even know anymore who doesn't even know who she is now," Liam said. "She's walked toward him, keeping everyone else at arm's length, for years now."

"I had daddy issues once," Veronica said, "but then I turned thirteen and got the fuck over it."

"Then you will both be pleased I am likely to die soon and take my pathetic, distancing daddy issues with me when I do," Claudia said sourly.

"What a maudlin little thing you are," Veronica said. "Of the many differences between you and Gieo, I would say that is probably the most pronounced."

"Gieo, the pilot who took Fiona from her, the one she doesn't even like saying the name of?" Liam asked.

"One in the same," Veronica replied. "Although to say she took Fiona is inaccurate since Claudia never so much as told Fiona she might be interested. You see, our dark little dove here calls everything night. Gieo took failure after failure and spun them into positive successes. While Claudia, melancholy Claudia, managed remarkable survivals, great victories, and always treated them like crushing defeats."

Great, Claudia thought, her brain was so broken even her hallucinations were starting to talk strangely. "I think I'm going numb," Claudia said weakly. She wasn't cold anymore, her shoulder didn't hurt, and the tunnel of her vision was down to a tiny, dirty window looking out on the rubble-strewn street her feet were stepping toward.

"You might have been the best thing for her," Veronica said. "I was too much like her, too soured on the world to do her gloomy outlook any good."

"I died though," Liam said, "and my laughter with me."

This brought fresh tears to Claudia's eyes. She couldn't sense much now, but she could feel her weak sobbing ripple through her fragile frame and feel the tears welling in her eyes to roll down her tingling cheeks.

Madness, a common malady in the post Slark-invasion world, started to sound like a likelier and likelier outcome for Claudia. Veronica was right about her. She was once physically strong enough to pull herself through so much. After Yuba City and the radiation that scorched her lungs, this wasn't true anymore. Her body always pulled her through the struggles her mind was ready to give up on as though the machine was too tenacious to let the ghost's depression drag it down.

Her father had this same strength of body, but he combined it with strength of mind she simply didn't possess. When he suffered a loss, he rallied to fortify twice as hard around what he had left. Again and again he had done this.

"My father should have had a son," Claudia murmured. "I was ruined when my mother died."

"In a world of orphans, the girl who still has her father is wishing she'd never been born," Veronica said with a laugh. "I tried like hell to fuck a little happiness into her, but it never stuck."

"Maybe that was the problem," Liam said. "Maybe that's why she's been so reluctant to take on new lovers and so reticent to enjoy the one she's actually had since you. If she equates sex with your desire to bring a little light to her dismal outlook, best to avoid good sex entirely."

"It'd explain why she's run from love her entire life or picked seemingly unlovable or unattainable people to fixate on," Veronica said.

"Finally got her dad back and she can't even be happy about that," Liam said.

"It makes me wonder why she's even still walking," Veronica said. "It must be twelve hours or more of her trudging along without a goal in mind."

"Have to keep walking," Claudia said, completely devoid of an answer for any of what they were saying. Their voices were beginning to warble anyway. They'd started sounding like warped records played by a dirty needle on a slowly dying turntable. If they left her, she would walk on as it was the only thing left to do. If the grimy little window of her vision closed off entirely, she would stumble on. She might believe her every step was entirely futile, but she had too much Marceau blood in her to stop taking them.

Liam and Veronica were trying to shout to her to be heard, calling her name again and again as the only thing that made it through the sudden terrible raucous. Clanking, rumbling, shouting, and machinegun fire was drowning them out, but they never stopped yelling her name.

Her exhausted foot finally caught on something she couldn't see and she stumbled. She managed to stay upright for a moment, but her other foot went into a hole she'd also missed, and she pitched forward without even the strength to throw up her hands to deflect the ground rushing up to meet her. The impact with the hard pavement never came though as strong arms caught her and suddenly Claudia was lifted, turned over, and looking up into the sun breaking through the clouds, putting a halo of cold autumn light around a woman's head.

"*Savez-vous ma mère?*" Claudia asked the ethereal woman dragging her deeper into the din.

Chapter 26:
Cats Should be so Lucky.

Olivia went in for her daily visit to Claudia's room and monthly check up for her mechanical leg. Dr. Gatling took her to the mixture of a mechanic's shop and a doctor's office first, promising she could see the miraculous Miss Marceau when he made sure she hadn't done anything egregious to her leg.

Up on the table, with the inner workings of her leg laid bare to the doctor's pokes and prods, Olivia relaxed at the normalcy of the whole situation. Somehow it felt routine to have Claudia in a hospital bed and Dr. Gatling grumpy about damage done to prosthetics.

"How is our repeat customer?" Olivia asked.

"Physically, she's going to be fine," Dr. Gatling said, still tinkering with Olivia's worn knee joint. He could take the limbs off his patients, work on them in an entirely different room from the person the limb belonged to, and would likely get his work done much faster if he did, but Dr. Gatling insisted all the wearers of his prosthetic marvels be attached to their limbs while he worked on them. He said it made him feel more like a doctor and less like an appliance repairman; Olivia suspected it also helped the patients feel like whole people rather than freaks. "Cats don't have the lives Miss Marceau does. The combined weight of what happened to her was pretty significant, but it was all very fixable stuff. She probably had a concussion, a road map of bruises, exposure, mild hypothermia, three deep scratches, a blood infection from said deep scratches, dehydration, malnutrition, and signs of extreme exhaustion."

"That's the insane list I saw on her chart," Olivia said.

"Then you know she'll be fine," Dr. Gatling snapped. "Her infection responded to IV antibiotics, she's stitched up, hydrating nicely, and resting comfortably. Give her another week or two of bed rest and she'll be back to denying death in wholly unbelievable ways."

"You said *physically* she would be fine…"

Dr. Gatling adjusted the straps of his harness into his chair, which he always did when he was nervous about broaching a topic with Olivia. There was still his oath to keep private his patient's more intimate issues, although he considered Olivia something of a colleague even though she barely held the medical training of a candy striper.

"She's depressed, clinically, would be my guess," Dr. Gatling said. "It's the real reason she's so lethargic."

"I'll talk to her, see what I can find out," Olivia said. She'd suspected as much as well, but wanted a more professional opinion to confirm her diagnosis.

"Is it true? Did she stroll right into the middle of a war zone?" Dr. Gatling asked.

"Like she was on a constitutional in the park," Olivia said. "I've never seen anything like it. Slark shock troops meant to reinforce their western flank came across us in the ruins of Half Moon Bay. We were in the fight of our lives, surrounded on two sides with the ocean at our backs. Claudia came walking out of the south, right into the middle of the fight, and didn't seem to see any of it."

"Lucky you managed to get to her before they did," Dr. Gatling said with a low whistle of surprise.

"I had to race the Greek for the pleasure," Olivia said with a laugh. "He's quick for such a stocky little man. Once I had her back on the tank though, it took begging, ordering, and finally threatening to get the other commanders to withdraw. Not that I can blame them—the enemy was there and the ground was as good as any to make a fight of it."

"I would have expected more discipline from my military patients."

"It was a momentary and forgivable lapse," Olivia said. "Once they realized the war wasn't going anywhere, they withdrew in an orderly fashion. The Slark gave up the chase when they realized their numerical advantage was going to vanish quickly in the narrows along Highway 1."

"Good to hear," Dr. Gatling said. "On a similarly hard-headed topic, would you mind terribly getting that Chinican girl to go home and at least bathe? She's not eaten in days excepting the food I forced on her, and I can't imagine her constant fretting over Miss Marceau is doing anyone any favors."

"Yes, I'll see what I can do," Olivia said. "How is the leg, doc? Will I ever dance again?"

"Could you dance in the first place?" Dr. Gatling snapped the pieces of Olivia's leg back together and closed the plating. "It's in better shape than most of your Clockwork Warriors, but that's hardly a ringing endorsement of your maintenance. Tell your men, they may not feel the bullet wounds in their mechanical arms and legs, but that doesn't mean the bullets aren't doing damage."

The name for the amputee army under her command, Clockwork Warriors, wasn't provided by Dr. Gatling, but good old Bruce Coffey. Olivia knew it to be one of genuine admiration. Bruce said he intended to reference the British book and movie, *A Clockwork Orange*, since the men under Olivia's command were mostly British and fancied a bit of the ultra-violence, but Olivia didn't believe him. They were all at least partly mechanical and after the respect earned for their successful rescue mission of the commander's daughter that didn't seem like such a bad thing anymore.

She put her pants back on, checked her recently oiled and calibrated leg with a few bends, and headed over Claudia's room. Esme was still in the chair beside Claudia's bed, reading some old book likely given to her by Dr. Gatling. Olivia gave her a questioning look and tilt of her head.

"When was the last time you were home to sleep, bathe, or have a change of clothes?" Olivia asked.

"What day is today?" Esme replied, never looking up from her book.

"Wrong answer." Olivia snatched Esme's coat off the hook beside the door and walked it over to her. When Esme still didn't acknowledge her, Olivia took the book from her and replaced it with the coat. "Regardless of what you might think, I'm doing you a favor. Nobody likes a disheveled, smelly woman sitting constant vigil over them."

Esme took the coat and none too subtle hint. Before she exited, she gave Claudia's hair a gentle caress and whispered she would return soon. Olivia waited until Esme was well out of the room with the door closed behind before she said anything.

"You can stop pretending to sleep," Olivia said.

"Maybe I'm pretending to sleep around you too," Claudia said without opening her eyes.

"That's a hell of a thing to say to your rescuer."

"Who said I wanted to be rescued?"

Olivia sighed and sat on the edge of the bed right in front of Claudia. "Open your eyes, stop being a pain in the ass, and talk to me," Olivia said. "I've got a few questions for you and some news from the Ravens."

This brought Claudia out of her faked coma. "How?"

"There was a squad of Voron Daggers in Crescent City when we sailed back through."

"What were they doing up there," Claudia asked incredulously.

"Investigating, I would imagine," Olivia replied. "The camp had been wiped out by a massive mutant invasion—an odd enough occurrence to warrant their curiosity."

"Did they say who they were?"

"Just the officer, Captain Dylan Watson, and I believe one of the others had the last name of Garcia."

"I know them," Claudia replied flatly.

"Yes, they seemed to know you too, and they were under the impression you were dead."

"It would have been better if they'd gone on thinking that," Claudia said.

"They also had some rather unfortunate news from Tombstone…"

"Wiped out to the last woman?"

"It didn't sound like it, but they did specifically mention Veronica…"

Claudia began tearing up again, she couldn't help it and didn't feel the need to hide it in front of Olivia. She knew, on some level, she knew all along, but hope is sometimes a surprisingly difficult creature to kill. She'd cried over Danny and she'd certainly cried over Liam, but there was a strange heartbreak to her tears over Veronica. There was just something about the Raven Queen that spoke of an unduly difficult life, and Claudia, like so many other women who cared for her, wanted to give her some of the happiness so clearly denied to her for so long.

"Loving me is a dangerous occupation," Claudia said.

"What do you mean? How could you have had something to do with her death if you didn't even know she was dead?"

"True, I guess, and you could probably say the same of Danny. Perhaps it would be truer to say trying to love me is a waste of a life destined to be cut short, which should stand as a warning to you and Esme, and should have stood as one for..."

"For...whom?"

"Nothing, nobody, I'm tired."

"Yes, I'm sure you're simply knackered from sleeping for nearly four days, but I'm afraid we're not done here yet."

"I do not want to talk about it."

"That's fine since I'm not even sure what *it* is," Olivia said. "We will talk about us though, and if we must, we will talk about Esme. Do you realize what she and I both underwent to bring you back?"

"I'm sure my father played no small part in all of it."

"Your father has a city of more than a hundred thousand people to protect," Olivia snapped. "He did what he could, but he is not just your father anymore. He is everyone's father now."

The implications stung. Claudia didn't want to think of her father choosing between sacrificing his daughter or saving more than a hundred thousand lives. He'd clearly made such a choice though and he'd chosen the city. A small, insidious part of her felt betrayed.

"I made it clear to you both that nothing was exclusive," Claudia said, choking back a fresh round of tears already stinging at the corners of her eyes.

"Your honesty was greatly appreciated, but it didn't stop you from doing your best to romance and seduce us, nor did it keep us from believing you might one day care for us," Olivia said. "I saw through you, held my heart back to see if you might stop with the games and take me seriously as a person one day, but Esme made no such preparations. She is in love with you because she ignored your words and believed your actions. You don't have to love and cherish either of us, but for fuck's sake, stop playing with our hearts."

"You'll both live a lot longer if you forget about me." Claudia pulled her blankets up tight around her shoulder and rolled over to turn her back on Olivia.

Olivia left in a huff. Claudia could hear Dr. Gatling ask after her when Olivia was in the hallway. Before the door swung closed, she heard Olivia say, "Physically still fine, but I've managed to make everything else much worse."

†

Claudia hadn't lied about being tired. She'd slept out of pure exhaustion and only after reassuring herself she wasn't alone and it wasn't dark out. Even still, when sleeping in Esme's presence during the day, nightmares plagued her slumber. With Esme gone and night coming on, Claudia was determined to stay awake, especially since the tower darkened at night to prevent easy targeting by Slark artillery.

Before the lights went off for the night in the building her father came to her room with a companion. Her father looked as tired as she felt although in reasonably good spirits otherwise, which was apparently the work of the dog following closely at his heels. The lanky German shepherd appeared to have something of a limp on the mend, but otherwise looked happy in his surroundings so long as Commander Marceau was nearby.

"Who is your friend?" Claudia asked, forcing levity to her voice at an extreme personal cost. She'd never had strong feelings one way or the other about dogs until the night when the mutant hounds attacked her and Liam. Now they frightened her and harkened back to one of the darkest nights of her life.

"This is Roger," her father said. Roger wagged his tail as if to confirm. "I think Olivia intended him as a gift for you, but he's been spending time with me while you were recovering from your most recent adventure."

"You should keep him," Claudia said. "He looks like a good soldier at your side." She wanted to say she thought her father was who Olivia probably really wanted to give the dog to, but she assumed that would simply confuse him and wouldn't make her feel any better.

"I believe you are right," her father said. He snapped his fingers in front of Roger's face. The dog sat at attention and stayed stock still while the Commander crossed the room to Claudia's bed. "I am tortured by the choice I made to stay with the city rather than come for you."

Claudia took her father's shaking hand and smiled to him. "You would not be the father I know if you sacrificed lives to save mine. I could have left with my men...I should have left with my men."

"The time you bought them..." Her father sat on the edge of her bed, wrapping his other hand around hers as well.

"...I could have bought for them while remaining with them," Claudia finished for him. "As I find out now, the Hungarian brothers died anyway when one would not leave the other's body after he bled out, and there is..." Tears again came to Claudia's eyes and she couldn't even look at her father anymore.

"What happened out there?" he asked softly.

"What does 'skate' mean?" Claudia asked.

"Shorthand for message runners during the liberation of the city. We'd long since run out of paper to write things down on, so the runners had to memorize their messages. Slark truncated to SK and attack down to AT—they used the mnemonic device of making little sentences like 'skate down Market' to remember the information. Skate stuck around after as a way for veterans of that fight to call out a Slark attack. Why do you ask?"

"He said they were resourceful like that."

The lights for the entire building went off. Claudia jumped when the room descended into darkness. Her father gently caressed her hair and reassured her that she was safe with him there. Slowly her eyes adjusted to the faint glow of LED displays on the hospital equipment around the room, although she wasn't hooked to anything but an IV anymore. Roger let out one bark, which caused Claudia to jump again. Commander Marceau snapped his fingers once, silencing any further reports from the dog.

In the relative darkness, feeling the safety and protection of her father surrounding her, Claudia closed her eyes and spoke. "There was a man in the wilds, the shooter from Tractor 17," she began. "He sacrificed himself to save me."

She couldn't see his look, but she could feel it. He didn't believe her, not entirely anyway. She should have known he was too shrewd to take her blank comment as the deeper truth of what was bothering her.

"If you say that was all, I will believe you," he said.

It was a good father answer, and enough to make her think she shouldn't keep things from him of all people. "I cared for him," she said. "In such a short time, it is difficult to say how much. I felt warm and safe with him. It was overwhelming."

"I see. And now you are lost in what to do next?"

"Yes."

"Had he survived, had he made it back with you, what would you have done then? What would you have told Kingston and your donut shop girl?"

It was a question she hadn't dared ask herself now that the possibility was ripped from her and if anyone but her father had asked her at any other time, she likely would have lied. In the dark, holding his hand for strength and stability, she felt she could tell the truth.

"I would have told them I wanted to be his, if he would have me," Claudia said.

"That is a truth, and an important one, but it is not the truth you must tell people," her father said. "You keep that truth for yourself to know what was taken from you. If you lie to yourself in this, pretend as though it might have been anything lesser than it was, you dishonor his memory and your feelings. It will hurt to know what you lost, but you will not lose capacity to feel. Do you understand?"

"Yes," Claudia said and she truly did. So much of what her father was made sense in light of this advice. "You know you would have spent the rest of your life with mother had she lived—when she died, you didn't simply lose her; you lost the lifetime with her you could have had."

"You do understand." Her father gave her hand a reassuring squeeze. They sat in silence for awhile under the weight of the discovery. "Your feelings for this man might never have blossomed, or they might have, but it is important to know you wanted them to."

"But knowing what we lost, how do we move on, Papa?"

"This is the second question to lead you to another, more important truth," her father said. "You did not think I would leave you with a deep emotional cut, clean but still open, did you?"

"Of course not, Papa," she said with a tearful little laugh.

"Knowing what you lost, and knowing it is lost forever, what will you say now that you know you cannot have what you wanted?"

"That I must stop being childish, I must stop seeking attention for the sake of attention, that Esme is too timid to stir my passions and that Olivia is too withdrawn to truly know as I would wish to know her." She'd had plenty of time to think about the answer to a question she didn't believe anyone would ever ask her over the past four days. The words weren't kind to anyone, herself included, but she felt better simply saying them.

Roger leapt to his feet at a sound in the hall too soft to alert either Claudia or her father. He let loose with a barrage of snarls and barks. Claudia's father snapped around to the door and flicked on his flashlight. For a brief second, Esme's face was illuminated in the crack of the doorway before the door slammed shut.

A sinking realization came over Claudia—Roger's first tentative bark, the one silenced by her father's snapping fingers, had signaled Esme's arrival. The Mouse couldn't be silent enough to sneak up on such an alert dog, but clearly she was more than capable of eavesdropping on Claudia and her father long enough to hear several emotionally damaging things.

"Would you like me to go get her?" her father asked.

"So I might say…what? Beyond what I have already said?"

"In truth, I do not know," her father said. "I have only ever loved two women: my wife and my daughter."

"And they both loved you in return…" Claudia murmured. "I know unrequited love. I know what it is to adore someone you cannot truly have. I simply don't know what to say as she never said anything to me."

"Patience then, rest and think," her father said. "In this, as with many things, haste can lead to errors."

It was the same lesson the Owl apparently failed to teach her in Carson City. She was still making the same impetuous mistakes she'd always made and now it had cost her Liam. She needed to learn patience before her recklessness took anything else.

Chapter 27:
Lights Going Out in a Dim World.

Olivia went to her bar for solace after her disastrous conversation with Claudia. The floor was reasonably clear and nobody seemed interested in dust ups anymore. Many were still out on militia work and anyone present was likely on break from hard fighting. Bowlers, top hats, and bare heads tilted toward Olivia when she walked in. The truce between her and Bruce had filtered down to the respective sides and they were all suddenly friends.

Bruce Coffey wasn't the captain of the couple thousand militia members yet, but the writing was on the wall. Cavanaugh's brutal tactics, which matched Hastings' almost perfectly, didn't seem to mesh well with Commander Marceau's directives. The term 'extinction war' was on everyone's lips again, and Marceau's new focus was to maintain as much human life as possible while still inflicting casualties upon the enemy. A safe battle that resulted in no human losses, but also only killed a dozen or so Slark was much preferred to bloody attrition—the new glory came from survival. Bruce professed his support for Marceau's preservationist mentality as most of the men in the militia were personal friends. Olivia didn't know if this was truth or simple lip service, but she did believe Bruce would tow command's line better than Cavanaugh. She voiced her support for the change that seemed inevitable.

If Commander Marceau was battered by the storm of the reignited war, her own father was floundering on the edge of sinking. She'd only seen Professor Kingston twice in the week of resumed conflict. The first time was when he came to the surface to check the electrical systems of the sea wall defenses on the bay side after the mutants knocked out the auto turrets and weapons. He pronounced them unfixable by human hands.

The Transcended, as he'd explained it, were just that—too far above humanity for humanity to understand them or for them to understand humanity. He could no more fix what they had built than he could describe God's bathroom. With that, he'd returned to the lair miles beneath the earth to walk among the robots that were so unknowable. Olivia had gone down to visit him after returning from retrieving Claudia. Their conversation went much the same as most of their conversations did, but with an added edge of tension. She wanted to see if he could convince the Transcended to work on the wall if it was cleared of Slark and mutants. Things quickly deteriorated from there. He couldn't talk to the Transcended because they were above language now. He was sick of people asking him to violate the barrier between humanity and those above humans with the concerns of war. They'd transcended trivial things like violence and war. He didn't even think he could make himself understood to them on such a matter.

The door to the bar swung open, and a familiar, yet surprising face came strolling through. Actually, her steps were far more mincing than strolling, but Olivia thought it probably qualified as a stroll for Esme these days. She'd taken the advice to go home and get cleaned up to a level Olivia hadn't expected. Esme actually looked a little dolled up with some curls in her hair, a little eye makeup, and a cute, navy blue dress with a tight cinch around her slender waist.

"What brings you down here?" Olivia asked of her.

"I overheard Claudia talking to her father," Esme said, immediately making her way across the bar to Olivia's side.

"Nothing complimentary by the look on your face," Olivia said.

"She doesn't want either of us, maybe she never did since we're both apparently so flawed in her opinion," Esme said.

"That sounds like a familiar answer to a common problem," Olivia murmured.

"And there was a man, outside the wall, he died, but she wanted him, cared for him…"

This took Olivia by surprise. She knew Claudia had a history with men, specifically she'd mentioned a man named Danny or Manny or something in Tombstone. Claudia also had specifically said she preferred women. Olivia didn't think Claudia was lying when she said the words, but she also might have subconsciously meant she preferred women when suitable men weren't readily available, which would certainly describe the City of Broken Bridges as huge swaths of the male population were married, gay, or barking at the moon crazy...or all three in some cases. The mystery man was dead though and Olivia had poured more grieving on by delivering the Veronica news so soon after. Despite the jilting, the ingratitude of her rescue receiving such a frosty response, and the secondhand news from Esme that Claudia wasn't really into either of them, Olivia still felt sorry for her. It was shocking how much sympathy the little sniper could illicit without lifting a finger to seek it out.

"Do you still feel bad for her? Do you still want to do kind things for her to try to cheer her up?" Olivia asked, a little disgusted with herself that she did.

"Yes, but that's not going to stop me from doing this." Esme took Olivia's face in her hands and kissed her.

Olivia's hands came up to her waist and the kiss deepened in length and intensity as both women were holding on to prove to the other it wasn't something either wanted to pull away from. Scooting to the edge of her barstool, Olivia spread her long legs around Esme, and pulled her closer until they were completely entwined. They broke the kiss, both panting with roiling sexual desire, and simply held one another.

"When you protected me from Inspector Cavanaugh, I saw you, truly saw you for the first time," Esme whispered against Olivia's neck. "I meant to tell you that the morning I came out to watch you depart, but you seemed so focused on rescuing Claudia that I couldn't bring myself to say anything."

"I'm not her and I don't want to be a way to hurt her," Olivia said.

They pulled back from the hug to look each other in the eye. Olivia expected to find tears around Esme's large, brown doe eyes, but instead found an intense fire burning behind them.

"I don't want to hurt her. I want to help us."

Olivia's first reaction to the wonderful words was to take Esme by the hand and find some place they might do a proper job of helping one another, but she refrained for the moment, still not entirely trusting the shift in the romantic dynamic. Instead, she led Esme to an empty table, of which there were many, and beckoned for food and drink to be brought.

Sitting in silence across from one another they poked at the plates of food brought to them. It was meant to be similar to baked beans on toast with a fried egg, but instead of baked beans, the dish contained stewed chickpeas; instead of toast, the hollowed skin of a potato; and instead of being fried, the egg was scrambled with grilled sweet onions. As much as Olivia didn't want to immediately go to their one interest in common, she couldn't think of anything else to say to Esme to fill the growing silence between them.

"Claudia said the food here is a lot better than in Tombstone or Las Vegas," Olivia said.

"It's a lot worse than it was before the Slark," Esme said with a wry grin. "How does it compare to what they served you in the Navy?"

Olivia considered the strange forkful of potato, chickpeas, and egg. "I'd rate it a sideways move. The tea here is atrocious though. Worse after the antebellum supplies were used up."

Esme smiled to her, looking wistfully for a moment. "I love the way you talk."

"Yes, I've been told my Manchester accent hits a pleasing part of the American ear."

"It's not just that," Esme said quickly. "Your accent is lovely, sexy even, but it's the way you use words, and make it all sounds so important—like you don't say unimportant things."

"That was a product of growing up with my father," Olivia said, blushing a little under the dual compliments of sexy and articulate. "The man wouldn't let my brother, mother, or I get a word in edgewise. Every moment was a teaching moment for him and every conversation a speech. With such an economy of words afforded the three of us in the gaps between his lectures, we all became fairly adept at only saying what absolutely must be said. I think I've gotten a little better since."

"I spent so much time worrying that Claudia would see something in you that she didn't see in me. I never stopped to consider if I might see something in you," Esme said. "I'm glad I did. You're a very interesting person."

"Made all the more interesting through science and technology."

"Have you been waiting to bring up your mechanical leg?"

"It's not something everyone can get past."

Esme leaned forward across the tiny table, catching Olivia's eyes with hers. Her voice dropped to a soft purr. "I already have lusty thoughts about seeing you naked, metal leg and all."

Olivia considered pointing out that the comment sounded like one Claudia would make, that Esme must have picked up some tricks from their mutual acquaintance, but she discarded the thought as irrelevant. She'd certainly learned a few things from Claudia as well, and it wasn't the sort of thing to say to move the romance forward. Instead, she leaned in to cover the rest of the distance and kissed Esme's full lips.

"We'll have to see about turning those thoughts into reality," Olivia said, mirroring a statement she could hear from Claudia's lips.

They slid closer to one another around the edge of the table to nearly sit on the same side. Silence stretched between them as if neither knew where to take the seduction from there. Claudia had been such a driving force in their relationships to that point that neither Olivia nor Esme were particularly equipped to take control.

"I think my mental scars might be worse than your leg anyway," Esme said. "I know they've made me difficult to sleep with. At least three nights a week, I wake up screaming or don't even wake up for the screaming."

"After Cavanaugh called you Mouse, I asked around about you," Olivia said. The civilian freedom fighters and the remnant British military units that fought to liberate the city hadn't overlapped much. A few MPs, Cavanaugh included, were sent by General Hastings to keep the civilian combat operations from getting in the way. Olivia had thought that was the sum total of the influence Hastings had over the civilians, but hearing Bruce Coffey's telling of it, the civilian militia was often used as shock troops or suicide ops. The animosity between herself and Bruce made a lot more sense after their conversation. He didn't know that she didn't know what really went on.

"Of the twenty-five who started out as couriers and spies, only three of us survived," Esme said. "Shin killed herself a few months after the wall was built, but I still see Chandra sometimes. She's not doing as well as I am."

"It was abhorrent that Hastings or Cavanaugh would use children as soldiers. I promise I didn't know anything about it."

"I don't think many people did. Claudia said she wasn't much older than me when she started training as a scout sniper. She says this world doesn't have children anymore; everyone grew up when the Slark landed or they died."

"Claudia lives under a black cloud of that kind of thinking," Olivia countered. "It may keep her alive, but it also keeps her from happiness."

"There has to be more to it than that," Esme said.

"There are three kinds of people when it comes to war: those who were born for it, those who can muddle through it if they have to, and those who were never meant to take part in it. Strangely enough, it was General Hastings who told me this. As he explained it, the vast majority of people were the third type, most soldiers were the second, and the ones likeliest to become career warriors were the first. Claudia, her father, and Hastings are, or were, the kind of people who were meant for war. I brought the theory to my father and he said it was reasonably sound, although he postulated that the first type likely only comprised one or two percentage points of the entire population, while ninety or more percent is probably the third kind."

"Which type do you think you are?"

"The second. I don't thrive on conflict the way Claudia and her father do. It's a job and an important one. Sometimes it's boring, sometimes it's dangerous, but it's still just a job."

"Then why join the Navy before we even knew about the Slark."

Olivia shook her head and sighed. "It seems too silly now. I did it to upset my father."

"Did it work?"

"Not a bit," Olivia said. "He actually had this bizarre romanticized notion left over from his boyhood of taking to the seas for adventure. He read a lot of Joseph Conrad as a child."

"Who is that? I was a product of American public schools. We only read two books in high school: *To Kill a Mocking Bird* and *The Great Gatsby*."

"He wrote *Heart of Darkness* and a bunch of other adventure tales, mostly about sailing, all incredibly dense Victorian era stuff. My father must have been one of a tiny handful of twelve-year-olds who actually thought they were exciting. After he told me about his *Lord Jim* style fantasies about being a sailor, I tried to read the book."

"How was it?"

"I was back to reading my lesbian murder mysteries in a week," Olivia said.

"Getting back to the three types thing..." Esme began although the sudden rattling of bells and wails of alarms broke off the rest.

Olivia was to her feet immediately, followed closely by most of the rest of the patrons in the bar. She made for the door with Esme close on her heels. In the streets, the resting members of the militia were arming and heading toward the surface.

"It's a general mustering," Olivia said, shouting a bit to be heard over the alarms. "You should get home."

"I feel safer with you," Esme said.

The comment on its own might have been enough to pluck a heartstring, but combining it with Esme taking her hand and looking up to her with those beautiful doe eyes and Olivia was helpless to deny her. She led Esme toward the surface. Elements of Olivia's Clockwork Warriors came to her side as they walked. They were men whose names she didn't know yet although their faces were familiar. They distributed weapons among them, handing Olivia an old revolver.

The push toward the surface created chaos of its own on top of the clanging bells and wailing alarms salvaged from a dozen different sources like schools, ambulances, and carnival games. When they broke free of the subterranean tunnels into the cold night air, the chaos shifted from noise to full-scale war. A battle was raging in the bay and the shore forces were doing their best to provide support.

Olivia grabbed the first of her men that she recognized as an officer. "Gather who you can and get the heaviest artillery tractors we have to help support the sea wall," she told him. Esme released Olivia's hand, following closely behind as if waiting for an order herself.

The general push of militia was heading toward the bay and the sound of combat. Olivia and Esme followed along, waiting to see someone who might know better what was going on. As they neared the water, the sound of battle intensified and they got their first glimpse of Alcatraz ablaze on the water among a dozen other fires.

The mutant onslaught had abated over the past few days. The sea wall was secured against the Slark, albeit at a steep cost. And the bay was once again patrolled by human vessels. All this seemed to be changing in one very impressive nighttime raid.

Olivia found Bruce Coffey at the crest of a small hill ringed in by sandbags and armor plating. He was commanding the militia with remarkable competence in the absence of Inspector Cavanaugh who, to Olivia's knowledge, hadn't been relived of his command yet.

"Olivia, glad to see you awake and armed," Bruce said.

"Where can I help?" Olivia replied.

"If you can get your Clockwork Warriors and their tanks along the northern edge of the sea wall to provide fire support for the boats pulling out survivors, that'd be a great help." Bruce led Olivia to the front of the makeshift command bunker and pointed to the sandy area along old pier 43 and the remains of the Embarcadero.

"Consider it done." Olivia turned to find which of her men she might give the order to, but only found Esme still at her side.

"I can run the message," Esme said.

Part of Olivia wanted to deny her, to keep her safe at her side, but she couldn't see another way to move the order any faster. "Do it, but stay out of the fighting and get back here as soon as it's done," Olivia said.

Esme smiled to her. "I need your authorization phrase."

Olivia leaned in closer to Esme's ear to whisper it to her, but also to lay a brief kiss on her cheek. "Toxic tango."

With that, Esme was off and running, moving faster through the mobilized military units than Olivia would have thought possible. Once she'd started asking around about the Mouse, the reports couldn't have been more impressive. During the liberation of the city, the Mouse didn't get caught, didn't get delayed, didn't forget even a scrap of her message, and never left a trail the Slark might follow to her destination or her departure point. After talking with Esme, Olivia was convinced most of what had made her so competent was a healthy dose of fear. Strangely, being terrified by her work served to keep her from ever becoming overconfident in her obviously impressive and much praised skill.

"I'll understand if you want to keep her as your private runner," Bruce said, "but I could sure use her and a dozen more like her."

"So could the world," Olivia said wistfully. "What is the situation, Militia Captain Coffey?"

"The details I'm getting are pretty beggarly, but it's clear from this vantage point what's happening even without full military clearance." Bruce handed Olivia his field glasses and directed her to look down around the edge of pier 39 and out across the bay where the battle was still raging. "The Slark pulled back to the Oakland side of the bay once our patrols gained strength. We thought they were done with trying to cross after the casualties their attack boat squadrons took, but then earlier tonight, they launched a raid with a force we didn't think they had anymore. Once they broke our bay patrol, they ferried over a thousand mutants or more on cattle-barge-looking-things and landed them all on Alcatraz. It must have taken them weeks to corral so many freaks."

"The automated defenses..."

"Knocked out in less than an hour by the nuclear EMP bursts the damn mutants give off when they die," Bruce said. "We've been trying to reinforce the two hundred regulars still on Alcatraz, but the Slark are hitting us pretty hard in the crossing. The civilian fleet, including the Balclutha, made it out before the fighting got too thick, but by the look of it they won't be coming back anytime soon."

Olivia continued watching the battle raging in the bay, focusing specifically on the long, sleek shape of the Hercules as it comprised the tip of the spear for the human fleet. She saw the suicide swift boat attack from around the southern edge of Alcatraz before the crew of the Hercules could. Five Slark skimmer boats, likely loaded with explosives, shot down along the human fleet's flank, striking the Hercules and her three escort vessels broadside. The explosions lit up the night, obliterating the smaller ships entirely. The Hercules listed and began sinking bow first into the black water of the bay.

Olivia's heart froze at the sight of the Hercules going down with a hundred souls aboard. She was one of the last fine ships of humanity with no new vessels being built. The greater implications for their war effort aside, which were devastating, the loss of the 1905 tugboat turned destroyer was practically the death of a distant family member for Olivia. She'd sailed on her before she lost her leg, knew every bolt and bulkhead, knew the faces of her crew, and had lulled herself into the same belief so many had that she'd survived too long to sink now.

"That'll be it then," Bruce said, spitting angrily on the ground. "They've got Alcatraz and the bay."

Chapter 28:
Hardened Lines.

The battle raged on long after Bruce accurately assessed the killing blow that was the sinking of the Hercules. Olivia didn't know which captain took control of the tattered remains of the fleet once the command vessel was destroyed. She had a few theories, but she didn't imagine it mattered. The patrol fleet fought on with no hope of victory and no real option for retreat. The shore forces under Coffey, Olivia, and Commander Marceau did their best to support, but the night was already lost with Alcatraz and the Hercules.

They focused on pulling survivors from the water and covering their evacuation as vessel after vessel met its water end in the bay. Olivia wanted to move off the command bunker to find her personal tank, but Bruce held her back. Her men were better off with their leader in a position to see the whole field than leading them around by the hand. She'd left her running, and even a bit of Bruce's, to Esme who was perking up as the night wore on.

Bruce began the ball rolling, saluting Esme after he gave her an order to deliver. The respect for her work spread like wildfire through the militia and the military regulars who witnessed it. Under Coffey, the militia functioned far better than it ever did under Cavanaugh. They were motivated, organized, and determined in ways nobody had seen to that point. This manifested in respectful treatment of Esme and the other runners. When the Slark targeted her or one of the other message carriers, the militia, without orders to do so, gave covering fire, provided shelter, and guarded the lines of communication as though the messengers weren't simply disposable.

The hillside above the old wharf and the open ground between the water and the rise became a muddy, cratered mess. The fields of grass, orchards, and crops were obliterated by tanks, tractors, and troops on the human side, and bombardment from the Slark navy. Esme raced among the trails she could find in her increasingly tattered and dirty dress, boots, and leggings. After a time, Olivia stopped worrying after her and focused on the battle. Esme was clearly the least likely of all the people on the field to die, which included Olivia as mortars targeted the command bunker on more than a few occasions.

Once the last of their navy was obliterated, dragged on to destruction by some captain or lower admiral who survived past the command vessel, the real battle began in earnest. The Slark tried again and again to land an invasion group to gain a foothold on the beach. Olivia's Clockwork Warriors and their mountain goat tractor tanks played an integral part in repelling every attempt to establish a beachhead. The Slark moved their invasion force to a different part of the beach, and Olivia's men were there to greet them.

As the morning began to gray with the coming dawn, the Slark withdrew their navy from the harbor's edge to the open water to begin the process of bombardment to soften up the position. Commander Marceau gave the general order to dig in, string razor wire, fortify trenches, and build bunkers. Olivia watched Esme run the order, nearly getting hit on more than a few occasions by the incoming bombardment. She moved toward the edge of the command bunker reflexively only to be pulled back by Bruce Coffey's gentle hand.

"You've got to let her work," Bruce said. "Besides, with that leg of yours on these muddy hills, you'd only succeed in getting yourself killed and then her when she tried to save you." When Olivia didn't seem convinced, Bruce handed her his field glasses again and pointed her attention to a forward position near the ruins of the sea wall where a fiery young man with a shock of orange hair, dressed in the battle armor common to top hats of an iron breast plate and a leather uniform, was shouting orders to direct men in gas masks and heavier armor in the stringing of razor wire nets across the gaps in the wall. "The Hotspur-like figure you see down there is my husband, Jeremy. Could he get blown off that wall at any point? Probably. Will it do either of us any good if I go down there and tell him to hide? Not a chance."

Olivia looked back to the heroic figure on the battlements with a new appreciation. "He's beautiful," she murmured. When she looked back to Bruce, a broad, knowing smile was beneath his impressive black moustache.

"And believe me, he knows it," Bruce said with a wink.

Olivia finally pieced together why Esme was so energized by the work that was the same work that used to terrify her. She'd never had the respect, the support, or a share of the unified goal that made being a soldier worthwhile. That night, Bruce had seen to it that Esme received the support, but Olivia had to respect her enough to leave her to her work.

Olivia began to wonder why she'd ever thought of Bruce as an enemy.

†

Within a few weeks, the old tension along cold battle lines returned although with different boundaries as the Slark gained a lot of ground in taking Alcatraz and control of the bay. Treasure Island was lost, the last of the Bay Bridge was destroyed, and humanity severed another tether to the mainland. Olivia looked over her maps every night when she came home and again the second she awoke. With an entire army of Slark fortified outside the wall on the south, open ocean with no harbors left on the west, an occupied Alcatraz and no Bay Bridge on the east, the peninsula had effectively become an island. The mutants pushed the human defenders back to the last juncture in the BART tunnel that could still be sealed before their attack petered out. One more push by Slark or mutant underground and they would lose the tunnel as well. They had ships, but nowhere to safely dock them, the Golden Gate Bridge to the north that they couldn't use or repair, and an overwhelming enemy laying siege.

Esme came up behind Olivia at the kitchen table and wrapped her arms around her, resting her chin on Olivia's shoulder to look at the map as well. "All those red lines make things look really bad," Esme said.

"We're an island now," Olivia replied. "That shouldn't bother me as much as it does considering I grew up on one."

"Can we hold out?" Esme asked.

"At a diminished capacity, I suppose," Olivia said. "We can't re-supply from our outposts, fish, or use any of the fields on the eastern shore, but they can't close off the western beaches since the water there is too rough to land mutant attackers and the sea wall defenses have enough range to hit something twenty miles away."

"Why can't they shoot the bay then?"

"They only point the one direction and my father said the Transcended will only change that if they see fit to." Olivia began to wonder if her constant pestering of her father about the Transcended might finally be wearing on him in a bad way.

"For such a smart man, he sure falls back on the same answer a lot."

It was statements like that making Olivia fall for Esme. She hadn't really considered how important it was for her to be with someone who truly got her, especially the parts of her that she hid from most people, but Esme, without even trying, understood so much about Olivia and her enigmatic relationship with her father.

"I think I need to see something good on this table for once," Olivia murmured, kissing Esme's forearm wrapped around her.

"I could make you breakfast, anything you want," Esme replied.

Olivia began rolling up the maps to set them aside. "No, I think I'd rather see something else."

It took Esme a few moments to piece together what Olivia meant, but when Olivia had her pulled from her place behind the chair to the front of it, her ass pressed against the edge of the table, and Olivia firmly pressed against her, she seemed to figure out the intent of the comment. She kissed Esme fiercely, slowly lowering her back onto the table. Esme responded with aggressive kissing of her own, pawing at the front of Olivia's uniform jacket. Laid out fully on her back across the table, legs spread around Olivia, and her dress threatening to creep up her legs, Esme did indeed look a whole lot more appealing than the bleak maps she replaced. Olivia stood for a moment to admire the view, particularly liking the way Esme's hair was splayed across the wooden surface around her head. Olivia's hands made their way up the tops of Esme's thighs, pushing the bottom hem of her dress up as she went.

"I haven't the foggiest notion why I would look at maps every evening rather than you," Olivia said.

"It's morning," Esme replied.

"See how my exhaustion has confused me?" Olivia said. "It's a bloody catastrophe how addled I've been lately."

"Do you need some direction in your current task?" Esme asked, giving Olivia a coquettish smirk.

"I would adore some."

Olivia couldn't remember how the joke between them arose, whether it was out of Esme loving Olivia stoic British-ism as she'd put it, or if it was the difference in rank and position in the military, but a fun little game of role reversal increasingly became the norm. Esme had the power in the bedroom while Olivia gave the orders on the battlefield.

Esme continued the work Olivia started in pulling up the hem of her skirt. She hadn't finished getting dressed for the day when she'd decided to take a break to kiss on Olivia, and so her leggings, boots, and underwear were still in the bedroom, folded neatly on the dresser.

Esme traced her fingers along the soft, caramel colored skin on the interior of her thighs. "I think you should start by kissing along here," she cooed.

"Smashing idea," Olivia whispered, lowering her head between Esme's legs to do just that.

Esme responded with a sharp inhale and a long, slow, satisfied exhale as Olivia's tongue made its way up and down her legs, tickling at her in a delicious way. "I think you should lick me," Esme murmured.

"I already am," Olivia replied, returning to the taunting work. She knew what Esme meant, but she liked making her say the actual words as she said it in such an adorably bashful fashion. Even now, she could mentally see the blush rising to Esme's cheeks as she worked up the confidence to give voice to the request.

"Lick my pussy," Esme said barely above hearing. "Please?" she added almost as an afterthought.

It delighted Olivia right to her very core to hear Esme ask. It was something they both wanted, something they would both enjoy, the entire reason Olivia had laid Esme on the table in the first place, but to hear Esme ask for it you'd think she was requesting the world from the only person capable of granting it. Unintentionally, Esme had an unerring power to make Olivia feel special. And so she did as was requested. Taking several, gentle licks along the outside first to push away the faint hairs, then deeper into the unmistakable tang that Olivia had come to adore. She waited for it, licked a few times more to see if she could hear the words above the quickened breathing and moaning coming from Esme.

"Thank you," she finally heard her lover whisper.

It was all Olivia could do to not giggle. She wondered if Esme thought she could even hear the words or if she was so polite in everything that she simply couldn't say please without following it with a thank you when the request was granted. Regardless, Olivia had come to expect the little reward of the whispered gratitude and liked Esme a little more every time it was uttered.

Briefly, Olivia considered teasing another request out of Esme, one she'd managed in the past, but she was on a bit of a schedule that morning and what she really wanted was to hear Esme climax. She would have to cajole the unambiguous "please...?" that actually meant "please lick my clit" at some point in the future. She focused her attention entirely at the top of Esme's slit and the hard bead, eager for attention. She flicked at it in slow, even strokes of her tongue at first, picking up on Esme's cues to increase speed and intensity until she had her lover writhing and ready to explode. She pressed her lips over Esme's clit and suckled at it to finish what she'd started in a lovely series of strangled, embarrassed moans from Esme. With as much effort as Esme put into controlling her sounds of pleasure, Olivia always felt a sense of accomplishment at getting her to make enough noise to disturb the neighbors.

Esme's hands came away from the edges of the tabletop she'd been gripping at and began to caress Olivia short, already messy hair. "I need to do something nice for you," she said.

"Haven't you already?" Olivia asked, licking Esme's taste off her lips.

"Okay, but now I need to do more," Esme said.

"Such a giver." Olivia stood, admiring her handiwork of Esme's glistening pussy before sliding the skirt of her dress back down. "You can make me breakfast while I work out the week's duty rosters, and tonight, if you're still concerned about our balance sheets, you can do whatever you feel necessary to make us even."

Esme surprised her by sitting up quickly to prevent Olivia from walking away. Her hands found their way to Olivia's belt, pulling her back into the embrace of Esme's legs wrapped around her. Esme looked up to Olivia with sparkling eyes and a knowing smile.

"I want to draw you," Esme said.

The request was so abrupt and earnest that all Olivia managed was a 'huh?'

"Completely naked except your mechanical leg," Esme elaborated. "It's artistic, you're artistic, and you've inspired me to pick up something I thought had gone out of me years ago."

"I don't..." Olivia began. She didn't really know what to say to the request. She'd never considered any of what had happened to her as artistic. The leg was functional and necessary, but sexy and worthy of being immortalized in a sketch?

"Please? I love the way your leg is the mechanical counterpart of your other leg, perfectly matched in shape, but not in composition. It's like the face of Janus, but with a beautiful..."

"I've never heard you talk like this before," Olivia said, catching immediately on what word had stopped Esme's description. "With a beautiful...what?"

"You know." Esme blushed furiously.

"Do I?"

Esme took a deep breath and sighed. "With a beautiful pussy between them," she said very quickly.

"Yes, you can draw me." Olivia leaned down, cupped Esme's face in her hands, and kissed her gently. "Be kind though. I've not been immortalized in artwork to this point and I couldn't stand it if I thought you pictured me as undesirable."

"Be kind in return," Esme replied against Olivia's lips. "It's been years since I've drawn and now I have to try to capture your beauty along with Dr. Gatling's craftsmanship."

"A daunting task, but I have faith in you, Mouse," Olivia said.

"I love when you call me that." Esme grasped at Olivia, pulling her in for another kiss, this one far more erotically charged, and suddenly breakfast and the duty roster were forgotten.

Esme clearly had designs on something in that exact moment and Olivia was eager to see what it was.

Chapter 29:
Even Gods Can Die.

Claudia could no longer find comfort in anything but walking. The hospital room was oppressive, the districts beneath the ground were claustrophobia inducing, and sleep was nearly impossible.

Olivia and Esme still came by from time to time, although never together. Claudia doggedly pretended to be asleep when one would visit her. Esme remained silent, read awhile in the room, and then left. Olivia didn't believe Claudia's act for a second and always talked at her, unconcerned with whether or not Claudia would respond. Olivia explained about her and Esme's budding relationship, apologized for being so callous about Liam's death, and said she was available to talk if Claudia needed to. Olivia only ever asked Claudia one question: "When I found you wandering in the ruins, why did you ask me if I knew your mother?" Claudia was surprised that Olivia remembered the delirious comment spoken in French or that she'd found someone to translate it for her. Claudia didn't answer, couldn't really think of an answer other than to say she spent several hours talking to two dead people and so she thought she was dead as well; since that would sound crazy and would break her silent treatment, she opted to turn her back on Olivia and pull a pillow over her head. Olivia didn't come back after that, but Esme stopped by with books or donuts nearly every day. Claudia didn't feel like eating or reading.

Within a few weeks, Claudia was declared physically fit for duty, although her mental status remained a question. It galled Claudia to think a couple weeks was all it took for her to recover from an ordeal that killed Liam. She'd done so little to save him when he'd clearly sacrificed himself to save her and she was walking away with only a few faint scars on her shoulder from the scratches that in no way indicated she'd survived a life threatening attack. She couldn't keep from going back to that night again and again in her mind, wishing she'd done something different, anything really. She could have shot at the Gator and Liam as they fought; she might have hit him, or she might not. She could have waited for a flash of lightning to shoot. He could have kept the gun, shot the Gator, and then come to her aid. The more she thought about it, the more the list of ways out of the situation with them both surviving grew until it was impossible for her to think it wasn't entirely her fault that she'd walked away and he hadn't.

She asked Dr. Gatling for a gun. He gave her an identical sniper rifle to the one she'd lost with the only admonishment being not to lose too many more. Apparently it was an increasingly popular design.

Before Dr. Gatling would clear her to have ammunition for the rifle or rejoin the military, Claudia had to clock a few hours with the battlefield counselor. Claudia almost laughed that such a person still existed. It only took her ten minutes of talking with the bespectacled little British man to figure out he wasn't really a therapist or counselor, but a ship chaplain from one of the military vessels in Hastings' flotilla. All his questions were designed to lead Claudia back to the existence of a higher power and the invisible hand this godly being had in her life. Whenever he thought he'd led her to a particularly miraculous occurrence that he thought could only be explained by a specific Judeo-Christian deity, he waggled his eyebrows and waited expectantly on the edge of his seat to see if she would suddenly feel the power of the Holy Spirit and instantly feel better. When he'd done this in response to finally hearing about how Liam died, or more specifically when he read it to Claudia from the report she'd had to submit after her ordeal, she wished she had her gun to blast him off the edge of his sanctimonious chair. She walked out of the chaplain's office, up a few flight of stairs to Dr. Gatling's lab, and demanded he give her bullets for her rifle so she could put someone out of their misery. He asked if she meant herself. She explained she was more of a threat to the chaplain than herself. He gave her the ammunition and cleared her for active duty.

Apparently sanity was a relative term in the City of Broken Bridges.

Her father refused to give her a patrol anywhere near the beachhead. He also entrusted her care to Roger, stating he needed someone to look after the dog while he was in the command bunkers at the front. Roger cowered and whimpered incessantly when the Slark bombarded the human fortifications from Alcatraz, which happened three or four times a day, but he didn't seem to like being away from a Marceau for too long. Claudia suspected Roger was supposed to look after her too.

Claudia didn't figure out until Esme and Olivia were both gone that she hadn't developed any friendships beyond them, which was a shame since she really could use someone other than her father to talk to about her entire romance life's brilliant collapse. Roger was a surprisingly good listener on their long patrols together around the base of the Golden Gate Bridge entrance. They were the two things her father couldn't stand to lose and so he'd ordered them away from danger to watch out for each other. That was his way. Claudia was glad for the company and the sympathetic ear.

Claudia and Roger were discussing where Claudia should live while they patrolled one of the many old bike routes along the wooded area on the northern shore, just east of the bridge. She didn't want to stay in the hospital room anymore. She'd moved from that room into Esme's house the last time she'd left the tower, but obviously that wasn't an option anymore. She couldn't imagine taking one of the houses or apartments in the subterranean districts, nor did she feel like moving into her father's home. That left requesting a different room in the tower or joining the other Irradiated in their above ground tenements. Neither option was particularly appealing. Roger barked once as his only contribution. Claudia came to the slow realization that the real reason she couldn't find a comfortable place in the City of Broken Bridges was that she viewed her position there as being temporary. Even before Olivia relayed the full encounter with Dylan and her Voron Dagger squad, Claudia always felt like the Ravens would eventually come to reclaim her. Roger didn't have much to say on the conundrum.

Her real problem was that she didn't plan well. She was a reactionary. Even her simplistic ambush plan to attack the Slark supply convoy required Liam to finish it. Her grandest plan of leaving the Ravens to find her father could only generously be said to have three steps: steal Gieo's bike, leave Tombstone, find father. And it relied entirely on blind luck and coincidence to succeed. Now that she truly needed to devise a plan for the future, she was mentally less able and her only counsel was the dog at her side.

She broke free of the trees above a sandy patch of beach, a grassy area, and a neatly stacked field of corrugated sheet metal. The day was bright and sunny, the bay calm, and the wind just above a breeze. The scene was lovely and serene from her vantage point and she took a moment to drink it in. Roger sat at her side and smelled the air blowing in from the bay, clearly taking his cue from her.

Appearing, as if from nowhere, a Transcended ambled toward the stockpile of sheet metal. It was so long since Claudia last saw one, it was a little thrilling that one of the giant robots was out from its subterranean den to begin a functional and artistic art project involving metal sheeting apparently. She pointed to the Transcended and nudged Roger's shoulder with the side of her leg. Again, he took his cue from her and looked on with interest rather than fear.

She was in the middle of deciding whether or not she would follow the Transcended to see what it was working on when she saw the white vapor trails coming from somewhere across the bay. It took her a second to realize what they were and what they were fired at. All she could do was scream a warning to the Transcended that it couldn't hear or heed.

The missiles struck the shore with only a semblance of accuracy. They clearly weren't blindly hurled rockets meant for bombardment. The Slark had a target in mind, but even the massive Transcended wasn't a large enough for the semi-guided missiles, likely intended to hit ships, to hit dead on. The explosions raked the earth and scattered the carefully stacked metal sheets, which probably weighed five or six times what Claudia did, into the air like a house of cards blown by a fan. The attack was over as quickly as it begun and Claudia was far enough away that she only felt an increased rush of wind and a rumble beneath her boots. Half a dozen craters along the grassy expanse and beach bled white smoke into the clear day. Through the haze, Claudia picked out the bronze body of the Transcended among the metal sheeting fluttering to the ground.

She raced down the hill toward it with Roger quick at her heels. She stumbled through the brush, nearly lost her rifle repeatedly, and snagged her skin and her clothing the whole way down. She hit the field at a dead run, dodging between the smoking craters to reach the fallen Transcended.

It hadn't stiffened and fallen over like she thought a disabled robot would or wound down in a predictable pattern like a crippled mechanical toy might. It was simply lying on its side in what Claudia could only describe as a pained fetal position, holding its stomach as though it took a wound there. She approached the dead or dying machine. She touched its massive metal arm that was easily ten times as long as she was. The blue globe, which it held in its shoulder like a medal of honor, was dark and empty.

She fell to her knees, resting her head on its metal forearm, weeping softly for something so beautiful being destroyed so wantonly. "I'm so sorry," she whispered again and again to the dead Transcended. They were so gentle, peaceful, and artistic—it was as though the Slark had cruelly killed an elephant or whale simply because it presented a big enough target.

She remained in that position for close to an hour. She heard retaliatory strikes from human batteries exploding across the hillside of the opposite shore of the bay where the missiles came from. She doubted they would hit what were probably mobile launchers, but she also didn't think the Slark would risk firing the missiles again anytime soon. On such a clear day, the vapor trails pointed directly to where they were fired from.

Roger let out a single warning bark, drawing Claudia's attention from the robot she was mourning. Four other Transcended were gathered around her and their fallen friend. They didn't seem to see her or Roger. She moved aside when they reached for the dead robot. Roger whimpered, huddled behind her leg, and tucked his tail under as they respectfully hauled away their fallen comrade, disappearing into whatever hidden alcove they'd come from.

Claudia stood among the pressed down grass where the Transcended had fallen. A couple electric trucks rolled up from the south to investigate. A few army regulars asked if she'd seen what the Slark were shooting at. She told them about the dead Transcended. They ushered Claudia and Roger into the truck to return to the tower.

At the tower, Claudia relayed her story to Dr. Gatling, again to her father, and yet again to the chaplain after they demanded she speak with her mental health professional. With each retelling, she lost more of her composure until she was unable to finish the final recounting through her sobbing. Dr. Gatling and her father agreed it was entirely possible she confused something among the scattered metal scrap for a Transcended, but equally likely the Transcended would take care of their own if one fell. The chaplain insisted her story was just an allegory for her lack of faith. She felt like shooting him, but Dr. Gatling had taken her rifle, again.

She demanded to see Professor Kingston, believing he would support her account as possible, but she was denied. The lowest reaches of the city were closed off, sequestered by the Keepers to protect the power plant from Slark attack. Claudia didn't believe the reasoning for the reclusion and she could see in her father's face when he explained it that he didn't either. Regardless of their disbelief of the rationale, Professor Kingston and the other Keepers were out of reach.

Claudia was again taken off active patrols and restricted to safe zones. Dr. Gatling refused to give her rifle back until she'd completed another twenty hours with the chaplain. Claudia decided she didn't need a gun badly enough to suffer another minute with him.

†

It was a week later, Claudia couldn't even accurately say which day of the week it was or what underground level they were walking through, when her and her father saw the Transcended. They were walking among the mostly vacant

Victorian streets by the buzzing electric light of the 19th century lampposts.

"I've had to officially replace Cavanaugh as captain of the militia," her father said.

"The remnants of Hastings loyalists won't like that," Claudia said.

"They've already complained," her father replied, "but what else can I do? The man has been missing for weeks now."

"And...?"

"And Bruce Coffey is far more competent."

"I would lead with that rather than a mysterious disappearance of the last commander who was replaced by a known street gang leader," Claudia said.

"You were built for politics, my little dove," her father said. "Perhaps it was a mistake to send you back to war at all."

"Do you think Cavanaugh is dead?" Claudia asked, ignoring her father's comment about her being unfit for combat and his transparently false compliment that she had any sort of head for politics.

"I think he can make himself appear and disappear as easily as you or I breathe," her father said. "If he were dead, he would be much easier to find."

"He was the primary resistance to the military council accepting the existence of the new Slark classification of Gators," Claudia said. "With him missing, will more consideration be given to what I've seen?"

"Reports from the handful of survivors of Alcatraz's defense force resemble yours. Larger, smarter, more vicious Slark appear to be taking over leadership. They are still not willing to attribute Liam's death to one though," her father said.

"It had hunting dogs, mutant hunting dogs," Claudia said, her voice cracking at the end. "What else could it have been?"

"I am still struggling to get many of them to accept the existence of such anomalies within the Slark population," her father said. "Cataloguing the dangerous new set of skills these Gators seem to have is going to be arduous and fraught with misinformation. Soldiers tell tall tales of an enemy's prowess after sound defeats, which we are once again suffering."

"Do you think I'm telling tall tales?"

Her father shook his head. "I believe my daughter would not be so easily tracked if hunting dogs were not used and, after reading what little existed of Liam's service record, I don't believe a lone, normal Slark could have killed him. These are conclusions born out of knowing you and knowing hand-to-hand combat with the enemy. Not everyone has the education I do on those two matters."

She could hear in his voice how taxing it was to try to defend the city while the war counsel in charge of carrying out his commands were habitually making things more difficult. The majority of the officers within the city's military were the officers Hastings brought with him. Many saw the light of how valuable Commander Marceau was, but enough didn't to make everything more difficult for everyone. If her father didn't placate these potential separatists, they could take their men and split away, which would weaken the city in potentially catastrophic ways. They had unwarranted power as an unreasonable minority, and it was clearly starting to get to her father.

Their conversation was cut short by a giant, multi-ton robot standing directly in the middle of the street before them. Claudia and her father stared up at the Transcended, which somehow found its way into one of the lower wards, something none of the massive robots had done to that point. Moreover, it appeared to be looking at them, not through them, or past them, but at them. Almost instinctively, her father began guiding Claudia behind him to place his body as a protective shield in front of hers.

Transcended were all so distinctive that there was no way Claudia could mistake the one in front of her for any other. It was the same one she'd seen die on the beach after the missile attack, but something about the Transcended seemed different or off.

"It is the same one I saw on the beach," Claudia whispered to her father.

"It appears they repaired it," her father replied, never looking away from the giant robot looming over them.

"We should go," Claudia said.

Her father guided her around the Transcended, giving it a wide berth as they passed. As if to make sure they didn't mistake its intention of blocking their way earlier, the Transcended appeared to track their path around it with the glowing blue orb in its shoulder, turning fully around to watch them go after they were past it.

Chapter 30:
Deals and Drawings.

Olivia sat by in the flickering light of a dozen candles, waiting for Esme to finish setting up her drawing implements. Olivia waited until the last possible moment to get fully undressed, keeping her linen robe that had faded from red to something of a shade of desert rose over the years. Esme was all business in getting organized, barely noticing her girlfriend's reticence or her imminent nudity, far too deep in the process already.

Esme finished laying out her scrounged pads of paper, her charcoal sticks, pencils, and even a couple of pens she'd found that she liked. She turned to Olivia with a bright smile and glanced down to the robe. Olivia's bedroom was as romantically and artistically appointed as either of them could make it, but she still didn't feel comfortable in her own space or her own skin for what was about to happen.

"You promised," Esme chided.

"That's an interesting route to take with this," Olivia said.

"You're beautiful, you're exotic, and you promised. Better?"

"Better enough, I suppose." Olivia untied her robe and let it slip away. It fell to the floor around her feet and for a moment she held her hands crossed over her chest to conceal her breasts, although she couldn't precisely say why. Esme gave her a perplexed look and she took her hands away. Nudity between them hadn't been taboo in weeks. "What am I supposed to do now?" Olivia asked.

"Get comfortable," Esme replied. "I'm not a very quick artist so we might be here awhile."

"Are there any poses I should try?" Olivia asked. She was feeling a little of the naughtiness and romance slipping from the act and she desperately wanted to recapture it.

"I don't know," Esme replied. "I've never worked with a model."

"You're not working with one now. You're working with your girlfriend and you'd do well to remember that."

"You're right; I'm sorry."

"Splendid, now give me a little direction and your bedroom eyes to make sure I still feel like this is a good idea."

"Could you sit on the edge of the bed?" Esme asked.

Olivia did as she was instructed, letting her bronze leg jut forward a little farther than the other. She leaned forward a touch and smiled to Esme.

"Smiling is going to be hard to hold for very long, and you'll want to do something more natural with your hands." Esme began etching out a rough outline of Olivia's mechanical leg first.

"Give me something interesting to look at," Olivia asked with an impish grin. She set her hands to her on either side of her hips to grip the edge of the bed for support as she scooted farther toward the edge. "It's only fair, after all."

Esme sighed and pulled her loose wool dress off over her head. When Olivia only raised an eyebrow, she slipped off her bra as well, which seemed to satisfy. "What was the word you used the other day?" Esme asked as she returned to her drawing, topless with her dark brown hair cascading over her slender shoulders and across the tops of her small, perky breasts.

"Incorrigible?"

"I know you are, but what am I?" Esme said with a grin.

"You didn't even know what the word meant."

"And then you told me and now I do," Esme said. "You are incorrigible."

Esme finished drawing after drawing as Olivia shifted positions to lying down, to reclining, to standing, and then to leaning against the wall. The last one, standing comfortably, her bronze leg fully on display with the knee slightly bent, toe touching the floor, her hands tucked demurely behind her back and her head slightly bent, hair draped over her left eye, was definitely the one Olivia felt most attractive in. Moreover, the vantage point couldn't be beat. The active work of drawing with charcoal left black smudges across Esme's mocha skin in some enticing ways and the warmth of the room raised a glisten of sweat across her skin that the candles lit up like tiny diamonds. Olivia was remarkably turned on by the entire artistic endeavor by the end and from the scant few glances she caught of Esme's final drawing of the evening, it was becoming obvious her physical response of arousal was sneaking into the artwork as Olivia's artistically rendered self had the same perky nipples she was boasting.

Esme finished her last drawing and motioned with reluctant, charcoal stained fingers for Olivia to join her on the divan to see what she'd accomplished over the last few hours. Olivia stepped over her robe in walking across the room and sat beside Esme. They spread the drawings over the top of the chest Esme had been using as a supply table for her artistic implements.

Olivia hadn't ever thought herself particularly beautiful. She'd been called pretty, cute, and intriguing, but the compliments often came with the qualifier of pointing out how tomboyish she was or how she would be far more attractive if she wore a certain kind of makeup more often. Esme captured something in Olivia she hadn't really believed existed. The woman in the drawings was a muse, a goddess with human frailty, an icon of beauty and sexuality. Her mechanical leg was featured prominently in every drawing and Esme had done a masterful job of rendering the bronze-plated robotics in a way that made it look more attractive simply for being attached to Olivia's body.

"Is this how you see me?" Olivia asked in a hushed tone. She picked up the final drawing, the one of the pose she felt most beautiful in, and practically wept from the emotional impact it made on her. She couldn't even recognize the woman in the drawing as herself. It took her several moments to realize the source of the disconnect: the woman in the picture looked euphorically happy.

"That is how a lot of people see you," Esme replied. "I'm just the only one in a position to show you."

"Can I keep it?" Olivia asked.

"As long as you keep me," Esme replied.

It was difficult to reconcile the woman Olivia was with the woman Esme saw her as. Olivia was more than ten years older, a world traveler, educated, and refined—all of which didn't seem particularly impressive to Olivia as she'd lived a long time with her shortcomings, of which there were many, and knew they more than balanced her better attributes, but for some reason Esme acted as though she were perfection incarnate. She couldn't figure out a way to tell Esme how fallible she truly was. She also began to wonder if she really wanted to. There was something profound and cathartic about having someone think she was so important, special, and beautiful.

"Keep you? I'm planning on cherishing you," Olivia said.

Any further discussion of the drawings, the artist, the muse, or the relationship they all now shared was cut short when the buzzer for the door rang. Olivia reluctantly scooped up her robe and slid it on. The path to her door was increasingly worn over the weeks as the war demanded more and more of her attention and the telecommunication lines became less and less reliable. She left Esme in the bedroom to get cleaned up and dressed as their evening would no doubt be interrupted by some minor catastrophe to deal with or some major threat on the horizon to avert.

Olivia opened the front door a crack to see who was disturbing what she planned on turning into a heavenly night of sex by candlelight with the charcoal smudged artist in her bedroom. Bruce Coffey stood in his full military regalia, which was becoming increasingly ornate and interesting with epilates on his shoulders, a top hat adorned with medallions, and a few old watch chains draped across the front of his double breasted jacket. To add to the finery, he was wearing a peculiar smile beneath his marvelous moustache.

"Gobble up a canary on the way over, did you?" Olivia asked.

"Wrong color birds and I wasn't the one doing the gobbling," Bruce replied.

This was an interesting and lingering answer, which meant he probably had enough time to come in and explain himself. Olivia stepped away from the door far enough to allow Bruce access. He strolled in with a little trepidation not just at walking into the home of a former adversary but from the obvious state of hasty dress she was in.

"I feel like I'm interrupting something intimate," Bruce said.

Olivia shut the door behind them and guided him toward the mismatched furniture adorning her Victorian era living room. "You are, so keep that truth handy when you explain what brought you over here."

Bruce and Olivia sat across from each other in the two largest living chairs in the room. Before he could explain himself, Esme emerged from the bedroom wrapped in a nightshirt. Most of the charcoal smudges were gone from her arms, hands, and face, but a fine caking remained around the edges of her fingernails—it was enough of a reminder to set a smile on Olivia's face. Esme made her way over to Olivia and sat on the arm of her chair.

"Good evening, Mouse." Bruce nodded to Esme briefly before returning his attention to Olivia. "We've got the bare minimum of one bridge left in and out of the city, but someone decided to use it."

"You wouldn't be here smiling if it was another mutant attack and we don't have any friends left after Redding fell," Olivia said.

"We can't decide if they're friends, maybe more acquaintances since they seem to know you," Bruce said. "Commando women, a whole squad of them, climbed across the suspension cables lickety-split, and asked for you by name when the first patrol got to them."

"The Voron Daggers," Olivia murmured. "Where are they now?"

"On the bridge still, waiting for you," Bruce said. "None of our northern patrols are remotely capable of taking that bunch into custody, and, since they don't seem interested in going anywhere else, Commander Marceau decided they could stay there under guard until you arrived to find out what they want."

"They didn't ask for Claudia?" Esme asked.

"They asked *about* her," Bruce said. "They wanted to know if she was still alive and seemed satisfied in simply knowing she was."

"I'll get dressed and head over there," Olivia said.

"I've got a truck waiting near the Doyle exit."

"Do you want me to come with you?" Esme asked.

"No need for that," Olivia said. "You're comfy and warm. Stay in and I'll be right back." Olivia gave Esme a long, lingering kiss that appeared to make Bruce a little uncomfortable.

Olivia departed the living room, leaving Bruce in Esme's company. She got somewhat bundled up as quickly as possible and returned to find Bruce and Esme laughing about something. The quiet, unworthy part of Olivia instantly thought it was likely a joke at her expense. It took a moment for her rational mind to restore order, but her voice still sounded a little nervous and strained when she asked, "what's the gag?"

"A San Francisco native joke about tourists," Bruce said.

"I like jokes," Olivia said, still hearing the nervous strain in her voice.

"You've seen the damn bridge, so why are you spending a fortune to cross it?" Esme said. When Olivia didn't appear to understand the joke, Esme explained, "it's not really funny unless you know what it used to cost to live here and how single-minded tourists were about the bridge."

Olivia forced a smile and motioned awkwardly for Bruce to join her. "I'll be back as soon as possible," she said.

"I'll be waiting," Esme said, her voice dropping an octave, right before Olivia stepped out of the door.

"She's a firecracker," Bruce said once they were strolling down the subterranean lane toward the surface exit.

"She's fragile and she makes me feel fragile," Olivia said.

"Still worried about her safety?" Bruce asked.

"Yes, to increasingly neurotic levels, and now there's a new irritant to add to the mix—what would become of her emotional state if I died? Certainly, she might die, which is worrisome for me, but I've been worried more and more about how hard she might take it if I was injured or killed."

"You've got it bad for her," Bruce said with a clipped laugh.

"What do you mean?"

"It's nothing special to worry about a lover's well-being. You'd have to be pretty heartless not to. But worrying about what she might go through if you die is another level.

Obviously it wouldn't actually matter to you anymore since you'd be dead, but it's…hard to explain. I guess it's the post-apocalyptic version of the sentiment behind buying life insurance. Speaking of which, is there anything you could do to make her situation better after you're gone?"

"Glad to hear you have such faith in my imminent demise," Olivia grumbled.

"For a woman with one leg you're not very aware of your own mortality," Bruce chided her.

"Fair enough," Olivia said. "I guess I would hope people who I consider friends would see to taking care of her."

"That's a good start. If you promise to take care of Jeremy, I'll make the same vow when it comes to Esme."

Olivia smiled to Bruce. It was a good bond to further seal their friendship and one she felt honored to be asked for. She nodded her agreement. "Consider it done."

"Is there anyone who might seek to hurt her without your protection?"

Olivia's knee-jerk reaction was to say no. She couldn't think of a reason anyone would want to hurt Esme. She was a lovely woman with a needed, albeit fairly minor, skill in the city. "Cavanaugh," Olivia said without thinking.

"He'd be on my list of concerns too," Bruce replied. "Odd that nobody has heard from him in so long."

"As lucky as we've both been lately, it still wouldn't seem reasonable to hope he died somewhere and we'll hear of someone discovering his body any day now."

"I don't know what your history is with him, or what he has against Mouse, but my own troubles with him extends well past simply taking his position as militia captain. Jeremy has similar past transgressions to worry about. I think if it weren't for my wariness caused by you and your bowlers, I would have been an easy target for him to get rid of long ago."

"Perhaps, if he isn't dead, we can remedy that if he should resurface," Olivia said. In truth, she didn't like Cavanaugh, but the actual wrong he'd done to her didn't pass beyond that. She also didn't have a clear picture of what angered Cavanaugh so much about Esme. The only explanation Olivia could come up with was that Cavanaugh had wanted to use all of the couriers for suicide bombings and someone had stopped him, in which case Esme would be a constant reminder of an embarrassment or public failure. Regardless, Olivia didn't have the slightest qualm about killing him to protect Esme.

"You've read my mind, Kingston. If the actual work of the thing bothers you though…"

"No, I'm sure I'll be up to the task when the time comes," Olivia replied. She'd never killed a man before. She'd fought Slark for years and served in the military even before, but an actual battle with other humans was something she'd never experienced. Killing a man she knew in cold blood wasn't an act of a soldier anyway and certainly wasn't something she'd learned in basic training. Something about the way Cavanaugh grabbed at Esme the night they were to mount the rescue for Claudia spoke of a strange, vitriolic hatred that Cavanaugh had for Esme. Combining that with the new, maddening adoration Olivia felt for Esme, and suddenly killing Cavanaugh seemed almost like a necessity.

"In that case, we'll have to rock-paper-scissors for the honor," Bruce said with a wink. It was a cavalier dealing of killing someone, but Olivia didn't think either of them would take the task lightly.

The ride out to the bridge held an element of normalcy. She and Bruce were fast becoming friends. What was once an alliance born out of necessity on Olivia's part and ambition on Bruce's quickly changed to true amicability. He'd come to collect her several times in the past few weeks for something or other regarding the city's defense and they usually shared a pleasant conversation on the way there or back. The talk of killing Cavanaugh put a pox on the evening for Olivia and even Bruce's fanciful interest about the Raven commandos couldn't penetrate her gloomy mood.

As they approached the bridge, burn barrels were being used to keep warm the patrols charged with watching over the Ravens. The shattered bridge was in a gentle sway, set to motion by the cold autumn winds off the Pacific and the lack of a full compliment of stabilizing wires to keep it from doing so.

Bruce dropped Olivia off at the checkpoint on the bridge's base where the toll booths used to be. She glanced to him to see if he meant to follow.

"They were pretty clear about not wanting to talk to me," Bruce said. "I could get some guards for you if you want, but I don't think you'll need them."

"I don't think so either," Olivia said, remembering clearly that Dylan's Voron Dagger squad could easily have killed her on the beach outside Crescent City, but instead chose to have a reasonably pleasant conversation. If the Raven women braved the bridge crossing just to speak with her, they likely didn't mean her any harm.

Olivia nestled her head down into the collar of her coat, plunged her hands in her pockets, and began the long walk down the bridge toward the collection of the dark figures huddled around the base of the nearest support tower. The bridge's gentle swinging was unnerving, but no more a challenge to navigate than the pitching and rolling deck of the Balclutha in heavy weather. Her mechanical leg, with its stability gyros and internal balances, aided immeasurably in keeping her on a straight line down the middle of the bridge.

Three women came away from the main group. The two women flanking the statuesque Captain Dylan Watson were armed with assault rifles, but the distinct tall, lanky Captain wasn't armed with anything but the knife on her battle harness. As Olivia neared the group, the moon broke free of the cloudy night and illuminated the bridge just enough to see the friendly smile on Dylan's lips.

"If it isn't the British sailor," Dylan said. "How has November treated you?"

Olivia forced a smile in return despite the fact that every wind shooting across the bridge cut through her hastily assembled outfit and the swaying of the bridge was increasingly unnerving the farther she went out onto it. She hadn't really heard anyone call a month by name in ages. They still had a concept of time, but which month they were in wasn't nearly as important as it once was. They were in autumn in the City of Broken Bridges and that was about as specific as anyone cared to be.

"As well as can be expected," Olivia said.

"That's not what our scouting reports say," Dylan said. "From what we've seen, your city is on the brink of falling and you've lost all your outposts."

Word from Gold Beach and Winchester Bay was spotty at best and nothing had come across the radios since the reports of the civilian fleets arriving. "What do you mean we've lost our outposts?" Olivia demanded.

"They weren't destroyed," Dylan said. "They're just under Raven rule now. I recognized the black, red, gray, and white ship you were sailing on when we arrived in Gold Beach. I mentioned your name, said we were friends, and they were all too happy to start flying the black, red, and white of the Raven flag. Seems fitting, don't you think?" Dylan tapped the patch on the shoulder of her uniform of a black, red, and white flag, similar to the Russian flag if the blue was replaced with black. "Once they saw how friendly we were, they told us they were concerned about Winchester Bay and we sent a team to secure the fishing village."

"You're colonizers," Olivia said through clenched teeth.

"That's a hypocritical accusation from a Brit," Dylan said with a little laugh. "But you're right. We are and we want forward positions on the west coast, especially since we learned the true source of Slark fuel."

"What we use isn't the same as their salvaged fuel..."

"All the better." Dylan took a step forward and Olivia tensed. The tall captain took off her beret to run her hand over her tightly braided hair. "You may not know this, and I probably shouldn't even be sharing intelligence with you, but the Slark are producing their own fuel again."

Olivia didn't need to ask how. The City of Broken Bridges had spread its fleets thin in the past six months. Patrols rarely went south anymore and never went as far as California Baja Sur which is where she suspected the Slark were already making themselves comfortable. With how much easier it was to use humanity's refineries rather than build their own up again, she did wonder why.

"Why?"

"We destroyed a third of their production fields and refineries for diesel fuel," Dylan said. "They couldn't run their war machine anymore on what they had left and they didn't know how to rebuild Bakersfield, so they started constructing Slark fuel refineries. The Ravens are down to barrel scrapings on the salvaged Slark fuel and the handful of intact oil fields we managed to find in west Texas aren't nearly enough to keep us going especially since we have almost no understanding of how oil refining works. The Slark must have known they were going to turn the tide as soon as they finished building their refineries."

"…and so they had to destroy the only city that knew how to make its own Slark fuel," Olivia finished for Dylan.

"Precisely."

"I'd thought they were being pushed by the Ravens."

"They all but rolled out the red carpet for us to cross northern California. We hit a wall of those creepy mutants almost immediately and then suddenly they vanished too."

"They rounded them up and herded them into us," Olivia said.

Dylan nodded, which quickly turned into a slight headshake. "That was the minority opinion of what they were doing among our military leadership. It seems the Slark are recovering from the devastating blow their military took in the cascade."

"The rise of the Gators," Olivia said.

Dylan smiled. "Claudia told you that, huh?"

"That brings us all the way back around to the real question of what do you want and why did you want to talk to me?" Olivia asked, wanting to change the topic from Claudia for any number of reasons.

"Your city is about to be reduced to rubble when the Slark get their full artillery compliment onto Alcatraz," Dylan said. "We're offering you a team, specifically my team, that can get a big enough bomb onto the island to make sure that doesn't happen."

"We've survived their bombardment so far," Olivia said, not wanting to divulge just yet that the City of Broken Bridges was predominantly subterranean.

"You haven't seen artillery like the kind they're setting up and they haven't targeted your wall yet."

Olivia hoped the shock of the realization didn't translate to her face, but she suspected it did. If they targeted the great wall and blew a hole in it, the three divisions of Slark troops waiting outside it would flood through and the city would be lost. What's more, she suspected Commander Marceau probably already figured this out and wasn't telling anyone what he planned to do about it.

"What do you want in exchange?" Olivia asked. Her voice sounded flat and emotionless in her own ears. She knew the price was going to be steep and she knew the military command of the city wouldn't pay it.

"The city, the secret to refining Slark fuel, and a list of the most competent women warriors in your ranks," Dylan said. "I'll save you the suspense—you and Claudia are already on the list."

"You don't mind asking for the sun, moon, and stars," Olivia said, already knowing Esme's name would find its way onto the list at some point as well. She might have avoided being named a competent war asset if the last few weeks hadn't seen a resurgence of the fame of Mouse.

"When you consider we offer continued existence, it doesn't seem like that much, now does it?" Dylan said.

"I can take it to our military council, but I can tell you right now what their answer will be." Olivia turned to walk away. Dylan covered the distance between them and caught Olivia by the arm.

"If you're concerned about Claudia, you don't need to be," she said. "Tell her the new White Queen is Alondra and that the newly promoted Red Bishop Bancroft has vouched for her. When San Francisco is in Raven hands, and it will be in Raven hands one way or the other, Bancroft will be in charge. See if Claudia doesn't strive to change minds after she hears that."

Olivia knew the name from Claudia's stories of Carson City. Bancroft and the Owl was the husband and wife duo who had begged help from Claudia in killing the Gator and their gratitude apparently wasn't spent yet. Olivia swallowed hard and nodded her understanding.

"You'd cut a dashing figure yourself in our uniform," Dylan said, adding a wink so subtle in its flirtation that Olivia doubted anyone who hadn't been targeted by it would even feel its weight.

Olivia knew she was blushing but she hoped Dylan couldn't see it in the moonlight, or, if she could, would chalk it up to the cold wind biting at Olivia's cheeks. Olivia allowed herself an inward chuckle at the thought of Hastings' empire being conquered by women he would have deemed unfit for combat. When Hastings reduced the female soldiers under his command to breeding stock, he'd burned every last bridge he had with Olivia. Now, in seeing another option for her sisters in arms, Olivia wanted to deliver the City of Broken Bridges to the Ravens.

Olivia met Dylan's gaze, mustering her strength to follow through with a treasonous declaration. "The Lazy Ravens have a friend in the City of Broken Bridges," she said, "and with a little time, they'll have an army of allies."

Chapter 31:
Called Bluffs.

Claudia listened in on the military council debating the Raven's offer. There wasn't a single person arguing they should take the deal and only her father was arguing temperance in how they responded. Claudia was surprised at how easy it was to find a vent in one of the adjoining rooms in the tower to listen at. She'd only missed the first few hours and it didn't sound like anything was going to be resolved before morning.

It took her awhile of eavesdropping to even figure out what the offer was. Slowly she pieced it together based off what people were railing against. Her father had actually called the rest of the council an "Anglo-centric herd of mules" at one point, which brought a grim smile to Claudia's face. He could be so French sometimes. He was fighting for a measured response, a counter offer at the very least, or some effort to bring the Ravens to a negotiation table. The rest of the council, which was mostly comprised of British officers left over from the flotilla and a mishmash of Americans, were almost entirely set on the course of telling the Ravens to go fuck themselves. Claudia knew that would be a mistake none of them would live to regret. The Ravens were born out of a particularly brutal branch of the Russian mafia. They were a government only in the sense that there wasn't really a government overseeing what they were doing anymore. There wasn't any voting, nobody represented anyone's interests above the Raven collective, and when something insulted the command structure, that something tended to die horribly. They wouldn't let the secret of Slark fuel die with the idiots in the other room.

Of course, if Claudia was being honest with herself about her former and probable future compatriots, they weren't any likelier to negotiate with her father if he brought them a counteroffer. He was making good points though, and it wasn't her place to inform them that their entire meeting was an exercise in futility.

It took her awhile to figure out what they meant when they kept repeating the number 4.5 million. Apparently the command structure of the British military made several estimations of what would be left after the cascade and invasion. These survived longer than Hastings, and her father apparently made the top secret information public knowledge among the military council. Four and a half million was all there was supposed to be of humanity on the entire continent of North America. The estimate was conservative, but also seven years old. Claudia could update that number with information from the Ravens that would make it significantly lower. They kept insisting the Ravens wouldn't sacrifice nearly 100,000 people just to get the Slark fuel. They insisted the City of Broken Bridges was the largest remaining city on the entire continent and should be given deference for that very reason. Claudia couldn't help but chuckle at this. The Salt Lake City separatists had thought much the same thing up until their entire budding civilization was burned and enslaved by the Ravens.

Then the conversation turned back to the cascade and the ruins of mankind that were left over. This perked Claudia up. She didn't know much of the story since the Ravens didn't know much. She knew more about what was happening in the east since the cascade than they seemed to, but she didn't know how they came to be where they were. The smartest scientific minds, the best soldiers, and the greatest military leaders that could be assembled from every nation were brought together to make one last ditch effort to give humanity a glimmer of hope for survival—this was as far as she knew into the story.

"They knew that no national interest, no country could be put above the survival of our species," her father said. "They burned it all down, sacrificing themselves and everything we ever knew in the hope that the seeds of civilization left over might once again grow. One percent. That was all that was supposed to survive on both sides. If that one percent is scattered to the wind, arguing with each other, and ignoring the threat that drove us to destroy what took us ten thousand years to build, then they may as well have killed us all and let some smarter species rise up to take our place."

This Claudia hadn't known. She hadn't known that her father carried such horrible knowledge all this time. She knew things were dire to create the cascade, to burn most of the eastern seaboard, almost all of Europe, and who knows how many cities in Asia just to even the odds, but she didn't know it was done so deliberately with such clear knowledge of how damaging the nuclear base EMP weapons would be. She always assumed the people in charge of pressing the button that ended the world were taking a calculated risk that might leave hope for their own survival, the survival of countries and governments. She didn't know they were planning, all along, to slaughter most of humanity in the hope of preserving an improbable future for the species. The knowledge made her sick to her stomach and she assumed it was the same nausea her father carried all the time. One percent repeated in her head. They knew before they did it that one percent would be all that was left, but they did it anyway. No wonder he thought of his people as so astoundingly valuable.

"Extinction was the other option," her father said, "and it is true now as it was then. We must make hard, even distasteful choices to ensure the survival of humanity as they did."

To hear her father speak with such passion and resolve, it made Claudia believe, but it didn't seem to make a dent in the tired men of the military council who remained convinced the Ravens were bluffing. Bluffing—it was an interesting thing to imagine Ekaterina doing. Claudia knew the Black Queen to feint, but bluffing just wasn't her style. They would find out soon enough, Claudia surmised, when they were dangling from the ends of ropes as traitors to humanity. If she acted quickly, got some time alone to work on Dylan or Bancroft when they took the city, she could probably spare her father's life. His value was undeniable, even more so if she could convince him to burn Hastings' papers so the only copy of the intelligence would be in his head.

Remarkably, as the sun was rising, her father gained enough traction with the exhausted council to send a reasonable response. Olivia arrived to take the message. They told her to tell the Ravens that they seriously considered the offer, but ultimately would prefer to try to handle the Alcatraz problem on their own. Once the bay was retaken, they would negotiate with the Ravens to begin large scale production and exchange of manmade Slark fuel. Olivia seemed as surprised as Claudia that their reply was so measured.

Claudia waited until the boardroom cleared out and then snuck around the corner to find her father organizing paperwork on a table that looked like it had spent a hard night with angry men. Claudia waited until he noticed her.

"You listened in, I assume," her father said without looking up from his task of cleaning up his files. "It was a game you played when you were younger—eavesdropping and spying."

"It's gotten me into trouble before," Claudia said.

"A fact that never dissuaded you from doing something more than once," her father replied.

"What plan do you have to retake Alcatraz?" Claudia asked.

"A dangerous, flawed plan that will likely cost us dearly in lives we can't afford." Her father stopped his work, searched the organized pile he'd created, and slipped out a folder to set aside for Claudia to look at. She crossed the room and tentatively opened the file.

"Fire boats, bombardment, and a distraction assault on the amassed army..." Claudia gleaned from the plan it had a low chance of true success. The number of fireboats was too few, the distraction relied heavily on the militia to hold the beach in the real army's absence, and even the troop numbers seemed a little slapdash as some descriptions were incomplete like an ambiguous listing for "Kingston's contribution" without further information. The truth was the City of Broken Bridges didn't actually have the ordinance to blow up Alcatraz. It was rock, cement, and steel fortified from the inside to keep prisoners in at one point and then armored on the exterior after the war when it was used as a fortress in the bay. The plan looked like it might succeed in destroying a few artillery placements on the island, prevent a shipment of the larger guns, and slow the Slark plans down, but nothing about it would prevent the Slark from simply trying again later. "The council should know better than to think this plan will accomplish much."

"The council does not believe the Ravens are the force you say they are," her father explained. "Too much of Hastings' teachings settled in with them. They see women as cavemen saw women—it is an old ignorance that blinds them."

"So you will sacrifice men to attempt a temporary solution to a permanent problem?"

Her father slapped his hands on the table and finally looked at her with a ferocity in his eyes that belied what she thought was a dying fire after a long night of burning. "Do I have to convince you now too?"

"No, Papa." Claudia shied away from the topic.

They stood in silence on opposite sides of the table for a time. Claudia had nearly forgotten what kind of anger resided beneath her father's judicious surface. He didn't like being questioned and he'd spent an entire night being roughly objected to by men he thought his inferiors. He didn't need his daughter participating in the same foolishness, and she didn't like having him mad at her.

"I would volunteer for the distraction team," Claudia said, regaining an iota of her former defiance that somehow drained from her whenever she was near her father.

He clapped his hands together, not even close enough to her face to truly be dangerous, and held them there, all ten fingers pointed at her. She flinched, far more than would be reasonable for such a simple loud noise and abrupt movement.

"You are not ready," he growled, "and I do not have so many daughters that I could throw them away to indulge their foolishness."

"But, Papa…"

"I have spoken on the matter," he bellowed. "You will remain in the tower until it is over for good or ill."

Tears threatened at the corners of Claudia's eyes and she willed them to remain in place until after she took her leave. She couldn't let her father see her cry. "Fine, are we done here?" Claudia asked, her father nodded, and she managed to clear from the room before the tears rolled down her cheeks.

The tense anger and embarrassment roiling beneath the surface felt so impotent against the world. In one conversation, he'd reduced her to the small, weak child she truly was in comparison to him. All her years of survival, fighting, and soldiering paled in comparison to what he was. He would always be a commander and she would always be his dutiful daughter. She could never be the warrior he was simply because her gender would not allow it. He claimed it was old ignorances about gender preventing his military council from taking the Ravens seriously, but he was truly no better despite being more knowledgeable. She wasn't angry at him because he misjudged her; she was angry at him because he'd judged her correctly and told her so.

She stormed up to one of the higher, completely uninhabited levels. She sank into a quiet corner. Shortly, she was joined by Roger who slunk in as though he too had recently been yelled at. He crawled along his belly to her and gently rested his muzzle on her leg, licking his lips and looking up at her expectantly. She gently caressed the scruff of his neck. The anger drained from her. When she calmed enough to think rationally again, she remembered back on something strange in the plan. A list of assets for the diversion assault included something explained only as "Kingston's contribution" without data on strength of numbers or combat capability description. Claudia assumed it meant Olivia Kingston and her Clockwork Warriors, but if that were the case, it would have included the numbers she was adding like all the other platoon strength information. "Kingston's contribution" apparently wasn't human and didn't need to be numbered.

"Could it mean a Transcended?" Claudia asked Roger.

Roger responded by wagging his tail.

✝

Claudia awoke with a start to the sound of heavy cannons firing. She couldn't remember falling asleep in the abandoned storage room with Roger curled up at her side. It wasn't good news, although it wasn't unexpected either. Her father's plan could happen at any moment, relying entirely on the Slark trying to move artillery out to Alcatraz. Her waking mind was satisfied with the explanation, but something nagged at her. She couldn't be sure how long she'd slept; however, there was no way it was long enough to actually set the plan in motion.

The men guarding the beachhead were supposed to be revolved out of their positions and replaced with Bruce Coffey's militia. They were then to muster with other elements of the army and take the far west exit under the wall to come at the Slark's main force outside in a flanking maneuver meant to draw attention away from the bay. All of that would take a day at least. They couldn't be more than a third of the way done, which meant the artillery shelling was starting sixteen hours too early. Her musings on timetables and troop mustering failures were cut short when she heard the buzz of Slark weapons between the thunder of cannon fire.

There shouldn't be any Slark weapons firing on the inside of the wall.

Claudia leapt from her position of slumped against the wall. Roger jumped to as well. She raced to the window. The thunder wasn't from cannon fire—it was exploding mortars and Olivia's tanks detonating. The Slark must have been waiting for an opening to invade and the rotation of army regulars for militia was the perfect breech. Through the haze of war and extreme distance, she picked out the gray, multi-armed aliens already on land. Claudia raced from the room with Roger quick at her heels.

She burst into Dr. Gatling's lab and found him readying for an influx of wounds to flesh and mechanical body parts. He didn't even seem to notice the out of breath sniper and her canine companion.

"I need my rifle," Claudia said.

"I'm under orders not to give you a weapon," Dr. Gatling said without looking up from what he was doing, which appeared to be placing various lubricants and pain killers into syringes. Claudia idly hoped he wouldn't mix up the two.

"Then keep your back turned while I take one since you weren't ordered to stop me from stealing." Claudia crossed the room to where Dr. Gatling kept the front inventory of his armory, her eyes already locked on her sniper rifle in the rack on the end.

"Actually, I was," Dr. Gatling said.

Claudia's hand froze inches from the gun.

"But after a five minute conversation with the chaplain I can understand why you didn't want to continue your therapy," Dr. Gatling said. "I still think you're an emotional train wreck, probably mentally unstable by now, and worst of all, you're full of accursed Marceau blood, but if I started pulling people out of combat for those reasons, there wouldn't be anyone left to fight, including your father. Take the gun, go with Cthulhu, and give those gray bastards hell."

Claudia grabbed her rifle, briefly considered asking who Cthulhu was, but then thought better of it, and ran from the room.

Roger didn't struggle at all to keep up with her as she ran across the fields and hills toward Telegraph Hill and the steep incline up to Coit Tower. If she could find some rocks or rubble to hide among, the shots would be long, but with an excellent line of sight. A mile or under as the crow flies from her emplacement to her targets—with a normal rifle and an above average sniper, this would be unimaginably difficult. But she had a technological marvel as a weapon and she was a superb markswoman.

Roger barked and urged her up the hill as she labored to keep up her pace once the grade became too steep. By the time she crested the ruins on the hill, the sounds of combat were closer and she imagined she wouldn't have to make any shots over a half a mile. She found a perfect position behind the trunk of a tree, lying out on a slab of concrete that was jutting from the shattered earth at a thirty degree angle. The tentacle pod on her rifle found a solid grip on the edge of the cement and she took her first survey of the battlefield below.

They were through the defenses and pushing hard to solidify their hold on the beach. The militia wasn't in full retreat, but they were on their heels and losing ground fast. Claudia scanned the human lines first to find her father or Olivia. The army regulars were turning back from their mustering point well to the rear to create a new line of defense and even gathering for a counterattack under her father's direct command. Olivia's Clockwork Warriors on their miniature tanks were trying to reinforce and provide covering fire for the militia's retreat, although it looked to be costing them dearly and she couldn't find Olivia among them with her cursory scan.

Claudia turned her attention to the Slark line with a cold certainty hardening her resolve. She started first with the mobile turrets giving the retreating militia such fits. The heavy, repeating weapons sat on the backs of smaller crawlers that looked a little like spiders. It took two Slark to fire the weapons effectively and two to drive although they were nearly unstoppable over almost any terrain. The Ravens typically targeted them at the outset of any conflict with rocket propelled grenades; apparently the soldiers of the City of Broken Bridges hadn't figured this out yet.

Claudia centered her reticule over the first gunner's center mass, adjusted to ticks over and one up for the wind, and fired. The shot struck high on the alien's chest. He jerked and spasmed a few painful times, trying valiantly to hold onto the gun's controls, but ultimately ended up falling backward off the spider-pod. She clicked in another round, found the second gunner, similar to a human reloader but with more responsibility in angling the gun, and fired before he could even get out of his crouched position. Her shot, after making another set of adjustments based on her first, punctured the Slark high on the upper shoulder and tore a satisfying green chunk of flesh off near his neck when it exited.

She continued her grim work of striking from a distance. She found a target, calmed her breathing, steadied her aim, watched for shifts in the wind patterns, fired, and repeated the whole process again and again. She ticked off her misses as rare until she'd counted out nine of every ten rounds landing on target, seven of ten resulting in a kill on the first shot. She had their spider-pods unmanned and useless within twenty minutes of work.

Her gun was heating up in her hands and her nerves were beginning to fray. The Slark pushed forward, which made her shots easier, but also put them closer and closer to the base of the insurmountable hill she was on. They might not be able to climb up to get her, but she'd seen Slark bombard an entire city grid with artillery to get rid of one sniper—shelling the hill she was hidden on wouldn't be a stretch if they pieced together where she was. Dr. Gatling's guns were remarkable in two importantly clandestine ways when compared to traditional firearms: they were a fraction as loud and boasted no muzzle flash to speak of.

Before she could begin her search for Gators among the Slark ranks, something strange happened. Two knives out of the human force began cutting two bloody swaths into the Slark position. Claudia focused back on the human counterattack to find two surprising sources of the pushback. The resurgence in the south followed an unimaginable spear tip in the Transcended she'd seen die and resurrect with the strange proclivity to see humans. The Transcended was the unstoppable killing machine everyone always said they would be if they could be convinced to join the war. Slark guns and explosives were of little use against its armored skin and it was outfitted with an astonishing array of weapons that seemed to fire accurately in every direction at all times. The bronze juggernaut rolled through the Slark as though they were of little concern. People had likened Transcended to gods and the one that finally joined the war certainly seemed to boast the wrath of one.

Claudia shifted her focus to the other front, expecting to find a second Transcended, but instead spotted her father, leading from the front. She'd never seen anyone fight the way he did. She knew he was an exceptional soldier before the war even began. He was decorated, first in his class at every training series, and spoken of in hushed, reverent tones by other Special Forces soldiers, but now he was a warrior of fabled capability. He moved faster than she would have thought a man could move across the muddy field, found targets she would have thought outside his field of vision, and wielded the massive machinegun as though it were little more trouble to wield than a garden hose. He skipped from cover to cover, feinted, gave ground, redoubled his attack, raced through openings in the Slark line, and devastated their ranks whenever they showed the slightest hesitation. She thought she should record what he was doing to show to the Ravens.

Instead, she focused on helping ease his path. She traced the likely area he would head, and looked for hard targets. She found a Gator at long last, but before she could fire on it, her father had riddled it with bullets and was racing over its blood splattered corpse.

"So, that's how it is going to be," she muttered to herself, moving farther out to find another target her father couldn't possibly reach before she fired.

A Gator, recognizable by his massive size and height, was directing reinforcements from a series of landing craft to shore up a failing defensive position. She faintly spotted the blue light lines of a communicator on the back shoulder of his improvised body armor. The beams were leading back to the ships and relaying out to the island. Claudia catalogued the information as interesting, but not particularly pertinent to the current fight. She wanted desperately to blow the Gator's head clean from its body, but didn't think she could manage it at over a mile's distance. She thought of the astounding feat her father was performing though in defense of the city and decided to try. If he could match the killing power of a Transcended, surely she could cleave one head from one body.

She took a deep, calming breath and held it, willing her heart to quiet to an unobtrusive thump only once a second. The wind died out enough for a single shot, a tiny window of stagnant air across a fairly windy battleground. She gave the trigger the gentlest of squeezes, prayed to Apollo or Cthulhu or whoever might be listening, and watched as the shot landed perfectly on the top of the Gator's muzzle, ricocheted off something hard inside its head, and exploded out the side, taking most of the Gator's skull with it.

Without their commander, the reinforcements looked lost and rattled. Then, a few moments later, when her father's force reached them, they looked dead.

The triumph of the moment was tempered by the realization that, while they repelled the Slark assault, it cost them dearly and certainly spoiled any possible chance of affecting their plan now. Her father and the Transcended were mopping up the beach when the sun began to set, casting the shadow of the hills of old San Francisco across the bloody field.

Claudia slipped from her sniper's nest, achy, tired, dehydrated, and starving. To her surprise, when she scaled the edge of the embankment she'd slid down, Roger was still there, standing guard over her exit. He hadn't been lying down only to stand at her return, but stood proper vigil, only turning his head from his guard duties to see her when she returned.

"Good boy," Claudia said by way of reward. Maybe the next time she faced a Gator using hunting hounds, she would have a canine sidekick of her own to even the odds.

Getting back down the hill was less time consuming and exhausting than scaling it was. She circled around wide to come in well from behind to survey the total damage as she walked the field. Their battle-ready forces were dwindling as it stood and she wanted to estimate how many they'd lost in regaining a defensive position they shouldn't have lost in the first place. This was when she heard the resumption of battle.

No new Slark boats were landing, the wall wasn't breached to the south, and there certainly wasn't enough of a Slark force left over from the original assault to warrant so much gunfire. She raced over one hill, leaping over bodies as she went, Roger ran at her side. As she crested the last hill before the dip down into the old wharf, she spotted the source of combat. The Transcended was chasing a small, dark-haired woman across the battlefield and men were hurling themselves at the violent, metal god to stop it from catching her.

Claudia slid in the mud, coming to rest behind a sandbag wall. She trained her rifle first on the source of the chase, only to find Esme ducking and dodging as the Transcended hurled everything it had at her. She was fast and intuitive in avoiding fire. The men assaulting the Transcended were helping some, but they were too easily felled to truly harm the crazed monstrosity.

Claudia targeted the Transcended. Human bullets weren't doing much better at piercing its armor than the Slark. A retaliatory strike by her father's squad, this time properly led from a distance by the no-doubt exhausted commander, managed to slow the Transcended, and Esme finally slipped away into what Claudia could only guess was an entrance into the under city that only a handful of people knew about. Claudia sighted in on the only soft spot she could think of—

the blue orb in the robot's massive shoulder. It was guarded somewhat since she'd last seen it, with a few chunks of metal mesh around the edges, leaving only an apple sized exposure in the middle. Her first shot, taken in haste, struck off the armored edges and succeeded only in telling the Transcended something potentially dangerous had located its weak point. The metal juggernaut turned its attention to Claudia and charged, scattering mud and dead bodies as it barreled up the hill.

She snapped in another round, sighted, held her breath, and fired. The shot hit low and to the right, bouncing off the metal mesh. Soon it would be in firing range to retaliate and she wasn't nearly as fast as Esme and certainly didn't have her stamina. She had time enough for one more shot, maybe two if she snapped off a wild prayer, before the Transcended would obliterate her hiding spot. She could see the weapons powering up and a swarm of red laser sight dots painted her as she brought the rifle to bear, found the blue orb in her crosshairs, and fired, anticipating the Transcended's gait as it broke free of the smoky haze collected across a low point in the battlefield. The shot hit home, shattered the glass, and spilled a stream of blue gel from the bullet wound. The Transcended died for a second time in a way befitting a human, staggering forward weakly through the mortal wound before crumpling forward with an arm pinned beneath.

Claudia promptly threw up from the stress and fear colliding with her already knotted stomach. Not having eaten that day, it was all acid and bile. Roger gave her a questioning look. "Don't eat that," Claudia croaked when she was done.

Her father was at her side shortly after. He helped her from the foxhole she'd hidden in and gripped her in a hug that would be her only wound for the day when her father left two tiny bruises on the backs of her shoulders from the overzealous and adrenaline-fueled hug.

She followed him down the hill as he stormed toward the fallen Transcended, shotgun in hand, meaning to do it more harm if it so much as shuddered. Claudia felt safer walking a step behind him, remarkably so after seeing what he was truly capable of on in combat. He was an ancient Greek hero, an Achilles figure among already battle-hardened veterans, and now she knew why he was shown such respect in the City of Broken Bridges.

"Get it rolled over," her father commanded of the men approaching the fallen Transcended with anxious, mincing steps. "I mean to see what is inside this thing once and for all."

Getting the Transcended rolled over onto its back was a Herculean task, requiring a tow chain and one of Olivia's tractors turned tank, to finally get it moved. Muddy and still leaking the peculiar blue gel, it required cutting torches to get through the armor seamlessly incorporated into the robot's shell around its shattered blue orb. Claudia and her father looked on as the men finally pried away the plating, broke out the last of the glass with a hammer, and began scooping out the remaining gel with their bare hands. The three workers surrounding the Transcended recoiled in slow, muted horror at what they found inside. They looked to Claudia's father as they backed away.

Claudia and her father stepped forward together, climbed the Transcended's arm, and gazed into the gaping hole in its shoulder where the blue orb once was. A vaguely human form, stripped of skin and most of its flesh, lay twisted in the bottom of the hole. A perfect bullet hole cracked the skull above the left eye socket which was a nest of wires in lieu of an eyeball.

To Claudia's shock and dismay, and likely everyone else's around her too, her father reached into the Transcended's wound, grasped the skull in his mighty fist, and tore it free both from the wires and braces holding it in place but also the remains of its spinal column and neck. He held the modified head in front of him as though he were about to address it in a Hamlet fashion. He glared hard at the wires, tattered flesh, and the blue goop still clinging to the head and his hand. He stared hard into the bullet hole that clearly was its demise as if the answer might be hidden within.

He stormed out of the gathered halo of concerned and curious soldiers with the head in one hand and his shotgun in the other.

"Papa, where are you going?" Claudia asked.

"*Pour obtenir des réponses de professeur Kingston,*" he said in a tone so cold Claudia shivered inwardly.

Chapter 32:
The Broken Machines of War.

Claudia caught up with her father in time to join him on the elevator down to the sanctuary of the Keepers. He'd said he was going to get answers from Kingston and she judged from the twitching muscles in his jaw that he was likely to turn violent if he didn't so much as care for the phrasing of one of the answers. The wire-riddled skull was still clenched in his hand at his side, dripping blue goop onto the elevator's metal floor as they descended into the earth. She wondered if he knew he still had it.

She couldn't think of a thing to say to him that wouldn't make him angrier. The potential harm to her the Transcended posed was likely only part of the rage. Professor Kingston had sent the Transcended into their midst, and clearly her father was holding Kingston responsible for every death and injury caused by the mechanical creature when it went insane. Claudia got the feeling from the head in her father's hand that Professor Kingston probably also lied to her father about what the Transcended really were since he seemed determined to carry proof to the Professor's door.

Upon arrival on the lowest level, after winding their way through the blackened tunnels in silence, they came upon the main chamber above the thermal vent. Few students roamed the stone walkways and no Transcended were anywhere to be seen. Professor Kingston beckoned to them from across a causeway before vanishing into an arched door in the natural rock wall. The fact that Claudia's father was holding a mangled, blue head didn't seem to perplex the handful of Keepers and students they passed.

They entered the doorway Professor Kingston vanished down, finding a winding stairway into a deeper recess. The pathway was large, much larger than would be necessary even for Transcended to use it. The walls also showed signs of metal scrapings in the rocks, which was odd considering how smoothly the Transcended shaped rock when they cut it. They exited the passage into a large room dominated by the skeletal remains of what looked like an alien submarine. Professor Kingston was standing with his back to them and the doorway, hands folded behind his back, gazing up at the derelict spacecraft.

"I think it's time you met our wayward traveler that has taught us so much," Professor Kingston said, gesturing to a chamber near the top of the vaguely fish-shaped vessel. In a holding chamber, similar to the one in the shoulder of the Transcended, was a desiccated Slark corpse with wires jutting from its limbs and eye sockets to connect it to the ruined chamber surrounding it.

"You told me it was under control," her father bellowed at Professor Kingston, not nearly as interested in the marvel before him as Claudia was.

"I told you it was as safe as it could be made," Professor Kingston replied. "Desperation colored how you interpreted that statement."

Her father hurled the skull at the floor near Professor Kingston's feet. The blue head bounced and rolled in a meandering manner, finally coming to rest slightly in front and to the right of Professor Kingston. The Professor looked down at it without alarm.

"Who was that?" Commander Marceau demanded.

"Inspector Cavanaugh," Professor Kingston explained. "He was of the original group who found the spacecraft wreckage and helped us bring it here. He kept our secret for so long that I actually forgot he knew it. Then, when Feinstein died, Cavanaugh was suddenly at our doorstep making demands in exchange for his silence."

"Who is Feinstein?" Claudia asked, not wanting to step on her father's interrogation, but needing an answer she already dreaded she knew.

"The Transcended you saw die on the beach in the Slark missile attack was Keeper Feinstein," Professor Kingston explained casually. "We think he was planning on building an aqueduct."

"You turn people into those monstrosities?!" Claudia said, her voice becoming shrill.

"It is the next form of evolution," Professor Kingston said, finally turning to face his interrogators. "People work for years to become worthy of their ascension. They build their shells with care and must display a mental discipline and moral clarity worthy of being lifted to the next level of life."

"Inspector Cavanaugh didn't seem all that mentally disciplined or morally clear and he didn't build the shell," Commander Marceau said. "You scraped out the remains of Feinstein and shoved Cavanaugh in."

Professor Kingston sighed and looked down at some minor flaw in the stone floor. "I was pressured from all sides to provide support from the Transcended. We'd never had one die before. We didn't really know what to do with Feinstein's shell or his body. Cavanaugh offered to become the first warrior Transcended ever in exchange for never telling anyone what was really going on down here. It seemed like a single solution for two problems."

Claudia's stomach did a somersault. Olivia was one of the people who pressured her father into the catastrophic decision. Claudia knew she could never be told what her father had done or why, in part, he had done it. As distasteful as the entire thing was, the incident would need to be swept under the rug for the good of the entire city. She had no idea what they would tell the Ravens when they inevitably took the city.

The rage was gone from her father and she could tell the answers he'd sought were far more devastating for him than he expected. She hadn't heard him pressure Professor Kingston about the Transcended, but from his body language, she could tell he was weighed down by his part in all of it. She placed her hand on his arm and smiled weakly up to him when he looked to her.

"How do you even know how to do this?" Claudia asked of Professor Kingston, taking over the questioning from her drained father.

"This is why I wanted you to meet the traveler, which is what we've been calling him." Professor Kingston again gestured to the Slark corpse in the ship resting against the far wall. "We found the wreckage in the earliest days after the cascade and we brought him down to the caves only a few of us knew about to study his secrets. As we unlocked the secrets of the ship, our knowledge of robotics jumped forward a thousand years. Their technology didn't survive the purge, but we were able to build simulacrums of it and that is how the Transcended came to be."

The Professor motioned for them to join him in his slow, reverent approach on the mostly dismantled ship. He stood a few feet below the compartment holding the nearly mummified Slark corpse. It lacked skin and sensory organs as Cavanaugh had, but it seemed a little more intact than the human skeletal remains in the dead Transcended, which only had a thin layer of tissue on the bones.

"He isn't like the foot soldiers and laborers you know," Professor Kingston said. "His head is larger by nearly two-thirds, his arms are longer and thinner, and there are no ocular nerve endings. Don't you see what that means?"

Claudia and her father shook their heads.

"He was born to be this!" Professor Kingston exclaimed. "We select our Transcended from the worthiest, the smartest, the most creative, and enlightened people we can find, but the Slark grow theirs in genetically altered embryos. The traveler hatched and was immediately hooked to the ship that would be his true body for his entire life. He saw the stars and the cosmos as no living thing could. He flew through space as a fish swims the sea or a bird flies through the air. This higher form of Slark wasn't just how they got to earth, it was probably how they even found us. What's more, I think they sent scout ships and I think we intercepted at least one."

"Like the Roswell autopsy?" Commander Marceau scoffed.

"Nothing that old," Professor Kingston said. "It would have been recent, a few years at most. Didn't it seem strange to you that we just happen to have a weapon capable of wiping out an advanced alien invasion force in the middle of a war we were losing badly that was less than a year old?"

Claudia could see the realization come over her father's face, but she didn't follow the epiphany that apparently was already part of Professor Kingston and her father's knowledge.

"What did you figure out, Papa?" she asked.

"If they captured a scout ship with one of these things in it, they would have thought all Slark were cyborgs for lack of a better word," her father said. "The EMP weapons were meant to wipe out a species believed to be partially robotic."

"Precisely!" Professor Kingston said. "They didn't learn until after the invasion began that these Transcended forms were only the leadership and thinkers of the species. The flesh and blood Slark foot soldiers were still the bulk of the population, which is why they added the nuclear radiation and firestorm elements to the cascade. They didn't have time enough to formulate a more targeted weapon as we were on the brink of extinction already and the combined weight of the United States and her allies had already spent nearly all the resources they could muster in building the cascade in the first place."

"They built the cascade before the invasion even happened?" Claudia asked.

"Probably," Professor Kingston said, "but just barely. The modifications to add nuclear weapons, strengthened by Slark technology robbed from ships, were likely an un-researched and unproven plan done after humanity became a cornered and wounded animal. The existential and ethical crisis the scientists who worked it must have faced...remarkable" Professor Kingston trailed off and for a moment Claudia could see the philosophy professor he once was, marveling at the inner workings of human thought from his lofty, academic perch.

Her father sighed and clenched his jaw again. "You have to destroy the empty shell and you cannot make any more Transcended."

"Nonsense," Professor Kingston protested.

"Papa, we can't afford to throw away something so potentially valuable," Claudia said. Both her father and Professor Kingston looked at her in shock at what side she came down on when it came to the issue.

"Cavanaugh went insane from the stimulus in part because he was probably insane when we put him into the shell and partially because his mind wasn't capable of handling the massive influx of information," Professor Kingston said. "The mistake was mine, and I will answer for it, but that doesn't mean the process is dangerous. The flaw was always in humanity in Cavanaugh's weakness and my rush to judgment. My own ascension will be pushed back years because of my part in this."

"Wait, you're planning on becoming one of them?" Claudia asked. "What about Olivia?"

"It is the goal of all Keepers to transcend someday and Olivia will lose her father to time and decay regardless. I do this for her so I might build a better, safer world for her as is the expressed goal of all Keepers who undergo ascension. We have an oath that explicitly says this and it is programmed into the shells themselves. Because Cavanaugh did not believe in any of it, forgoing the ritual entirely, he was not soft or hard coded to be an egalitarian—what soldier truly could be?"

Claudia didn't need to point out the obvious insanity of what the Professor was saying. He was too far gone to see it and her father likely didn't need her help catching that the Keepers were all completely off the deep end. Still, Claudia was trying to amass bargaining chips to exchange when the Ravens took a superior position within the city and there was a treasure trove miles below the surface if she could figure out how to use it all.

"Fine," her father grumbled. "We will split the difference. The shell will be returned to the sanctuary, but a moratorium is ordered on creating new Transcended until the peninsula is secured again."

"It goes without saying that the secrecy must remain as much as possible," Claudia said, thinking again of what the information might do to Olivia.

"That'll be a difficult prospect considering how many men saw me rip most of a human head from the body of one of those things," her father said.

"When the Ravens land, and they'll have to now, there will be a compelling distraction," Claudia said. "We're all about to have a much bigger and much more immediate problem."

†

Olivia was pulled from the wreckage of her tank in better shape than she would have thought possible considering the blast obliterated the entire center of her formation, centered on her tank. The Greek of all people was the first to grasp her reaching hand and drag her from the twisted, burning metal. He was burned and bleeding as well, but in fine spirits otherwise.

"The blast threw me from the tank. I landed in the nice soft mud over there." He pointed in the direction of a patch of mud twenty or so yards away where there was indeed a large, Greek sized impact crater as evidence for his landing.

Olivia, aside from being thoroughly shaken and dinged up, felt fine. She tried to stand, but her mechanical leg came apart at the knee, raining gears and widgets from the gaping hole where her lower leg should have been. Maybe it was Esme's drawings that made her mechanical limb suddenly seem beautiful or maybe it was the trauma of losing her leg all over again, regardless of the source, Olivia burst into tears at seeing the tattered remains of her mechanical leg falling apart fast before her eyes.

"Where are Alfie and the rest of the crew?" Olivia asked through her tears.

The Greek hauled her well away from the wreckage before he set her down in a makeshift foxhole lined with sandbags, several of which were punctured and bleeding their grimy sand across the muddy ground in front. He sat down hard beside her in the little alcove as they waited for aid. He dabbed at a few oozing cuts and burns along his arms and a particularly bad scrape under his wide chin. His reluctance to answer was answer enough, although he added a small shake of his head all the same. That made sense to Olivia. If he only survived by being blown free of his gunner position and she only survived by losing a limb, albeit a mechanical one, then it was extremely unlikely anyone else would have made it.

The battlefield seemed to be returning to a state of normalcy after the botched changing of the guard. Medics were moving among the wounded, soldiers were returning to their posts, and combat engineers were repairing defensive positions as best they could. Olivia strained her neck to look up over the sandbag alcove to find Esme and her bobbing dark braid as she ran messages among the troops. She spotted other runners, lithe women and small, agile men, racing down new paths as the battle had torn down old routes, but she didn't spot Esme among them.

"Where is Esme?" Olivia asked.

The Greek shrugged his massive shoulders and shook his head. "The flying and landing rattled my brains a bit. I take too much time figuring out I am not dead to see how the battle end. Then, when my head work again, I come find you."

"Find her, and if you can't find her, find Bruce Coffey and see if he can help you," Olivia said. When the Greek looked at her with concern, she pushed his shoulder to no appreciable effect. "Go, I'll be fine."

The Greek stood on shaky, tree-trunk legs, and took off in his strange waddle run that was remarkably quick despite the power-walk look it had. She watched him go for a time until he vanished into several of the large groups of troops moving about. A combat medic team spotted her a moment after and she waved them over.

They hoisted her into the bed of a truck heading up to the tower alongside a dozen other wounded. The old army rig bounced and jostled them all the way up the muddy, rutted slope before the battlefield's muck gave way to a proper trail. Even then, for the first few dozen yards, the truck flung great hunks of mud from its tires as it tried to fully shake free of the mire it emerged from.

The other wounded around Olivia were in much worse shape. The wound she suffered was one that wouldn't threaten her life. She couldn't walk, but she wasn't likely to bleed to death on the back of the rattling old truck. The wounded around her had no such luck in which body parts were blown from them. None of them were her Clockwork Warriors originally, but, judging from some of their current wounds, they would be if they survived.

Civilian volunteers at the tower were waiting and ready to aid the medics in transporting the wounded into the safety of the tower. The chaos within hadn't hit its full stride yet as Olivia was among one of the first groups of wounded to be hauled from the field, although she suspected a second battle would soon be waged in the operating rooms and expanded hospital to save the injured from death. She was quickly looked over by a male triage nurse who had sharp blue eyes and a thick, muscular neck. He deemed her green card and set her aside in a waiting area for officers with minor wounds.

Olivia sat in the side room on a surplus army cot with no mattress. The other five officers in the room, scattered among the twenty or so cots, were all lying down, trying to catch up on sleep or at least appeared to be. Olivia couldn't even force herself to rest until she knew Esme was okay. She sat up as the only defiant action she could take.

Eventually, Dr. Gatling came down to find her, no doubt having received word she was among the wounded. He wheeled into the room on his elevated chair, wiping his hands clean of some mechanical grime or other with a clean rag. He clicked his tongue at seeing the state of her leg. As he rolled up to the side of her cot, he made a quick, blasphemous sign of the cross as he was a devout atheist, and shook his head.

"That leg is done for," Dr. Gatling said.

Olivia let out a strangled, stressed laugh. "That's the same bloody thing you said to me when I lost it the first time," she said. "Your bedside manner hasn't gotten any better after all these years?"

"No, and I don't suspect it ever will," Dr. Gatling said. "You'll be on crutches, maybe with an antebellum peg-prosthetic if I can find one, but I can of course fit you with another leg eventually."

"Splendid, I'll take the crutches now if it's all the same to you, and I would appreciate if you rebuilt this leg rather than start from scratch," Olivia said, scooting to the edge of the cot as though her departure was imminent.

"Got your medical degree without telling me? I should have liked to come to your graduation, Dr. Kingston," Dr. Gatling snarked. "You'll wait until you're medically cleared to leave and I'll do what I damn well like when it comes to restoring your limb." He pushed a lever on the side of his chair to lower the hydraulics enough to get a closer look at her ruined mechanical leg all the same. He prodded the stump with a few fingers, popped open a dented panel, and let out a frustrated sigh. "You realize this leg probably saved your life. If it were still made of flesh and blood, you would have bled to death in a matter of seconds when your femoral artery was severed. If it wasn't so sturdy and partially armored, the shrapnel would have shot up through your hips, likely shredding your lower organs. Yes, any leg but this one on your body and you'd be fitted for a body bag by now."

"All the more reason to save it rather than throw it upon the scrapheap," Olivia argued.

"Fine, fine," Dr. Gatling said. "Unhook the blasted, heroic limb and I'll see to its salvage."

Olivia eagerly unstrapped the leather clasps and braces that held what remained of her bronze limb to the small stump left over from her original leg. It came free from the tattered ends of her trousers and she handed what little was left to Dr. Gatling who slipped the whole mess into a leather bag along the back of his marvelous wheelchair. He raised himself back up to his original height on the hydraulics and began to wheel away, muttering to himself. "If I had another friend, any other friend, I wouldn't have to tolerate such outlandish demands from that girl. Blast it all, I need to get out of my lab and make another friend, even one more so she would have to think twice before…" was all she heard before he was out of range.

She sat back, a little calmer now, but not nearly enough to lie down. There wasn't any way she could convince anyone to give her crutches, certainly not in defiance of what would be very explicit orders from Dr. Gatling not to. The medical staff, even the temporary members, thought he walked on water with legs he didn't even have anymore.

Hours later, a medical assistant came through to clean up her cuts, take her blood pressure, check her breathing, and basically strip off her clothes to give her a once over. The little old woman was something of an anomaly in the City of Broken Bridges. Most of the elderly died out during the guerilla war waged to retake the city after the cascade. Many volunteered for dangerous tasks that would certainly lead to death at once or eventually in radioactive zones. It was remarkably noble and courageous, but resulted in few people over the age of 65 after the city was delivered. The elderly Chinese woman treating her likely had seen her share of these tasks as her left hand didn't have a full compliment of fingers anymore.

After Olivia's wounds were cleaned and dressed and her vitals recorded, she slowly redressed in hospital clothes provided by the woman. "Thank you, wise grandmother," Olivia said to the woman as she was packing her gear. It was the Chinician tradition to call the remaining elderly among their kind by such a revered title, regardless of whether or not the person was a grandmother or grandfather. As Esme explained it to her, in both cultures, Mexican and Chinese, when a person reached a certain age and respectability within their village, they were thought of as being everyone's grandmother or grandfather. Reverence for the elderly was part of what helped meld the Chinese and Mexican citizens into a single Chinican people.

"You are welcome, precious child." The woman smiled and nodded to her before moving on to the next soldier in the quickly filling beds.

It was another few hours before the Greek found her and with him was Esme, unharmed in every exterior way. They both came to Olivia, weaving through the crowded room of cots filled with wounded. Esme practically threw herself onto Olivia when she arrived. The Greek stood at the foot of her bed, fingering a woolen cap he'd taken off upon entering the room. His bushy hair was sticking up in most places and still had a bit of mud clinging around the right side where he no doubt landed on his hard noggin.

"Thank you so much for finding her," Olivia said to him, looking over Esme's shoulder as she held her in an intense hug.

"She did not want to be found, I think, but the people who knew her told me which way I might be going to find her," the Greek said. He replaced the cap on his head, tipped it to them, saluted, fidgeted a bit more, and took his leave.

Olivia held Esme close for a time and while the embrace seemed to do Olivia some good, Esme didn't stop quivering in her arms no matter how long they remained entangled.

"What's wrong?" Olivia asked.

"The Transcended tried to kill me," Esme said.

Olivia pushed Esme out to arms length a moment to look her in the eyes in hopes she hadn't heard correctly. "What did you say?"

"The Transcended your father sent to help us," Esme repeated, "it tried to kill me after the battle was over. If it weren't for people trying to stop it, I think it would have caught me too."

"What happened to it? Where is it now?" Olivia demanded, a fierce anger rising in her voice not only at the metal creature who tried to kill her beloved, but also her own father for sending something so potentially dangerous into the midst of an already vulnerable army.

"I don't know where it is now, but the word passing among the soldiers is that Claudia killed it and her father gutted it," Esme said. "The myth of Marceau among the men is starting to include Claudia now. They'll be erecting statues to both of them if things keep on the way they're going."

Olivia smiled to Esme, losing track of the conversation a little. "You're starting to talk like me."

"It's such a stylish, interesting way of speaking," Esme said. "I can't help it." In a shockingly intimate gesture that took Olivia completely by surprise, Esme reached her hand up the empty leg of Olivia's pants to place her hand on the stump of her lost leg. "Your beautiful leg was broken?"

"Dr. Gatling said he would repair it," Olivia said, blushing furiously at how remarkable it felt to have Esme touching the ruined remains of her old leg in such a loving way. Olivia usually took her mechanical leg off to sleep as it caught on bedding something fierce, but Esme hadn't ever touched the stump until that point.

"Until it is, let me be your legs," Esme said. "I'll get anything you want."

"Right now, I want to get out of here, and get answers from Claudia, Commander Marceau, and my father," Olivia said. "With how much went wrong, someone must know why."

Esme smiled brightly, kissed Olivia with an elation that could only come from two lovers finding each other relatively whole after something traumatic, and stood from the bed when their lips parted. "I'll get you crutches right away."

Chapter 33:
Rebirth After Death.

The elevator ride to the surface was slow and sullen. Claudia's father finally became aware his hand was covered in the strange blue goop straight up to his elbow and the realization seemed to make him uncomfortable, or perhaps it was because of the larger untenable position with no real appealing options left.

"The plan would not have delivered Alcatraz," Claudia finally said, breaking the silence between them. She was back in the opposite corner of the basket from him, both of them standing more in the shadows than out.

"I had an alternative plan," her father said. "I might have seized control in what would no doubt have been a bloody coup, but the loss of life would have been lower than what it ended up costing us in failure, and now..."

"...the same people will have to die regardless," Claudia finished for him.

He nodded.

"You are afraid of making the same mistakes the people who implemented the cascade made; you are afraid of making the same mistakes Hastings made," Claudia said. "This is admirable, but you have an option neither of them did. You can preserve your city at a much lower price."

"By trading what we have for totalitarianism?"

"The military oligarchy we have now is hardly superior to the military oligarchy the Ravens offer," Claudia scoffed. "If it were, they would be on the brink of destruction, and the City of Broken Bridges would be secure."

"You are the only counsel I have left. What would you have me do?"

She hadn't heard her father speak with such defeat since her mother died. It was horrible to hear the doubt and resignation in his voice. Perhaps her melancholy outlook on the world wasn't entirely derived from her mother.

"I will bring the Voron Daggers to take care of Alcatraz and you will undertake your coup so they will have a proper figurehead of power to deal with," Claudia said. "If the military council remains intact, they will burn it out and their rule of the city will be as unfriendly as their reception was made by that bunch. If you are solely in charge, you can make them feel welcome and they will be welcoming in response."

"What do the Ravens do with traitors?" her father asked.

"Hang them," Claudia replied, unsure if he was asking after her future or his own.

✝

Claudia and Roger waited in the darkness on the beachhead near the park where the Transcended had died. The craters remained from the missiles that missed and nobody had bothered to clean up the metal sheeting scattered from the pile the Transcended was trying to harvest from.

Claudia slid the flare gun from her pocket and fired it into the air. The red flare streaked into the sky and began its slow, flickering descent over the water ahead of her. The waves lapped at the sand in the darkness and the wind blew in from the ocean across the bay. Before the hissing flare made its fizzling impact into the black water of the bay, Claudia heard the motors of boats coming toward the beach.

Olivia wasn't happy about giving over her contact duties, nor was she as resigned to Claudia's fate. Claudia assured her that she was as safe as inevitability would allow anyway. This hadn't made Olivia any happier.

Claudia didn't know Alondra, although she knew of her. She was a much softer colonizer than Veronica, or so the rumors went. Claudia also didn't truly know if Bancroft was even still alive. Counterintelligence was something the Voron Daggers excelled at and whatever Dylan told Olivia could easily be lies intentionally planted to set Claudia at ease. It was all masturbatory to even wonder though—Claudia had nowhere else to run and the Ravens would take the city rather than let it fall into Slark hands. She was caught.

Rubber speed boats struck the sandy shore, three in all, fully loaded with Voron Daggers in full combat regalia. The boats slid up far enough onto the shore to stick from the force of the drive in and the commandos leapt free to secure the beach against an unseen enemy despite the fact that the only welcoming party they were to have consisted of an unarmed woman and her unimpressed dog.

"I guess I shouldn't be surprised when you show up anywhere," Dylan said as she strode out from the group of warrior women. "It's good to see you again, Marceau."

"Is it really?" Claudia asked.

"Keep your wary shield up if you like, but the sisterhood of the Voron Daggers isn't so easily broken by one of us taking a vacation," Dylan said. "Garcia, why don't you tell Claudia how many times we've had to find you off on some random adventure?"

Libby Garcia emerged from the line, stripped away her night vision goggles, and immediately scooped Claudia into her arms for an earthy hug. Claudia hugged back, surprised to find her long lost friend and spotter still lived. They held each other for some time before Dylan cleared her throat to end the reunion.

"Four," Libby said. "The last time was going to be a wedding leave that I left on a little early."

"With Alec?" Claudia asked.

Dylan stifled a laugh.

"Alec was three guys ago," Libby said sheepishly.

"You see, Marceau?" Dylan said. "The Voron Daggers put up with all sorts of nonsense if you're one of the sisterhood." Dylan stepped between Libby and Claudia, and gently cupped Claudia's face with one of her gloved hands. Claudia looked up to the tall captain and smiled. "If it comes down to it, we will protect our own."

"I appreciate that," Claudia murmured.

"Your appreciation is appreciated," Dylan said with a smile. "Now, you didn't call us over here simply to see if we would be happy to find you alive, did you?"

"I'm here to negotiate a…" Claudia began, but it wasn't a genuine negotiation and she wasn't authorized to negotiate on behalf of anyone. If she was to truly rejoin the Ravens, and she would need to in order to save her own life and protect her father, she would need to talk with Dylan as though she were already back into the fold. "…they tried to retake Alcatraz and failed spectacularly. The city is now out of even bad options. Everything can be taken with only minor bloodshed if we act quickly."

"Ms. Olivia Kingston seems to think your father would be an excellent figurehead and guardian to leave in charge of the city," Dylan said. "Can he be brought into the flock, as it were?"

"He's pragmatic and amenable," Claudia replied. "Moreover, he would be an exceptional asset if his needs could be seen to."

"What needs might those be?" Dylan asked, taking a half step back, folding her arms over her chest.

"Simply let him decide how best to protect the people of the City of Broken Bridges," Claudia said. "He has taken his stewardship of these people very seriously and it would likely be devastating for both groups if they were torn apart."

"I couldn't see why the Raven command would care so long as he knew his place," Dylan said. "We like the port and want the Slark fuel—beyond that, the people here can do as they like. From what we've seen, these people lack anything but a quickly withering technological advantage. I'll take the request to Bancroft, mention it's specifically from you, but I don't see why she wouldn't approve that deal. You know the Ravens—why wait for a consensus of a bunch of people when you only have to talk to one, if you catch my meaning."

Claudia nodded her understanding of the universal truth of the statement. The Raven model was Eastern European to its very core, especially in regards to the consolidation of ultimate authority into just a few hands. Of course, Veronica had pointed out, and accurately so, that this was also a very American concept. For all the boasting of freedom, equality, and democracy, the United States before its fall was little more than a plutocracy dressed up like a Republic. These were terms Claudia's father had used before, but until Veronica explained what it all really meant, Claudia hadn't truly understood. The world was in flux and continuing a plutocracy where wealth and birthplace dictated power seemed a complete frivolity when compared to the Russian model of strength of leadership above all else. Claudia never understood patriotism and was glad when it died with so many other institutions in the cascade. Her allegiance only went as far as survival, which was only as far as the Ravens ever asked of anyone. Perhaps she wasn't as French as she thought.

"My father's practicality and strength to rule will meld well with the Raven ideals," Claudia said.

"Excellent," Dylan said. "Then I don't see why the city shouldn't remain under his command once all other obstacles are removed."

Claudia glanced over her should to the solemn silhouette of the tower to the south. She expected to see either the single green light of the coup having started, signaled from a window nearest the top, or perhaps even the two green lights, one above and one below, that would signal the successful completion of the coup. Instead, only the aircraft warning lights flashed along the spire in slow, repetitive intervals. The blood in Claudia's veins ran cold—the coup was on shaky ground and likely to fail. To reinforce what she hoped was a mistake she heard the distant pop of rifle fire.

"Is something wrong?" Dylan asked, apparently putting things together in part.

"How fast can you take out Alcatraz?" Claudia asked, whipping her head around to address the Captain with proper urgency.

"We could have done it yesterday if someone asked nicely enough," Dylan replied. "We could do it right now if you sent us someone who knew the ins and outs of the island even in the dark."

"I'll find you that someone, I swear it," Claudia said, "but the island needs to fall tonight for the city to be delivered by morning."

Dylan gave her a withering, skeptical look, and, for a moment, Claudia doubted she would acquiesce. "Very well," Dylan finally said. "Keep in mind I'm putting more trust in you than is entirely warranted in this situation."

"The guide's name is Esme, and she'll carry the old identify friend/foe of the Ravens," Claudia said. "They tore it down…"

"…so we could build it back right," Dylan finished for her. "Now go. I'm guessing you have a fire to put out."

Claudia took off at a jog with Roger by her side. She hoped her lungs would hold out long enough to reach the rally point for the coup, and she hoped Esme was with her father and Olivia when she arrived.

†

The list of things Olivia never thought she would live to see added a dozen or so things in the past hour. She was fighting alongside the fabled Commander Marceau, which was a good thing, but they were losing badly and were being chased up Telegraph Hill toward the ruins of Coit Tower, which wasn't how she'd expected that moment to play out. She was firing a carbine one handed, trying to keep steady on crutches, and struggling with even basic footing on the steep incline up the hill's ruined face—a new experience to be sure since she'd long since lost the feeling of having a fully missing limb. When she faltered, which was often, Esme of all people was the one to take up a weapon and defend her; another occurrence Olivia never thought to see. The final, and perhaps the most bizarre, was in seeing Dr. Gatling out of the tower. The doctor's advanced wheelchair scrambled easily up the hill on its articulating wheel arms in a way that most mountain goats might envy. Stranger than seeing him out of the tower, which was plenty crazy on its own, Dr. Gatling was fighting alongside them, and doing a thumping good job of it. It was easily the weirdest night in Olivia's memory.

"Bruce's rallying cry must be hampered by something," Esme shouted above the firefight that was slowing to a dull roar as the rebels took the high ground of Telegraph Hill.

Olivia hoisted herself over a disturbed chunk of cement, abandoning one of her crutches in the process. She didn't need both anyway—she still had one good leg. When she was in the safety of her new cover, she reloaded her carbine and took a moment to breathe. "I didn't have the time to rally the former women soldiers to full strength and the mustering plan for them was hasty at best," Olivia replied. "We'll have to hope

Bruce is as determined and persuasive in this as he is in most things."

While Commander Marceau's plan was still in its infancy, arming and readying the various pieces on the chessboard, the rest of the military council enacted their own coup. They'd gotten it in their heads that Inspector Cavanaugh was silenced by the rebels after discovering Commander Marceau had killed General Hastings. Both accusations seemed entirely preposterous to Olivia even as the soldiers who came to arrest the lot of them uttered the charges. To her further chagrin, Commander Marceau, defiant as ever, admitted his daughter had killed Inspector Cavanaugh and that he had indeed killed General Hastings to save his daughter's life. Moreover, he wasn't sorry about either action and he wasn't about to surrender. In the firefight that ensued, Commander Marceau obliterated the men sent to arrest him, seizing on the split second of hesitation caused by the surprise of hearing him admit readily to both crimes. At close range, with knives and his shotgun, all he needed was their momentary distraction.

The commander was already cresting the hill with the rest of his defensive line of rebels falling behind him. This was when hell began raining down on their pursuers. From the elevated position at the top of the hill, with a weapon cache no doubt secreted away for just such an eventuality, Commander Marceau fired rockets, incendiary grenades, and a deluge of bullets down upon the pursuers, changing weapons rather than reloading and moving among the different armaments as though he were Zeus with a full compliment of lightning bolts for the mortals on the ground below.

Olivia looked up to him, flashing in the fires he was raining down, and saw in him the terrifying figure of a warrior with nothing left to lose and swords enough for all his enemies at his fingertips. Dr. Gatling came to her side, impelling her up the hill under the cover Commander Marceau created.

"When you're truly free, you're bound to get a little weird," Dr. Gatling said to her. "In me, this has been freeing, but in him, this weirdness is a little frightening."

With the entire dozen of the remaining rebels atop the hill, Commander Marceau quickly saw to fortifying their defensive position. He situated everyone in highly precise ways, making maximum use of the weapon cache he'd planted for just such a purpose. The hill was so steep, the cover so slanted toward defense, and the armaments so impressive that Olivia didn't doubt it would take a hundred to one advantage for anyone to knock them from the base of Coit Tower, which made it all the more surprising when Claudia and Roger appeared seemingly out of nowhere.

Claudia and her father embraced, a meager passing of words took place, and then they were off to find Esme of all people. Olivia desperately wanted to abandon her post to see what Claudia was telling Esme who seemed more than a little disturbed by the orders. She took her leave without so much as saying goodbye to Olivia, scampering away into the darkness to disappear in much the same way Claudia appeared.

Dr. Gatling delivered a sniper rifle to Claudia and pointed to the ruins of Coit Tower. Claudia vanished into the tower as though this was always part of the plan.

Olivia sat in her defensive position with her numerous carbines and rifles laid out beside her and wondered how much of this plan she really was privy to. Apparently, Commander Marceau was guilty of the treasonous act that Olivia defended him against for months and the entire plan of killing Cavanaugh concocted by her and Bruce Coffey was already rendered pointless by Claudia at some point, possibly weeks ago since nobody had seen or heard from Cavanaugh in ages. What Olivia really needed to understand was why.

Against orders, and with little more than a meaningful glance to the two men flanking her defensive position, she abandoned her post to hobble on a dented crutch and a single leg to get some answers out of the godly Commander Marceau. She'd built up a head of steam on her way over, which she didn't end up needing as the commander didn't seem remotely surprised at her approach or her leaving of the line.

"Make your questions quick, Kingston," Commander Marceau said.

"Why did you kill General Hastings?" Olivia demanded, happy to oblige the Commander's request of bluntness.

"He intended to throw Claudia off the Golden Gate Bridge when she arrived, claiming she was little more than another worthless mutant," Commander Marceau said flatly. "Her life is far more valuable to me than the General and his men, so I killed them."

There was a coldness in the battlefield calculus that made Olivia shiver a little. After seeing Commander Marceau fight, she didn't doubt that General Hastings and his private guard wouldn't be a match for him. She also knew the General to be a massively arrogant man who likely wouldn't have believed anyone capable of disobeying an order he gave, even including "please don't kill me."

"Fair enough," Olivia said. "Why did Claudia killed Inspector Cavanaugh?"

This answer came slower as though the Commander wasn't as certain in the truth, or perhaps the truth was ugly and not as wholly owned by him in this case. "He was inside the Transcended that attacked the donut shop girl; Claudia killed him to save her life."

It was a judicious response, and one Olivia knew lacked important elements to be fully understood. "What are you even talking about? Cavanaugh was inside a Transcended?"

"The Transcended *are* people," the Commander finally said. "Your father can explain more if you need more."

The finality of the statement left little room to continue along that line of questioning, so Olivia moved on. "Are you planning on delivering the city to the Ravens?"

"I'm planning on preserving as much human life as I can with the options left to me," the Commander replied. "At the moment, that means a transfer of power from the military council to the Raven command. I have tried to make the process as bloodless as possible."

"That's not going well so far," Olivia said.

"Isn't it?" the Commander replied. "The people we are killing would have been hung as traitors anyway. Isn't it better that they die on their feet fighting rather than dangle from the ends of ropes?"

"Where did Esme go and why didn't she say goodbye?"

"She is helping the Ravens in their mission to destroy Alcatraz. In what ways, I do not know. As for her lack of a farewell to you, that is a question better answered by her when she gets back."

"I have other questions but I'm afraid to ask them."

"Then you have as much information as you need." Commander Marceau guided Olivia back toward her defensive position.

†

To call the night eventful would be an astounding understatement. Claudia picked off attackers from her hiding place in Coit Tower as the loyalists tried again and again to take the hill. Only once did they break through the defenses in a mad rush to capture or kill Commander Marceau.

Her father wasn't easily taken dead or alive. Claudia managed to eliminate two of the five men sent for him on a suicidal run. He killed two more in close combat and Roger felled the fifth with a running attack-dog tackle followed by a very wolf-like tearing out of the man's throat. Claudia hadn't even seen Roger's entrance into the fray and neither had the man he felled in defense of her father.

The brilliant feint followed by an overwhelming assault mounted to provide cover for the five men sent for her father seemed the last gasp of a failing counter-coup. The attacks from then on out barely scratched at the midway point of Telegraph Hill before being driven back under superior fire and a remarkable defensive position.

Amid the chaos below, Claudia finally found in her scope the line of Olivia's Clockwork Warriors and Bruce Coffey's militia making their best push toward what Claudia guessed to be the loyalist command post as the sun began to rise across the bay to her back.

Before the true dawn could even fully break, a titanic explosion rocked the entire bay. Rocks and shrapnel rained down miles away when Alcatraz exploded. Claudia knew it was likely several charges set at different places, but the detonation was so simultaneous that is sounded simply like a multi-toned single explosion. She let out a deep sigh of relief, letting her guard down at the wrong moment as a final death gasp of the failed counter-coup began their bombardment of the hill.

Chapter 34:
Metal Birds of Mercy and Prey.

Claudia barely had enough time to recognize what the sounds were before the first shell struck the tower. Her attempted evacuation lasted only a few seconds. The crumbling ruins of the tower were already looking for a reason to fall and a few direct hits from artillery gave the perfect opportunity for the whole thing to come crumbling down. The stonework beneath her feet shifted and fell away even as she raced along it, trying to find any exit she might hurl herself from. She ran for the back of the tower, the side facing the wharf, in hopes it would survive the bombardment coming from the city side. She leapt for the outer wall on the far side even as it was falling away from her. She managed to grasp a gloved hand onto the edge of something, possibly a window or vent, and pulled her body flush against the stone surface that was quickly going from vertical to horizontal.

Dust and explosions overwhelmed her senses shortly after and soon she wasn't even sure whether or not she was still falling or had already landed. When rocks and brickwork didn't rain down on her, she suspected she'd selected her escape route well. She covered her head with her free arm all the same. Her mind was racing, but the world around it was going even faster. She impacted the ground with the crumbling wall beneath her in answer to her short-lived wonderings of whether or not she was still falling. Despite her best efforts to hold onto the ledge, the wall came away from her when she bounced free and her handhold failed. The air exploded from her lungs and refused to refill, which she thought might be for the best as she couldn't even see a foot in front of her face from the dust kicked up in the destruction of the tower, making her think breathing would probably be a gasping, choking affair anyway.

She tried to roll free of the rubble raining down, grasping her ribcage painfully as her lungs tried again and again to refill from having the wind knocked out of her. A tree trunk stopped her rolling before it even began. She wrapped herself around the tree, placing the stout trunk between her and any further debris coming down. Something must have gone wrong in her hasty plan to escape. The tree line on the wharf side of the tower was well away, meaning she must have dropped out of the northern side into the old garden.

Her lungs were recovering from having the wind knocked from them and the dust was settling when the second barrage hit. The tree trunks around her, barely visible in the tan cloud of dust kicked up by the tower's collapse, started exploding in showers of splinters and shattered earth. She huddled in closer to the tree she'd selected as her shelter, hoping it wouldn't be targeted as she really didn't know what else to do.

Between the distant pops of cannon fire, the whistling of shells descending, and the earth-shaking explosions when they impacted, she heard people shouting to one another, a few even calling her name, and Roger was barking somewhere. She was glad of the other survivors and glad she hadn't lost any hearing in the explosion that took down the tower. When she tried to shout a response though, her mouth filled with blood, choking off her words. She felt around in her mouth to see if she'd broken any teeth, which was her primary concern, only to recoil from her tongue painfully. She'd bitten the tip, hard, likely when she landed, and she hadn't even noticed in the adrenaline rush and turmoil.

A third salvo, which she dreaded would be the end of the top of Telegraph Hill and everyone on it, never came. Bruce's men must have finally pushed through to the loyalist artillery positions to silence the cannons. Still, Claudia clung to the rough bark of the tree trunk, waiting to see what new catastrophe might befall her. The sound that finally pried her eyes open was more disorienting than alarming.

The drone of airplane engines filled the air. Not blimps, which she'd seen and ridden in since the Slark invasion, but actual airplane engines. She pried her eyes open to search the sky through the hazy dust clearing around her. Out of the east, soaring through the smoke pillar coming off the ruins of

Alcatraz, were a dozen or so World War II bombers. She recognized the fuselages from the History Channel programs her father used to love watching with her. Most were heavily modified B-24 Liberators but among the flock of strange birds were a handful of the larger B-17 Flying Fortresses—they were her favorite when she was a child.

She watched the bomber formation as it winged its way toward the part of the peninsula south of the wall. Before bombs could even begin raining down on the target that she suspected was the assembled Slark army, white streaks of rocket pods fired off. They were flying so low and so quickly, Claudia wondered if maybe the engines weren't really jet-props running on Slark fuel. The machine gunner pods on the planes, originally intended for aircraft defense, appeared to be replaced with rocket placements, which made sense since there wouldn't be any fighters attacking the bombers. She could see the hand of Gieo in the bombers—brilliant and eccentric with a strangely creative practicality.

Her admiration of the tiny bomber wing was cut short when her eyes scanned to follow them. Roving through the dust cloud, large and frightening in the obscured field of view, were the silhouettes of several Transcended climbing the hill. The terrifying image of Cavanaugh's shell charging her remained at the forefront of her mind and she couldn't help but huddle to hide away from the metal giants. They began plucking something from the rubble and it took Claudia a moment to figure out through the slowly settling haze that they were picking up people. The human figures being delicately harvested from the destroyed hilltop were so tiny in the Transcended's colossal arms that it sent another shiver of fear through Claudia. She skulked down the edge of the hill and found a proper hiding place among the fallen trunks of several trees, well away from the main group, and there she waited, hoping she wouldn't be discovered.

The sounds of the metal giants sifting through the debris seemed to go on for hours, but never came any closer to her than a few dozen yards, which was closer than she would have liked. Eventually, after an interminable wait, the Transcended lumbered off the hill in a slow trickle. Claudia waited for several minutes more before slipping from her hiding place.

The dust was settled by then and the hilltop was an entirely alien landscape from what she remembered. Coit Tower was little more than a pile of scattered stones. Only a handful of trees remained, including the one she suspected she hid behind. Craters dotted the landscape where a dozen or more shells landed. She scanned the area for other survivors to no appreciable effect. Her tongue still hurt, but a thorough examination of it with her fingertips confirmed she hadn't bitten through it, or probably even far enough to require medical attention. Still, shouting would hurt, so she tried clapping her hands. The clap immediately brought a familiar figure out of a similarly brilliant hiding place.

Roger shook the dust off his coat and ran to her. Somehow, he'd secreted himself away in an alcove beneath the bronze statue pedestal. She knelt to receive him and embraced his dirty, but happy frame, when he nearly knocked her over in his joy at finding her.

She spent an hour searching the hilltop for other survivors with Roger's help. When their thorough examination of the area yielded neither body nor living person to dig free of the wreckage, she started looking for a path down. The eastern side of the hill was still a sheer cliff face for all intents and purposes, which made it a lousy option, and so she focused her attention on the northern side as she didn't want to try for the western where there may still be loyalist soldiers.

She found the trail she'd used to first infiltrate the rally point the night before was in reasonably good shape, although she had to climb over a few washouts caused by rockslides jarred free during the bombardment. Roger's spirits never flagged as he stuck close by her the entire lengthy descent. She wondered if he had any idea how uncertain she was about what they were doing.

A patrol of soldiers almost immediately discovered her when she reached the bottom of the hill. The field on the northern side that she'd crossed the night before sat barren after what she guessed was a grain harvest, leaving her nowhere to run or hide when she spotted the soldiers and their truck rumbling across the expanse toward her. She placed her hands on her head in surrender knowing she couldn't escape back up the hill before they caught her and she didn't have a weapon left to fight them with if they turned out to be loyalists.

The men were dressed in military regular uniforms, but they seemed happy to see her. One of the men spoke into the radio that they'd found her. The others exited the beat up pickup truck armed, but were apparently more interested in guarding her than securing her as a prisoner. One of the men, as young as she was and also as battle hardened by the look of his face, pressed a pistol into her hand.

"There are still pockets of resistance," the officer in the passenger seat told her as she was ushered into the cab of the truck.

She nodded her understanding and allowed herself to be positioned in the center of the bench seat between the driver and the officer. She glanced down to the pistol. It was a standard issue .38 revolver of some kind, likely from an old police stockpile. She'd started to wonder if she would ever use a gunpowder weapon again, which reminded her of other survivors, including Dr. Gatling who had built so many marvelous guns.

"Did anyone else make it off the hill?" Claudia asked as the truck pulled away with Roger in the back and her in the cab.

"Most everyone," the officer said. "Your father is commanding the forces taking back the Transamerica Pyramid as we speak and the rest were hauled down into the Keeper sanctuary by a group of Transcended."

"That's where I'd like to go," Claudia said, noting the officer's use of the White Tower's proper name—he must have been a native San Franciscan.

"Your father requested we take you back to heavily guarded areas," the officer said, "but I suppose the sanctuary would qualify."

Claudia's primary concern was defending Olivia against the knowledge of what was really going on in the bowels of the Keeper's labs, but she suspected she would be too late judging from the way Professor Kingston was coming clean about so many things lately. The truck wound its way through the fresh war zones that had gone quiet. The strange landscape of San Francisco that went from city to farmlands had made another transformation into a World War I battlefield with impact craters, barbwire barriers, and sandbag bunkers. Claudia hated how quickly conflict could ruin so many things.

The soldiers parked the truck at a subterranean entrance, which was guarded by other troops loyal to her father, and escorted her through the tunnels to one of the elevators leading down into the sanctuary. There they took their leave from her, promising they would remain and wait for her to come up no matter how long it took. They offered to watch Roger for her as well since no amount of calling or cajoling could convince the dog to step onto the rickety miner's basket.

The elevator ride down took longer than she expected. She wondered if it was because she was using a different route than she'd ever used or if it just felt that way because of the urgency of where she was going. The ride did give her a second to wipe the dried blood and dust from her face and ruffle chunks of wood and debris out of her hair. She suspected doing a proper job of cleaning away the grime of what she'd just been through would take hours. Tending her battered vanity was a relatively pleasant distraction for the rest of the elevator ride into the under world.

If the elevator ride felt longer, the darkened tunnels where she had to feel her way toward the end seemed much shorter as she almost immediately popped out in the hellish glow of the thermal vent and the enclosed canyon above it. Her wanderings came to an abrupt stop when one of Professor Kingston's students, a young woman who looked like any grad assistant a person might meet on a university campus, came running up to greet her.

"They're about to start and Professor Kingston said you might want to see," the woman said, grasping Claudia's hand to drag her along.

They raced through the labyrinthine series of tunnels and causeways over the lava filled vent. The woman seemed to know precisely where they were going, although Claudia was almost immediately lost. They came upon a great chamber off one of the smaller tributary fingers of the lake of magma beneath them. The hand of the Transcended was obvious in the room as it was almost a perfectly smooth sphere, large enough to hold several city blocks. Machinery lined the room, looking like a combination of the steam-powered vents and tubes created by the Transcended and the entirely alien technology favored by the Slark, which was a cross between watery waves and insect chitin. On a large platform in the center of the sphere, the shell of the Dr. Feinstein Transcended, briefly inhabited by Inspector Cavanaugh, was awaiting a new occupant.

Claudia cried out, making her bitten tongue sting. It was a wordless utterance that served its purpose of grabbing the attention of the people gathered beneath the altar that was clearly used in the creation of new Transcended. Olivia, still hobbling on one crutch and one leg, came away from the crowd of a dozen or so students and Keepers. She looked as haggard and battered as Claudia felt, and she looked angry at Claudia's interruption to boot. Esme followed her from the crowd, keeping a respectful few steps behind the woman she had clearly come to love in ways she never loved Claudia.

"This is a quiet moment," Olivia hissed to her when she got close enough.

"Your father promised to put a moratorium on the creation of new Transcended," Claudia protested, although she dropped her voice an octave or so.

"You and *your* father interpreted his silence that way, but that doesn't mean he agreed to the order," Olivia said.

"Do you know what…?"

"Yes, my father explained everything and I don't need you trying to explain it a second time," Olivia said. "Dr. Gatling is about to ascend and we've all come to wish him well on his journey to the higher plane of existence."

"They're putting Dr. Gatling into that *thing*?"

"No, Dr. Gatling is going willingly into a new life as he has outgrown this one."

"Your father put a mad man in the very shell he's about to put Dr. Gatling into!"

"My father is a deeply emotional and highly intelligent man with a greater understanding of the world than I ever gave him credit for," Olivia said, "while *your* father is just a warlord in a world that values warlords more than philosophers."

The accusation stung Claudia more than she thought it could. If her father was just a warlord, then she was just a warlord's daughter and sole heir to a bloody throne. It was a shift in Olivia's opinion of the world that surprised Claudia. No longer did Olivia wish to be like Commander Marceau and look upon her own father, Professor Kingston, with disdain. She'd learned more of both men and made a startling choice in Claudia's estimation. The shock and hurt, clearly visible on Claudia's face, tempered Olivia's anger.

"You don't understand what it is to be part machine," Olivia said, her voice lowering to a softer, explanatory tone, abandoning the harsh edge of accusation. "Dr. Gatling and I have lived for years now in a hybrid state, relying on mechanics for what our flesh and blood could no longer do. The Transcended are the next logical step in this process. Even you must have known this on some level as my father said that you said destroying the shell was too much."

"I can't…"

"No, you can't see and you probably never will," Olivia said. "Dr. Gatling is dying. Normally, they would not allow a person to ascend simply to save their life, but it has long been believed that Dr. Gatling was ready for his ascension and so the rules have been amended in his case. I am only sorry I will never be able to follow my father into the higher plane."

"Why not?" Claudia asked. She didn't understand, but the tone of Olivia's voice spoke of a true longing and part of Claudia wanted her to have what she wanted even if she didn't understand.

"A soldier's mind is altered by war in ways that make it forever incapable of certain things," Olivia said. "One of these things is the ascension to the higher plane. This was discovered in the autopsy of what remained of Inspector Cavanaugh's brain. My mind will forever be tarnished by the things I've done in battle. Violence ruins the parts of our minds required to see the world with loving eyes, which is paramount for the Transcended. You're ruined, I'm ruined, and your father is completely ruined. I didn't understand this truth about the commander until your father explained the math of killing so many to protect you; killing is a physical exercise from him, disconnected from morality of any kind.

My father still has a beautiful mind capable of seeing altruism and aestheticism in the world. Shouldn't we want minds like that to persist?"

"I suppose..." Claudia said. Whatever else she might have said didn't matter and she knew it. She felt far dirtier after Olivia's explanation of what was truly wrong with Claudia and her father than she had even after the entirety of Coit Tower and most of Telegraph Hill was dumped onto her. She wandered away stunned and confused until the grad student woman took her by the arm to guide her back to the elevator.

She couldn't tell the Ravens what really went on in the Keeper's sanctuary and she knew her father wouldn't want to either. She suspected the Keepers and the Transcended had ways of defending themselves, isolating their underground world if the need should arise, but Claudia also knew the world, specifically the City of Broken Bridges, would suffer far more in the severing of that bond.

Winter was coming, the season of slaughter where the warm blooded humans would gain the advantage over the cold blooded Slark, and she knew when the Ravens pushed south toward Los Angeles, she needed to be with them. She hoped to put a lot of distance between herself and the City of Broken Bridges before spring broke.

Chapter 35:
Epilogue.

The conversation with Olivia clung to Claudia long after Dr. Gatling made his ascension. The math of war Claudia's father used, described so harshly by Olivia, put people's lives in danger if Claudia should remain in the City of Broken Bridges. When Bancroft and her burned husband, the Owl, made their brief appearance in the new Raven city to deliver a flag and officially welcome Commander Marceau into the flock as the first Black King, Claudia made her decision to rejoin the army she'd abandoned. It was a little surprising to her how easily they accepted a male figurehead, although she also knew no man had ever had so much to offer the Ravens.

Dylan was more than happy to welcome Claudia back into the Voron Daggers and promised to allow visits to the City of Broken Bridges whenever Claudia got to missing her father. "Just let us know when you need some family time and we'll work something out," she'd said. "We don't want to have to chase you down again since you've got quite the knack for making it a long way before anyone knows you're gone."

Despite every desire to bring Roger with her, Claudia left the marvelous German shepherd in her father's care. As they parted ways, she took the dog's face in her hands and instructed him to defend her father with his every breath. She didn't think she needed to even give the order for the loyal dog to carry it out after seeing what Roger was capable of when it came to guarding his master. She hugged her father next and told him to take care of her dog until she came to visit. Letters from the front would let him know when she could get a bit of leave time.

The bombing run on the Slark by the fledgling Raven air force made good headway in scattering the three divisions of troops beyond the wall, but didn't have the decimating effect everyone hoped they would. The Ravens used the City of Broken Bridges as a staging point for the push south down the peninsula, and Claudia joined the Voron Daggers as the tip of the spear, relying heavily on her experience in the wilds with Liam. The march south included a stop at the little league fields south of Half Moon Bay to find and bury what remained of him. The distance Claudia thought she had from the tragedy evaporated and she wept openly not only for Liam, but Veronica as well when they finally laid the Scottish footballer to rest.

✝

Olivia wore her wedding band on her right ring finger so whenever she held Esme's hand their rings would click against each other. As they rode one of the many strange street cars through the chilly fields of winter tilling done when the rains softened the soil, she lifted Esme's hand to her lips to kiss it. They looked upon one another and smiled.

The Dr. Gatling Transcended had a few moments of recognition when it came to Olivia in the weeks after the ascension, but the instances faded quickly and he became just like all the others, looking into a world beyond humanity with a single, hopeful blue eye. Olivia had thought this would mean she would need to find another way to repair her leg, but a couple days after the Dr. Gatling Transcended stop recognizing her, she found her old leg completely repaired and upgraded, sitting on her porch.

Her wedding with Esme was a city wide affair. Bruce Coffey served ably as her best man/maid of honor. Her father gladly gave her away, joking he was glad to make his hard-headed daughter Esme's permanent problem. Olivia had nearly forgotten her father's wonderfully irreverent sense of humor until his hilarious toast to the happy couple. She and Esme almost immediately started screening possible sperm donors for their first child. Esme insisted she be the one to carry their first baby, although she made it very clear to Olivia the next one was hers and that they wouldn't be waiting too long. The renewal of her relationship with her father gave

Olivia more hope in having a large family where she formerly would have felt unease at the expansive plans Esme had for building their family.

The street car wound through the former battlefields of the week-long civil war following Commander Marceau's nearly catastrophic, but ultimately successful, coup attempt. The trenches, bunkers, and barbwire were replaced with the new refineries meant to create Slark fuel and munitions. The Transcended Dr. Gatling worked constantly on building automated systems to create the fuel from raw materials inserted by workers and even began constructing other machines that would build his wonderful weapons in large numbers. He was the closest thing the city had to a true guardian Transcended even when he was alive, and after his ascension his efforts were no longer hampered by his physical disability or the pesky need for sleeping and eating he'd always complained about getting in the way of his work.

As they rounded the new refinery, heading down to the old wharf to oversee the creation of the fishing fleets the Ravens commissioned, Olivia caught sight of the familiar Transcended. She pressed her hand to the glass in something of a wave to the Transcended Dr. Gatling. The giant, bronze robot stopped in its work of welding together an elaborate pipe system. It waited patiently for a handful of crows that had landed on its arms. The jet black birds took their time while the Transcended held perfectly still; finally the crows took wing to hunt bugs and snails in a nearby fallow field and the Transcended resumed its work.

The End

Continue the Raven Ladies Saga Winter of 2012 With the Next
Installment:

About the Author

Cassandra Duffy spent most of her childhood being precocious, which stopped being entertaining or impressive when she grew into an adult, at which point she had to start being precious. After being an outcast child prodigy it was no surprise when she graduated from one of the many fine University of California schools a year early to follow her girlfriend in a cross country move.

She writes a free-lance sex advice column found in various lesbian magazines and dating websites. Her short story collections and novels can be found on her website.

Two of her greatest prides are being a true California girl and author of some truly naughty things. She is a dutiful partially-Asian daughter who is beloved by her fairly traditional Korean father who thinks having a gay daughter is just fine as long as she keeps playing coed flag football. She is a stereotypical younger sister, and an adoring aunt of a hilarious little boy. Being a modern techno-freak, gamer-girl, she spent most of her childhood dreaming of being a video game designer, but changed her mind and brought her dreams of world building and story-weaving to writing unique romance novels.

Cassandra is a gleefully monogamous girlfriend to an earthbound goddess who was once her high school bully, but has done a magnificent job of making up for all the school girl nastiness ever since. When she isn't being an avid fang girl (vampire fan girl) or tormenting people in online gaming, she lives and writes in Winter Park, Florida with her partner and soul mate Nichole and their two cats: Dragon and Josephine.

6280941R00187

Printed in Germany
by Amazon Distribution
GmbH, Leipzig